Books by Norman Collins

THE
HUSBAND'S
STORY

THE HUSBAND'S STORY

Norman Collins

ATHENEUM

New York

1978

Library of Congress Cataloging in Publication Data

Collins, Norman, 1907-
  The husband's story.

  I. Title.
PZ3.C6958Hu   1978   [PR6005.036534]   823'.9'12   78-3594
ISBN 0-689-10898-2

for Kathie and Lew

Author's Foreword

This isn't a particularly nice story because even the very nicest people don't always behave very nicely; and it isn't a particularly happy story because human happiness has always been notoriously haphazard. But, by and large, it probably works out somewhere around the national average – better for some, and not so good for others. And that's where the luck of the game comes in: in all spectator sports there has to be someone who loses, and it isn't always the favourite who wins.

Contents

PREFACE

Introducing Mr Cheevers

I

You couldn't have fitted another one in.

The Press Box was packed solid, elbow-to-elbow, as it always was when one of the really big cases came on. For the past two-and-a-half hours, the place had been a cramped, oak-panelled factory, with ball-points and propelling pencils all working flat-out to be ready with the finished product for the breakfast-table and commuter markets next morning.

Not that there could be much more to come.

It was now only the sentence, the sheer, hard arithmetic of it, for which they were all waiting. And the alert had just been signalled. Mr Justice Streetley had brought the tips of his fingers together and was nodding his head like a metronome in time with the words that he was speaking – always a sure sign with him that he was about to pronounce.

The old hands, the experienced ones, had thrust themselves back as far as they could go from the schoolroom row of desk tops, all with their little let-in inkwells, and were sitting on the edge of their seats with their notebooks gathered up in their laps in readiness. The men from the news agencies and the evening papers had already left their places and were standing alongside the policemen by the doorway nearest to the telephones.

As always happens at such a moment, the body of the Court had become frozen. The ushers, feet together and eyes front, were as motionless as snowmen, and even Counsel had stopped fiddling with their headpieces.

It had all gone quiet, too; quiet and church-like and muffled. It might have been the blessing that they were hearing, and only just hearing it at that. Mr Justice Streetley was a notoriously soft-spoken Judge. His faint, precise tones, with all emphasis and emotion ironed out of them, were never more than barely audible. The Clerk of the Court himself had to lean forward to make sure that he was not missing anything.

When His Lordship had finished – and his voice had dropped almost to a whisper as the words 'Eighteen years' came out – someone up in the other gallery, the Public one, shouted 'Shame'; and, out of sight down below near where Counsel and solicitors were sitting, a woman uttered a little cry – half gasp, half sob – and there was a noise that might have been caused by someone falling, or a chair overturning.

Mr Justice Streetley ignored both interruptions, did not even seem to have noticed them in fact. He was feeling tired; tired and relieved that it was all over.

In getting ready to rise, he had separated his finger-tips and was now closing the embossed folder on the polished table-top in front of him. Under the fullness of the wig, his creased grey face was expressionless. Face and wig might have been made of the same material.

But it wasn't yet quite over. The policeman standing duty outside the dock had opened the door leading to the cells, and the other police-man, the one who had stood there throughout, tapped the prisoner on the shoulder to let him know that it was time to go below.

The prisoner, however, took no notice. He was trying to say some-thing. Mr Justice Streetley ignored him too.

Even so, the prisoner persisted.

'Thank you very much, my Lord,' he said. 'I'm deeply sorry to have put you to all this trouble and expense on my account.'

II

Even though the curtain was already down, it was really the key speech of the whole performance. It contained everything. That was why it was such a pity that, in the rush, the agency men and the evening-paper reporters missed it altogether.

Not that it really mattered: the Stop Press, with the smudged lines saying 'Eighteen Years', was the only bit for which their readers had been waiting.

But there was one person who hadn't missed it, one very special person who recognized it immediately for the courtroom treasure that it was.

And he was still sitting up there in the Press Box, a brooding, con-centrated observer, with a discreet bow-tie and neatly combed-back hair. There was no panic scramble to the telephone-booth for him. He could afford to wait; just sit there, sucking up the last few drops, and savouring them.

That was because he wasn't a common Court Reporter like the rest of them. He was Mr Cyril Cheevers, Crime Correspondent of the *Sunday Sun*. He was a somebody. His pieces carried a signature line. It was to him that his paper turned when they wanted the big, human-interest, heartbreak stories, the behind-the-scenes disclosures.

The Old Bailey was Mr Cheevers's special province; practically his preserve. Even if he spent most of his time hanging round Scotland Yard and enjoyed it, it was only when he turned left off Ludgate Hill towards the Central Criminal Court that he felt really at home. And he always made a point of going there on foot from his office because he liked the walk so much, because it was so full of happy memories for him. Faces of past swindlers, bigamists, spies, arsonists, murderers, extortionists – many of them now dead and mere images – kept passing through his mind in nostalgic succession.

Every time he mounted the worn stone stairs, the policemen at the door greeted him like one of themselves. And for good reason. His latest book, *I Condemn . . .*, was by way of being a best-seller in the paperbacks; and his earlier works, *Blind Justice, Cases Famous and Infamous* and *The Old Bailey: Lore and Legend* were still on the shelves of all the Public Libraries.

I Condemn . . . was largely about Mr Justice Streetley himself. Of all the Judges whom Mr Cheevers had watched, studied, analysed and written about, Mr Streetley came out nearest to his ideal. On every count, too. His presence, his manner, his imperturbability, his perfectly modulated phrases, his great, grey face, his aloofness, his severity, his occasional flashes of sly, sarcastic humour, even the finger-tip posture, all added up to something very near perfection. Mr Cheevers had offered to dedicate *I Condemn . . .* to Mr Justice Streetley personally, but His Lordship, though flattered and appreciative, had felt impelled to decline.

As well as being a keen student of human nature, the Crime Correspondent was something of a stylist. It was some years now since he had coined the word 'Crimeograph' for his full-length descriptive pieces; and, combined with the name of the paper he worked for, the phrase was now copyright. It was something to live up to, and he did not forget it.

Even as he sat there watching the back of the departing prisoner, he could feel the scene transforming itself inside his mind into little isolated globules of prose: 'Court Number One today had never seen the like . . . an event unparalleled in the bleak, darkly-chequered history of the dock . . . the graven, Sphinx-like face of the Judge beneath his flowing and archaic wig . . . condemned to a sentence that left Mr Jeremy Hayhoe, QC, Counsel for the Defence, a stunned, bewildered man . . . within the Court, a rasp of protest and a scream of pain . . . a boyish, upright figure calmly and politely saying thank you to someone who had just deprived him of his prime of life . . .'

Mr Cheevers remained quietly confident. He did not doubt that, over a cup of tea in the Canteen, the gem fragments already in his mind, and others as yet uncut but just as sparkling, would all come together, and almost automatically rearrange themselves, paragraph by paragraph, into the sort of tabloid jewellery which was expected of him. Typed out in double-spacing on one of the office Remingtons, another brilliant and characteristic 'Crimeograph' would have been completed.

The piece, moreover, would appear in the same issue as the exclusive, two-part, double-spread revelations that the Features Editor had got all signed-up. They were the wife's revelations, of course: the readers of the *Sunday Sun* were always interested in what wives had to say. And Mr Cheevers was very pleased about them, too. He had a nose for such things, and had tipped off the Features Editor long before the rest of Fleet Street had spotted what a story they would make.

Because the Features Editor set great store by Mr Cheevers's judgment and discretion, he had asked him to be the go-between. The go-between and the ghost. That was how Mr Cheevers first met the tall, distracted woman with the red-rimmed eyes and the elaborate hair-do.

The partnership had been a brief but fruitful one. Two sessions of an hour-and-a-half apiece, and Mr Cheevers had got all that he needed. That was because of the knack he had. He knew just the right questions to ask; got her to remember all sorts of things that she would otherwise rather have forgotten, re-opened old wounds that she had thought were long-since healed.

Mr Cheevers felt now that he could relax. Professionally, he was satisfied. A bachelor son, he looked forward to returning to his mother's small house in Dulwich.

But the journey home did not prove to be a quiet one. The image of the man who had just been sentenced rose before him, and remained there. He could see again the pale blue eyes which kept closing momentarily when he replied to anything, as though he were trying hard, really hard, making a great effort of it, to give the truthful answer; the way his hair rose up in a little quiff on one side, giving him a strangely youthful, even rather jaunty, appearance; the sagging, shapeless lapels of the inferior, ready-made suit that he was wearing. He could even see him holding up his hand politely like a schoolboy before making that final thank-you speech to Mr Justice Streetley.

As the train bumped and rattled over the points, the pale blue eyes continued to stare into Mr Cheevers's own dark brown ones. It was then that his great idea came to him, his moment of revelation. With the hard, plastic buttons of British Rail upholstery pressing into his back he was on his way not to Dulwich but to Damascus.

He knew now what his life's work was to be. It had been made plain to him. Instead of merely pursuing cases in which the Police had already become interested, or studying the actions and behaviour of men brought up before the law, he would select one particular wrong-doer and go back to the origin of things, trace events to their starting place and lay bare the very roots of crime.

In the notebook which he always carried he had got the wife's telephone number. It was a new one, of course; fixed up by him with the Post Office so that outsiders shouldn't bother her. He'd give her a ring as soon as he got home; say something consoling, hold out at least a token promise for the future. She'd need a bit of bucking-up, he reckoned.

Then, when she had learnt to live with herself again, had come to grips with separation, they could get down to some serious literary work together. This time it was not the wreckage of her life in which he was interested: it was her husband's story.

And he knew that it was only from the wife that he could hope to get it.

BOOK ONE

A Garden with Gnomes

Chapter 1

Because it was raining so hard, really hard, Stanley Pitts put down his parcels on the wooden settee in the booking-hall and then, one by one, fitted them into the side pockets of his raincoat. Even in the short walk down the platform the fancy wrapping-paper had become blotched and uninviting-looking.

But Crocketts Green was like that. No proper protection for the passengers in bad weather; not even a covered footbridge over to the Elmers Road side. And it was important to Stanley Pitts that his parcels shouldn't get ruined. They were presents. He wanted them still to have the original boutique-and-salesgirl gloss about them when he reached home.

Even on fine nights, it was a brisk ten minutes' walk; ten minutes exactly, that is, if he turned off at the Launderette and cut across the service area by the Post Office – longer, of course, if he carried straight on past the Bank and down Westmorland Crescent. Over the years he had got into the habit of timing it; keeping himself up to scratch as it were. This evening, all bundled-up and with his hat pulled down over his forehead, it might take him as much as twelve to twelve-and-a-half; even thirteen, possibly, if the downpour persisted.

As he turned into Kendal Terrace, he already felt himself at home. There was something so wonderfully welcoming about the little row of villas, all precisely the same and all so startlingly different. For whereas the woodwork at No. 10 was painted a light heliotrope, No. 12 was olive green, and No. 14 had favoured rich chocolate. It was the same, too, with the front doors. Going down the street, you came on plain black; green; green with the panels picked out in cream; royal blue; even canary yellow, flat-surfaced and modern-looking, with aluminium-finish knocker and letter box. At No. 16, where Stanley Pitts lived, it was different again: shining white paintwork and the only front door in Kendal Terrace with a glass panel and a Spanish-type ironwork grille on the inside.

But there was more to distinguish No. 16 than the front door. Stanley Pitts's house had concealed lighting for the bell-push. As soon as night came, the device shone out in the darkness like an illuminated fruit-gum. There were also the gnomes. There were three of them stationed there in the front garden, all dressed in red and all heavily bearded. The one with the longest beard – he was a replacement, actually – held a fishing-rod dangling over the miniature, heart-shaped pond; the second in seniority was seated, legs crossed, on top of a heavily speckled toadstool; and the youngster of the party, by the look of him, lounged flat-out, with his chin supported on his hands, simply looking on.

At one time there had been another quite outstanding feature, too, up beside the flowerbed next to the house – an eighteen-inch, fibre-glass windmill, all in imitation weather-boarding, with scarlet sails that would have turned merrily if any passing gust could have got down low enough to reach them. But the mill was there no longer. It had simply disappeared; vanished overnight from the surrounding elfin landscape. And not by magic, either. The general view of Kendal Terrace was that it must have been the holiday-relief milkman who had pinched it, along with the rock plants from No. 17, on his early delivery round one August Sunday morning.

That was why the gnomes were now all firmly cemented in.

Tonight, however, Stanley Pitts hardly gave them a thought. Nor did he have to; even in that dampness they could idle their time away in perfect safety. The piece of copper tubing let in two inches below the brim of the pool saw to that. Before he had fitted it, anything might have happened. After one sudden summer cloudburst, he had known the angler up to his armpits in flood-water, the toadstool entirely marooned and nothing showing of the little lazy one except the tassel on the top of his cap. As it was, Stanley Pitts could hear the reassuring gurgle of the drainage-system as he stood there in the shelter of the porch, and knew that everything would be all right.

Soaked through, Stanley Pitts uttered a sigh of sheer contentment as he felt the key in the Yale lock begin to turn beneath his fingers. Remembering the presents that he had bought, he must have been one of the happiest men in London.

'That you, Stan?'

Because it was coming from the far end of the little hallway where the kitchenette-cum-diner was, and because the electric mixer was electrically mixing something, the voice sounded a trifle muffled and indistinct. And, at the moment, it carried just the faintest note of tension, of anxiety even. To an eavesdropper, it could have sounded as though, after a whole day's waiting for him to come home, his wife had suddenly suspected that it might be someone else.

But Stanley Pitts knew every intonation in that voice. And he had learnt to make allowance for it. There was nothing to it, really. It was simply that she was the highly-strung, keyed-up kind. Things affected her more than they did other people.

'Coming, Beryl,' he told her.

The glass bead curtain over the alcove parted, and Beryl herself stood there. Silhouetted against the background of built-in, Viceroy-range domestic units, and with the tubular light fittings, all bright chromium, shining down on her, she looked beautiful. Friday was the day for her regular hair appointment. And there she was, with it all piled up and gleaming, raven-black and perfect, above the long white nylon overall that she was wearing.

He started to come forward so that he could kiss her, but she stopped him.

'Oh, my goodness,' she said breathlessly, 'you're all soaking. Is it raining or something? You stay just where you are until you've got those things off. You're dripping over everything, you are.'

Obediently, he stepped back onto the doormat. Beryl was quite right, of course. With the side pockets of his raincoat crammed full, the rain-water was trickling down in little channels on either side. He was standing in a puddle already.

In the state he was in, Beryl told him, he had better take his shoes off on the mat while he stood there. Then he could go straight up to the bathroom and hang his raincoat on the hook behind the shower curtain. What's more, he'd better put his trousers straight into the press while they were still damp so as to get the creases out, she added; otherwise they'd look like nothing on earth when he came to wear them again.

It was all said in a rush as though it were a single sentence that she was uttering. And halfway through the electric mixer, which was automatic, abruptly turned itself off. That was why towards the end she seemed to be speaking so much louder; almost as though she were scolding him.

When he did reach the bathroom, however, he couldn't open the door because little Marleen was still in there. Not that the door itself would have been locked: Beryl was against locked doors in bathrooms because of the dangers of fainting fits and sudden collapses and drownings. But she was also against her husband going in when Marleen had nothing on.

'I mean, it's got to stop sometime,' she had only last week explained to him. 'It can't go on like forever, can it? Our Marleen's getting to be quite a madam, remember. We don't want her to think that things like that don't matter, do we?'

Naturally, he was grateful to Beryl for having pulled him up in time. Because, left to himself, it would never have occurred to him. For as long as he could remember, he had enjoyed the moments he'd had sitting there on the cork-tipped bathroom stool, reading her favourite chapters from *Black Beauty*, or the latest Enid Blyton, or whatever it was that she'd happened to be keen on at that time.

When he did at last get into the bathroom and put the trousers into the press he noticed that the turn-ups had begun to fray. They were not yet ragged, but already wispy. And this was disturbing because it was his best office suit that he was wearing; the one in which he would be facing the interview board. He wanted to be well turned out for that.

Though they don't actually say so, dress is one of the things they notice in the Civil Service: more than once he'd seen quite promising careers go sour because of a fountain pen clipped on the outside pocket or a pullover where a waistcoat should have been.

It was with a feeling of real relief, of putting the whole of his working life behind him, that he changed into his sports jacket and his Burton's cavalry-twill. The cavalry-twill was anything but new; nearly four years old, in fact. But fresh from the cleaners it might have come out of Savile Row only yesterday. It made him feel a different man.

Gathering up his parcels, he went downstairs to celebrate. After her bath, Marleen looked pink and fresh and pretty. She undeniably was a pretty child. And this was strange considering that she mostly took after Stan's side of the family, and not after Beryl's. Blue eyes, peaches-and-cream complexion, and fair hair: that had all come from him. But the good bone structure, the high cheek line and the tantalizingly deep eye-sockets had been her mother's gift.

And it was Beryl, of course, not Stan, who had taught her how to make the most of herself. No make-up, naturally; no lipstick or eyeshadow. Not yet. Just a pat or two on the forehead with a powder-puff to get rid of the schoolgirl shine, and the little ringlets of pale gold hair pulled forward to make a frame for the small, eager face. Also, done that way it helped to cover up the ears. The ears were rather large and outstanding; another of the legacies from Stan's side.

At the sight of him, Marleen rushed forward to give him her special Daddy-come-home-at-last kind of hug. It always pleased Beryl to see it happening: it showed what a united family they all were. That was why she encouraged it, often giving Marleen a little shove in the small of the back as she heard Stan's key go into the keyhole: encouraged it, that is, unless the hug went on too long, and got rough and silly. But, even then, she made a point of reminding herself that despite the tiny wrists and the golden ringlets, at heart Marleen was really just a high-spirited, old-fashioned tomboy.

'I've got something for you here,' Stan said. 'Something for both of you.'

'Whatever is it?' Beryl asked, her voice rising a little as it always did when she was excited.

As she was speaking she came round from behind the ivory enamel louvre that cut off the cooking and washing-up part from the dining area. It was another from the Viceroy range, that louvre. Even in the catalogue Beryl had fallen in love with it; and, once in place, it was possible to step from the sink into society simply by slipping past it. She had already removed the white nylon overall, leaving it behind her in the chores section. Underneath, it was her red and gold housecoat, the one with the big Mexican-looking buttons, that she was wearing. They were Sun-God buttons and they glinted as she came towards him.

Even so, Marleen had got there first. She was already reaching out for the present that Stan had brought her. Beryl gave the back of Marleen's hand a little slap because the child was grabbing out so, just the way she'd always been told not to.

'No snatching like,' she said sharply. 'This isn't the monkey house.'

The wrapping-paper on Marleen's parcel had not yet quite dried off. As she tore it open, it made a sticky, sucking sound.

Stan turned towards Beryl.

'And this is for you,' he told her. 'I . . . I hope you like it.'

'Oh, if you chose it like, I'm sure I shall. What a lovely surprise.'

She did not, however, open her parcel immediately. Not because she didn't want to, but just because she was watching Marleen; making quite sure that whatever she had been given was suitable.

Not that she need have bothered. It was one of those chunky, raw-

25

leather bags with a thick shoulder-strap; the sort that *rancheros* carry about with them. All the girls of Marleen's age had a bag just like it. Beryl had seen them in her copies of *Woman* and *Woman's Own*, and in *Vogue* and *Harper's Bazaar* at the hairdresser's. She was relieved, and even a trifle surprised, that Stan should have thought of it; because, in the ordinary way, she was the one who seemed to care about such things.

Then she turned to her own parcel. It was a big square envelope with a top flap that folded into itself to make a carrying handle. On the outside she could read the words *Chez Miss, branches in Kensington, Chelsea, Streatham, Victoria and Purley* all set out in fancy type on the striped paper.

Because of the rain, the handle part had become stuck together; it was so firm it might have been gummed. But she persisted, easing it up ever so gently so as not to tear it. She was funny about that: ever since childhood she had always made a point of saving things; keeping a little stand-by store of whatever it was for tomorrow.

There was a layer of tissue paper as well, and she re-folded that, too. Then she took out the silk scarf that had been inside and, holding it at arm's length in front of her, daintily shook it out of its creases. It was a pleasing, black-and-white design that Stan had chosen, printed all over one side with views of London – St Paul's, the Tower, Buckingham Palace, old shops in Holborn, the Houses of Parliament, Nelson's Column; the lot. The other side was covered with grey taffeta which meant that you could see that it was a good one, the assistant had said.

'It's lovely. Really it is,' Beryl told him, her voice falling a little. 'It's just what I . . .'

She went over to the wall mirror. But the scarf just didn't go with the housecoat; she had known that before she even looked. But she didn't want to hurt his feelings. And, when it just looked silly up against the brocaded collar of the housecoat, she tried it as a headscarf instead. But that was no use either. She didn't want to crush down her new hair-do; and, just letting the scarf rest there on top, the two ends hardly met beneath her chin. She took it off again just as carefully as she had put it on, folding it back into its original folds, relieved to think that she wouldn't have to go further than Streatham if, in the end, she should decide to change it.

It was then that she noticed the other parcel, the one that had not been opened. And immediately she brightened up again.

'And whatever's that?' she asked.

Stan smiled. He'd been looking forward to this, thinking about it all the way down in the train; and he had no intention of being rushed. Slowly, he untwisted the screwed-up roll of brown paper.

'Bo-zho-lay,' he said. 'A bottle of Bo-zho-lay. That's for both of us. Something to celebrate with.'

Beryl stood there, staring at him. Two little spots of colour had appeared in her cheeks the way they always did when she was excited about anything. Suddenly she looked younger. Her lips were half-parted, and for a moment Stan thought that she was going to kiss him.

'Stan,' she said breathlessly. 'It's happened like. It's really happened. You've got it. And you never told me.'

She had come up close to him by now, and Stan had to put the bottle hurriedly down on the table-top to avoid dropping it.

'No. Not that, dear,' he told her, edging away as he was speaking. 'Not yet. That's not until next month, like I said.'

'Like you said what?' Marleen asked.

There was a cold, accusing note in her voice as she asked the question, and her pretty blue eyes had gone hard and narrow. She had stopped playing with her new bag, buckling and unbuckling it: the bag just hung limply there with the front dangling wide open. She moved round so that she could face him. If there was one thing that she could not bear, it was the feeling of being kept out of a secret.

Nor could her mother. Still holding the silk scarf in her hand, Beryl simply flicked Marleen out of the way.

'Well, *something's* happened,' she insisted, 'I know it has. Don't you tell me . . .'

She stopped because Stan had taken a small white card from his breast pocket, and was holding it out to her.

Reading it took her some little time. That was partly because, though she didn't like to admit it, she should have worn reading-glasses, and partly because she was naturally just a rather slow reader.

'Well, I never,' she said at last. 'Not like again this year. Two years running. Just fancy that.'

But all the excitement had gone from her voice; there was even the faintest note of disappointment.

She passed the card across to Marleen as she was speaking, pausing long enough to make quite sure that Marleen would wait for it to be given to her properly.

Marleen was better than her mother at reading; top of her class, in fact. And her eyesight was young and perfect. She held the card straight up in front of her.

'Civil Service, Admiralty Division,' she read out. 'Photographic Society Annual Exhibition 1965. First Prize, Five Guineas, Stanley Pitts (Contracts Filing)'.

Then she paused, too, her eyes narrowed up again.

'What's Contracts Filing?' she asked.

But Beryl was growing a trifle tired of Marleen's questions; even, for that matter, a trifle tired of photographic competitions.

'It's what your father does,' she told her. 'File contracts like. And now give it back to him. At once. He doesn't want dirty, sticky marks all over it, does he?'

But Stanley Pitts did not really seem to mind. He had not yet quite finished what he had in store.

'And we had the Press along,' he said. 'I think they liked *Hoarfrost* best. One of them gave me this.'

It was a smaller card that he took out of his pocket this time, a visiting card, and he did not let go of it.

' "Max Karlin, London representative, Pictures International",' he read out. 'Said he'd be getting in touch with me.'

'What about?' Marleen asked.

She still felt that there was something fishy somewhere, that she wasn't being told everything.

'About buying some of my work for the papers,' Stan told her. 'For the high-quality ones, of course.'

'Coo!'

It was an expression that Beryl didn't like Marleen to use. It was vulgar. But she could not help being a bit impressed herself. It had never occurred to her that there might be money in photography. Secretly, it had always seemed to her to be just another hobby, like toy boats or model railways; something inexcusably selfish that made him set off by himself on Sunday mornings when he could have been indoors, like other husbands, helping her.

'Well, let's only hope he does,' she said. 'You've certainly been at it long enough. It's about time . . .'

The buzzer over the automatic cooker had sounded to tell her that the Oven-Fresh Old Style Farm House Cornish Pasties were ready. She'd set the automatic dial at '3'; and that usually took care of things, unless Stan's train was really late, of course. But tonight they'd hung around undoing all those parcels. If she'd known, she would have set the dial at '2½' or even '2'.

She turned and went back behind the ivory-enamel louvre. A sudden feeling of flatness – that awful has-it-really-got-to-be-like-this-forever-until-I'm-dead? sensation – had come over her. She'd been expecting Stan's big news, the news that was going to make all the difference to them, that at last he had got his promotion. And all that she'd got was talk about photographs again.

From the other side of the screen, she could hear him still going on about them.

'The *Swans* was last year,' he was telling Marleen. 'They're the ones in the lounge. *Hoarfrost on Wimbledon Common* was the year before. This year I sent in *Apple-blossom Time*. Can't afford to go on repeating yourself, you know. If you're a good girl, Marleen, next year, perhaps it'll be you. You, in your ballet skirt. Up on your points. Against a neutral background. Holding a Chinese lantern, or something.'

Chapter 2

You can't expect to run around picking up big photographic prizes every day of the week; not Firsts, of Civil Service standard, that is. Even the most gifted competitors have to content themselves with a Second here or an Honourable Mention there, or even a Specially Commended; and usually that amount of acknowledgment has to see them over the whole twelve months.

In consequence, the rest of January came as a bit of an anti-climax for Stanley Pitts. There was the usual round of congratulations as the non-photographers in other Departments came to hear of his success; and the local paper carried a whole three-inch piece about him. But that was all. There was an undisguisable feeling of flatness to everything; flatness, and a sense of nervous expectancy about next month's Appointments Board.

Deep down in his own mind he kept telling himself that he had nothing to worry about; that the job was as good as his already. But little niggling doubts kept returning to him, and he was always glad in the evenings to get back to the warmth and security of Kendal Terrace. Friday evenings, of course, were best of all.

Like this particular Friday, for example. He hadn't been kept late at the office; the train had been on time; he'd changed into his week-end clothes; the meal was just over and, there in the small dining alcove, he and Beryl and Marleen were clearing the table to get it ready for breakfast next morning.

It was then that the front-door bell rang. No ordinary ring, either. *Ding, ding-a-ling-ding, ding-ding,* it went. And, at the sound of it, Beryl's heart turned right over; it went *bump-a-bump-bump,* like the door bell. That was because she knew it must be Cliff; her own, original Cliff, and no one else on earth.

She was thankful now, really thankful, that she had never had musical chimes installed instead of an ordinary door bell. Admittedly, in the ordinary way, they were more warm and welcoming. But they only went *ding-dong* no matter how you played about on the door bell-push.

She turned to Stan.

'Well, aren't you going to answer it?' she asked.

Then she turned to Marleen.

'And up to bed you go,' she told her. 'It's ever so late. You know it is.'

It wasn't really very late: not late at all, in fact. But, now that they were going to have Cliff with them, she wanted to keep the whole evening as close and concentrated as possible. Much as she loved Marleen, even the presence of one child could, she knew, somehow produce a strangely diluting effect.

'May'n't I just . . .?' Marleen began.

'No, you may'n't. Upstairs like I said.'

Marleen went over and gave Beryl her obedient, good-night kiss. Then she moved slowly over to the doorway and hung about there.

'Oh, hullo Uncle Cliff,' she said as she stepped through the bead curtain. 'I was just going up to bed. Perhaps if you ask Mummy . . .'

But Uncle Cliff turned out to be on Mummy's side. He'd had a long day already, and didn't in the least want to spend the rest of it with an eleven-year-old hanging about in the background; didn't even particularly want to go on being called Uncle Cliff for the rest of the evening.

'Now just you go on up,' he said, giving a teasing tug at the light gold curls as he was speaking. 'And go off to sleep.' He kissed her twice on the forehead, cupping her face in his hands as he did so. 'And if you're a good little girl you may find a present beside your bed in the morning.'

Then, because he was such an old friend of the family, practically one of them as Beryl was always saying, he slapped Marleen playfully on her little bottom. It was not the sort of thing of which Beryl, in the ordinary way, would have approved; but, coming from Cliff, she would have known that it didn't matter in the slightest. He was more like a second daddy, really.

And she had deliberately made a point of staying behind where she was in the dining alcove, and not rushing out to meet him in the hallway. This was important. Because she didn't want Stan, or Cliff for that matter, to think that she minded in the slightest whether Cliff came to see her, or whether he didn't.

But it was different, quite different, as soon as he was standing there in front of her. He had such an irresistible way with him. Like never actually speaking her name, just saying, 'Hullo, Beautiful,' as if 'Beautiful' really were her name; and saying it so casually, too, as though what he called her didn't matter to either of them.

When they had kissed, brother-and-sister fashion, he stood back and looked at her.

'Been slimming again,' he said. 'Just like I warned you not to. No point in taking chances. Wake up one morning, and you won't be there. All because . . .'

It was Beryl who stopped him.

'I'm enormous,' she said. 'You can see I am. I just don't know what to do about it.'

She swung round as she said it, so that the Sun-God buttons jangled, and the folds of the Mexican housecoat spread out around her heels. It was a brave and daring gesture. But she knew perfectly well that it was one that she could afford. Thanks to Mincal biscuits at lunchtime and no milk, no sugar in her tea at breakfast, and no tea even at tea-time, she had lost nearly seven pounds since October. Naturally, living with her all the time, Stan hadn't even noticed. Cliff was the one who had.

But she was no longer thinking of *her* appearance. She was thinking of Cliff's. And she had to admit that she had never seen him looking quite so marvellous. The new, long hair style for men might have been designed specially for him. There was something so raffish about it; so correct, too, in a vaguely naughty sort of way. And he had never before, to her knowledge, worn a shirt with thick horizontal pink lines running right across it; or a plain white collar. But she had to admit that they both went wonderfully with the broad blue pin-stripe that had turn-up cuffs on the jacket, and the double-breasted waistcoat, and the big, thin wrist-watch with the black face, and the chunky cuff-links and the dark chocolate of the laceless suede shoes. Only someone like Cliff, she reminded herself, could have carried the whole thing off so perfectly.

But already Beryl had remembered her manners; had realized to her dismay that she was just standing there. She gave him her quick, hostess smile.

'A bite to eat?' she asked. 'We've only just finished like. But it wouldn't take a jiffy. Not be any trouble, I mean.'

Pictures of the outsides of tins went flashing through her mind as she was speaking. Veal loaf, Spam, sardines in tomato sauce, salmon, celery hearts, baked beans, corned beef, Hungarian goulash – she could see them all. Left to herself for a few minutes she knew that she could produce the sort of meal that any Woman's Editor would have applauded.

Cliff, however, was busy refusing.

'No food, thank you,' he said. 'Not good for me. I've got something in my bag outside. Something I brought specially.'

He turned to Stan, and let his hand rest lightly on his arm for a moment.

'Be a good fellow and go and get it, would you?' he asked. 'It's the little one. The air bag.'

He waited until he was out of the room, and then jerked his head over his shoulder in Stan's direction.

'And how's the photographer?' he asked. 'Taken any more nice pictures lately?'

Beryl frowned, bringing the corners of her mouth down as she did so.

'You're not to talk about Stan like that,' she said. 'I've told you that before. I don't care for it.' She paused. 'As a matter of fact, he's . . .'

Stan had come back through the bead curtain by now, and was holding out the BEA air bag. Suddenly, Beryl felt sorry for him.

'I've just been telling Cliff about your prize,' she added. 'He's ever so pleased like, aren't you, Cliff?'

'Ever so,' Cliff assured her. 'Congratulations, old boy. We'll be hearing about you one day. You'll be famous. You'll hit the headlines.'

He had unzipped the bag while he was talking and had brought out a bottle of four-star Cognac.

'Try this instead,' he said. 'And don't thank me. Thank the Customs. Duty free, and no questions asked. Daylight robbery, I call it.'

His hand was on Stan's arm again.

'Glasses, please,' he added. 'Ladies present, remember. Ladies present. No swigs.'

That was another of the things that Beryl liked about Cliff. He made everything seem so carefree and cheerful. Even right back in the old days, that were so far away now, things had always gone with such a swing when Cliff was anywhere around. But now, least of all, was the time to remember. Living in the past was fatal, as she had often reminded herself.

She tugged the belt of her housecoat in tighter.

'Well, I'm sure I don't know what we're all doing out here like,' she said brightly, bringing out her quick hostess smile again. 'Why don't we go through to the lounge? That's what it's there for, isn't it?'

Beryl led the way, with Cliff following after her carrying the bottle of Cognac. Stan had to stay behind to collect the glasses. This took a moment or two because they were on the top shelf of the special glass-and-china unit. He was quite sure that it would be the best ones that Beryl would be wanting, and he had just got them all set out nicely on the matching tray that went with the set when he heard Cliff calling to him from the lounge.

'Bring the bag along, too, would you, old chap,' he said. 'I've got something else in it.'

That was the authentic Cliff all right: as long as he'd known him, Cliff always had got something else. Samples, mostly; or discontinued lines, or broken ranges, or Army surplus, or rejects, or seconds, or miscellaneous bankrupt stock. That was Cliff's great strength, his versatility. If Cliff could buy it, Cliff could sell it. Wireless sets, watches, lingerie sets, garden hammocks, tape recorders, costume jewellery, indoor fish-tanks, binoculars – they were all one to him. And that was only half the story. Package tours, second-hand cars, insurance, the employment agency business, home loans: he had tried them all.

There had been ups and downs, naturally; but distinctly more of the ups. And he was clearly on an ascending curve at the moment. He was, in fact, becoming quite big in the discount trade. And, so far as he was concerned, it was all strictly cash; no credit, and scarcely any book-keeping.

It is not all that easy to get through a bead curtain when you are carrying an air bag and three crystal-cut glasses balanced on a shiny tray. Stan took his time, and did it the sensible way: backwards. It may have looked silly, but it worked.

When he reached the lounge, Cliff was in the Swedish swivel chair with the black leather cushions that wheezed as you sat down on them, and Beryl was sitting sideways, half on and half off the couch, her knees together and her hands folded demurely in her lap.

Cliff held up the brandy bottle as Stan came in.

'Forward, St Bernard,' he said. 'Mountain rescue team approaching.'

Beryl glanced up for a moment, almost as if she had expected that there could be something wrong.

'You've forgotten the coasters,' she told Stan. 'The flower ones. And better bring a mat like for the bottle.'

Then she turned back to Cliff.

'Just fancy,' she went on. 'I can't believe it. Really, I can't. Three hours ago you were in Paris, and here you are now . . .'

But Cliff wasn't listening.

'Give us another kiss,' he asked.

Beryl shook her head. She had already heard the click made by the spring-catch on the door as Stan closed the mat cupboard, and she wasn't moving.

'You stay where you are,' she said. 'Sit still and behave yourself.'

Brandy, Stan reflected, *is* a good after-dinner drink. Not just centrally-heating and agreeable. There's a secret of some kind inside it; something of the feel of a fine sunset, or a loving hand left resting lightly in your own. Stan had allowed Cliff to fill his glass again up to the criss-cross pattern on the side, even though Beryl had only just begun to sip hers, pecking at it warily, like a bird.

After his day at the office, Stan suddenly found himself feeling better. Much better. He had even forgotten about the Appointments Board. This was the way life ought to be, he kept telling himself; the way he would have liked it to go on being forever. With the knife-edge crease of his newly cleaned cavalry-twill showing over his crossed legs, Stanley Pitts was beaming.

'Well, mustn't forget what we came for, must we?'

Cliff had thrust himself up from the breathing Swedish upholstery, and was rubbing his hands together like an auctioneer about to open the proceedings in a saleroom.

'Just you pass that air bag over, young man. Nothing in it for you, I'm afraid. Only for the girls.'

The first thing that Cliff pulled out was a big, transparent pochette of sugared almonds. Bigger than big, in fact. As he held it out in front of her, Beryl thought that it was the biggest pochette of sugared almonds that she had ever seen; a pound of them, at least; even, remembering how much sugared almonds weigh, possibly two pounds. And all tied-up round the top with an expensive-looking satin ribbon, finished off in a rosette with a gold label, bearing the maker's name, *Fleurette*, in the centre. Just like Cliff, Beryl was thinking: whatever he did was always on the grand scale.

35

'For little Marleen,' Cliff said. 'In case she wakes up in the night. Good for her teeth.'

At the sight of so many sugared almonds, Stan felt even happier still. He knew that Marleen liked sugared almonds, and he was pleased for her sake. But he felt quite sure that she would like the chunky, raw-hide satchel even better, and that pleased him too. What pleased him most of all, however, was thinking about Beryl. She needed little peaks of excitement in her life. It would mean a lot to her, having a private, unexpected birthday just when she had been sitting down to an ordinary Friday evening like every other one.

Cliff seemed to be happy, too. He winked across at Stan.

'Would you believe it?' he asked, reaching down into the air bag. 'Silly me, I've left it behind. No, must have been stolen. Lot of sticky fingers at the airport these days. Serve in Customs and grow rich, that's what I say.' He broke off suddenly. 'There it is,' he announced. 'Just where I hid it. Underneath the cocaine. Knew I'd put it somewhere safe.'

This time the parcel was flat and soft and yielding. There was no name of a shop on the outside; but there wouldn't be, Beryl reflected, because Cliff would have bought it through the trade, naturally. Cliff had trade connections everywhere.

And, when she opened the layers of plain paper inside, she could not restrain a little gasp. Just couldn't help gasping because it was so beautiful. It was a white silk headscarf with an enormous scarlet peony embroidered in the middle. The scarf was enormous, too; just the way it naturally would be if Cliff had chosen it. And pure silk; the sort of silk that sends tingles up your fingertips as soon as you touch it.

Beryl didn't waste a moment. The mirror over the mantelpiece was only an ordinary mirror, oval, picture-sized and with a magnolia-coloured glass frame to it. But it was quite large enough. She put the scarf over her head, turning sideways as she did so, Carmen fashion, and then loosely brought the two ends together beneath her chin. Even if she had knotted them it would have made no difference. It was such a huge headscarf that she knew that she could wear it any way she liked without upsetting her hair-do.

Because she was so happy, she spun round, took another look at herself in the mirror and went across to give Cliff a kiss. It was just a fleeting kiss, the sort of kiss that any wife could give to any man in front of any husband.

Then, seeing how disconsolate, how out of it Stan was looking, she crossed over to kiss him, too.

It was late now; really late. Getting on towards midnight. Cliff had gone off with a tremendous *vrmmp-vrmmp* in his new Jaguar, and Kendal Terrace was quietly settling down for the night. Stan double-locked the front door and put the safety-chain in position.

It may have been simply because it was bedtime. Or because of the little kiss that she had given him. Or simply because of the Cognac that he had been drinking. Or possibly because of all of them together. Whatever it was, Stan went through into the bedroom feeling suddenly young again.

Beryl was seated on the low stool in front of her dressing-table. It was all part of the same suite, that stool; ivory-white, with lyre-shaped, curving legs. The dressing-table was nearly all mirror, except for a pair of small ivory-white drawers on either side. The bedside tables, with their matching lamps, were ivory-white, too. And so was the waist-high, bow-fronted cabinet that had photographs of Marleen, right back to the time when she had been a tiny toddler, arranged on the glass top.

Not that it was a cold-looking room. Beryl's natural eye for interior decoration had seen to that. The fitted carpet, the curtains, the shades on the matching lamps and the bedspread were all old rose: they glowed. And tonight there was another splash of colour as well. Across the end of the bed she had draped the white scarf that Cliff had given her. The scarf was really white, white as marble, with the great scarlet peony blazing in the centre.

Stan approached her gently, lovingly. It wasn't exactly the moment to speak to her because she was cold-creaming her face. She was all shiny and sticky-looking, and he waited patiently until she had cleaned herself up with the last of the face tissues.

Even then it wasn't easy because she immediately poured something out of a little bottle into the palm of her hand and began patting it into her cheeks with short, vicious slaps, as though she were intent on hurting herself. Her hair, too, made it difficult for him to speak to her. Naturally, she didn't want to risk getting face cream onto it the very day it had been done. That was why she was wearing the biggest of her bath caps. It was of flowered muslin, practically balloon size. Stan had

37

to edge right round it before he could even see her.

He put his hands on her shoulders. As he did so, he felt a little tremor, almost a shudder, go through her. She folded her own hands in her lap and sat there motionless, saying nothing.

'I do love you,' he said.

His hands were passing beyond her shoulders by now. In a moment, they would be sliding down inside her nightdress. But again there was that tremor, that shudder; and it really was a shudder this time. She quickly brought up her pale, sticky hands to force his large dry ones away.

'Not tonight,' she said. 'I just don't feel like it. Besides, I've got a headache. I feel terrible.'

'I don't,' he told her. 'I feel pretty good.'

He gave a little laugh as he said it; a short, silly sort of a laugh. It was not like his usual laugh at all.

All that Beryl did was to shrug her shoulders. She had already begun to pour some more of the stuff in the bottle out into her open palm.

'Well, perhaps it agrees with you,' she said. 'Brandy, I mean. It just upsets me. It does some people. I shall never get to sleep. Not tonight I won't. I know that. I can feel it like.'

She was staring hard at herself in the mirror, searching for a fresh place to begin slapping.

'Why don't you sleep in the dressing-room?' she asked at last. 'You won't get a wink in here. I shall have my light on all night.'

The word 'dressing-room' was entirely Beryl's invention. It was simply the spare room really. But calling it the 'dressing-room' made the whole house seem so much larger and nicer, somehow.

Stan did not reply. Instead, he went over to his side of the bed and lifted up the pillow to get his striped pyjamas. He put them under his arm and walked over to the door.

On the way, Beryl stopped him.

'You do understand, don't you,' she began. 'It isn't that . . .'

'All right. I understand.'

'Well, good night, then. Sleep well.'

'Good night.'

The door was already half-closed behind him when he heard Beryl call.

'Sta-an.'

It was the break in the middle that made him stop so suddenly. That was just the way she always said his name whenever she was really fond of him.

He turned, and stood there waiting. Beryl's big, dark eyes were looking at him out of the mirror.

'Which branch was it you got it at?' she asked. 'The little black-and-white one, I mean.'

Chapter 3

February is usually the most miserable of months, with Winter still grizzling away in the background and Spring far off and improbable.

But not this February. At least, not for Stanley Pitts. He felt relieved that it had come. That was because it was the month for the Selection Board. Ever since the date had been announced, way back before Christmas, Stan had been looking forward to it as if it had been his own birthday. Very nearly was, in fact. Next month he would be thirty-six. And thirty-five was exactly the right age to move up a Grade: quite senior enough to be able to show a record of good, practical experience – nearly nineteen years of it, in his case – and still sufficiently young for there to be a note of undetected promise, of brilliancy even, in the application.

In his mind, as he sat there in the staff canteen, stirring his mid-morning coffee, he kept going over the details of the advertisement. He knew the whole text by heart already, and he could see it as though it were all printed out in front of him: *Senior Records Officer (Contracts)* it ran: *Salary £1,850–£2,250. Candidates will be expected to have first-hand experience of modern filing systems and procedures, and be familiar with the requirements of other Service Departments. London based (Hammersmith). Application form P/11/372 from Chief Personnel Officer, ext. 347. Closing date, January 15th, 1965.*

It was really quite remarkable. The whole thing fitted so perfectly that it might have been drawn up specifically with him in mind. More than once he had wondered how on earth they could have expected to fill the post if, by sheer good fortune, he himself should not have happened to be around.

Even so, he wasn't leaving anything to chance. Ever since the advertisement had appeared, he had given his present job all he had. And more than *his* job, really: the Senior Records Officer's job as well. The Senior Records Officer was coming up to retirement age. That was why the post was falling vacant, and it was only natural that he should have slowed down a bit and been prepared to leave more and more of the work to his assistant. After all, Stan had been trained by him. The

Senior Records Officer knew perfectly well that even if he dropped dead tomorrow, the reputation of the Department would continue untarnished so long as his pupil was still around.

'£1,850–£2,250': that bit might have been printed in red, it stood out so vividly. They were very reasonable people, too, the Civil Service; that is, once you got to know them properly. They always took age and experience into account. What they were after was a real winner, and the more suitable the candidate, the further up the financial ladder they started him. By the time of his thirty-sixth birthday, Stan should be a two-thousand-a-year man. Even £2,100, possibly. And then it wouldn't matter if Beryl still wanted to have the small back garden paved all over and made into a patio, complete with teak furniture and a place for the plug-in electric barbecue.

Even though the last grains of sugar had long since dissolved, Stan was still vacantly stirring away at his coffee, thinking about the whole bright future and his own peculiar good fortune.

But back in Kendal Terrace, things were by no means so good.

The day had started off badly, from breakfast onwards in fact, with Marleen splashing the milk for her cornflakes all over the front of her new school uniform; and then, on the way to school, when she and Beryl had got as far as the corner of Derwent Gardens, having to go right back to the house again because she had forgotten her dancing-shoes.

What made it all so hard was that other mothers did not have to put up with it. Most children of Marleen's age went to school on their own. But not Marleen. Beryl knew that it was silly of her, but she couldn't help it. Eight forty-five in the morning, broad daylight, too, wasn't a particularly dangerous sort of time. Not like evenings. But, all the same, there were some very strange people about, and Beryl would have been ready to stand outside the school gates all day if necessary just to make sure that nobody nasty got a chance of going up to her Marleen.

There was another thing that made it so much harder for Beryl. That was because she always made a point of dressing properly before she went out anywhere. Half the mothers at Marleen's school just wore anything in the mornings, not even troubling about a hat mostly. Beryl herself always wore gloves and, on mornings like this, carried an umbrella. It was one of the new short, chubby ones.

On the way back from school, Beryl did her shopping. Not that there was much of it; not on a Tuesday. Just soap flakes, sponge wafers for Marleen's tea, a new rubber nozzle for the tap in the sink, and a tube of toothpaste. But it still had to be done, and she liked to be through with it early. That was why she always popped the nylon-mesh shopping bag into her proper patent leather handbag before setting out.

It was still not yet nine-thirty when she got back to Kendal Terrace and to the life of which husbands know nothing. They just slam the front door, these men and, with the morning paper under their arm, go off to the station imagining that the breakfast table clears itself and does the washing-up, that beds are re-made without touching them, and that whole rooms give themselves a thorough going-over with the Hoover when there is nobody around.

On good mornings, it gave her a rather pleasant feeling of superiority, a consciousness of her own efficiency, that she could make it *seem* like that. She always went straight upstairs to change the moment she got in, hanging her shopping dress up in the wardrobe ready to wear again when she had taken her afternoon rest. Then, dressed in almost any-thing – an old jumper and skirt, usually – and with her stockings rolled down so that they wouldn't ladder when she had to kneel, she got down to it. Really got down. Vim, Mansion Polish, Windolene, Brillo soap pads, the daily sprinkle of Harpic in the lavatory pan – she used them all.

A couple of hours later when she had pulled her fingers ever so carefully out of the rubber gloves that she always wore when she was working, she was exhausted. Utterly exhausted. But it was better that way, she told herself. Even if she felt breathless sometimes – faint too at times – it meant that she would be free by lunchtime. She could relax. Become a human being again. Enjoy the very things that she had been cleaning, and scrubbing away at, and rubbing down and polishing; enjoy them, that is, until twenty-to-four when she had to go round to Kendal High to pick up Marleen.

Lunch itself was nothing really. Just two Slimmits, and an apple. Then a cup of plain Nescafé. With a figure like hers, Beryl had to be perpetually careful, on the alert the whole time in case the red line on the bathroom scales even threatened to go above the nine-six mark.

The afternoon rest had, for years now, become the most important thing in Beryl's life. It was so entirely her own. And she deliberately kept it so. Even if anyone came to the door selling something, she remained where she was, ignoring the bell, pretending that she was out. A proper little burglar's paradise the house was, she often told herself. But it was quite safe really. She always went round checking that the ground-floor windows were properly fastened and put the safety-chain on the front door into position before she went upstairs.

Then, lying stretched out on her bed, with only the eiderdown over her and with the Venetian blinds half-closed to shut out the houses opposite, she could begin her own separate existence. Sometimes she read a few pages of a library book. Sometimes she nibbled guiltily at a Mars Bar which, in the shop, she had told them that she was buying for Marleen. And, even then, as she kept reminding herself, it wasn't that she was being self-indulgent, not just giving herself a furtive, schoolgirl treat. She knew that there was more to it than the sweetness. It was the actual sugar energy that she needed. Nearly always these days, she was battling against a strange wilting-away sort of feeling. Sheer fatigue, she supposed it was; just wilting away and wondering how, and for how long, she could still keep going.

Quite often, she couldn't bear it any longer, and had to give way to tears; simply rolling over and sobbing, all alone, onto the pink pillow-case. Those were the occasions when, after school, Marleen used to notice how made-up her mother's eyes were, almost as if she were going out to a dance, or something.

And today it was remembering the peony on the white headscarf that set her off. There had been a time, so far off now it seemed, when Cliff would have gone on giving her presents like that every day if she had let him. He had been so mad about her. And she had been mad about him, too. It was only her parents, for some reason, who had been against it. They kept warning her that Cliff wasn't the sort of young man to be relied on. And, in the end, he had made his brief, disastrous marriage to a common waitressy kind of girl, while Beryl – on the re-bound, she supposed it must have been – had married Stan. Her parents were both dead by now. She had lost them, just as she had lost Cliff. All she had was Stan and Marleen now. Just that, and nothing else. She herself didn't matter any longer. She had realized that for years.

At the thought of Stan, she suddenly sat up. She had stopped feeling sad and miserable by now. She was angry. He'd made so little of himself, had Stan. That's what she couldn't stand. And with all the advantage she'd given him, too. It was her house really they were living in: Stan could never have afforded even Kendal Terrace if it hadn't been for the money that poor Daddy had left her.

That's why she was keeping her fingers crossed about the new appointment. More than once, she had thought of going along herself to see the Personnel Officer. Not to cause trouble; not to give him a piece of her mind. Nothing vulgar or unladylike like that. Just so that he could see the sort of person that Stan was married to. So that he should realize how ridiculous it was for a woman like Beryl to be married to a bottom-Grade clerk, or for a bottom-Grade clerk like Stan to try to keep up socially with a woman like Beryl. It was, she reckoned, something that the Personnel Officer owed to the Lords of the Admiralty to get his sense of values right.

The onyx alarm clock on the bedside table – Beryl always set the hand for three-thirty just in case she should happen to drop off – gave a little warning click that meant that it was about to start ringing. She pushed the button down on top, and went over to the dressing-table to re-do her face.

At least, for once, she didn't have to rush. On Tuesdays, because of dancing, Marleen didn't come out until nearly quarter past.

It was Beryl's only other quiet moment of the day. The evening meal was over. The plates and dishes were in the automatic washer. The television was on. And Marleen was safely tucked up at last, up in her little chintzy bedroom; tucked up, but not necessarily asleep, Beryl kept reminding herself. That was why she was keeping one ear open. Sometimes the little monkey switched the bedside lamp on again, and went on reading long after her mother had kissed her good-night and left the room in darkness. But Beryl was wise to her. Even above the television, she knew that she could still hear if there was the least tiny sound from Marleen's room. Leaning over to take another book from the shelf that Stan had fixed up for her would be quite enough to get Beryl beside her in a flash.

Because they were watching television, Beryl and Stan were both sitting half sideways in their chairs. It is like that in most homes – just one of the natural hazards of television – that there is nowhere really right to have the set. Except in the fireplace, that is. And this was out of the question in No. 16 because it was only last autumn that they'd had the new convection gas-fire fitted. As it was, all the furniture faced one way, confronting the gas-fire; and the television set, smart and

44

good-looking in its own way, was stuck right over in the corner.

Beryl turned towards him.

'I don't suppose like you've heard anything, have you, Stan?' she asked. 'About the job, I mean.'

She hadn't meant to ask him at all. The question had just slipped out, sudden and unintended. But then she hadn't really been watching. More just sitting there, thinking. Going over things in her mind; things like wondering how much longer they would have to put up with a black-and-white set when so many of Marleen's friends had already gone over to colour; and what it would cost to get Marleen properly fitted up with jodhpurs and ankle boots and a tweed jacket and one of those black, peaked caps that were so severe they looked almost saucy.

Turning towards him had made no difference. Stan hadn't really been watching either. Just thinking. Even his eyes had gone glazed. He might have been marooned on some desert island, he seemed so far off.

Even so, she wasn't going to be ignored, not treated as though she didn't even exist. So, naturally, she repeated the question. And this time she could tell that Stan had heard because he half raised his hand in a sort of waving-away gesture to shut her up, as though she were a child, or something.

That was why she shouted at him; shouted even louder than she had intended.

'Well, if you don't care, I'm sure I don't,' she could hear herself saying, her voice rising all the time. 'What do we want with the extra money? We don't need it, do we? We're rolling in it. We're rich. That's what we are – rich.'

She was sorry afterwards, of course. And surprised at herself. The outburst had been so entirely unexpected. But it showed how run down she was, how close to breaking-point. And naturally she did break down and cry; cried the way she did in the afternoons when she was all alone.

But perhaps it was just as well. She had noticed before that somehow she always seemed to feel better after a good cry. And Stan was so kind and loving, so understanding. He went over to the couch to put his arms round her. So confident, too.

'Everything's going to be all right this time,' he told her. 'It's . . . it's in the bag.' He paused for a moment remembering his past un-successes, and then resumed. 'Nothing to it really. I've been recom-mended. I know that for a fact. Just a formality, advertising the job.

So that it doesn't look like favouritism, you know.'

Beryl squeezed his hand. Then she fumbled about in the pocket of her housecoat to find a handkerchief.

'Don't take any notice of me,' she said. 'I'm just being silly. I must be tired, that's all it is. It's only that I couldn't bear it if . . .'

She had broken off, and Stan could tell that she was listening to something. Upstairs, so she thought, she had heard the sound of a bedside lamp being clicked on. They waited in silence, both of them listening hard. Then Stan got up and returned to his own chair.

But it was only a false alarm, and Beryl resettled herself.

'I mean,' she resumed, 'that if anyone else got it like, I think I should kill myself. For your sake, I mean. Because if anyone ever deserved anything, you do. Working away all those years down in the basement with no proper fresh air or anything, and everyone else getting promoted all round you. It's simply more than I could take. It's only because I love you that I care so much.'

Chapter 4

There is more to a terrace house than simply living in it.

For a start, you have neighbours. And naturally, you get to know them. You can't avoid it, in fact, particularly when the builder has planned it so that the front doors are set next to each other: two front doors with a front room on either side, then two more front doors and two more front rooms, and so on right down the street.

If you don't meet one lot either coming in or going out, once you're inside you're practically one big family with the other lot. Only a wall's width away, remember; and only a thin dividing-wall at that. If No. 14 had the radio turned up, Beryl could set her watch by the time signal; and, if the old-fashioned two-panel front door at No. 18 was banged shut instead of being closed gently, the hat-rack in No. 16 always rattled. The same upstairs, too. But worse. Shared noises like bath water running. Or plugs being pulled. Even snoring, sometimes.

For years now, Beryl had been saying that they ought to move right out somewhere. Into a little bungalow, preferably. No stairs. And, above all, no next-door neighbours. As things were, however, she had to admit that she was lucky in the neighbours she had got. Down the road it was different. At No. 35, for instance, there was a family with five children; five children in a three-bedroomed house: Beryl didn't like to think what it must be like there when any of the children got ill. And No. 28 was openly sub-let, with two bell-pushes for everyone to see. Then there was the house at the end that always had the blinds drawn, and never did anything about the front garden; and three doors down on her own side there was a red-haired woman, apparently without a husband, who gave parties and had the oddest-looking collection of friends who said noisy goodbyes on the pavement and woke up the whole street by slamming car doors before they went home.

More than once Beryl had wondered if it could be that the whole neighbourhood were going down, slipping away socially the way some places do. She hoped not, because she could not bear to think of spending money on the house if property values were falling. And, she had decided, almost decided that is, to have the outside re-painted in pale apple-green. She had even got so far as wondering what colour the curtains would have to be to go with it.

Not that either No. 14 or No. 18 would be likely to mind very much either way. Mrs Thomson in No. 14 was an invalid; and, as she never went out, she could hardly be expected to see anyway. And, on the other side, there were the Ebbutts. Mrs Ebbutt was as nice a woman as you could meet. But married to a schoolmaster. And just not interested. All that they cared about in No. 18 was homework and revision and 'O' Levels and that kind of thing.

If Beryl were to go mad and re-paint the woodwork pink or violet, Mrs Ebbutt would probably not even notice.

It was the letter from the Bank Manager that upset Beryl.

And it came on a Saturday of all days – one of the only two days in the week when she had a moment to herself in bed and wasn't rushing round all the time doing things for other people. Over the week-end Stan had always made a point of bringing her breakfast up to her; it had started right back from the very moment when, ever so long ago, they'd returned from their honeymoon. And now, of course, he had Marleen to help him: she looked after the toaster while Stan made the tea. It gave Beryl quite a lump in the throat sometimes to see the two of them come trooping into the room looking so pleased with themselves just because, instead of the other way round, for once in a while she allowed them to wait on her.

It was because it was a Saturday that the letter was there, propped up against the teapot like an invitation. And not knowing what it contained, she had opened it before she had taken so much as a sip of tea. In consequence, her whole mouth became bone dry as she went on reading.

If she had been fully dressed and with her make-up on, she wouldn't have minded so much. She could have coped. But, with just a short frilly jacket over her nightdress and her hair not even seen to, she felt defenceless.

The letter wasn't written in the way that Mr Winters usually wrote to her. All his old-time niceness seemed to have gone out of him. In hard, black typing he simply said that her account was now overdrawn by one-hundred-and-seven pounds and that the Directors had instructed him to see that it was put in funds again. He asked therefore that she should arrange to come and see him as soon as possible, and hoped that in the meantime she would not be proposing to draw out any further amounts.

It made her go cold all over, that letter, and she could see the sheet of paper fluttering in her fingers as she lay there. What made it all so much worse was that, until now, she had always thought that Mr Winters was her friend. And now this horrible letter showed that he simply did not understand; come to that, never could have understood the first thing about her. Because her private bank account meant more to her than anyone else could ever realize. Her whole self-respect depended on it. It was what made her different from all the other wives in Kendal Terrace; different from all the other wives in Crocketts Green, she didn't wonder.

First there had been the money from her father's will. Nearly two thousand pounds of it. Then buying the house – Mr Winters had encouraged her in that. Then all the expense when Marleen had been so ill and Beryl had thought they were going to lose her. Then the re-wiring when, without warning, the electricity people said the place wasn't safe. Then all the things she'd done to the house to make it a nice home for the three of them. That was when Mr Winters had offered – yes, actually *offered* – to arrange a mortgage. And she had been forced to go back to him a second time because otherwise there would have been no way to pay for summer holidays or winter clothes or even odds-and-ends like skates for Marleen when half her form had started going along to the ice rink, and naturally Marleen had to go, too.

It wasn't her fault that now there was nothing left. Nothing for anything. Now, whatever it was she wanted, she would simply have to do without. Or ask Stan for it. Even for the hundred-and-seven pounds to pay back to Mr Winters. And then where would she be? Just like all the other wives. Utterly dependent.

But what more could she have done to make things right? Heaven knows she'd been on to Stan often enough, begging him, imploring him, nagging – yes, actually nagging – him to do something about getting himself promoted. He'd tried twice already, once for a job on the Stores side, and once for something to do with Pensions and Sick Pay; and then only because she'd made him. But both times they'd turned him down.

And really she didn't wonder. You only had to look at him to see that there was nothing there. No real ambition. No confidence in himself. Not like Cliff; not a leader. No drive. It was just like Stan to have to hang around and wait for someone else to retire before thinking of getting anywhere. Left to himself, he'd have been perfectly content just to go on forever doing whatever they asked him to do, being paid whatever they cared to pay him, provided he was left free to get on with his photography.

'Oh, my God, Stan,' she suddenly heard herself say out loud, 'you don't know what you're doing to me. You're killing me. That's what you're doing, killing me. Slowly, deliberately killing me.'

Even after the outburst, she was down at nine o'clock as usual, dressed in her blue shopping suit, properly made-up and her hair re-done exactly the way Monsieur Louis had shown her how.

But she wasn't really there at all. This was only the mechanical part of her, the machine that she had turned herself into just so that things shouldn't get out of hand and go sloppy. The true Beryl, the one with feelings, the one who loved and got hurt, was miles away. Up on a cloud somewhere, thinking about debt and Mr Winters; and by how much Stan's salary would go up when he got his promotion; and what life would have been like if, when only nineteen and still with a long pigtail down her back, she had agreed to run away with Cliff the way he had wanted her to.

And it was like that all day. She was two entirely different people. The one who trundled the metal trolley round the Supermarket picking up the giant economy sizes, the special offers and the new range packets, simply wouldn't have understood if the other one had suddenly come up and thrown her arms around her, bursting into tears because life was all so frightful, so hopeless.

Because Beryl was strangely silent at lunch, Stan asked if she was feeling all right. Only, of course, he was asking the wrong person. The sensitive, mature woman who had just sliced up a banana for Marleen and poured Express Dairy cream over it, and couldn't have been more in control of herself. And this was strange because at that very moment, face down and with her long hair trailing behind her, the one he didn't know about was already floating downstream somewhere, unconscious, to some hidden, watery grave, simply because she had decided to end it all.

It was not until the evening, after Marleen had gone to bed, that Beryl finally spoke to Stan. And by then she was pleased with herself to find how calm and considerate she was. She crossed over to the television set and turned it off.

'Sta-an,' she said, the word coming out rather slow and appealingly, 'you don't mind not looking for a moment, do you? I just want to say something to you.'

But it happened to be another of those times when Stan had not even noticed that she had spoken to him. And she saw now that she need not have bothered to turn off the set. He hadn't even been watching. Instead, he was going, paragraph by paragraph, through the Used Equipment pages of *Amateur Photographer*.

'Sta-an,' she said again. 'I'm talking to you.'

He looked up.

'Yes, dear?' he asked, keeping the tip of his finger up against the small ad: *Zykton-Matic lens inc. case and adaptor 200 mm f. 3.5 auto, £25 19s 6d* that he had just been reading.

Beryl came over and, going up behind him, leant forward and spread her hands flat out across the page.

'I want you to pay attention,' she said, making it sound all light and playful. 'It'll only take a moment. Then you can go on reading your silly old magazine again.'

While she was standing there looking down at him, she could not help noticing that his hair, still wavy in front, was getting strikingly thin on top. His pale, pink skin kept showing through underneath, and she realized that in a year or two – say five at the utmost – he would be bald, really bald, like her own father. The sight rather shocked her. It was another of those awful reminders of how old they were both getting. It wasn't so far off now, that unthinkable moment when she would wake up one morning knowing that she would never see forty again.

But, with Mr Winters's letter in her handbag, she could not let thoughts like that distract her.

'It's about the bank account,' she said. 'You know, my private one. I've gone and overdrawn it.'

Her hands were resting on his shoulders by now. It seemed better that way, impersonal but still friendly. She was glad that she wasn't actually looking at him because, as soon as she even mentioned the words 'bank account', she could feel him suddenly tightening up, could detect that all his muscles were contracting. And she remembered that it had been the same last time: Stan was always jumpy whenever they started talking about money.

'But you can't have,' he said. 'Not again.'

'Somebody's got to pay for things,' she snapped back at him. 'They don't just deliver them free like. Not nowadays they don't.'

Hurriedly she checked herself. This was just the kind of thing that she had meant not to say. It was why it had all gone wrong so often before. She dropped her voice, and began speaking more slowly.

'It was the curtains mostly,' she went on. 'The ones with the pelmets, I mean. And the upstairs carpets, the fitted ones. You said yourself we had to have them. It just wasn't safe like. How would you have felt if Marleen had caught her foot in one of the bad places? She might have injured herself for life, she might really.'

Stan had got up, pushing away her hands as he did so. He threw his *Amateur Photographer* back into the chair, and stood facing her.

'How much?' he asked.

She was looking straight at him by now. It was exactly what she had been wanting to avoid.

'I'm afraid it's rather a lot,' she told him.

'How much?' he repeated.

'You're not going to be cross if I tell you?'

As soon as she had spoken, she wished that she hadn't said it. It sounded so absurd. She was behaving almost as if she were afraid of him. And the idea of anyone being afraid of a little shrimp of a man like Stan was just plain silly.

'Go on. Tell me,' he insisted.

'It's a hundred pounds,' she said. 'Just a bit over. Anyhow, you can see for yourself if you like. Here's Mr Winters's letter.'

She didn't want Stan to see that her hands were trembling as she opened her bag, and she pretended that there was something wrong with it.

'It's that stupid, cheap clasp stuck again,' she explained. 'It's always going wrong. It's foreign. French, or something.'

The letter itself had got a bit crumpled. That was because her first instinct had been to screw it up and throw the beastly thing away. Stan had to smooth it out before he could read it properly.

Then, having read it, he stood there not saying anything. It was Beryl who had to speak first.

'Well?' she asked.

And still Stan did not speak. He had drawn in one deep breath and then another, and was simply staring down at the half-sheet of paper.

When he did speak, the words came out all in a rush, and Beryl couldn't help noticing how common, how downright uncouth, his voice could sound.

' 'S'no use asking me,' he told her. '*I* can't help you. I haven't got it. 'S'matter of fact, I'm a bit overdrawn myself.'

This was too much for Beryl. Just for a moment – and only for a moment – she forgot how quiet and dignified she had intended that they should keep their conversation.

'Well, if you can't I'd like to know who can,' she demanded. 'The man-in-the-moon, I suppose.'

But Stan wasn't listening to her. Instead, he was repeating the words 'a-hundred-and-seven-pounds'; saying them over and over again to himself as if they were some sort of incantation. In the end, Beryl had to stop him.

'I know what it says,' she reminded him, being careful to keep her own voice low this time. 'I told you. And it's no use just going on about it like. We've got to do something, haven't we?'

'Like what?'

'Like going to see Mr Winters, like he asks,' she told him. 'Like telling Mr Winters about the new job. Once he knows your salary's going up, he'll stop worrying.'

'But I haven't got the job yet,' he reminded her. 'It's only the interview, remember.'

'Well, it's the same thing, isn't it?' she asked. 'You as good as told me. Mr Winters doesn't expect to be paid back tomorrow. All he wants to do is to make sure.'

She gave a little laugh as she said it because everything suddenly seemed so much better. The old, awful feeling of misery merging into despair had gone completely. In its place a new, placid confidence had settled in. She felt relieved, even carefree. And, because Stan was still wearing his dumb, hopeless expression, she tried to reassure him.

'After all, that's what a bank's for, isn't it?' she added, 'to lend money like.'

Chapter 5

If there was one thing on which she could legitimately pride herself, Beryl had often reflected, it was that she never bore anyone a grudge. Not even Stan. She wanted everything to be all right for him; all right for all of them, that is. And she could guess how awful he must still be feeling because of the way he had been so horrible to her about her overdraft. She decided, therefore, that, in her own way, she would show that she had forgiven him. Frankfurters, the small kind, with Sauerkraut and spaghetti, had always been a favourite meal of Stan's: she could have gone along to the High Street and picked the right tins off the shelf, blindfolded. If that was what he found waiting for him when he got back home, he would know that everything was warm and loving again.

What spoilt it for her, however, was that when Stan did get back, she hardly recognized him. And this was a pity because he had only been trying to make the best of himself. Not wishing to appear shaggy and unkempt at tomorrow's interview, he had gone along to Dan's Gent's Saloon in Hammersmith and asked for a general clean-up. The mistake, he had realized immediately afterwards, was to have bought a copy of the mid-day *Standard*, and to have sat reading it, while Dan's assistant worked on him. The man had certainly been nothing if not thorough. Leaving the quiff untouched, even deliberately brushing it up a bit, he had reduced everything else to stubble. And he had finished off enthusiastically with the electric clippers. Across the nape of Stan's neck there now ran a sharp, hard line, bristly brown above, and raw, naked pink beneath.

It made him look all of ten years younger, Beryl reckoned. Like a newly-graduated Boy Scout. And Cliff, she couldn't help remembering, had taken to wearing his hair rather longer just lately; at the sides, especially.

There was worse to come, too, on the morning of the Appointments Board. There was Stan's tie. She wasn't for a moment saying that he didn't need one. It was just that particular one that he didn't need.

Plain blue, it was; and rather a bright blue at that. It looked as if it had been meant to go with some kind of uniform, like hospital staff or a railway guard. Left to herself she would have bought him something in silk, dark with a contrasting stripe; or one of the new flowery kind; even Paisley, possibly.

But it was too late now to do anything about it. Besides, she didn't want to mention it for fear of upsetting him; when you were dealing with anyone like Stan the last thing that you would want would be to undermine his confidence. All that she said when she kissed him good-bye on the doorstep was: 'Well, good luck, Stan. I'll be thinking of you. And remember to keep your coat buttoned up, won't you. It looks so much more businesslike that way.'

Now he was setting out, Stan was surprised to find how calm he was. It had not been so last night. Far from it. Nothing but doubts and un-certainty until about twelve-fifteen when he dropped off; and then panic verging on despair when he woke up around three and couldn't get off to sleep again. In the ordinary way, he'd have got up and made himself a cup of tea. But he didn't want to risk disturbing Beryl: it had been only since she had forgiven him that she had said that he could move in with her again. It was better sleeping on the Vi-Spring in her room than in the rather hard three-footer in the dressing-room, and he was anxious that she shouldn't regret it. As it was, he had just lain there wondering about the other candidates, and listening to her breath-ing.

But now, in a corner seat on the eight-ten, he was an entirely different man, confident, unruffled, resolute. He had caught sight of his reflection in the window of the big radio shop up by the station. And what he had seen had looked just right: freshly barbered, and with the knot of his bright blue tie showing clearly above the neat white collar, he did not doubt that the impression that he would make on the interview board would be a pleasing one.

And that was important. There were bound to be some there who hadn't met him before; hadn't worked with him, maybe hadn't even heard of him. They weren't to know how conscientious and hard-working he was. Or how loyal. Filing Contracts wasn't just a job with him. It was a career; something that he had chosen and mapped out for himself. Even while he had still been at school, it was the Civil Service that he had been aiming at. And with his School Certificate showing five subjects with two Credits and one Distinction he reckoned that, in him, the Commissioners had picked up a bit of a bargain.

In even the largest of modern, purpose-built business premises, the architect always forgets about things like Appointments Boards.

Important as they are, with so much depending on them, they usually take place in somebody else's office, with the furniture re-arranged as if for a court martial, and no ashtray for the candidate who is probably feeling a bit nervous and might like a cigarette. In Frobisher House, for instance, there wasn't even a proper waiting-room. Just a row of hardback chairs in the corridor beside the door to office No. 737.

There were two others already waiting there when Stan arrived. One of them, the thick-set, surly one, had come up all the way from Chatham. He wasn't due to be called until three-fifteen. With his legs stuck out in front of him, he kept his chin down onto his chest, and glowered. The other was slight, birdlike and jumpy. He kept looking at his watch and then taking out a small plastic comb to preen himself. They were five minutes late for him already. Then the door opened, and an important, bank-managerial sort of person emerged. He was smiling all over, and still saying goodbye to someone in the room even after he was outside in the corridor along with the rest of them. The width of the smile seemed ominous.

The birdman had already hopped down off his perch and was giving himself a final peck before going in. As the door closed behind him, they were joined by the three-thirty appointment. This one was tall, with a long, sad-looking face and lips pursed together as though he were sucking something.

Stan wondered where, short of a television series, they could have found them. And apparently it had been like that all day. From ten o'clock onwards a steady stream of candidates had been passing through at the rate of four an hour. That meant, he reckoned, that there were anything up to a couple of dozen, all putting in for the job that had practically been promised to him. He straightened his new blue tie, and waited.

But not for long. At the butts inside the interview room it had only taken them ten minutes to bring down the birdman. He came fluttering out, clearly winged. And a bit ruffled. He was already reaching for his pocket-comb as he departed.

'Mr Stanley Pitts.'

56

As the senior Personnel Officer's secretary said his name she gave him one of her best professional smiles. It made the fourteenth of them that she had already handed out that day. But it was her job, and she was good at it; the last smile of the day was always every bit as cordial and welcoming as the first. Stan squared his shoulders, gave another tug at his tie and followed.

After the half-gloom of the corridor, the room seemed unnaturally bright. And the chair that they had set aside for him – it was a hardback like the others outside – had been placed so that it exactly faced the window. Stan felt himself screwing up his eyes as he sat there.

It was all a bit more formal, too, than last time. That was because it was such a senior post that was being advertised, he supposed. The members of the board had their names clearly printed out on white cards in front of them – Mr Rawlings, Mr Hunter-Smith, Mr Miller and, at the end of the table, at a right angle to the others, Dr Aynsworth. They all had identical little memo pads and yellow, stationery-issue pencils. Mr Hunter-Smith, because he was chairman, had Stan's file open in front of him. He also had the water carafe.

'Ah, Mr Pitts,' he began, 'I believe we've met before, haven't we? You were once thinking of branching out into the Staff Pensions side, I seem to remember.'

It was not a good beginning. Mr Hunter-Smith had wrong-footed him before the game had even got started. Stan wanted the board to recognize him for what he was, a career man in Filing; one of the single-purpose, dedicated kind. And now he had been made to sound more like a common adventurer. But there was nothing that he could do about it. Mr Hunter-Smith was too preoccupied. He had licked his fingertip and was flicking through the pages of the personal file like a bank clerk counting Treasury notes. Then, happy at his discovery, he looked up again.

'And before that it was Catering Stores. That was back in '59, I see.'

The others turned and looked at Mr Hunter-Smith admiringly. His powers of memory were a legend that ran right through the whole Service. Mr Miller caught Stan's eye and winked at him. That was when Stan began to feel better again.

And the rest of the interview didn't seem to be turning out badly at all. There wasn't much point in asking him questions about the Filing job because they knew that he would know all the answers. Even Mr Rawlings, who was Establishment, couldn't find anything to go on about. Apart for a few days off during the last 'flu epidemic and an odd tonsillitis or two, Stan's record was constant and unblemished as far back as you cared to go. No matrimonial troubles. No personal loans. No change-of-base difficulties. No special allowance claims. Nothing. Mr Rawlings just gave up.

For a moment, Stan felt apprehensive. At this rate, they'd have him out of the room again faster even than the birdman. But, so far, Dr Aynsworth had not spoken. Dr Aynsworth was a recent addition to these Appointments Boards, and he was by way of a refinement. Industrial psychology was his line, and he had his own skilled approach to staff interviews.

Round-cheeked and spectacled, he lit up like a lantern whenever his turn came round. Stan was conscious that he was now being beamed on.

'Now if you had the choice,' he began, 'of being in charge of a small department, say half a dozen in all, or being number two in a big one, thirty or forty if you like, which one would you prefer? Don't think about the money. Just think about the job.'

Stan ran his tongue across his lips. This was one of those googlies that you could see coming at you from a mile off. And he didn't intend to be bowled out by it. He pondered. But already Dr Aynsworth was at him again.

'It's whichever you like, remember.'

His voice was high and rather squeaky, Stan couldn't help noticing: the more patient he was being, the more impatient he sounded.

'To be in charge,' Stan told him.

Dr Aynsworth bent down and made a little tick on his memo pad. It was not like all the other memo pads. He had squared his off in the manner of a chessboard.

'And suppose the small department wasn't doing very important work and the big one was. Would that make you want to change your mind?'

This time Stan was careful not to keep Dr Aynsworth waiting.

'I'd rather it was important,' he replied.

The beam flickered and went out for a moment. He made another mark on his memo pad. This time it looked like a circle.

'That isn't quite what I asked you,' he said, reprovingly. 'But never mind. We can come back to it. Now tell me something else. Which would you rather do – work in a department where everything goes smoothly, or in a department where things keep going wrong and you're the one who has to put them right?'

Stan could see that Mr Miller was watching him.

'I don't know,' he replied. 'I've never had to. Things don't go wrong in Contracts Filing. Not usually, they don't.'

Dr Aynsworth drew another of his little circles.

'Not quite the answer to the question,' he said. 'But never mind. Now let me ask you something else. Would you rather be in a highly paid job where you didn't like the work or in a less well paid one where the work interested you?'

'The less well paid one.'

Dr Aynsworth had already begun to make his tick when Stan spoke again.

'That is, if it isn't too badly paid, I mean. Not too much of a difference.'

Dr Aynsworth's pencil turned the tick into a cross.

'Would you call yourself an ambitious man, Mr Pitts?' he asked.

'I suppose so.'

'Only suppose?'

'No. I mean "yes". I'm very keen to get on.'

'And if it was a choice between you and your best friend applying for the same job, would you do anything to spoil his chances, make it harder for him?'

Dr Aynsworth was clearly enjoying himself, and the beam had grown brighter. His voice, too, had risen higher, squeakier. And he could hardly wait to hear the answer. He began tapping with his pencil.

'Well, I wouldn't do anything mean,' Stan told him. 'Not like . . . like going behind his back, I wouldn't.'

Dr Aynsworth drew two more of the symbols that only he could understand. One was another circle, and the other a circle with a cross in the middle. He looked down at the result, and nodded. If he had been designing nursery wallpaper, he could not have seemed more pleased. Then he looked up again.

'Now tell us about your pleasures, Mr Pitts.'

'My pleasures?'

'The things you enjoy. What you get out of life.'

Stan hesitated. Not that it mattered. To Dr Aynsworth, hesitation was every bit as significant as a reply; very often more so, in fact. He counted six, and helped Stan out again.

'You are married, are you not?'

The picture of Beryl rose up sharp and clear in Stan's mind; Beryl,

59

in her Mexican housecoat with the big Sun-God buttons, and with her hair piled high on top. He only wished that she could have been there to show them.

'Oh, yes,' he said, 'I'm married all right.'

Dr Aynsworth awarded Stan one more tick as soon as he heard the words, 'all right'. They might not have conveyed very much to other people; indeed, they would probably have passed entirely unnoticed. But, to a properly skilled psychologist, they said a lot. They meant that the little fellow with the blue tie and the crew haircut was one of the lucky ones. Unquestionably he was living in the security of a marriage that was cloudless.

'And have you any children?'

It was all down in black-and-white in the staff file in front of Mr Hunter-Smith. But Dr Aynsworth was careful never to read any of the personal particulars before an interview. The answers to questions, even the apparently aimless ones, were always so much more revealing.

'Just one. A girl. Marleen. She's eleven.'

Even though Stan did not know it, he had just come up with another winner. Dr Aynsworth always gave half a point whenever the candidate confided in them by mentioning the name of a child. It was all part of the same secure family pattern.

'And now about yourself, Mr Pitts. Have you any hobbies?'

This was the point at which Mr Hunter-Smith found that he could stand it no longer. He disapproved of all psychologists, and had been against having this one. The man had simply been forced on him from above and, in his opinion, he had wasted quite enough of the board's time already.

'Mr Pitts is our prize photographer,' he explained. 'You win the competition nearly every year, don't you, Mr Pitts? Three Firsts and two Special Mentions, I believe it is . . .'

But the intervention had been fatal. The whole train of Dr Aynsworth's questioning had been destroyed. It had ruined everything. The light inside him flickered and went out. Pushing his pad away from him, he sulked.

'No more questions, thank you, Mr Chairman,' he said.

The sun had come out while he was speaking and was now shining full into Stan's face. He screwed up his eyes again. Dr Aynsworth started. He had just remembered his real role at interviews like this. It was, with his trained mind, to spot things that ordinary laymen might otherwise miss.

'One supplementary, Mr Chairman, please,' he asked. 'Do you ever feel the need to wear glasses, Mr Pitts?'

That was all there was to it. A moment later Stan was back in the corridor, and it was all over. Fifteen minutes flat, he made it. And those fifteen minutes had taken it out of him more than he had expected. He felt all drained and empty; like a blood donor coming away from a transfusion station. And depressed. Depressed by the very thought that, in Room 737, they would have restarted the stop-watch, and the race would be on again. By now, Mr Hunter-Smith would be re-membering all about the man from Chatham, and Dr Aynsworth would be getting ready to ask more unanswerable questions in that Little Bo-Peep voice of his.

It was eight floors down to the sub-basement where Stan worked. But, when he got to the lift, he pressed the button to go up. It was the canteen that he was making for. He needed a cup of tea just to revive himself; and, by way of a little comfort, he picked up a chocolate cup-cake at the service counter. Then, sipping and munching, he thought about all the things that he would have liked to say to Dr Aynsworth if only he had been given the opportunity.

Stan sat on in the canteen longer than usual. That was because he knew just how it would be. As soon as he got back to Records they would all start asking him about it. He was right, too. Even Miss Mancroft, a temporary from the typing pool who couldn't have cared less about what happened to him, looked up from her machine as soon as he came in.

'They kept you long enough, didn't they?' she said. 'Was it third degree, or something?'

But Stan took no notice of her. Just shrugged his shoulders, and walked past. Stan's desk was over in the corner by the radiator. It occupied the best position in the open office. Stan remembered envying it when he had first joined the department; and now it was his through sheer seniority. What's more, with Mr Miller still up in the interview room, Stan was exactly where he wanted to be. He was in charge.

It was nearly quarter to six when Mr Miller came down and went through to his private cubicle for his hat and coat and scarf and gloves and umbrella. Mr Miller was a conscientious dresser, and believed in being well-protected. He was clearly tired, and a bit surprised to find Stan still sitting there. Stan usually left at five-thirty exactly.

But he could guess how Stan must be feeling. And, with the office empty, he could speak freely.

'I shouldn't worry if I were you,' he said. 'No one else suitable in that lot. Not the right experience. But there it is: once they've applied you've got to see them. It's staff regulations.'

The words comforted him. Stan was glad then that he had waited.

Even with so much going on, there had been no difficulty about getting time off to go and see the bank manager. It was simply that Stan had been reluctant to ask. He didn't like to think of what might be happening in the department if he wasn't there to keep an eye on the place.

Ten o'clock was when Mr Winters had said that he could see them; and that was one comfort. It meant that, with any luck, he'd be able to get back to Frobisher House before midday; it was in the afternoons when people were beginning to slack off a bit that things mostly went wrong.

In the end it was her medium-length black dress with the high collar, the almost new one, that Beryl chose, because that meant that she could wear her long black coat with the big cuffs. Admittedly, gloves and shoes were a bit of a problem. Black was, she felt, quite out of the question because the whole effect would have been too dismal, too funereal. Pale beige was what she finally settled on. And, though she had never liked beige with black, particularly when it was one of those warm, rather biscuity shades of beige, she knew instinctively that they would serve to brighten things up. And her beige handbag with the zip. Beige earrings were something that she hadn't got. But that didn't really matter. Because she had her large flat white ones that showed up so strikingly against the sheer blackness of her hair.

Then, at the last moment, she remembered Cliff's headscarf with the huge red peony. She didn't actually wear it; just carried it loosely festooned across her forearm as a decorative afterthought. And, standing in front of the long mirror in the bedroom, edging further and further back so that she could see more of herself, she felt satisfied.

On the way round to the bank, Beryl decided to have a word with Stan.

'And when we get there,' she told him, 'you'd better let me do the talking like. I want you to be with me because it'll look nicer that way. But I'm the one to tell him. About the job, I mean. I can say things you can't.'

Because Beryl didn't want there to be any possible doubt about the outcome, she decided to make her announcement straight away. As soon as she had sat down and put her handbag on the floor beside her, she gave Mr Winters one of her fullest, most confidential smiles.

'I expect my husband will soon be having a piece of news for you,' she said. 'Good news for all of us like. It's about his promotion.' And, just to show that she had remembered that she had brought him with her, she added: 'Won't you, Stan?'

Mr Winters was smiling, too, by now. He swung round in his swivel chair so that Stan could tell him all about it. He had always had rather a liking for Stan. There was something so modest, so unassuming about him. And it was gratifying to think that he should have chosen one of the professions where diligence and hard work were properly rewarded. Somehow, Mr Winters couldn't have seen him surviving for very long in the cut-price, short-measure, stab-in-the-back world so many of his business customers seemed to live in.

'Ah, is that so, Mr Pitts?' he began.

But he had turned his chair too soon.

'Of course, there's nothing definite yet,' Beryl was saying. 'Not yet, there isn't. But it's as good as. You know what the Civil Service is like. Always keep you waiting. It's Head of the Department, you know. And he's earned it. He's been there eighteen years. Haven't you, Stan?'

'And when do you expect to hear?'

This time, Mr Winters looked for a moment at Stan. Then back to Beryl again. And he was right to have done so.

'Well, I mean it's got to be soon, hasn't it. I mean they can't keep you hanging about for ever like. Stan's boss goes in April. They'll have to announce it before then, won't they?' She paused and stroked her gloved finger thoughtfully across the crimson peony on her arm. 'Of course, it'll mean more money. Like I said, it's Head of the Department. It's a different Grade, and everything.'

Mr Winters smiled back at her.

'Then you and your husband have every reason to be pleased,' he said. 'You must be very proud of him.'

'Oh, I am,' she told him. 'Aren't I, Stan?'

Mr Winters had taken out his gold, presentation pen and was fiddling with it, twisting it round and round in his fingers, as though he were winding it.

'Now about this overdraft,' he said. 'I wonder what we'd better do. Because we can't let it go on like this, can we? It'll just mount up and up if we don't keep a check on it. That's what we're all here for, isn't it?'

It was a speech that he had made many times before, smooth, considered and unvarying.

'Just look at those heavy withdrawals,' he went on. 'I'm afraid we can't have any more of those. Not for the time being, that is.'

Beryl found herself getting indignant. It showed that Mr Winters just didn't understand.

'Well, I mean like there won't be any more, will there?' she replied. 'Not just now, there won't. We don't want to go on putting new carpeting down all the time like, do we, Stan?'

'And this one,' Mr Winters pointed out to her, tapping the entry with his pen as he did so. 'Seventeen pounds, four shillings.'

'Well, they're new, too,' Beryl told him. 'The curtains, I mean. With the pelmets, that is. We shan't be needing new curtains again. Not for years and years, we shan't.'

She had, she felt, satisfactorily disposed of that. The last thing she wanted was for him to imagine that she wasn't careful. She cared every bit as much about money as he did. More, probably.

Even so, he wasn't satisfied.

'Then what do you suggest we should do?' he asked, keeping carefully to the plural to make it clear that they were shoulder-to-shoulder in the matter.

'Well, we can't send them back like, can we?' Beryl reminded him. 'They wouldn't take them. Not now they've been fitted, they wouldn't.'

The toe of her pale beige shoe began twitching. She could feel herself getting upset, just the way she always did whenever Marleen was being difficult.

Mr Winters turned again towards Stan. He was perched right on the edge of his chair as though he hadn't yet had time to sit down properly.

'I take it you don't want to clear things up with a single deposit?' he asked.

Stan wondered why Mr Winters had even suggested it. He must have known perfectly well that it was out of the question. Mr Winters was Stan's bank manager, too. He had only to press the bell for his statement to be brought in and laid down alongside Beryl's.

'I couldn't do it,' he said. 'Not possibly.'

'Then shall we say something every month?' Mr Winters enquired. 'What about ten pounds a month? Then it'll be out of the way by . . .' Mr Winters had put down his pen and was drumming out the months with his fingers, '. . . by Christmas.'

Stan shook his head.

'It wouldn't leave us enough to get along on,' he told him. 'We can only just manage as it is. Sometimes I don't know where . . .'

Mr Winters was still being kind, still smiling.

'Then what about eight pounds? That's only two pounds a week, remember. I'm afraid the Inspectors wouldn't like it to be less than that.'

'Does it have to start now?'

The words had been blurted out. He had started saying them almost before Mr Winters had finished.

But there was no rush about it, Mr Winters explained. No one was putting any pressure on him. Just a transfer from next month's pay cheque into his wife's account. That's all it was. If Stan would simply sign the form, the three of them could then forget about it.

It was evidently the way Mr Winters had expected the interview to end because he had one of the forms lying there ready in the folder. All that he had to do was to take the cap off his pen and fill in the amount.

'Eight pounds a month it is, then?' he asked.

Stan merely nodded. He couldn't bring himself to say anything. It was Beryl who spoke for him.

'It won't make any difference really, will it?' she said. 'Not with the promotion, I mean. Not with Stan's salary going up like at the same time.'

As soon as Stan had signed the form and handed it back, Mr Winters turned again to Beryl.

'There you are,' he told her. 'That's all settled then. It didn't take long, did it? And it'll all be cleared off by next year.' He paused. 'No more cheques, of course, in the meantime please. Not till the account's in the black again. Otherwise we'll just be back where we started.'

It was Mr Winters who was smiling now. And it was then that Beryl noticed what a nasty, toothy smile it was. Like some old crocodile grinning at you, she thought. Just for his own cruel kind of pleasure, he was taking it out on her, and enjoying himself.

But secretly she was pitying him. Even though he didn't know it, he'd got it coming to him all right. As soon as Stan's promotion was through and the overdraft was paid off, she was going to close her account and move across the road to Barclay's.

Barclay's was bang opposite. Mr Winters wouldn't be smiling quite so much when he saw her drawing up across the road in the sort of car that the wife of the Head of the Department would be driving.

Chapter 6

It was on Sundays, especially, that Stan wished that he had a dog.

He'd brought up the matter any number of times, suggesting something big and muscular like an Alsatian or a Boxer to protect Beryl when she was alone in the house, or something small and affectionate, such as a Peke or a Cairn for Marleen's sake. But Beryl had been adamant. Dogs, in her view, were destroyers, vandals who went round chewing things, scratching on door panels, leaving patches on fitted carpets. That was why, on Sunday mornings, after he and Marleen had brought down Beryl's breakfast-tray and put everything away again, Stan had to set out alone.

Alone, that is, except for his camera. At week-ends, his camera was part of him. Indeed, some of his best studies – *Deserted Platform, Winter, Coming back from Church,* and *The Paper Seller* – had been obtained simply by mooching around Crocketts Green with his eyes open.

More than once, towards the end of the month when funds were low, he would sling his second-hand Pentax over his shoulder knowing perfectly well that there was no film in it. And that is something that only a fellow-photographer, one of the priesthood, could understand. Because it's the feel of the instrument that counts. Once you know that the skill is yours, there's nearly as much pleasure in framing-up and focusing as there is in actually taking anything. It keeps the eye in. And it's cheaper.

In earlier days Beryl hadn't minded in the least if Stan took Marleen out alone for little Sunday morning outings. Had rather encouraged it, in fact, so that she could have a few minutes to herself just to catch up with things. Even so, it had been only on condition that he didn't let go of her hand, not even for a single second. Marleen, however, was too big for that sort of thing now; hand-in-hand stuff at her age would simply look silly. And Marleen herself had lost all interest. Going as far as the Memorial Pond in one direction, or out past the allotments and the recreation ground in the other, somehow no longer held the charm that she had experienced so keenly when she was five. She preferred nowadays to stay at home, and read. Or lie on her bed, and think. Or finish her homework. Or help Beryl. Anything, in fact, rather than look at ducks or beans growing.

Not that Stan really minded. Photography is a solitary and full-time business. You can't concentrate, can't detach the mind sufficiently, if you've got to keep a conversation going. And, above all, you can't stand still as often, or for as long, as you want to if the other person asks what it is that you're looking at. Enjoyable though they had been for both of them, the years from four to eight in Marleen's life had been about the least productive in Stan's.

And there was another reason why Stan did not mind. That was because, on his way back, he used to call in at the Bull and Garter. Not secretly, either. Nothing furtive about it. 'Daddy's little drinkie' was how Beryl always referred to it; and she liked herself every time she said it. It showed that she wasn't the self-centred sort of person some people might take her for. Nor jealous. She didn't mind in the least if Stan was out enjoying himself while she was indoors working. Indeed, she felt that it was right for a man to have his own circle of friends: there was something so . . . so manly about it. A lot of marriages in her view would be a good deal better for it if only wives allowed their husbands to have a bit of a spree sometimes. And twelve-thirty to about ten-to-one on Sunday mornings was the time that she had allocated to Stan for his.

Beryl herself had never been inside the Bull and Garter. Stan, more than once, had suggested it. But Beryl had declined; and been firm about it, too. She was glad for his sake, she said, that it was nice enough for him to want to take her there, but just imagine what one of the teachers from Marleen's school would think if she were passing at the time and happened to see her coming out, and on a Sunday of all days.

It was certainly the only pub in Crocketts Green that Stan would have considered going into himself. That was because it was still recognizably a part of old Crocketts Green, a reminder of what the place must have been like when it was still a village. It had atmosphere. There were two others, the Station Arms (severe, run-down and melancholy) and the Kon-Tiki (smart, chromium and musical). Saloon prices were the same in all three; same proprietary brands, same measures. But everything else was different. The regulars went to the Station Arms and to the Kon-Tiki for the drinking – large pink gins in the Arms and vodka-and-pineapple-juice in the Kon-Tiki. Round at the Bull and Garter it was the company that counted. An altogether better class of customer, too, even though it was mostly only keg and draught that was drunk there.

One of the things that Stan liked best about the Bull was the old, familiar smell of the place. It was a mixture of floor polish and freshly-cooked sausages and beer frothing out into thick glass tankards and tobacco smoke. A thick, blue haze like Channel mist always hung over the whole bar by closing-time. Because of the low ceiling it was noisy, too. Even with only a handful of customers, it sounded as though there were quite a good party going on.

It had already begun to fill up by the time Stan got there: they were two deep all along the counter. Stan knew every one of them by sight. He would, in fact, have been surprised if any of them hadn't been there. But he made his way past them as though they were strangers. They didn't belong to him at all.

His group, just the four of them, did their drinking over by the palm in the corner. They were four friends, four bosom friends, who saw each other regularly once a week, wouldn't for the world have missed the reunion, and didn't give each other so much as a thought on the other six days.

Come to that, they didn't even know very much about each other, either. One of them was something to do with insurance. Another, the blue blazer and bow-tie member, was vaguely in sales. And the third was mixed up with the rental business. All three knew that Stan was a civil servant. They even made jokes about it. But beyond that, outside the Bull, their lives were their own private and individual mysteries.

And today, as he raised his tankard and said 'Cheers', Stan wasn't for the moment interested in any of them. That was because right across the bar, on the other side where only casuals went, he thought that he saw somebody he knew. It was nothing definite. Only a glimpse. And it took him a second or two to remember. Then it all came back, and he was certain.

The man who had just put his glass down on the counter opposite was the nice Mr Karlin, the representative of the international photo-press agency, the one who had said that he would be getting in touch with him. Stan was all ready to go over and ask him why he hadn't. But the bar was full by now. Stan couldn't squeeze his way past. And, in any case, Mr Karlin was just leaving. His smooth, pink, friendly face was turned away by now, but his raincoat had his own personal stamp upon it. It was the same raincoat that he had been wearing at Frobisher

House on the day of the photographic exhibition. There weren't too many of them about, not Continental-style raincoats with shoulder-flaps and a deep V-shaped seam running halfway down the back.

Stan was sorrier than ever that he hadn't been able to catch up with him. Because right from the start there had been something about Mr Karlin that he had liked. There was genuine warmth there, an outgoing quality that, even at first acquaintance, made you feel as though you had known him for years.

Very few people were gifted that way, and Stan was anxious to keep up the friendship.

Chapter 7

You can't work in a Service department without facing up to the fact that security, like the weather, is something that you have to learn to live with. Not that it should come as anything of a shock. Because unless you have been checked, counter-checked and then re-processed you couldn't be in a Service department at all.

Even so, like everything else in life, security has its ups and downs. There can be weeks on end, months sometimes, when you would think that the entire MI6 side had been disbanded. No warning notices, no reminders, no personal visits. Nothing. Then somebody gets himself arrested in Chatham or Dartmouth or somewhere; and, overnight, the whole place is swarming.

It was the Gareloch affair that had done it this time. Down in Frobisher House, four hundred miles away, it all sounded far off, improbable and rather silly. But not to MI6 it didn't. Apparently, they had come on a young stores clerk, Grade 3, who had been passing on details of the daily delivery sheets. Endless lists of tinned foods, condensed milk, coffee essence, toilet rolls, medical supplies, tooth brushes, all for the Polaris crews. On the face of it, nothing very exciting there. But MI6 knew better. At this very moment, they did not doubt, there was an Eastern Commissar, with a computer on one side of him and an abacus on the other, working out detailed plans in case anyone on his side of the Iron Curtain might want to build a Polaris of his own. Or, at least, so MI6 pretended. Otherwise there could have been no possible excuse for a spot security check on Central Records at nine-thirty on a Monday morning of all times.

It was all right for Stan because he was always one of the early arrivals. The eight-ten from Crocketts Green gave him a good ten minutes to himself before the department was officially open. And this morning he needed those ten minutes. Exactly on the half-hour, Mr Miller was due upstairs in Room seven-three-seven for the interviews with the last batch of applicants. In the meantime, there were the three sets of keys to hand over.

Records and Classified each had its own bunch. But Top Secret was a different matter altogether. It even had a key to itself, and the bunch was kept in a leather box in Mr Miller's own private safe. There was no key to that one: Mr Miller's safe had a combination lock.

At nine-twenty-eight, Mr Miller, with his buff-coloured folder under his arm, went out saying that it shouldn't take long to polish this lot off. And thirty seconds later, Security walked in.

Stan was still the only person there. He had just folded up his *Daily Express* and put it away in the drawer in case he felt like a second read at lunchtime. The day-ledger was open on the desk in front of him, and his ball-point was lying beside it at the ready. In the whole of Frobisher House there could not have been a more perfect little cameo of Civil Service punctuality and efficiency.

Even so, the men from MI6 were not pleased. They were a dour, rather unprepossessing pair, a Commander Hackett and a Mr Clegg. Commander Hackett played the part of the wise one. Head thrust forward, he asked all the questions and, every time he received an answer, he raised his eyebrows slightly and glanced knowingly across at Mr Clegg. The Commander had asked so many questions in his time that he now had two deep furrows running right across his forehead.

After they had identified themselves and had got Stan to produce his own pass, Commander Hackett began enquiring about the keys. Was Stan an authorized person? Had he signed for them? How could he be sure that none of them was missing? Had they been handed over in the presence of a third party? Didn't he know that it was a breach of security for a single person, unattended, to have access to Top Secret documents? Up and down went the eyebrows every time, and every time Mr Clegg nodded thoughtfully.

The rest of the staff had arrived by now, and Commander Hackett and Mr Clegg went round examining their passes. The fact that they had all shown them at the front door as they came in was apparently without significance. For all the Commander knew, they might have swapped them in the lift coming up, or carelessly left them lying about on the ledge in the lavatory when they had gone to wash their hands, even tossed them out of open windows into the outstretched hands of enemy agents waiting down below.

Then, when he could find nothing wrong with the passes, Commander Hackett suggested that they should go into Mr Miller's office. And, once inside, he asked Stan to close the door. There were only two chairs for visitors. That meant that Stan had to sit in the swivel chair at Mr Miller's desk. It was the first time that he had ever done so. Remembering what was going on at this moment in Room seven-three-seven, the omen seemed a distinctly good one.

And by now Commander Hackett had evidently revised his opinion of Stan. He began to treat him as an equal. Tucking his thumbs up into the armholes of his waistcoat and thrusting his legs straight out in front of him, he invited Stan to be indiscreet. Were there any irregularities that had come to his notice? Had any member of staff ever done or said anything that had raised a doubt in Stan's mind? How many of them did he know socially? Were there any money difficulties he knew about? Did he ever hear political views expressed? Could he suggest any way in which the running of the department might be tightened up a bit?

The eyebrows were no longer working so hard, and it was only occasionally that he and Mr Clegg exchanged glances. The words 'tightened up', however, brought him fully back to life again. Tightening up was the whole guiding principle of Commander Hackett's life. He used the phrase as a mechanic might have used it, even giving a twisting, spanner-like movement of his hand as he said the words.

It was getting on for ten o'clock by now. The queue of messengers at the counter had grown longer and, outside in the general office, the telephones were ringing. Commander Hackett and Mr Clegg looked at their watches and announced that they would look in again when Mr Miller had returned. Stan went back to his own desk over in the corner.

It was nearly lunchtime before Mr Miller got back, and Stan hadn't been any too happy about the delay. But Mr Miller seemed far from despondent. He called Stan into his office straight away, and told him so.

'Well, you're on the short list,' he said. 'Just three of you. That's what they've got it down to.'

'Short list.'

Stan heard himself repeating the words.

'So you mean they haven't decided anything yet?'

Mr Miller took off his spectacles and wiped them. It had been a tiring morning, and he had come away with a headache. Eye-strain, he put it down to.

'Not yet, they haven't. That'll be next week some time. They'll want to see the three of you again. Just to make sure, that is.'

He had put his spectacles back on. But it was no use: his headache was as bad as ever, and the edges of the blotter looked all blurred and wavy.

'Nothing to worry about,' he added. 'It's just that it all takes time.'

Childless himself, Mr Miller felt strangely paternal at this moment. He had known Stan for a long time; had brought him up, practically. It pleased Mr Miller to think that, after his retirement, the department would go on along the lines that he had so carefully laid down; would, so to speak, remain something of a family affair.

'Well, he wouldn't have said it like if he didn't mean it, would he?' Beryl asked. 'Not that bit about not having much to worry about.'

At that moment, she was really rather proud of him. It was pleasing to think that out of all those hundreds of thousands of other civil servants there were, besides her Stan, only two others who were regarded, even remotely, as worthy of being considered for the post.

'And I've got a piece of news for you,' she told him, after she had made him repeat Mr Miller's words about not worrying. 'They want our Marleen to go in for the dance contest. The junior one like. It's national, you know. The under-twelves, that's what her teacher said Marleen ought to try for.'

She went over to the mantelpiece and took down a printed leaflet.

'It's all there,' she explained. 'The dates and the prizes and everything.'

The lettering was in gold, and the cover showed a dark, Italianate-type princeling, in white tie and tails, two-stepping with his English rosebud partner. The couple were framed in one of those filigree-lace designs that come up every year on Valentines; and, inside, were set out the names of dance band leaders of whom Stan had heard, and judges of whom he hadn't. Page three had a picture of a little girl rather like Marleen holding up the sort of cup that is displayed at Wembley. And on the back was the entrance form that had to be posted to an address in Blackpool. The registration fee for juniors was one pound.

'D'you mean Marleen's got to go all the way up to Blackpool?' he asked.

'Only if she's short-listed like her Daddy,' Beryl replied. 'And she will be. Her teacher says she holds herself so well like.' Beryl straightened her own back as she said it, and gave a little loosening wriggle with her shoulders. 'The elimination round's in Croydon. At the big hall.

Marleen's Southern Counties, you see. They go on all over the country. It's national, like I said.'

Stan turned the leaflet over and found himself looking down again at the princeling and the rosebud.

'What's it all going to cost?' he asked.

Beryl had expected the question. It was exactly the kind of thing Stan would say. And she had the answer all ready.

'A pound, like it says,' she told him. 'That's all it is. Don't tell me we can't spare a pound for our Marleen. It's her career, you know. She's got to make a start some time, hasn't she?'

'I mean all the travelling and things.'

But that didn't bother Beryl either.

'Well, we don't know she'll have to, do we? She may change her mind, or something. It's quite an ordeal out there in front of all those judges. She's only a baby, remember. I wouldn't blame her if she got stage fright at the last moment, not at her age I wouldn't.'

It was Marleen's ball dress that she was thinking about while she was speaking. White satin it had to be. And she wanted the skirt to be as full as possible; full, and pleated. What she had in mind was the sort of skirt that would stand out like a lampshade if you swirled round in it. Rather high, almost Empire, was how she saw the waist; plain line in front, and gathered in at the back with a sash. Beryl liked sashes because you can make such beautiful bows out of them, and the bow that she was going to make for Marleen would be something special. She'd noticed for some time that, though Marleen's tummy was as flat as a board, her little behind did tend to stick out rather. With a bow like that there wouldn't be a judge in the place who could tell where her little Marleen left off and where the bow began.

As it happened, Stan was thinking about ball dresses, too. He had turned back to the picture of the other little girl who was rather like Marleen, and he was looking at the dress that she was wearing. It looked rather an expensive sort of dress to him.

'But we'd have bought the dress by then, wouldn't we?'

Beryl pulled down the corners of her mouth.

'I wasn't going to anyhow,' she said. 'Not buy it like. When the time comes, I'll make it. There's hours of work in a ball dress. That's what you pay for. It's not the material, it's the time. Any dressmaker knows that.'

'You couldn't make the shoes,' Stan reminded her.

Beryl found the remark irritating.

'Well, she can't dance without shoes, can she?' she asked. 'She's got to have shoes like. There's no point in me wearing myself out making that dress if she hasn't got the shoes to go with it, now is there?'

Silver for the shoes: it had come to Beryl in a flash as she stood there.

'What'll shoes cost?' Stan persisted.

Beryl was inclined to brush the point aside.

'It isn't the shoes that cost the money,' she told him. 'Like I said, it's the dress. That is, if you just go out and buy one. But I'm making it, aren't I? We save all that to start with. And she won't need the shoes. Not yet. Not until she's got the dress, she won't. They wouldn't be any use to her. Not just the shoes. Not without the dress, they wouldn't.'

Stan folded the leaflet and put it back on the mantelpiece.

'I still don't see why it's got to be this year,' he said. 'Not now we're economizing.'

But Beryl had the answer to that, too.

'Well, she can't go in for the under-twelves if she's over, I mean can she? It wouldn't be fair like. And they'd never allow it. Her teacher knows how old Marleen is because she told me. She'd never have mentioned it if she thought we weren't going to do anything about it, now would she?'

Stan did not reply immediately. He'd only just got in, and he was tired. He wasn't really thinking about dance contests at all. His mind was still full of short lists and second interviews. There was another whole week stretching ahead of him before he'd know anything.

'Oh, all right. I suppose so,' he said. 'But only the registration. Don't go ordering anything.'

Beryl was smiling again. She looked radiant.

'I knew that's what you'd say. Now I've explained it, that is,' she replied. 'I told Marleen it'd be all right. She's ever so excited. And she won't let us down. Not our Marleen. She's set her heart on it.' She paused. 'Then I'll leave it all to you, then. You'll have to send off the cheque, though. Because I can't, can I? Not the way things are, I can't. Not till we've paid off Mr Winters, that is.'

The thought of the ball dress and of Stan's promotion had made her happy. Already she could hear the applause, the thunderous applause. And she could see it, too: everybody waving programmes and getting up onto their feet, and the judges all holding up their cards with 'sixes'

76

on them, while out there on the great dance floor, oblivious of all the excitement, would be her Marleen in the centre of the spotlight, curtseying like a little white-and-silver angel.

Beryl was glad to think that by then the ugly metal brace would have been taken off her two front teeth.

Chapter 8

Just at the moment things weren't going too well for Cliff. Personal-
wise, that is. Businesswise, they could hardly have been better. It was
his private life that lay shattered. And all because of the last-minute
cancellation of charter flight No. 562 from Heathrow to Nairobi.

For the past year or so, everything had gone on pretty much as in
other past years. Whenever one of his girl friends had moved on or got
married or simply faded on him, there had always been another girl
standing by, prepared, ready to step in and take her place. And sometimes there had been more than one. Ever since last summer, for
instance, there had been two, Estelle and Zena.

Estelle, tall, ash-blonde and cautious, was a model by occupation.
It was the wholesale side of the trade that she was in; evening gowns,
mostly. M'Ladye Mayfayre the house was called. It was one of the
smaller firms, just basement and ground floor, on a side turning off
Great Portland Street, stuck down between the two giants, Gayrex
International and Teenage Associates.

In M'Ladye's service, Estelle doubled up her modelling duties with
those of receptionist-cum-telephone operator. That meant that any
time up to mid-morning when things were slack, Cliff could be sure of
getting hold of her. It was only in the afternoons when the buyers were
around that it was difficult. Estelle was professionally engaged by them,
doing her endless walkabout, up and down the strip of blue Wilton
between the dress racks. That was when Cliff usually had to hang on a
bit.

But, almost invariably, it was worth it. The buyers, particularly
those from the north of England, were a pretty zestful lot. They came
down from Leeds and Bradford, like Vikings with the glint of conquest
in their eyes. And, once past the ticket barrier at Euston, they demanded
invaders' privileges. Estelle knew the whole process by heart: the
suggestion of a quiet dinner, the mention of a night club afterwards,
the hanky-panky in the taxi, the abrupt and unasked-for stop at some
hotel that she had never heard of, the display of five-pound notes as the
driver was paid off, the heavy breathing. It was *dane-geld* on a modern

cash-and-carry basis, and Estelle had always felt that she was worth something better than that. That was why she was so glad of Cliff. It helped to cut propositions short without offence when she could say: 'Pardon me, I'm wanted on the phone. It's my fiancé.'

Not that Estelle was formally engaged to Cliff. Nothing like that. Nor could she be. Because Cliff was still married, and Estelle's own divorce had not come through yet. There was just an understanding; an arrangement. And Estelle herself did not want to rush things. She could not afford at her age – coming up twenty-nine next birthday – to have life go sour on her a second time: it suited her to play it cool. She liked Cliff; liked him very much; could see herself going crazy over him. But that was all. The trouble was that she didn't trust him, not out of her sight for a single moment, she didn't.

Cliff, naturally enough, had never mentioned Zena to Estelle. Zena was simply another number in Cliff's private phone list, written in below those that had already been crossed off. She appeared on the very next line to Estelle because Cliff had met her at the same party. But that was as close as the two girls had ever got. There was, in any case, nothing that they had in common. Zena was small, dark and intense. Also, intermittent. Her air-hostess duties made her so. Phoning Zena was well-nigh impossible, because she spent so much time in places like Jakarta and Caracas. It was a matter of ringing up and leaving messages. But she was a good caller-back. And usually after these long trips she was lonely.

Some of the most agreeable interludes in Cliff's life had been shared with Zena. Difficult to arrange, confirmed at short notice from airport call-boxes, the reunion always had its own special, poignant quality, a fleetingness that somehow brought out the best in Cliff. Towards Zena, he was never other than gentle, tender and considerate. And this was just as well because as well as always feeling lonely on arrival, she nearly always felt frayed. By the time she had handed in her flight-sheets and checked out at the air charter office, she was all in little pieces and jaggedy.

It was not, in fact, until after her second drink that she ever really came to life again. Then, with her shoes off and her legs tucked up under her on Cliff's couch, the evening would begin. That was when Cliff always moved over and squeezed in beside her.

This evening, however, Zena was absent, already booked up to be amid the stars, air-bound for Nairobi. Next Thursday was to be her night, and she was going to confirm the time when she reached the terminal. In the meantime, it was Estelle, with her legs tucked under her, who was sitting there. Estelle's legs were longer than Zena's. This meant that with Estelle he always had to squeeze in from the other side.

The evening had been a relaxed and pleasant one – dinner at a Chinese restaurant, two of the best seats in the cinema for a Hollywood musical, an ice-cream for Estelle in the interval, and then back to Cliff's place for a drink. Off the Edgware Road was where Cliff lived.

It was a new block, smart and expensive. The front door was of glass with a large circular steel handle, and there was an illuminated fountain playing in the tiny courtyard. The front hall, mostly marble and mirror, certainly lived up to the fountain. So did the lifts. It was only as you got out at one of the upper floors that you felt that the architect had somehow exhausted himself down below. The corridors were long, plain and rather narrow. A child could have designed them. Just so many doors, so many bell-pushes, so many strips of concealed lighting.

But it was quiet; even snug in a modern, chromium-and-black-leather kind of way. And the evening was proceeding as placidly as it had begun. Estelle somewhat half-heartedly said something about having to get back to Ealing, and Cliff equally half-heartedly offered to bring the Jaguar round again. But Estelle stopped him. It wouldn't be fair, she said, not after he'd been drinking.

That was why, when he suggested that she should stay the night, Estelle quite readily agreed. And it was at moments such as this that Cliff's natural, easy charm always came to the fore. As a host, he was perfect. He simply invited Estelle to go through to the bathroom first, and told her that she would find a new toothbrush in the cupboard over the basin. Just that. Estelle had always liked men who were nonchalant.

When she emerged, she was wearing Cliff's St Tropez wrap that she had found conveniently hanging up behind the door. And Cliff himself was down to his string vest and college underpants. His restrained pin-stripe suit, his pink shirt and his bold and rather striking tie were draped neatly over the chair by the window, with his brown suede shoes on the floor beside them.

Cliff put his arm tenderly about her, and they started to go through to the bedroom together. They had got only as far as the end of the couch, however, when the front-door buzzer sounded. The note startled him. Telling Estelle to stay where she was, he padded barefoot into the hall. It was definitely on the late side for visitors. There was no safety-chain on the door, and he was careful to lean his shoulder up against it as he turned the knob.

But it was only lonely Zena. And after the frustrations of the airport, the endless cups of coffee before the flight cancellation was finally confirmed, she was dangerously close to breaking-point. At the sight of Cliff, all stripped-down and masculine-looking, she uttered a happy little cry and sprang at him. The door flew open, and there he was clasped in the cherry-red uniform of Charter Airflights.

It was over Cliff's shoulders that Zena saw Estelle. And the sight of those long, white legs under the St Tropez bath-wrap was too much for her. She was still carrying her overnight air-bag with the name of her employers printed on it. And it was heavy because it contained a carton of duty-free whisky that she had intended as a present for Cliff. Slipping the bag off her shoulder, she shortened her grip on the strap and hit out at him. Cliff, all but defenceless in his string vest and college underpants, backed away. Then he saw that Zena was making for Estelle, and he tried to stop her. That was when the cherry-red uniform got torn. The occasional table went over. And Zena was swinging out again. This time it was at Estelle. But by now Estelle was prepared. She had picked up one of Cliff's brown suede shoes, and was defending herself.

Looking back on the whole episode, what Cliff resented most was Zena's and Estelle's attitude towards him. When the fight was over, they had gone through to the bathroom together, and had stayed there rather a long time. While Cliff was putting the occasional table back on its feet again and picking up the cigarette ends from the ashtray that had gone over with it, he could hear taps being turned on and off, and the basin cupboard being opened and shut again. Because Estelle would hardly be using her new toothbrush now, he imagined that it was aspirins or sticking-plaster that they were after. Then the bathroom door opened and they walked straight past him. The last that he saw of either of them was as they went down the corridor towards the lift. They had their arms round each other by then, and Estelle was carrying Zena's air-bag for her.

That was how it was that Cliff was free to see so much more of Stan and Beryl. With Estelle and Zena both gone, and with no one else on call at the moment, the flat seemed strangely desolate and empty. By comparison, Kendal Terrace was a haven. There was real warmth there. He might have been one of the family the way Beryl greeted him. And, low in spirits as he was, more than once on the way down in the car he had reflected on how things might have been.

By rights, it should have been Stan who was dropping in on him and Beryl.

Chapter 9

It was in the second mail delivery, the one that usually reached Contracts Filing at the same time as the tea trolley, that the buff, internal office envelope addressed to Mr Stanley Pitts arrived. It was marked 'Private and Personal'. And, the moment it came, Stan pounced on it.

He had been sure that he would hear something during the day. It made him feel all bright and cheerful inside. And it had showed. During breakfast Beryl had even accused him of holding out on her, saying that he must know more than he was telling. Otherwise he wouldn't be like that, she had added: not at breakfast, he wouldn't. And the same happy, expectant feeling had persisted all the way up in the train.

Now that the letter had really come, however, he found that he couldn't bear the strain of it all. It meant too much to him. He just stood where he was, with the buff envelope in his hand looking down at it. Then, because he didn't want to attract attention to himself, didn't want any of the juniors in the department to wonder what he was doing, he picked up the letter-opener and slit open the envelope with a flourish as though it didn't matter.

He was still standing as he unfolded the paper and began to read, and he did not sit down again immediately. He wasn't even looking at the letter any more. He was staring straight ahead of him; not really seeing anything, either. Eyes simply fixed in space, oblivious of everything. And he was quite still, except that now his hands were trembling.

When he did at last sit down it was because he suddenly felt sick. A strange sensation of not being there, of not being anywhere, had come over him, and he wondered if he were going to faint.

Because his fingers were still twitching, he found it difficult to fit the letter back into its envelope. But all that he wanted was to get it out of his sight. What it said was his secret and, for the time being, that was how he wanted to keep it. Opening his jacket, he pushed the envelope deep down into his inside breast pocket, along with his wallet and his season-ticket and his comb. He could hear the scraping, grass-

83

hoppery sound as the teeth of the comb came up against the flap of the envelope.

But it was no use. In his mind's eye, he could still see the hard, black typing on the inferior, brownish paper. '*. . . regret having to inform you that your application has been unsuccessful . . . post has accordingly been otherwise filled.*' And just so that there could be no mistake about it, no careless blunder up in Personnel, there was the reference number, *P/11/372*, that he knew by heart, plainly set out in the same hard, black typing. He could have done a drawing of the whole letter from memory.

The palms of his hands had moisted up and become sticky, and he went down the corridor to the staff lavatory. As he passed the temporary girl from the typing pool, the one he knew rather liked him, he heard her ask if he was all right. But he didn't even answer. Then, when he looked at his reflection in the big plate-glass mirror over the washbasins, he saw why she had spoken; all the colour had gone out of him.

After his second cup of water, drunk out of a limp, cardboard container, he felt better. Not so sick, but still shaky. Then he went over to the window, and leant up against the wall beside the roller-towel machine. Despite that drink of water, the whole inside of his mouth felt dry again.

He was thinking of what he would say to Beryl when he got home that night.

Because Stan still wasn't feeling well, Mr Miller sent him home early. A quiet evening in front of the telly followed by a good night's rest and he'd be a different man in the morning, Mr Miller told him.

It was four o'clock when Stan left Frobisher House. Going out at that time gave him an unreal, strangely guilty feeling and, as he passed the security check, he was careful to speed up a bit, stepping out as though he were going somewhere important. But, now that he was out there on the pavement, he didn't know what to do with himself.

Then he remembered that he hadn't eaten any lunch. He had felt too ill for lunch. Besides, up there in the canteen he would have met too many people.

There was a Wimpy Bar at the corner, and he went in and ordered a cup of coffee and a hamburger. The coffee was all right. But he couldn't manage the hamburger. He didn't feel strong enough. Long before it had gone cold, he had pushed it away from him right up to the far end of the table-top as though someone else had made the order and then forgotten about it.

Stan wasn't thinking about food at all. He was thinking about Marleen's dance contest, and the rates that were due next month, and the overdue electric light bill that he hadn't yet paid, and the new pair of shoes that he needed for himself, and the cost of Beryl's weekly hair-do, and the overdraft repayments, and the price of colour film, and his own turn-down by Personnel and Establishment.

With a start, he realized how late it was getting. Leaving the office at four was one thing; idling about in Wimpy Bars was quite another. If he had hurried, really hurried, he could have been at Cannon Street in time to catch the two-minutes-past-five or even, with luck, the four-forty. As it was, he was in danger of losing his usual train. And by the time he reached the station the barrier on Platform 4, his platform, was already closing.

The sight of the gate as it was pulled across in front of him produced an odd sensation. He realized that, instead of feeling angry and frustrated, he was grateful. Positively grateful. The plain truth was slowly beginning to dawn on him. He wasn't merely reluctant to go home, wasn't simply trying to put off telling Beryl.

He was afraid.

Chapter 10

Until the moment of Stan's return, it had been undeniably one of the better days in Beryl's life.

Marleen's cold, which had looked like developing into a real, old-fashioned streamer, had cleared up overnight as if by magic, and Beryl didn't even have to press a spare hankie into the little hand when she said goodbye to her at the school gate. Beryl herself was happy, too, because she was so sure that Stan was happy. She had felt it all day. Ever since breakfast time, in fact. That was when, for the first time, she had been certain, really certain, that Stan would, at last after all that waiting, have something definite to tell her when he got home.

In consequence, she had been in high spirits. A strangely young feeling had come over her, a sense of lightness. And every time she saw herself reflected in the shop windows in the High Street the whole effect pleased her. Last season's camel-hair coat still looked almost new, and her patent leather handbag sparkled. That was because she had given it a thorough going-over with Min-Cream after she had finished polishing her dressing-table. But what she liked best about those reflections of herself, what was so reassuring, was that no one catching a glimpse of her could have imagined for a single moment that she was the sort of woman who ever had to turn her hand to house-work. People would never have believed that less than an hour ago, rubber gloves and all, she'd been down on her knees wiping over Marley tiles like a skivvy because the plastic handle had come clean off her Dainty Maid Handymop.

It was entirely for Stan's sake that she had gone into the Supermarket and bought him a deep-frozen Cornish chicken pie. Chicken pie, provided it was one of the deep-frozen kind, was one of Stan's favourites. And clearly he deserved a bit of a treat. It had been cruel – yes, downright cruel – of the Civil Service to keep him in suspense like that. Fortunately for him, he wasn't the highly-strung type. Even so, it must have been a strain on him, too, she reckoned. For some time now he hadn't been looking what she'd call well; not really well, that is. He was in need of a tonic, something to brace him up a bit. Just thinking about it made her feel strangely loving towards him. Almost maternal.

And during her afternoon rest, her regular shut-away-from-the-outside-world siesta, the same mood of lovingness persisted. She felt warm and blissful. There wasn't so much as a trace of one of her silly old headaches, and she really believed that she had found the right hand-cream at last. When she had peeled off her rubber gloves before going out shopping, she'd noticed it straight away. And it was the same now that she was holding the Mars Bar. Her fingers round the packet looked soft and white and delicate. Not a bit like a housewife's. More like a young bride's, she thought. Next to her hair which, as Beryl always said whenever the subject came up, was the best thing about her, she had always been very proud of her long, slender hands.

The copy of *Woman's Own* was open on the bed beside her; and on the pillow, the pocket radio, turned down so as not to be disturbing, was quietly saying something to her. But Beryl was neither listening nor reading. She was thinking. Annoying and irritating in little ways as Stan was, she ought to try to be nicer to him, she kept telling herself. Her role as a wife was to build him up, give him self-confidence, make him feel important.

And it was all going to be so much easier on his new salary level. For a start, it meant that she would be able to take him in hand and do something about his clothes. Just because he was stock size, standard small gentleman's that is, he didn't have to go around reminding everybody about it. Even his best suit, the brown one, was somehow too ordinary. Something in dark grey flannel with a chalk stripe and rather wide lapels was what she had in mind for him; and definitely striped shirts, instead of plain ones. And a blue-and-white polka dot tie; big dots, not small ones, of course.

On nice days nothing but nice things seem to happen; it was little Marleen who had once said that, when she had still been quite tiny. And it was true. By six-thirty, everything was ready. The table in the dinerette alcove had been re-laid after tea, the Cornish chicken pie was in the oven with the switch set low, Marleen had finished in the bathroom and Beryl was in her Mexican housecoat with the Sun-God buttons.

Even on ordinary days it was one of the moments that Beryl liked best. There was a sense of leisure, of luxury almost, in just being able to sit there quietly in the lounge for a few minutes. Idly, more to pass the time than anything else, she re-read the article in *Woman's Own* on attic conversions. Not that she was thinking of doing anything about it; not just for the moment, that is. Not until they had settled up with Mr Winters. But some time next year, perhaps. One huge, enormous room stretching the whole length of the house was how she saw it, with divan-style furnishing and a lot of big, lumpy cushions; and a squat, glass-topped table; and low-key lighting; and bare boards, naturally, with a rug or two set at strange, odd angles to complete the effect.

Carefully, so as not to disturb the rest of the magazine, she tore out the supplement and put it in her desk. Later on that evening, after Stan had told her his news of course, she would get it out again and show it to him. So far as possible, she liked him to share in all her long-term planning.

But Stan had really done it this time. He had missed the six-thirty-two as well.

It was only partly his fault. After all, the gates on Platform 4 had been closed in his face and, simply to make something to do, he had walked across to the station buffet and ordered himself half-a-bitter. Half-a-bitter can't take anybody very long to drink; and Stan had a full thirty minutes in hand, remember.

He had actually left the bar with quarter of an hour to spare, when he turned back. That was because he had started trembling again. Quickly making up his mind, he decided that he needed something to settle his nerves. Beer was no use this time; too much of it. So, expensive though it was, he asked for whisky. By now, the barmaid knew him by sight and gave him one of her bright, barmaidish smiles of recognition. Then, to his surprise, Stan heard himself say: 'Make it a double.' In the ordinary way, whisky was something that Stan never drank. He didn't even know which brand to ask for, and didn't particularly like the taste of any of them. But tonight it seemed that he needed it.

And the stuff seemed to work all right. There was no denying that. He could feel it going down inside him, powerful and fiery. In between gulps he breathed out rather noisily, opening up his lips every time like a goldfish; and undeniably the whisky had done him good.

It was so obviously just what he'd needed that he ordered himself another one. The trembling by now had ceased altogether. He said good night to the friendly barmaid and left her there against the background of bottles. It came, therefore, as something of a shock to find that the seven-two had left nearly five minutes ago.

This time, however, he was taking no chances. He sat down on the station seat nearest to the barrier, his eyes fixed on the departure board. He was first at the barrier when he saw the name 'Crocketts Green' come up on the indicator, and he walked practically the full length of the platform so that he would be right for the exit at the far end. The rush-hour was already over, and he had the whole compartment to himself. This was just as well, because by now he was rehearsing what he was going to say to Beryl; rehearsing it over and over again, out loud.

It didn't seem like Crocketts Green when he got there because there were none of the regulars around. The station had a shut-up, gone-out-of-business look; and it was the same all the way home. Just street lamps and empty pavements. To keep his spirits up and give him the inner strength that he was needing, he began to hum. The music came first, and then the words. By the time he had turned into Kendal Terrace he was not humming any longer. He was singing. Softly, but audibly, he was in full song. The refrain was 'Firm but gentle, that's the slogan', and he was endlessly chanting that one line to the tune of 'Men of Harlech'.

The catch on the gate of No. 16, normally so simple to operate, had turned stiff and awkward this evening. He had to joggle it repeatedly up and down before he could hear the familiar click that he was waiting for. And, on the front step, he stumbled. Another few inches, and he'd have been clean through the glass panel over the Spanish grille.

But, now that the moment had come, he felt perfectly calm. Calm and forceful. He had stopped singing, and had composed himself. With his key in his hand, he paused long enough to make sure that his tie was knotted properly. Then he went inside.

'Wherever have you been?'

The words reached him before he'd even time to close the front door. And he detected the note of impatience.

'Coming, dear,' he told her.

'Do you know what time it is?'

He did not answer immediately. He would have liked to explain about how he had missed lunch, and about the uneaten hamburger and how he had gone back into the buffet only because he hadn't been feeling well. But he wasn't sure that, without some kind of introduction to it all, she would understand. He was still wondering what to say to her when she spoke again.

'Well, do you?' she repeated.

She had come out into the hallway by now, and was facing him. What she did not know was that he was having trouble with his overcoat. One of the sleeves had turned itself completely inside out and, even when he did at last manage to struggle free, the whole thing came slithering off the hook as soon as he hung it there.

By now she had noticed how flushed his face was. He might have been running a fever, sickening for something. Rocking slowly back and forth on his heels, he stood there staring at her. Then, without warning, he began. He was speaking very fast, as though he had wound himself up and then suddenly released the spring. He was indistinct, but unstoppable.

'Now I just want you to listen to me,' he told her, 'and I don't want you to interrupt. I don't want you to interrupt either of us. I've got something to say to you, and I want us both to listen very carefully. Because what I'm going to say is important. Estremely important. That's why I don't want any interrupting. Just no interruptions at all.' He made a sweeping, scythe-like gesture with his hand as he said it, and the effort nearly unbalanced him. But he kept straight on. 'I was on the short list. And then they never even had one. No short list at all. They just did it – like that.' He tried to snap his fingers to show her how, but there was no strength left in his hand: his thumb and forefinger merely slid over each other. 'So we've got to go on as we are. Erzackly as we are. No change. Nothing different. Everything the same as before. The way it's always been. That's what I'm telling you.'

Beryl had not moved. She was standing quite still, her arms folded across her bosom, regarding him. And letting him go on. It would be something to remind him of forever.

Stan, however, had already finished. He had no more strength left. That long speech of his had finally exhausted him. He was now conscious only of a strange floating feeling, an up-and-down, drifting sensation as though he were ballooning. Pushing his way past her, he went through into the lounge and stretched himself out upon the couch.

'Iss not your fault, dear,' he said, his voice fading gradually away as he was speaking. 'Iss nobody's fault. But iss too late to essplain things now. Mush too late. We're both of us very, very tired. Esstremely tired. I'll tell you all about it in the morning.'

Then he closed his eyes and went to sleep.

It was just after one a.m. when he woke up. He had a headache, and the inside of his mouth felt dry. But his mind was clear enough. It all came back to him. The bad news. The drinks. The trains that he'd missed one after another. Everything that he wanted to forget. Until the very moment of his homecoming, that is. All that he could remember about that was how the sleeve of the overcoat had turned itself completely inside out and how the overcoat itself had kept sliding off the hook every time he went to hang it up.

He tidied up the couch, and turned the lights off. Then, very quietly so as not to disturb anyone, he made his way upstairs. He tried the bedroom door handle, but it was no use. Beryl must have turned the key on the inside. But Marleen's door was open. And, though the bed had been slept in, it was empty now. Evidently Beryl had taken Marleen in with her.

Then he noticed something else. It was his bedroom slippers and pyjamas in a heap on the floor outside the dressing-room. They looked as if they'd just been flung there.

Chapter 11

The name of Mr Miller's successor, the outsider who had come up from nowhere and beaten Stan at the finishing-post, had just been announced in the Staff Gazette. Mr Miller called Stan in specially to show him. And he had gone to some trouble over it. Using his felt-tip pen he had enclosed the entry in a pair of thick, black brackets to make it stand out better.

'Well, there it is,' Mr Miller said as he handed the paper over to him. 'That's the one. Now you know as much about it as I do.'

It was all set out clearly enough: '*Senior Officer (Records), Frobisher House*' the paragraph ran. '*Mr Anthony Parker (Administration), Admiralty, Whitehall, to succeed Mr R. J. Miller (retiring). Effective, 1st July, 1965.*'

'Anthony Parker'; Stan began repeating the name to himself, pulling down the corners of his mouth as he did so. It was a perfectly ordinary name, the sort of name that would slip through any directory unnoticed. But already Stan found himself disliking it. The more he said it, the more aloof and superior it sounded.

But already Mr Miller was speaking again.

'Not to worry,' he said reassuringly. 'If it doesn't work out, you can always apply for a transfer. There shouldn't be any difficulty about that. Not with your record, there shouldn't.'

Stan felt a sudden little tremor run through him. The muscles of his stomach contracted and went slack again.

'D'you . . . d'you think it'll come to that?' he asked.

Mr Miller was cautious.

'Hard to tell,' he replied. 'Won't be the same, of course. Not like it has been. Different approach altogether. Business School training. All very modern. May suit you, or it may not. Just have to see how the two of you get on together.'

But that only made it worse. Much worse. Because Stan could see that Mr Miller was warning him; and being very careful to be nice about it. What he was really saying was that if the new man stepped up the pace a bit he doubted if Stan could take it. Stan found himself beginning to doubt it, too. And this was ridiculous, because only last month he'd been thinking about one or two quite important changes of his own that he'd be introducing as soon as he was really in charge of the place.

An altogether new fear had come into his mind.

'How old is this Mr Parker?' he enquired.

Mr Miller tapped on the desk with his pencil before replying.

'About your own age,' he said. 'Bit younger, in fact. Not much in it. Only a month or so.'

That piece of information left Stan in pretty low spirits; the very lowest of the low, in fact. He now felt despondent about everything. And, if it was like that in Frobisher House, it was worse still back in Kendal Terrace. Ever since the night when he had made that disgraceful exhibition of himself, Beryl had hardly spoken to him. If he said anything to her, she didn't seem to hear him; at any rate, didn't answer. And, if he went through to the lounge when she was there, she promptly got up and went out. She was even careful to take Marleen with her, too, if the child happened to be anywhere around at the time.

It was the deliberate erection of this shield around Marleen that Stan found particularly hurtful. And he could see that it was having its effect. During the long silences at meal-times, she had taken to eyeing him. She had large, expressive eyes, and the look that had come into them lately was one of brooding incredulity. Knife and fork held in mid-air, she kept inspecting him. 'Get on with your meal, Marleen,' Beryl would say, without looking up from her own plate while she was speaking. 'We don't want to have to sit here all day, do we?'

What with being ignored by his wife and stared at by his daughter, Stan couldn't help feeling uncomfortable nearly all the time.

Then, on the Thursday, two days after the Gazette had appeared, something nice happened; something really nice, and entirely unexpected.

Stan was on his way home at the time. Gloomy and downcast as ever, he was back in Cannon Street rather wishing that he could find some excuse for missing his train again. And it was just as he came out of the exit from the Underground that, quite accidentally, he ran into Mr Karlin. Or rather, Mr Karlin ran into him. Mr Karlin was going down at exactly the moment that Stan was coming up. They collided.

It was clear that Mr Karlin was in a hurry. He muttered a quick

'Pardon' as he tried to push his way past. Then he stopped suddenly, and turned.

'Isn't it Mr . . . Mr Pitts?' he asked, searching round in his mind for the surname.

Stan had stopped short, too. He would have recognized that soft, grey-flannel voice and that Continental-style raincoat anywhere.

'Mr Karlin.'

The steps of the Underground were no place for trying to carry on a conversation. But Mr Karlin seemed to have forgotten all about the hurry he was in. He was holding out his hand in welcome.

'Well, isn't that extraordinary?' he said, his big, smooth face pink with excitement. 'I was just thinking about you.'

He paused and looked round him for a moment.

'What about a drink?' he asked. 'Somewhere we can talk. Then I shan't have to write you a letter.'

Stan glanced up at the station clock. It was all right. He was on the early side tonight. He could afford to let the six-two pull away without him. And he was certainly curious to know why Mr Karlin should have been going to write to him at all. Even so, he was cautious. Extremely cautious. He couldn't afford to have things go wrong a second time.

'Well, just a quick one,' he said.

As they went into the bar, Stan was afraid for a moment that the barmaid would remember him. And he didn't want Mr Karlin to think that he was one of the quick-nip kind. But he need not have worried. The barmaid was working away at high speed, like a lady-conjurer, too busy with her glass-and-bottle tricks to spare a smile for any of the audience.

'What'll you have?' Mr Karlin asked.

'Half a bitter,' Stan told him.

Mr Karlin, it appeared, was not a hard drinker, either. He ordered two half-pints, and then moved away from the bar so that others could get served. There were some pretty impatient ones among them, too; they might just have come in from the Sahara they were so thirsty.

'Cheers.'

'Good luck.' It was Mr Karlin who had wished it. 'It's about that photograph of yours,' he said. 'The one that got first prize. Cherry blossom, wasn't it?'

'Apple blossom,' Stan corrected him.

94

Mr Karlin seemed disappointed with himself.

'I'm no good on flowers,' he admitted. 'I just know when they're beautiful. And that's what your photograph was – beautiful.' He paused. 'Have you got any more like it?'

'Fruit trees, you mean?'

Mr Karlin smiled.

'Don't have to be. Just nature stuff generally. Or animals. Pets, you know. Pets with children. Open air studies. It's not the subject. It's the treatment. That's where someone like you comes in.'

'There's *Swans at Teddington Weir*,' Stan told him. 'That's about my favourite. Two firsts and a special mention.'

'I'd like to see it sometime.'

'And there's my *Deserted Platform, Winter*,' Stan went on. 'And *Coming Home from Church* and *The Old Paper-seller*. And all my snow pictures. *Jack Frost in Kensington Gardens* got a first, too.'

'Did it, now?' Mr Karlin was nodding his head approvingly. 'Then I was right about you. I guessed straight away. You're not amateur class. You're professional.'

Stan found it very pleasant being appreciated like that; very agreeable and consoling, after everything that had been happening to him. It was like being stroked.

'You really think so?'

Mr Karlin shook his head this time.

'I don't think. I know,' he said. 'It's my business. We place a lot of pictures. News and action mostly. But there's always a market for the other kind. In the quality papers, that is, and the glossies.'

'And would mine be good enough?'

'Properly handled, they would be. Got to have the proper contacts, of course. No use just sending them in. Have to know the picture editors.' He paused. 'Ever thought of starting it up as a sideline?'

'Not really.'

It was untrue. Up alone in his darkroom and mooching about outdoors with his Pentax slung over his shoulder, he'd thought about little else. Ever since he'd been a schoolboy with an old box Brownie, he'd known that a camera was a part of him, that his life and photography were somehow all linked up. But he wasn't going to let on to Mr Karlin.

'There's money in it, you know,' Mr Karlin was telling him, his voice growing warmer and more confiding as he spoke. 'Ten guineas here. Fifteen guineas there. Twenty if it's a cover piece. Colour supplements – they're the ones to go for.'

'And how do I do that?'

'Get the right representative,' Mr Karlin replied.

Stan looked down into his glass. Already it was half empty. Two more mouthfuls, and he'd have finished it. But he was careful not to hurry. He was playing it cool, very cool.

'Would you care to represent me?' he asked.

Stan was rather pleased with the question. It made him sound like a professional already.

'Proud to,' Mr Karlin replied.

And then he paused. It was rather a long pause. And, when he resumed, Stan could see the reason for it. Mr Karlin was embarrassed.

'It's only that I wouldn't want you to be disappointed in me,' he continued. 'It can happen, you know. A big fat cheque one month, and then only a fiver or a tenner next time. Got to take the rough with the smooth, you know. It can't be over the hundred mark every time.'

Over the hundred mark! Even though at that moment Stan wasn't drinking, he swallowed. But he was careful to go on wearing his professional expression. And, when he spoke, his voice was quietly business-like. He doubted if Cliff could have done better.

'What commission do you charge?' he asked.

'Ten per cent. Or buy outright. Whichever the client prefers.'

He saw that Stan was looking at his watch, and that reminded him that he was running late himself. He reached into his breast pocket for his wallet.

'Tell you what,' he said. 'You send me a selection. Just the best ones. Then I'll see if we can make you an offer. Advance against royalties, if you prefer it that way. We're easy.'

He had taken his card out of the wallet, and was holding it out for Stan to take.

'You gave me your card last time,' Stan reminded him.

'Then tear it up,' Mr Karlin told him. 'It's out of date. We've changed the box number.'

The farewell handshake was a hurried affair because Mr Karlin was so late. But he found time to give Stan a pat on the shoulder as they parted.

Stan looked after him. Mr Karlin was still wearing that Continental-style raincoat with the big gusset V in the back. There weren't many raincoats like that in London. He was quite sure now that it had been Mr Karlin he'd seen in the Bull and Garter that Sunday morning. Perhaps, without knowing it, they were neighbours. Stan liked the thought of having someone as nice and friendly as Mr Karlin living near to him.

Chapter 12

If the past month had been a bad one for Stan it had been worse, much worse, for Beryl. Watching Stan leave for the office in the mornings, she had envied him. He was able to get away from it all, whereas she was stuck there, imprisoned; trapped in the pit that she had helped to dig for herself. She was helpless.

And she had given up caring. She told herself that she didn't mind how the house looked. On some mornings, instead of Hoovering and polishing, she would just go through to the lounge and sit there, doing nothing. If it hadn't been for little Marleen, she'd have been along to the new drug store weeks ago. It was their largest bottle of sleeping-tablets that she had in mind. And, when she got back home, she'd have swallowed the whole lot at once, cramming the tablets into her mouth one after another, like peanuts, so as to end it all.

Gloomy and woebegone as these thoughts were they were not, however, entirely without compensation. She got a lot of satisfaction out of thinking about what her sudden death would do to Stan. As soon as he saw her stretched out, cold and lifeless, on the bathroom floor, he'd know at last what he had done to her. Because he was the one who would have driven her to it; that made it murder really, not suicide. And just in case he didn't see it that way she would leave a note on the washbasin pointing it out to him.

Thinking about Stan had another useful side effect. It made her angry. And when she was really angry, she couldn't be miserable at the same time. Instead of moping, she began to call him names.

'You silly, stupid, little man,' she said out loud. 'What good do you think you are to anyone? You're no good to me, that's for certain. No good now, and never have been. You're just a creep, that's what you are. A common, selfish little creep. And no good at your job either, or they'd have promoted you. You head of the department, indeed! Don't make me laugh. You're not fit to run a winkle stall.' It was an expression that she'd once heard, and she rather liked it. On occasions such as this it came in useful; it was so apt. And merely saying it made her feel angrier still. 'That's why everyone laughs at you,' she went on.

'Me, and Marleen and the Ebbutts. And secretaries at the office, too. I bet they laugh at you behind your back. I know I would. There's nothing to you – that's your trouble. You're just a pipsqueak. You haven't got the courage of . . . of a nit.' It was a nasty word, a word that, in the ordinary way, Beryl would never possibly have used. But by now she was saying all the things that, for years and years, she'd been storing up inside her, and she was feeling all the better for it. 'I don't just despise you,' she finished up. 'I hate you. D'you hear me? I hate you. Hate you. Hate you. Hate you.'

She was so tired when she had finished that she had to sit down. She was breathless. But she felt better. A sense almost of calm had come over her. She made herself a cup of Nescafé and drank it slowly, thoughtfully. Then, as she wetted her fingertip to gather up a few caffeiney grains that had spilled into the saucer, an idea came to her. It was so obvious that she wondered why it had not occurred to her before. Leaving the cup and saucer unwashed, she went through to the lounge where the telephone was standing.

It was only because of her strength of mind that they were on the telephone at all. Stan had been against it from the start. He regarded the phone as an unnecessary extravagance. But because of emergencies she'd been able to talk him into it. He'd given way in the end when she'd asked him how he'd feel if Marleen suddenly got a burst appendix or something and, because they weren't on the phone, she hadn't been able to save her life. It was the sort of domestic tragedy, she insisted, that was an everyday occurrence in middle-class households. Ivory-white like the kitchen cabinets was the colour that she finally chose for the instrument.

Even so, as it turned out, the installation of the telephone had proved a bit of a disappointment. Beryl had seen it as opening up a whole exciting new world to her, a world of gossip with old friends, shared confidences, surprise invitations. And nothing of the sort had happened. There were practically no calls at all, either incoming or outgoing; apart from the occasional wrong number, there were some weeks when the bell never rang at all.

All the same, Beryl wouldn't have been without it. She liked being able to say to the mothers of Marleen's school friends: 'Give me a tinkle some time. You've got my number, haven't you?'

And, of course, it served to keep her in touch with Cliff. It was

Cliff's number that she was dialling this morning.

'Clifford Hamson Group,' the switchboard operator answered, and Beryl felt a pang as she heard her. It just showed the heights that Cliff had climbed to; and all by his own efforts, too. Cliff was right at the top already; not like someone else she could mention.

And, though she had to hold on a moment because he was speaking on another line, she could tell at once how genuinely pleased he was that she had rung him.

'Hullo, Beautiful,' he greeted her.

The quick intake of breath told him how eager she was.

'Oh, Cliff,' she said. 'I want to see you. I need to.'

'On my way,' he answered, and she could hear the pages of his desk diary rustling. 'What about Friday? Usual time?'

'No. You don't understand,' she told him. 'I want to see you alone. Not with Stan there.'

It sounded like a low whistle from the other end.

'Do I smell burning?' he asked.

It was exactly the kind of thing that she'd always liked best about Cliff. He was so much on top of things, so humorous; and deep down, of course, so understanding.

'I'm in trouble, Cliff.'

'At your service.'

'Can I come and see you?'

'Name the day. I'll be here.'

'What about tomorrow?'

'What about *lunch* tomorrow?' he corrected her. 'Where d'you like – Ritz, Savoy, Dorchester?'

She paused. She would have liked any one of them, even all three on successive days if that had been possible. Her medium-length black with the pale beige would have been exactly right for a West End luncheon engagement. But she wanted Cliff to realize how much in earnest she was, how serious.

'Just somewhere quiet, please. Somewhere we can talk.'

For a moment this seemed to have put Cliff at a disadvantage. He didn't seem to know many quiet places. Then he remembered just the right one.

'D'you know Soho?' he asked.

'I know where it is.'

'D'you know Greek Street?'

'I can find it.'

'Well, write it down. El Morocco in Greek Street.'

'One o'clock?'

'Why keep me waiting? I'll be there at quarter to.'

Beryl felt suddenly like crying. She gave a little sniff.

'Oh, Cliff,' she said, 'you are nice. You're so good to me.'

This time there was the sound of a kiss blown down the telephone.

'Listen, Beautiful,' he told her. 'I haven't started yet.'

Mrs Ebbutt was ever so good about it, or Beryl wouldn't have been able to go up to town at all.

It was Marleen who was the trouble. But Mrs Ebbutt said that she didn't mind a bit: she knew just how Beryl felt about letting a pretty little thing like Marleen walk home alone, and it wouldn't be the slightest trouble going round to the school gates to collect her. Then she could stay with them at No. 18 until Beryl got back. The only thing that Mrs Ebbutt hoped and prayed was that the specialist would tell Beryl that it wasn't.

The specialist had been a sudden, happy invention on Beryl's part, one of those smooth white lies that make life so much easier. She'd thought of it just as she was putting the telephone down. And, to set her mind at rest, she'd gone next door straight away. The note of urgency was all too apparent, but Mrs Ebbutt couldn't help admiring the way Beryl played it down, made it sound as though it didn't really matter.

'It probably isn't anything,' she had said. 'Not really. It's just that he wants a second opinion like. I mean doctors can't be expected to know everything, can they? You know me, I wouldn't bother. But it's gone on for such a long time now . . .'

After she had heard Beryl's news, Mrs Ebbutt insisted on keeping her there while she made a cup of tea. It came as rather a relaxed and pleasant interlude, chatting over the hazards of womanhood; and Mrs Ebbutt couldn't help admiring Beryl even more when she said that she didn't want even the least whisper to reach Stan because he'd worry himself half-demented just thinking about it. That was when Mrs Ebbutt said that she was glad, downright glad, that the doctor was being so careful because she'd noticed that Beryl hadn't been looking quite herself for some considerable time now. This rather upset Beryl.

But Mrs Ebbutt had a heart of gold: no question about that. She was even there next morning waiting at the window to give Beryl a good-luck wave as, so calmly, so bravely, she set off for the station as though it were any ordinary kind of day.

At the station Beryl bought herself a copy of *Home Hairdressing* to read on the train. It was only a stray thought so far, a partially-formed fancy still locked in the away part of her mind that had prompted her. But if she wanted to, she didn't see why she shouldn't; just try it out like, she kept telling herself. And, with hair as raven black as hers, the effect should be quite something. Any day now, without saying a word about it first, she would tell M. Louis in Railway Approach to take two thick tresses on either side and bleach them pure snow white just for the contrast. She wished now that she had made her mind up sooner so that today's hair-do could have been like that for her lunch with Cliff.

Her mind was not entirely on hairdressing, however. It kept straying back to what Cliff had said when he had invited her. She found herself wondering if he had really meant it when he had suggested the Ritz. She would have liked casually, as a kind of throwaway line, to be able to say to Marleen's teacher: 'When I was lunching at the Ritz the other day . . .' And now it would have to be: 'There's a little place in Soho I go to sometimes when I'm in town . . .' Still good, but not so good. Either way, however, she was looking forward to saying it. And then, with a pang, she remembered: today's lunch was secret. If it had been in the House of Lords or Buckingham Palace she could never, so long as Stan was around, possibly refer to it.

She would have liked to take a taxi from Cannon Street, but it was the expense that stopped her. The fare to town had been more than she had expected, and she now had only fifteen shillings in her handbag. By the time she had collected Marleen's shoe-repair on the way home, she would be down practically to a handful of small change. It was humiliating.

Because she couldn't afford a taxi, the choice was between a bus and the Underground. And it was the Underground that she chose. This, as it turned out, was a mistake. When she asked for a ticket to Soho, the booking-clerk told her that there was no such station, Piccadilly Circus was the nearest, he said. There was humiliation in that, too: it was yet another painful reminder of how suburban, how much out of touch with things, she had allowed herself to become. She winced as she picked up the ticket.

Finding her way from Piccadilly Circus to Greek Street presented its own special problem. Once she had turned off Shaftesbury Avenue she would have liked to ask the way, but the only people she could see were exactly the sort of people that she wouldn't have cared to be seen talking to. Foreigners mostly; and not very nice foreigners at that.

Usually, if you wanted to enquire about an address, you could just pop into the nearest shop. But here in Soho it was different. They were such extraordinary shops. So frank, so explicit, and so single-minded. She only hoped that Marleen would never get taken past any of them. Not until she was married at least. And even then only if she had found herself the right kind of husband.

In the end, it was a window-cleaner that she asked. He seemed respectable enough. And the El Morocco, when at last she found it, was distinctly reassuring; a piece of real old Marrakesh sprung up in WI. The proprietor had indulged his own hot Mediterranean taste. The front was painted deep ochre, and the shutters and jalousies were striped in yellow. On either side of the doorway hung twin baskets of fern and geraniums, and the glass panel of the door was decorated with the display cards of Diners' Club, American Express and the Société Gastronomique de France. Beryl had known it all the time: Cliff would never have dreamed of taking her anywhere that wasn't of the best.

Even so, it seemed dreadfully dark inside. The blinds were kept permanently drawn and the only light there was came from the little dangling lamps like incense-burners. The shirt-front of the waiter showed up all right but, when he turned to lead her to the table, she almost lost sight of him again. That was why it was wonderful to hear Cliff's voice saying 'Hullo Beautiful', coming from somewhere in the blackness ahead of her.

The tables were set in small alcoves all round the room. Getting in was a bit of a scramble. The tables had to be pulled out first but, once they had been pushed back again, there was no denying that there was a wonderfully intimate, close-up kind of feeling. Beryl had never sat on a couch instead of on a chair in a restaurant before.

At first she said 'no' she didn't want a drink, really she didn't, not at lunchtime like. But Cliff refused to listen. A drink was exactly what she needed, he told her, adding that this was something else they had in common. And he insisted on ordering for her. The wine waiter was smiling and dusky and wore a fez. He and Cliff appeared to be old friends, and Beryl found herself wondering who Cliff usually brought with him into the alcove. It was the sort of place where even comparative strangers would get to know each other very quickly.

They were Vodkatinis that Cliff ordered, and in sign language he indicated that they should be large ones by separating his thumb and forefinger as wide as they would go. Whatever Cliff did always had style to it.

It was the same, too, with the meal. She let him choose. But there was really nothing else she could have done. The menu was written out in French on thick parchmenty paper and, in the thick twilight of the El Morocco, she couldn't make out a word of it. This saddened her because it meant that any day now she might need reading-glasses. But the prices stood out plainly enough; and she could hardly believe them. Just thinking of what Stan told her that he had to pay for lunch in the canteen at Frobisher House reminded her of the two different worlds that Stan and Cliff lived in. That was what was so marvellous about the way all three of them were able to go on being such good friends.

The Vodkatinis were not only large, they were powerful; like gin, only different. And more relaxing. And when Cliff suggested that a bottle of hock would go best with what they were having, she was ready to agree with him. She had finished the Vodkatini by then, and she felt better; happier and more secure. Just sitting there on the little semi-circular couch with Cliff's knee pressed up against hers, was enough. She knew that everything would be all right now, and even wondered what she had been worrying about.

Cliff made no attempt to rush things. He knew women. Those long silences were always the prelude, at any moment now she would break out and tell him everything. And once again he was proved right. Leaving the Parma ham only half-eaten, she turned to him.

'Oh, Cliff,' she said. 'I simply had to see you. You're the only one I can tell. You can't imagine what I've been going through. Really you can't.'

He put his large, strong hand with the big signet ring on the third finger over hers, and left it there.

'That's what we're here for,' he told her. 'We're not just friends.'

And, to show that he meant it, he gave her hand a little squeeze as well.

'It's Stan,' she went on. 'I'm sorry for him. Really I am. But, I mean, it's no use pretending, is it? He just isn't up to it like. That's what's wrong with him.'

Cliff removed his hand for a moment because Beryl wanted to finish up her melon. It was the pink kind that came from Israel, and she was particularly fond of it.

'And he knows it,' she resumed. 'I mean, he must do, mustn't he? Stan's not stupid. He minds. You can tell that. It's what gets him down like.'

The wine waiter in the fez had removed the hock bottle from the ice-bucket and was uncorking it. Cliff was very particular about wine. When the waiter had poured a little, he first sniffed and then sipped. Next he raised his glass.

'To both of us,' he said.

In the ordinary way, Beryl liked drinking out of long-stemmed glasses. They seemed somehow so much more festive than the other kind. But today she scarcely noticed.

'That's why he's gone to pieces,' she said. 'Like the night they told him he hadn't got it. You've never seen Stan when he's drunk. Well, I have. I've never been so ashamed in all my life. That's why I had to take little Marleen through to my room. So that *she* shouldn't see. That's the kind of time I've been having. Only of course I couldn't let on like, not even to Marleen.'

None of it was in the least what she had meant to say to Cliff. All that she had intended when she set out from Crocketts Green that morning had been a straightforward conversation about money. But she had not reckoned on the Vodkatini and the hock. And, in the event, if she had been lying out on a psychiatrist's couch she could not have been more confiding.

'And you can imagine what I felt like next morning taking Marleen to school,' she went on. 'It's a wonder I even dared show my face. Supposing someone we knew had seen him. Marleen's form-mistress like. That would have been nice for me, wouldn't it? I mean . . .'

It was the waiter who interrupted her. He was bringing the *kebab*. And one glance at him was enough to show that he was exactly the type that would go in for eavesdropping. A single indiscreet remark from her, she realized, and it would be all round the Arab world tomorrow. She sat on in silence until he had finished serving.

'It isn't as though I'm demanding,' she explained, as soon as he had gone away, 'because that isn't the way I'm made. Not that it would make any difference if I was. Because, if it isn't there, you can't have it, can you? I've got used to going without. But it doesn't mean that you don't still want it.'

If Beryl had not taken up her knife and fork, Cliff would have put his hand over hers again. As it was, he pressed his knee in closer and rubbed it up and down a bit.

'And all this time you never let on,' he said. 'That's what I call loyalty. Real loyalty.'

'Sometimes I think I'm going mad,' she told him. 'I just lie in bed at night thinking about it. Because it'll never get better. Not married to Stan, it won't. That's why I thought of you.'

Cliff had put down his own knife and fork, and was sitting back watching her. She certainly looked cool enough; and he admired her for it. In all his experience he had never had anything quite like this happen to him before.

'You know how I feel about you,' he said. 'I always have. Always.'

What Cliff found strangely unnerving was that Beryl was so clearly enjoying her *kebab*. And it was worse with the salad. She was munching it.

'So I decided I had to do something about it,' she told him between mouthfuls. 'I'll repay you all right. You needn't worry about that. It's just that I've got to have it. And I've got to have it now.'

This time it was the waiter with the sweet trolley who made her break off. In the end it was the *gâteau* she chose. She knew when she asked for it that she shouldn't have done so. With a figure like hers she had to be on guard all the time. But she liked chocolate *gâteau*, and somehow it didn't seem to matter so much with Marleen not there to see her eating it.

Then she turned back to Cliff again.

'There's one thing you've got to promise. You're not to let Stan know. If Stan gets to hear of it, he'll try to stop it. I know he will.'

Cliff promised.

'And it can't go on any longer,' Beryl told him. 'Because they won't cash any more cheques like. Mr Winters said so.'

'Mr Winters?'

Cliff heard himself repeating the name. It meant nothing to him.

'Well, it's not Mr Winters really,' Beryl went on. 'It's the head office. At least he says it is. But he would, wouldn't he? And it comes to the same thing, I mean. Not being able to write a cheque like.'

Cliff shifted further back into the couch and eased his knee away from hers.

'Are you asking me for money?'

The question came as a surprise to Beryl. After all that she had been telling him, it seemed impossible that he shouldn't have understood. But she was ready to explain things more clearly if that was what was needed.

'It's been going up, you see. That's the whole trouble. It didn't matter the way it was because it always had been. But it's more now. That's why I've got to do something. Stan can't. Not on his salary. Well, he couldn't, could he? He's not mean. He just hasn't got it.'

'How much?'

There was, Beryl noted, something strangely flat-sounding about his voice as he asked her. She supposed it was something to do with his business life. After all, buying and selling things, he was probably talking about money all day.

'It's a hundred and seven,' she told him. 'Not counting the new covers, that is. And they've got to be paid for some time. I mean, if you don't pay you can't go there again, can you? It stands to reason. And they're cheaper than anywhere else. You've only got to look at . . .'

Cliff wasn't listening any longer. He had taken out his cheque book and was writing something with his thick gold-looking pen. He tore off the cheque and pushed it across to her.

'Would this help?' he asked.

As soon as she looked down at it, she knew that she had been right to ask him. There was nothing small or mean-minded about Cliff. Whatever he did had his own distinctive gesture to it. The cheque was for one hundred pounds.

This time it was Beryl's hand that reached out and squeezed Cliff's.

'You are sweet,' she told him. 'I'll give it all back, like I said. Stan's bound to get a raise sometime, isn't he? I mean, they can't expect him to go on forever, not the way he is now. Not forever they can't.'

Cliff looked at his watch.

'I've got to be getting back,' he told her.

Chapter 13

In the end it was Mr Miller's feet that did it. By now they had become strangers to him; useless and unfeeling, they had no life left in them. Even resting on a hot water bottle they remained icy. In short, Mr Miller was bedridden. His doctor spoke of extended sick leave and wrote out a medical certificate. Not that Mr Miller minded very much. He'd done his bit. His sick leave entitlement carried him comfortably over his April retirement date.

It was only Stan that he was worried about. He'd have liked to be there to make things easier at the time of the hand-over. He was pretty well set in his ways, was Stan: that was what made him so dependable. But how he would feel about modern management methods, fresh classifications, even possibly an entire reallocation of work duties, Mr Miller was not so sure.

Waiting for his successor to arrive did not make for happiness. Stan liked sitting at Mr Miller's desk and having everyone come up to him; and it was nice to have a cupboard all of his own. But now, just when he'd got used to it all, it was going to be taken away again. They were an insensitive lot up there in Establishment: the way they behaved, human feelings didn't come into it.

The manner of Mr Parker's introduction was another example. It was mid-morning when it all happened. Stan was tilted back in his chair drinking his eleven o'clock cup of tea. That was one more of the privileges that he was enjoying: everyone else had to drink out of crinkly plastic things with fold-away handles, but Mr Miller had his own cup and saucer. And it made all the difference. The tea even tasted like tea. That was why Stan was taking his time and sipping it.

Then, without warning, the door was thrust open and Stan saw the Deputy Controller standing there. And not only the Deputy Controller. There was a tall young man behind him. A six-footer, Stan reckoned; and a very well-dressed six-footer at that. He was wearing a light grey suit with a striped, expensive-looking tie.

Because he was leaning so far back in his chair, Stan came down with a bit of a bump as they entered. The cup was still more than half full and the tea splashed up at him. As soon as he had shaken hands he had to get out his handkerchief and start mopping up. The blotter now had large brown patches like a skin disease all over it.

'We didn't mean to disturb you,' the Deputy Controller was saying. 'Simply that Mr Parker wanted a little chat with you before he takes over. Everything's been arranged. Mr Parker is with us from now on.' The Deputy Controller smiled his smooth, office smile and glanced down at his watch. 'Well, I've got to be leaving you. You know where to find me if you want anything, Mr Parker. You'll put him fully in the picture, won't you, Mr Pitts?'

Stan stuffed his handkerchief back into his pocket. It now had tea stains all over it like the blotter, and he felt sure that Beryl would have something to say about it. What's more he could feel that Mr Parker was watching him; observing everything about him, drawing his own conclusions. Stan tidied up the desk and pushed the swivel chair back into position. But, when he began to move away, Mr Parker stopped him.

'No, no. You go on sitting where you were,' he said. 'I'll stand. I've been sitting around upstairs.'

He drew himself up to his full height as he said it. And it was obvious that Mr Parker possessed charm. While he stood there he was scattering a little of it over Stan like confetti.

'I've been hearing all about you,' he said. 'Doesn't sound to me as though you need any help in this department. Can't imagine why they brought me round here.'

'I think you'll find Mr Miller left everything in order,' Stan told him.

But Mr Parker would have none of it.

'That isn't what they were telling me upstairs,' he replied. 'They say you're the one who's been running the show. After all, Mr Miller hasn't been here lately, has he? They know that all right.'

It was clever, too, this use of 'they'. It indicated, without stressing it, that there were levels in the Civil Service in which Mr Parker moved and Stan didn't. They were the levels at which confidences were exchanged, and big decisions arrived at.

'By the way,' Mr Parker went on, 'What's been done about paying you?'

Stan was puzzled for a moment.

'I've been paid the same as usual,' he said.

Mr Parker shook his head and brought out a little memo pad. It was rather a handsome little memo pad, with a pigskin back and bright gilt corners.

'That's not good enough,' he said. 'Acting Head. Extra responsibilities and all that. I'll mention it to them. Look better coming from me. Can't promise anything, of course. But we'll see what we can do.'

Then, almost as though he were rebuking Stan for detaining them both, he broke off quite suddenly.

'Well, we mustn't just stand round talking all day,' he said. 'I want you to introduce me to people. First names as well, please. Pet names, too, if they've got them.'

They had reached the door by now, and Mr Parker was regarding it somewhat critically. It was a perfectly ordinary door, plain, painted deal beneath and half-glazed in the upper part. Even a bit better than ordinary, because Mr Miller had asked to have a door-spring fitted so that it wouldn't get left open.

But apparently with Mr Parker it was different. He pulled the door wide, and surveyed the open office in front of him. Then he turned towards Stan.

'You might arrange with Works to get this door taken off, would you?' he asked. 'I like to know what's going on.'

Mr Parker had been there for a full week now.

And it wasn't only the smart pigskin memo pad that he used, either. Mr Parker was way out ahead of the rest of the Civil Service. He had his own personal tape-recorder. Japanese and duty-free, it gave an air of brisk efficiency to the whole department.

But, for the most part, it was staff relations that Mr Parker was working on. He made regular tours round the place just to talk to people. He'd remembered all the names and rather deliberately made use of them. It was to the older secretaries that he was particularly attentive. With the juniors he knew that he didn't have to worry. After the elderly and limping Mr Miller, it was strangely exciting having a boss who came into the office carrying a couple of squash racquets and a canvas sports-case. Two of the juniors were, in fact, already in love with him. They were the same two who had wished Stan good luck when he went along to the Appointments Board. They had really wanted Stan to get the job. But, now that they'd seen the real thing, it was different. Nice as Stan was, they could see that he wouldn't really have been up to it.

Back at his own desk Stan had become part of the general office again; and, to his surprise, he rather liked it. What he did not like was that, with the inner door off its hinges, he was right in Mr Parker's line of vision. He couldn't even enjoy his eleven o'clock cup of tea properly because of the thought that Mr Parker might be watching. It gave him an uncomfortable, prickly sort of feeling.

And this was a pity because in Mr Miller's day Stan had always looked on the tea-break as being by way of an unwinder. It meant that for those few odd minutes he could relax and think about other things. Photography mostly. Some of the best titles for his competition pieces had come to him during tea-break. But it was not about competitions that he was thinking now. It was about the professional and commercial side. He had made his own selection of his best work as Mr Karlin had asked him, and he felt pleased with himself. Even rather impressed. There was more good stuff just lying about in his workroom than he had realized. Mr Karlin was going to have a surprise coming to him.

It would have come to him already, in fact, if Stan had been able to go out and buy all the printing paper and mounts that he needed. But good quality paper for art work has always been expensive. And so have mounts. High-grade card with a china finish can be nothing less than prohibitive. Stan had managed to save up for the art paper by cutting out canteen lunches, and making do with a sandwich. But the mounts were a different matter altogether. He'd been forced to use old ones, prising off the original prints with a razor blade and then smartening up the dirty edges in the guillotine. It was the stationery side that had been taking up the time.

He glanced up at the Ministry clock on the wall, and re-set his watch by it. In another hour-and-forty-minutes he'd be on his way home. With luck, he reckoned, this evening he'd be able to finish the pasting-up and re-mounting. After that it would just be a matter of putting them into the press overnight to flatten them.

Re-setting his watch, however, hadn't done any good. The thing had stopped altogether. It was an old watch, and Stan knew the kind of tricks it got up to. He took it off his wrist, gave it a series of little shakes and pressed it hard up against his ear. Then, when he could hear nothing, he got out his penknife and eased the back off. He was peering down into the works, blowing on them, when Mr Parker spoke to him.

'Having trouble?' he asked.

Mr Parker's voice came from right over his shoulder, and Stan wondered how long he had been standing there. The uncomfortable prickly feeling returned. It broke over him in a hot wave like nettle-rash.

Returning to Kendal Terrace in the evening had become more like old times. Beryl appeared to have forgiven him and they were on speaking terms again. Not particularly friendly speaking terms; no endearments. But still, it was better than one long militant silence. And Beryl seemed in herself to have become more tranquil and contented. It was almost as though, for the time being at least, she had given up worrying about Mr Winters.

In any case, he kept telling himself, it wasn't going to be long before things got better. When Mr Karlin saw the selection – and it was only a selection – of the prints that Stan had prepared for him he'd know that he was on to something. Then they'd both be able to forget all about Mr Winters and his two-pounds-a-week repayment plan.

That was why Stan didn't allow things to slacken off. Immediately he had helped Beryl with the washing-up he went back to his workroom again. And he was very nearly through. He'd divided up his photographs into categories as Mr Karlin had suggested. There were now five neat little piles of them, all in folders and all labelled. When Mr Karlin came to undo the parcel he'd find 'Four Seasons'; 'London, Old and New'; 'Child Studies'; 'Character Pieces'; and 'Animal Kingdom'. 'Animal Kingdom' made up quite an impressive album all on its own. In addition to his already famous *Swans* there were *Donkey-time on Hampstead Heath*, *Blackbird on Nest*, *Poodle Parade*, *Kensington Gardens*, *Jo, the Zoo Gorilla*, and *Mother Love*. *Mother Love* was a singularly tender little piece, showing the Ebbutt cat with her five kittens all in a wicker basket dumped in the middle of the back lawn on a fine Sunday morning in September.

It was nearly eleven o'clock when Stan brought down the blade of the guillotine for the last time. The little slither of cardboard spiralled onto the floor and the old mount, brought up to date and refurbished, was all ready to receive *Picnic Party* in the 'Child Studies' section. Except for the mopping-up, Stan's work was finished.

And, because he was tired, he wasn't really looking where he was going when he came downstairs. He nearly bumped into Beryl as she was leaving the bathroom. Her face was all pink and shiny with conditioning cream. She was wearing her flowery bed-cap and, seen through the printed muslin, the two white side-streaks that she had made M. Louis put in showed up like scars.

Beryl paused halfway across the passage. From her expression it was evident that he was not yet entirely forgiven.

'You still live here?' she asked. 'I'd forgotten. Really I had. I thought I'd been alone all the evening. Only I can't have, can I? Not with you around the place, I can't. And please don't think of putting yourself out on my account. Please don't, I say. I'm used to it. I'm only glad one of us is happy.'

Her door closed behind her, and Stan went along to his dressing-room. On the way, he peeped in to see Marleen. She was asleep, with her arm curled round the big Teddy-bear that she always took to bed with her. The composition was perfect. So, too, were the colours; pale, but contrasting. All pastel shades, in fact. Marleen's hair was almost pure flaxen and Teddy's was distinctly reddish even for a bear. If it hadn't been that Beryl might object, he'd have liked to take a flash of the two of them as they lay there. Just head-and-shoulders and a bit of pillow.

Beauty and the Beast, he reflected, would make a nice caption. Either that, or play safe and call it *Land of Nod.*

Chapter 14

Ask anyone who travels by Southern Region and you'll hear the same story. A month or two at the most of smooth running – scheduled timetable stuff – and then trouble again. If it isn't the signals, it's the points. And if they're both all right, there's an engine breakdown. Or a derailment. What's more, it doesn't have to be your breakdown or your derailment. Southern Region is like the blood circulation system, all veins and arteries. Thousands of miles of them. It may be somebody else's thrombosis in a different county altogether that makes your particular limb go dead and useless.

It was like that this morning. When the eight ten got in to Crocketts Green it was already eight seventeen. And, when it pulled out again, the station clock showed eight twenty-five. Even if they'd had a clear run ahead of them they could never have made it up. But it wasn't a clear run. This time it was one of Southern Region's real monumental hold-ups. When Stan reached Cannon Street it was already nine twenty.

Mr Miller had always been very understanding about that kind of thing. He was a rail-traveller himself; he knew. And naturally Stan expected Mr Parker to see it Mr Miller's way.

He sat down straight away at his desk, and was surprised therefore when Mr Parker came out and spoke to him.

'Do you mind coming into my office?' he asked, without even a 'Good morning' to start things going.

Stan followed him. The two juniors looked up as he went past, and he heard one of them give a little giggle and whisper something to the girl next to her.

Mr Parker folded his arms, and sat down in Mr Miller's chair. It was a comfortable chair. Mr Miller's cushion was still in it. The chair on Stan's side of the desk was an ordinary office hardback. Even so he didn't ask Stan to take it.

'Well?' he asked.

'Well what?'

'Do you know what time it is?'

Stan knew exactly. It was two minutes past ten. He'd been counting up the minutes ever since he had left Cannon Street. But he wasn't going to tell Mr Parker because he felt perfectly sure that Mr Parker knew already.

'The train was late,' he explained. 'There'd been a hold-up or something. They were all running late this morning.'

'Does this kind of thing often happen?'

'It's not my fault,' he told him. 'I can't tell when it's going to happen. There's nothing I can do about it.'

Stan was beginning to feel aggrieved by now. In all his life in the Civil Service he'd never been spoken to like this before. And it was clear that Mr Parker intended to go on with it. His eyes were fixed on Stan as he was speaking. They were hard, sportsman's eyes.

'Oh yes, there is,' he replied. 'You can catch an earlier train. Give yourself a safety-margin.'

Mr Parker, however, simply didn't understand. Beryl would never hear of it. As it was, she disapproved of breakfast at seven thirty. In her view that was when the working classes had breakfast. Anything earlier than eight o'clock smacked of commonness.

But, in any case, Stan wasn't going to be pushed around like that. He was not prepared to have Mr Parker re-making his domestic arrangements for him, and he was determined to make that clear.

'It may interest you to know that, at the moment, I leave the house at five to eight every morning,' he said.

Mr Parker's eyes did not move.

'And this morning that was half an hour too late, wasn't it?' he asked. 'There was no one in charge of the outer office until ten.' He paused. 'It didn't matter, of course, because I was here. I'm only glad that no one else spotted it.'

Stan felt himself trembling. It had always been the same: whenever he was upset about anything he started to twitch. Already little electric currents were running up and down his fingers. He steadied himself.

'Is that all?' he asked.

And he was pleased with the way he had asked it. He'd kept his voice deliberately flat. It had come out polite but indifferent-sounding. No one could have guessed how hurt he was inside.

Or perhaps Mr Parker did guess it. He was the complete youth leader, and knew that there was something more to leadership than discipline. He came over and put his hand on Stan's shoulder.

'Sorry to have to speak to you like that,' he said. 'I'm not blaming you. It's simply what you've grown used to. They told me things had got pretty slack round here. It's up to the two of us to put that right. You're not going to let me down, are you?'

Stan could feel the hand on his shoulder give a little squeeze as he finished. It made Stan feel faintly sick. He'd not forgotten that the door had been taken away. For all this hand-on-shoulder stuff, Mr Parker had succeeded in making a public spectacle of him.

Outside, the two juniors were giggling and whispering again.

In that one brief conversation, Mr Parker had managed to destroy nearly eighteen years of sheer routine happiness.

And that was where Stan found the photography side of things such a refuge. Photography was something that was private; something that belonged to him alone. Photography was his own secret world into which Mr Parker did not enter. Come to that, nor did Beryl. Photography was his one-man planet, blissfully spinning away in space with only him on board.

Not counting Mr Karlin, of course. He was welcome. And, on his part, eager. Mr Karlin had made that clear. The appointment to see him had been fixed for six o'clock next Thursday. In such a friendly way, too. It had been Mr Karlin's suggestion that, instead of making a purely business matter of it in Mr Karlin's office, they should meet in the lounge of the Brava Hotel, Bayswater. It would be so much quieter there, Mr Karlin told him.

And this suited Stan perfectly. Because he didn't want to be rushed. To show the prints off properly, he and Mr Karlin would have to go through them one by one, taking their time over it.

The Brava Hotel stood in that part of Bayswater where family life had died out long ago. All the houses were hotels by now; and some of the hotels seemed to be in danger of dying out, too. The Brava was one of them. The white stucco on the outside had flaked off in pieces, exposing a dark chocolate-brown layer underneath. And the twin pillars by the front door looked as though they had been nibbled at. Altogether it had the air of an old and second-hand wedding cake.

There was no one at the reception desk when he went inside. But Stan didn't need anyone. A neon sign that someone had forgotten to switch on said 'Lounge and Bar'. And there was an arrow pointing straight ahead. Stan followed it.

It was then that he found out what Mr Karlin had really meant by quietness. The lounge had once been the drawing-room. It still had the original red wallpaper; most of the furniture appeared to be original, too. The bar itself was clearly an afterthought. It had been fitted in over on the far side like a corner-cupboard, and two red stools on bright chromium stalks had been screwed into the floor in front of it. The stools were both empty, and apparently the barman had not yet come on duty.

Stan wasn't the only person in the lounge, however. There was someone sitting in an armchair by the window, holding an evening paper open in front of him. Stan could only see his feet. They were small feet in narrow, highly polished shoes. Then the evening newspaper was put down, and Stan found himself facing a slim, rather shadowy young man, pale-complexioned and polite-looking. The young man folded up his paper and came over.

'Mr Pitts?' he asked.

'That's right,' Stan told him.

'I'm Mr Karlin's assistant,' he explained. 'Mr Karlin's been delayed. He asked me to apologize for him. He shouldn't be long now.' The young man pointed at the parcel under Stan's arm. 'I expect you'd like to put that down and have a drink,' he said. 'What's it going to be?'

Stan would have liked to order beer. But it didn't look like a place where anyone drank beer. All that he could see behind the bar was a row of upside-down bottles and small glasses.

'Whisky, please,' he replied, adding 'with water' to make it sound as if whisky was what he always drank.

The young man was looking at the parcel again.

'Are those the pictures?' he asked. 'Mr Karlin's told me all about your work. He is very excited.'

He had delicate, expressive hands and, with them, he managed to convey some hint of Mr Karlin's excitement.

Stan smiled professionally.

'Just a selection,' he said. 'Plenty more where these come from.'

This clearly pleased the young man.

'You're what we've been looking for. To keep up the supply. There's not much good stuff about nowadays.'

At the sound of voices, the barman had opened up his corner cupboard and put the light on. The place looked gayer now. It had transformed itself into a small, illuminated shrine, complete with siphon and ice-bucket.

When he had returned with the drinks, the young man spread out his hands with the palms held upwards.

'Shall we begin talking business?' he asked. 'You know our terms. Either outright, or on commission. It's entirely up to you.'

Selling outright was something that Stan knew about. He'd read the warnings in all the better photographic magazines.

'I never dispose of the copyright,' he said. 'Never.'

In itself the reply was enough to show the young man that Stan wasn't by any means a beginner. It was evident now that there were two of them there in the faded back lounge of the Brava who could talk business.

'Then, if we handle them on commission, what advance do you want? They've got to be exclusive to us, of course.'

Stan blew his lips out. This was the moment he'd been waiting for. He took a sip of whisky and cleared his throat before answering.

'How about a hundred pounds?' he asked. 'Exclusive licence for one year.'

This time he wished that it could have been Mr Winters who was listening to him.

The young man did not seem in the least surprised.

'I'll put it to Mr Karlin,' he said. 'Money's his department.'

'Of course, he'll want to look at these first, I imagine.' Stan tapped with his forefinger on the parcel as he was speaking.

'Naturally,' the young man replied. 'They're what he's paying for, aren't they?'

'Those, and more like them.'

While he was sitting there, his confidence had returned to him. At that moment he was pleasantly conscious of being in the master class.

The young man looked at his watch.

'Another drink,' he suggested. 'Mr Karlin shouldn't be long now. He must have been detained in Fleet Street. It's not like him to be late for an appointment. I only hope . . .'

But the young man need not have worried. Mr Karlin might have been outside the door listening for his cue. He came in, smiling his big warm smile, before the young man had finished speaking.

'Those Editors,' he said. 'Never let you go once they've got you there.' His handshake was big and warm like his smile. Just being gripped like that made Stan feel welcome and important. 'Has he been looking after you properly?' he asked. 'I told him you might be a client of ours.'

Stan smiled back at him.

'I've brought the photographs,' he said. He started to undo the parcel, but Mr Karlin stopped him.

'Not in here,' he told him. 'Light's not good enough. Couldn't tell anything in here.' He turned to the young man beside him. 'Don't I get a drink?' he enquired.

While the young man was at the bar, Mr Karlin widened the conversation.

'How's the Civil Service?' he asked. 'Still overworking you?'

'Not really,' Stan replied.

'Don't know how you stand it,' he said frankly. 'Not with an artistic nature like yours. But if you're happy there that's all that matters.'

When Stan said nothing about being happy, Mr Karlin continued.

'I see you in a studio of your own,' he remarked. 'Somewhere you can develop your talent. And that's where we may be able to help you. We use a lot of photographers. Stringers mostly.'

Stan didn't know what a stringer was, and he did not choose to ask. But it sounded a good sort of thing to be.

'How's the family?' Mr Karlin asked. 'What have you got? A boy and a girl, isn't it?'

Stan corrected him.

'There's two of Marleen in there,' he said. 'One of 'em in her birthday suit and the other as The Little Milkmaid. Fancy-dress stuff, you know.'

'I'll look out for them,' Mr Karlin assured him. 'Always a good sell, children.'

The young man was back again. He'd brought Stan another drink as well, even though Stan had not yet finished his first one.

'Did you get round to terms?' Mr Karlin asked.

'Commission,' the young man replied. 'Hundred pounds advance against royalties. One year licence.'

Mr Karlin wrinkled up his nose.

'I don't like the year's licence bit,' he said.

The young man seemed temporarily put out.

'What's wrong with it?' he asked.

'Too long,' Mr Karlin told him. 'Suppose we don't get on together. What happens if he doesn't like us? We don't want an unhappy client round our necks.' He turned to Stan. 'Cheque or cash?' he asked.

As he was speaking, Mr Karlin had thrust his hand into his breast pocket and produced a wad of something. He didn't bring it right out into the open, but kept it half hidden under the width of the lapel. Then he ran his thumbnail across the top. It made a noise like a pack of cards being shuffled.

'Cash,' Stan told him.

Mr Karlin slid the bundle across to him.

It was the first time he'd ever had a hundred pounds actually sitting there in his hand.

'Thank you,' Stan said politely. Then he reached up to his breast pocket for his Biro. 'I expect you'd like a receipt,' he said.

But this seemed to amuse Mr Karlin. He pointed at the parcel beside Stan's feet.

'Why?' he asked. 'I've got these, haven't I?'

Stan saw the point.

'OK,' he said.

Mr Karlin was smiling again.

'Better count it,' he told him.

The notes were old ones, tired and grubby-looking, and Stan was a slow counter. The young man picked up his evening paper, and Mr Karlin signalled to the barman to bring him a drink.

'Forty-five, fifty.'

Stan had got halfway. He set up a separate little pile of them, and then started off on the second batch. To make it easier for him, he began with 'five' again.

Then he looked up.

'There's a hundred here,' he said.

'Well, don't spend it all on the way home,' Mr Karlin said. 'And keep clear of the girls. I don't want you to go getting yourself into trouble.'

He got up and stretched out his arm to give Stan another of those great big warm handshakes of his.

'Mind you, don't rush things,' he told him. 'Give us a ring at the end of the month. Then we'll both know how we've been getting on.'

There was no reason why he should not have told Beryl straight off where the money had come from. It would have made everything far simpler that way. But of late, she simply hadn't been nice enough about his photography for him to want to share any part of it with her. The hundred pounds was for her, of course; and for Marleen, too. It was family money.

How he had come by it, however, remained his affair. This was something else that belonged to his private world; and he found being secretive was rather enjoyable. For the moment, he was keeping the bundle of notes in his own possession. They were concealed under the lining-paper of his developer drawer. Merely thinking about them, stowed away up there, made him feel aloof and superior. He could afford now to look down on other people, even people like Mr Parker who had only their regular salaries to draw on.

And, what was more important, Beryl wouldn't be looking down on him much longer. In the meantime, he knew that it was his position in the Civil Service that she minded about. She had taken that last turn-down personally. And not simply because of the money. It was status as well as money that counted. No woman who knows instinctively that she is cut out to be a Number One likes to be reminded that she is married to a husband who is essentially a Number Two.

And now, thanks to Mr Karlin, he could see a way of putting things right. He would choose his moment carefully, pick a good time when he hadn't recently done anything to annoy her, and then quite casually tell her that he had been up-graded. True or false, it would be just the sort of tonic that he felt she needed.

What's more, with all his photographic artwork out of the way for the time being, he reckoned that it shouldn't prove too difficult to find the proper opportunity. Nowadays, as soon as he had seen to the washing-up and emptied the trash-can into the dustbin, he came through to the lounge to join Beryl. Ever since their big row, they didn't have very much to talk about together. And two-and-a-half hours' silence in closed surroundings can seem like a long time. That is where television comes as such a blessing. With a television set on, two people can sit side by side for a whole evening, not speaking and hardly aware of each other. Many couples prefer it that way, and many marriages have been saved because of it.

As it happened, however, Beryl would hardly have been aware of him anyway. She had Cliff on her mind. What she couldn't make out was why he had been so sweet to her at lunch and then had dropped her so completely. After the way in which she had confided in him, she would have expected the next move to come from him.

Mr Karlin's hundred pounds came in useful in another way, too: it was a shield against events within the department.

Mr Parker, having bided his time, was really getting into his stride at last. There were big changes afoot. Already, in place of the old In-and-Out Book that Stan had kept for years, there was now a Daily Register. Everything that came out of Filing had a little card attached to it. The card bore the signature of the clerk who had asked for it as well as the signature of the clerk who had handed it out. Both these details were entered into the Register before the Requisition Slip was honoured. There was a space on the back of the card for the messenger to sign. Then the card and the Requisition Slip, which already had the signature of the clerk-on-duty on it, were clipped together and filed separately. How else, Mr Parker asked, could you ever hope to keep track of anything? If Moscow had implanted its own agent right there in Central Records, Mr Miller's easy-going, old-fashioned methods would never have revealed it.

Mr Parker was very hot on Security. Being Security-conscious was, with him, a religious condition. The last time he had assembled the staff for one of his informal pep-talks he had put it to them straight from the shoulder. 'By all means, love your neighbour,' he had told them. 'But that doesn't mean that you have to trust him. In fact, in your job never trust anybody. Just follow the rules. And, if it isn't in the book come and ask me. That's what I'm here for.'

Off-the-cuff sermons like that came naturally to Mr Parker. They were best, he had discovered, if you kept both hands thrust deep into the trouser-pockets and perched yourself up against the edge of the desk. The other method was to turn a chair round back to the audience, and then sit down as if you were riding it. Either way worked. All that mattered was producing the right gather-round-I'm-one-of-you kind of atmosphere.

What Stan was not prepared for was the scale of Mr Parker's revolution; or, indeed, his ruthlessness. And somehow Mr Parker made it all that much worse by being so friendly about it, so understanding. It was after office hours, when the whole department had gone quiet, that Mr Parker liked best for his person-to-person chats, his pow-wows. That way there was the seal of privilege and confidentiality about them.

At five twenty-five, Mr Parker sauntered over.

'You in any particular hurry to get off?' he asked.

'Nothing special,' Stan told him.

It wasn't true. As a matter of fact, he'd promised Beryl that he would have a look at the electric tin-opener when he got home. For some extraordinary reason, instead of attacking metal surfaces like a shark, the instrument had suddenly become docile. When given a tin to hold, it merely purred at it. Stan was clever with his hands and reckoned that half an hour with a screwdriver ought to get it back to its savage and aggressive state again. But he was a conscientious Civil Servant. If his superior wanted him, he knew where duty lay.

'Then what about my room?' Mr Parker asked. 'Easier in there.'

To show how informal it all was, Mr Parker ignored the chair with Mr Miller's cushion still in it. Instead, he took one of the two hard-backs on the visitor's side of the desk. It seemed a good moment for his horseman-astride position, and it left Stan looking rather prim and reserved as he sat upright facing him.

'Make yourself comfortable,' Mr Parker invited him. 'Have a cigarette if you want one.'

Of course, Stan wanted a cigarette. He'd wanted one for years. But smoking was something that Beryl had asked him to give up when Marleen was born. At moments like this, Stan found himself missing it more than ever.

'I've been having a good look at the O and M side,' Mr Parker began.

'O and M?' Stan asked.

It sounded like another department. Operations and Something-or-other. Stan wondered what sort of work it did.

'Organization and Method,' Mr Parker told him. 'The way the wheels go round. Or don't, as the case may be.'

'Oh, that.'

'In this department,' Mr Parker went on, 'clerks have been folding up papers and filing them away in pigeon-holes ever since Nelson's day.'

'I suppose they have,' Stan agreed with him.

It was an agreeable thought: there was the authentic smell of history and romance about the whole idea. He liked Mr Parker for bringing in the Trafalgar touch.

Mr Parker turned his clear blue eyes upon him.

'Well, it's not going on like that much longer,' Mr Parker informed him. 'It's all right here in the outer office. I can keep an eye on what goes on. Down there is where the trouble starts.' He swung round in the saddle and pointed towards the safety-door behind him. 'That's our factory. That's where our product comes from.'

'I know,' Stan answered. 'I did my first twelve years in there.'

'That's why I want you to go back,' Mr Parker told him.

'Go back!' he repeated.

Mr Parker couldn't know what he was saying. Or, if he did know, he was simply trying to humiliate him. Everyone in the department would know what a move like that meant. It was returning him to the ranks. And worse than that. It was putting him away out of sight where Establishment and Personnel could forget all about him; once inside those steel safety-doors, it was the end.

Mr Parker's eyes were still fixed on him.

'That's what I said,' he replied. 'I need you there.'

Stan remained very calm about it. He was still only trying to explain.

'Mr Miller always said . . .' he began.

But Mr Parker stopped him.

'Mr Miller isn't here any longer, is he?' he pointed out. 'What Mr Miller used to say doesn't matter any longer. We're going to do things my way now. The modern way. The efficient way.' Mr Parker pushed the chair away, slid his feet out of the stirrups, and straightened himself.

Stan knew that, at any moment, he would feel the horseman's hand come down onto his shoulder, and it came.

'It's all a matter of team-work,' Mr Parker reminded him. 'Everyone in the team has to do something he doesn't like sometimes.'

Chapter 15

Nothing had worked out in the least as Stan had intended.

Even though he had plenty of time on his hands at the moment, the right opportunity for telling Beryl never presented itself. Either Beryl felt a bit tired and went up early to bed, or Marleen found herself unable to sleep and came downstairs to join them. Just when he was getting round to the bit about his surprise re-grading, something always prevented it.

In the end, he gave up. And, because it did not seem safe to leave a sum of money like that hanging about, he waited for Saturday morning to come round again and then went round to pay it into the bank.

He'd meant it to be just a simple, over-the-counter transaction. But Mr Winters immediately spotted him. Mr Winters prided himself on his good personal relationship with his customers. He felt like a father towards all of them.

'Coming in to see me, Mr Pitts?' he asked.

Stan shook his head.

'Just paying some money in,' he told him.

Mr Winters liked to see cheques being paid in. It showed that his customers in Crocketts Green were doing nicely. And he was particularly pleased that, this time, it should be Stan who was at the right end of things.

'Let me attend to it,' he offered.

He took the bundle of notes from Stan's hand and started to walk over to the counter. Then, when he saw that they were all fivers, he stopped.

'Oh, but I think you *do* want to see me, Mr Pitts,' he said. 'Or, at least, I shall want to see you. You've got about a hundred pounds here.'

'It's a hundred exactly.'

'Mr Pitts's file,' Mr Winters called over his shoulder. 'Mr Stanley Pitts.'

He pushed open the frosted-glass door of his office, and stood back for Stan to pass. Mr Winters was rubbing his hands.

'I take it you want to pay it into your wife's account,' he said. 'Then we shall be able to stop those monthly deductions. This'll more than clear things up.'

Stan stared at him.

'Not by itself, it won't.'

Mr Winters beamed back.

'Perhaps Mrs Pitts forgot to tell you,' he said. 'She's probably keeping it as a surprise for you. Your wife paid in a cheque for a hundred pounds last month.'

The file had come by now, and Mr Winters bent over it.

'As I thought,' he went on. 'A hundred pounds last month, and now this hundred today. No withdrawals, because we agreed to stop them. Your wife is ninety-three pounds in credit, Mr Pitts.'

He picked up the monthly deduction form that Stan had signed, and wrote 'Cancelled' across it.

'That's better, isn't it, Mr Pitts?' he asked. 'No deductions, and no interest on the overdraft. Mrs Pitts *will* be pleased.'

Stan tackled Beryl the same evening. It seemed a good moment. Marleen had developed another of her colds, and was up in bed with a supper-tray across her knees. Beryl herself couldn't have been better. She'd had the two white streaks in her hair brightened up again, and she was wearing the Mexican housecoat with the Sun-God buttons. Stan thought that he'd never seen her looking more beautiful. Beryl was rather pleased with herself, too. She had taken longer at her dressing-table than usual. It had crossed her mind more than once during the day that, because it was the week-end, Cliff might possibly drop in.

Stan braced himself.

'I went to the bank today,' he told her.

'Did you, now?'

Beryl did not even look up as she answered. She was reading a story in an American magazine, *20th Century Romances*. And really it was quite extraordinary; almost spooky. Because in the story there was this deeply sensitive, unhappy woman married to an inadequate, well-meaning sort of husband. And, in the background, there was Ed, the successful baseball coach. Ed had just taken her to one of the World Series matches, and now they were driving back recklessly through the night in his new Tornado.

'And I saw Mr Winters,' Stan continued.

Beryl only just heard him.

'I wonder you dared,' she said, and went on reading.

Her mind was divided right down the middle. One half was on stand-by ready to attend to Stan's silly interruptions, and the other half, the absorbed half, was there in the new Tornado with the successful base-ball coach. Their team had won, and Ed was celebrating. He kept reaching for his hip-flask, and Beryl was pleading with him. Just ahead lay the State Highway intersection. Ed's foot was hard down as the Caution and Slow Down notices flashed past them.

'He says you paid a cheque in.'

Beryl was still reading.

Joe Moskovitch was in the left lane, travelling fast. The day's schedule had been cruel, heartless. He had already driven three hundred kilometers since breakfast. It would be another hour before he could switch off the diesel, and take Mandy's fresh young body in his arms again. Behind him, the sixty-two-foot-long liquid oxygen container, cushioned on its twelve giant wheels, loomed sinister like a warhead rocket. The warmth of the cab made Joe feel sleepy. He knew the road, recognized the eating-joints and the car-lots. For a moment, Joe closed his eyes.
(*Continued on p. 77.*)

The two parts of Beryl's mind came together.

'He says I did what?'

'Paid a cheque in.'

'Well, suppose I did.'

She did not care for the tone of Stan's voice. It sounded rude and accusing, and she certainly wasn't going to have him talk to her like that.

'Where did you get it?'

This time there could be no doubt about it. He *was* accusing her.

'That's my business.'

She put *20th Century Romances*, still open, face downwards in her lap, and turned towards him.

'And don't look at me that way,' she told him. 'I don't like it.'

Usually when she spoke to Stan in that way he knew, at once, that he had gone too far. It stopped him immediately. But this evening it was different.

'I want to know,' he said.

'Then you'll just have to go on wanting, won't you?'

To show that, so far as she was concerned, the conversation was over, she picked up the magazine and began searching for page seventy-seven. It was somewhere near the end. By then, the stories were simply little panels of print wedged in between the advertisements.

But Stan hadn't finished.

'Did you get it from Cliff?' he asked.

Beryl had just found what she had been searching for.

The screech of the air-brakes rose above the roar of the Tornado. Joe struggled with the steering-wheel, heaving his twenty-ton chariot into a devastating arc. Below him in the searchlight glare of his headlamps he glimpsed two ghost-like, terrified faces staring up helplessly into the black interior of the cab.

'I asked you if you got it from Cliff,' Stan repeated.

The strain of being in two places at once, in the doomed Tornado and sitting there on the couch with Stan looking at her, was too much. She threw *20th Century Romances* down onto the floor.

'Well, what if I did?' she demanded.

'Then you've got to give it back.'

Beryl pulled in the corners of her mouth.

'Listen to Mr Millionaire talking.'

'I mean it.'

'Well, I can't, can I?' she snapped back at him. 'Mr Winters wouldn't let me. You know that as well as I do.'

This was the moment for which Stan had been waiting. And it had been touch-and-go: any instant now, and they might have been right back in the middle of one of the old-fashioned rows of the kind they used to have.

'I paid in some money myself this morning,' he told her.

'You never.'

'Hundred pounds, as a matter of fact,' he said quietly.

'And where did you get a hundred pounds from, I'd like to know?'

Beryl was rather disappointed in herself. She had simply blurted the words out the way Marleen might have done.

'Been up-graded,' he replied. 'Back pay. Annual bonus. That kind of thing.'

It was his innocent white lie, and he had come out with it. He still looked forward to the day when he would be able to tell her the truth; and, the way things were going, it needn't be so very far away. By then he wouldn't be just an ordinary Civil Service filing clerk. He'd be Stanley Pitts, the photographer, a name to conjure with in professional matt-finish circles.

Beryl took the news very calmly. She was pleased about it, but she was also indignant. That was why she did not congratulate him so much as raise further questions.

'Well, it's about time too, isn't it? I mean they couldn't have kept you waiting much longer, could they? Not after all those years. It wouldn't have been right like, would it?'

Stan started to get up.

'So I'll ring Cliff, and tell him,' he said.

Already Beryl had been bending over to pick up her copy of *20th Century Romances* as he said it, but she straightened herself immediately.

'Oh, I wouldn't do that,' she told him. 'Not right away, I wouldn't. It'll only upset him.'

'Why should it?'

'Well, I mean it wouldn't seem polite like, would it? Not after he's only just given it to me. It would look like I didn't really need it, wouldn't it?'

'You don't need it,' Stan said firmly. 'Not any longer, you don't.'

Upstairs in her bedroom, Beryl was still reading. She had at last re-found her place on page seventy-seven, and thereafter it was like riding in a steeple-chase to keep up with the story. It kept disappearing only to turn up again on a still later page among a whole different lot of advertisements.

But it had all worked out for the best. At the last moment, she had managed to kick Ed's foot off the accelerator, and stamp her own small one down firmly on the brake pedal. That was what had saved them both. Even so, the baseball coach was paralysed from the waist down. But that didn't matter so much because Beryl was there to look after him. Her whole life was devoted to him now.

Towards midnight, she dropped off to sleep, still thinking about their miraculous escape. Her last waking thoughts were of wondering what it would be like looking after Cliff if, by some chance, anything of the sort should happen to him, and how much the up-grading would mean in terms of Stan's salary.

She found both lots of thoughts strangely consoling.

Chapter 16

Beryl had been quite wrong about it: Cliff wasn't in the least upset. But then very few men would be when it comes to recovering a hundred pounds that had looked like being lost and gone forever.

All the same, he was surprised. Stan sounded normal enough on the phone. There were no signs of drink and violent temper that Cliff could detect. It even occurred to him that perhaps Beryl had been exaggerating, because Stan seemed so sure of himself. He spoke of returning the money as though it would be no trouble at all to him. And, when he suggested that Cliff should drop in for supper one night next week, Cliff accepted. It could be either a cheque or cash, just as he pleased, Stan told him.

As it happened, Stan had good reason to be sure of himself. He had just spoken to Mr Karlin, and Mr Karlin had invited him to go along to the Hotel Brava again. There was a new scheme that he had worked out, and he wanted to explain to Stan in person. It was something important that he felt would be right up Stan's street, he said.

On the whole, the Brava seemed to have gone down rather than come up since his last visit. Tomorrow morning's milk bottles were already ranged alongside the doorstep; and, as usual, there was nobody on duty at the reception desk. Stan made his way past the unlit sign, straight through to the bar.

This time, Mr Karlin was there before him. He was sitting up on one of the chromium stools, talking to a girl who was beside him. When he saw Stan he came over.

'That's what I like about you,' he said. 'Always punctual. Who says artists are unbusinesslike?'

Stan found it rather pleasant to be called an artist. It showed that Mr Karlin really appreciated his work. And Mr Karlin certainly could not have been more welcoming. He brought his hand down on Stan's shoulder and left it there. It was funny: Stan couldn't bear it when Mr Parker did that but, with Mr Karlin, it was different. Stan liked the feel of Mr Karlin's hand.

'Come here and meet Mr Pitts.'

It was the girl at the bar that he was summoning. And the way he called her over was in itself rather flattering. It made him the important one, the one for whom they had both been waiting.

'This is Helga,' Mr Karlin announced. 'She works for the agency.'

Helga had brought her glass with her. She raised it to her lips in a kind of toast, and smiled at him over it. Stan noticed that she had very pretty teeth.

'Happy to meet you,' she said. 'I feel already that I know you well.'

'She means your work,' Mr Karlin explained. 'She's mad about it.'

Stan smiled back at her. He was equally happy to meet Helga. She was small and dark and good-looking and, like Mr Karlin, very friendly.

'Let me get you a drink,' she said to him. 'Whisky?'

'With water, please,' he told her, remembering that whisky and water was what he always drank with Mr Karlin.

There wasn't room for all three of them at the bar, and Mr Karlin moved across to one of the couches.

'Make yourself comfortable,' he said, and took the armchair opposite.

When Helga came back, she sat down next to Stan. He was immediately aware of the scent that she was using. It was a strange, heady scent; close and jungly. Little feelers of it kept reaching out towards him. He wondered whether any traces of it would still be clinging to his clothes when he got back to Kendal Terrace and, to be on the safe side, he edged away a little.

'Well, I expect you want to know how things have been going,' Mr Karlin began.

Stan nodded. He was deliberately cool and off-hand about it. An artist of his standing could afford to be.

'Then ask Helga,' Mr Karlin told him. 'She's looking after your side.'

Helga turned her big brown eyes towards him.

'Slow. Very slow,' she said.

'You mean they're not selling?'

'Not yet, they're not. The editors are interested, but no sales.'

Mr Karlin reached out his hand towards Stan as though he were going to pat him.

'Give her time,' he advised. 'She's the best in Fleet Street.'

'It is not the treatment. That's very good. It is the subjects,' Helga went on. 'They are no longer fashionable. The readers do not require them.'

Mr Karlin nodded.

'State of the market,' he said. 'It's her job. Knows it backwards.'

'You mean you don't think there's a future in it?' Stan asked.

He had allowed just the wrong note of disappointment to creep into his voice as he was speaking.

'Not in them, there isn't,' Mr Karlin told him. 'There's a future in you, though. Start in right away, can't he, Helga?'

'Right away.' Helga's brown eyes were still on him. They were deep admiring eyes and, at the moment, they were smiling at him. 'Give me the right subjects, and I can place them.'

'What sort of subjects?'

They were both looking at him now. Mr Karlin was smiling, too.

'Nudes,' he said. 'Good, high-class, figure work.'

Stan shook his head.

'Not me,' he said. 'Don't go in for that kind of thing. Never have.'

The note of disapproval in his voice was obvious. He regretted that Mr Karlin should even have suggested it. In Stan's view, nude photography was something that had given the whole profession a bad name; had they been alone together, he would have told him so. But, with Helga on the couch beside him, all that he wanted to do was to change the subject.

Mr Karlin sounded disappointed.

'Pity,' he replied. 'Lots of money in it. That's so, isn't it, Helga?'

Helga put out her small white hand, and rested it on Stan's arm.

'A great deal,' she said. 'All the time a great deal.'

Because she was being so serious about it, she was frowning. Stan thought that she looked prettier than ever with her forehead wrinkled up like that. Then her face brightened, and she was smiling at him again.

'It would make me very happy to sell pictures like that for you,' she told him. 'Then you can be happy, too. We can all be happy.'

But Mr Karlin seemed to have gone stale about the whole idea. He sounded almost impatient.

'If Mr Pitts doesn't want to, we can't make him,' he reminded her. 'It's a free country.'

Helga removed her hand.

'I am sorry,' she said.

She sounded so upset about it that Stan felt that he ought somehow to put things right. He could see that she had her difficulties, too.

'No need to be sorry,' he assured her. 'Just doesn't happen to be my line.'

He heard Helga give a little laugh.

'How can you know if you have never tried?' she asked. 'Perhaps it is what you would be most good at.'

Her forehead was wrinkled up again, and she was leaning forward. The hot, close, jungly scent was all round him.

'Too late to take it up now,' he told her.

Helga was already shaking her head.

'For an artist, it is never too late.'

This time when she reached out it was simply to touch him. The pressure was there one moment and gone again the next. All the same, it was unsettling. Stan wasn't used to having a girl put her hands on him like that.

'It's no use,' he said. 'I don't even know any models.'

Mr Karlin raised his eyebrows.

'Helga knows models. Don't you, Helga?'

Helga nodded.

'I know many models. And there are always new ones. Tell me what type you want and I will find her for you. It is not difficult.' She sighed. 'They are like all of us. They need money, too.'

It was a deep sigh that Helga had given.

Mr Karlin jerked his thumb in Helga's direction.

'She knows,' he said. 'Used to be a model herself.'

But it was clear that Helga did not wish to be reminded. She shook her head sadly.

'That was a long time ago. I was young then. The body gets old so quickly. Mine would be no good now.'

'I bet it would.'

The words, uninvited, had suddenly formed inside Stan's mind, and he found himself blushing: what was worse was that he had so nearly said them out loud.

Mr Karlin did not seem to have noticed.

'Mr Pitts isn't interested,' he reminded her. 'It's not his line. He told you so.'

Helga did not reply to Mr Karlin. Instead, she put her hand back on Stan's arm again.

'Would you like another whisky, Mr Pitts?' she asked.

Stan was firm with himself.

'Not now, thank you. Time I was off.'

He looked down at his watch as he said it. But it was no use. The watch had stopped exactly where he had set it when he left Frobisher House an hour ago. It was always stopping nowadays.

This seemed to amuse Mr Karlin. He slapped his hand down hard onto his side-pocket.

'Nearly forgot,' he said. 'Present for you.'

It was a long, thin, imitation leather case that he brought out. The clasp was heavy, and looked convincingly like gold. He thrust the case into Stan's hand, and pressed Stan's fingers down onto it.

'See if you like it,' he told him. 'All automatic. No winding.'

Stan paused. He wanted a new watch very much indeed, but he didn't want to accept anything else from Mr Karlin until he had earned it.

'No, I couldn't. Really, I couldn't.'

He tried to hand it back, but Mr Karlin stopped him. He might have been reading Stan's mind all the time.

'Didn't cost me anything,' he said. 'Trade sample. Just try it on. Wear it for a bit, and see how you like it.'

The watch looked even more expensive than the case. For a start, it was large; a real grandfather-watch. Not that any space had been wasted. It wasn't only the time and the day of the month in Bayswater that it showed. By turning the bezel you could tell the time anywhere else in the world. It was the same, too, if you had other interests. There was a knob on the side for timing sports events. And, in case you tended to be a late sleeper, there was a little button just beside it for setting the alarm. With a watch like that on your wrist, you could go through life practically without having to call on outside assistance.

'So you don't care for it?' Mr Karlin asked. 'You think it's too big? It looks vulgar, is that it?'

He slid back his shirt-cuff as he was speaking and revealed another watch just like the one that Stan was holding. Mr Karlin, Stan noticed, had very hairy arms.

'It looks all right on you,' Stan told him.

'Look all right on you, too, once you're used to it. If you don't want it, give it to your Marleen. All little girls like presents.'

Mr Karlin was already getting up. He leant across the table and helped Helga to her feet.

'If Mr Pitts won't have another drink there's no point in hanging

134

around here, is there?' He paused. 'We got off cheap tonight. I was going to offer Mr Pitts a separate advance for his nude work. Now we don't have to, do we Helga?'

Mr Karlin had opened his jacket by now, and his hand was in his breast pocket. He kept drawing his thumbnail across something that was hidden there. It made a sound that Stan recognized; the one like cards being shuffled.

Helga looked up at him.

'It is a big pity. A very big pity. All that work, and you won't do it for us. So highly paid, too. I can place it anywhere. Think it over, Mr Pitts. For my sake, think it over.'

Mr Karlin was still smiling.

'That's right, Helga,' he told her. 'Let Mr Pitts think it over. We'll still be around if he wants us.'

Chapter 17

Because there had been no fresh cash advance from Mr Karlin, it had to be the cheaper kind of Beaujolais that Stan bought. Not that it was without character. On the contrary, strangely acid and at the same time distinctly sweetish, it dissolved in the mouth like a fruit drop. And the colour was quite remarkable, too: a deep, almost purple, amethyst-like hue that was opaque even when held up to quite a strong light. In short, at five-and-nine a bottle, it had everything that could reasonably be expected of it.

And Beryl had been at her most inventive about the meal to go with it. Even rather daring. This was because she had used a recipe that she'd been keeping by her for some time. 'Why Be Ordinary?' it was entitled, and it had come from a woman's magazine that she had read while sitting in her dentist's waiting-room. The friendly, understanding style of the article had appealed to her. And, because she had been alone in the waiting-room at the time, she had simply ripped the page clean out. With one swift *creech* it was hers and, folding it twice over, she had popped it into her handbag.

It came in particularly handy because it covered the whole course of the meal from lighting the joss-sticks before starting to serve, to offering little chunks of Turkish Delight, impaled on cocktail sticks, along with the coffee. And all three courses were just as thoughtfully conceived. It was the salad, in particular, that pleased her. There had been a colour illustration of it in the magazine and she had followed the design exactly. With the ingredients – the silvery sardines, the sticks of celery, the slices of carrot, the black and green olives, the radish discs, the banana strips, the segments of grapefruit – arranged radially, the effect was most striking. Seen from above, it was like the principal flower bed in a Corporation public garden.

Because Marleen wasn't sitting up for dinner, Beryl naturally didn't take quite the same trouble over hers. Not with the arranging, that is. But it was all there on her plate, Beryl assured her; a little bit of everything that Mummy and Daddy and Uncle Cliff were going to have.

As it turned out, the meal could not have been more successful. In fact, it was well-nigh perfect before it had even started. Stan had seen to that. Cliff had hardly got his coat off before Stan had handed him the envelope with the cheque in it. And he did it most gracefully. Even nonchalantly, in a way that made Beryl rather admire him for it.

'Thanks very much, old chap,' he said. 'Very good of you. Very good indeed. Much appreciated. But we couldn't take it from you. Besides, we don't really need it. Not now, we don't, do we, Beryl?'

The question caught Beryl unawares. The whole speech had been so polished that she had not expected it to end so soon. But she saw that some kind of reply was needed.

Pursing up her mouth into a little smile, she answered him.

'Well, not if you say we don't, we don't, do we?' she said. 'I mean it's not like having to have it if you haven't got it, is it?' She turned towards Cliff. 'But it was ever so sweet of you to offer. It was really. I shall never forget it. Never.'

Beryl was aware that, at best, it was a poor, stumbling kind of response. But, at least, it was entirely spontaneous. Stan's, on the other hand, had been most carefully rehearsed. In the train he had gone over it again and again, sometimes merely saying the words to himself, sometimes repeating them out loud until the other passengers had become uneasy and had begun to move away from him.

Chicken à l'Abraham Lincoln was what the woman's magazine had recommended for the main dish. Apparently the great liberator had been peculiarly partial to boiled fowl with a kind of thick white parsley sauce, and out there in the kitchenette of Beryl's log-cabin the chicken, deep-frozen, had been patiently thawing itself out all through the afternoon.

It was while Beryl was seeing to the parsley sauce that Stan showed Cliff the watch that Mr Karlin had given him. Cliff examined it carefully.

'Your friend got the agency?' he asked.

'Don't think so,' Stan told him. 'Said they were being given away.'

Cliff tapped his front teeth with his thumbnail. It was a habit of his while thinking.

'Find out who by,' he said. 'Good-looking watch. Might even be interested in handling it myself.'

He started tapping his teeth again. He could see it all so clearly: the small ads in the Sunday papers; the cash down and six monthly-instalments; the offer of money back if not entirely satisfied; the parchment guarantee certificate with the big red seal.

They were still talking about the watch when Beryl called them through to the dining alcove. At once she became interested.

'Did you find out about it like I asked?' she demanded.

'I couldn't,' Stan told her. 'I haven't seen anyone to ask.'

Beryl turned to Cliff.

'I just want to know if they do a lady's model,' she explained. 'I mean the same like. Only smaller. I thought perhaps . . .'

It was Cliff who changed the subject. The joss-stick that Beryl had so thoughtfully lit was fuming away inside the miniature china pagoda that had come along with it in the same packet. Up there on top of the free-standing kitchen unit, it provided just that rich, exotic note that Beryl had intended. Little lavender-coloured tendrils of smoke were drifting gently upwards through the tiny windows.

Cliff began sniffing.

'Hullo, hullo,' he said. 'Call the Fire Brigade. House on fire. I smell burning.'

Stan was grateful to Cliff for the interruption. He had already lied to Beryl about where his hundred pounds had really come from; and she had believed him. He could hardly expect her to believe that the Civil Service had suddenly decided to present him with a king-size chronometer as well. That was why he had invented a brand-new lie about having just won a photographic competition with the wrist-watch as first prize.

They were entirely white lies; both of them fully justified and thoroughly well-intentioned. All the same, they meant that for the first time in their marriage he was living another secret life entirely of his own.

Even though the Beaujolais had not been exactly pleasant it must have possessed a certain potency. There was now more colour in Beryl's cheeks than when she had sat down, and Cliff himself was in the best of high spirits. He told Beryl that her cooking was better than at the Ritz. He kept congratulating Stan on his promotion. He remembered his first motor-car, a grey Jaguar with red upholstery, and became sentimental about it. He showed them a balancing trick using two forks and a tablespoon. He spoke of an evening up in town just for the three of them. And, as soon as the old-style caramel whip – another, so the magazine said, of the dead President's prime favourites – was finished, Cliff suggested that the men should take their coats off and do the washing-up.

But Beryl wouldn't hear of it. Not with the Dishmaster standing there doing nothing, she wouldn't. It shouldn't take a jiffy, she said. And the saucepans were all the quick-clean kind anyway. What she wanted was to get the menfolk into the lounge so that she could see Cliff's face when the coffee was poured out and she produced the Turkish Delight impaled on the little cocktail sticks.

It was over coffee that Stan remembered about Cliff's Jaguar. That long-ago August Bank Holiday came back to him. He could see Cliff, bow-tie and sports jacket and all, sitting behind the long, low bonnet. And naturally he'd taken a few snapshots of the car. One of them in particular had been rather more than a snapshot. It was a composition. With the camera held at radiator height it made the bonnet look even longer, with Cliff away in the distance half-hidden by the steering-wheel.

A happy thought came to him.

'You two be all right if I just go upstairs to fetch something?' he asked.

As it turned out, he was away longer than he had intended; much longer. In the first place, Marleen's light was still on and he sat down on the end of her bed to talk to her. Not just an ordinary talk, either. It was fatherly, counselling stuff about not crying yourself to sleep just because you haven't been allowed to sit up for supper.

And it was the same upstairs in his workroom. That took longer, too. It wasn't because the print of the Jaguar wasn't indexed. All his prints were numbered and entered in the reference register. He was rather proud of that register. It showed that he maintained his high professional standards even in his hobby. But it didn't speed things up. It was simply that he found his other early work so interesting. 'Toadstools', for example. Or *Easter Parade*. Or a study of passengers waiting at a bus stop on a rainy day: *Les Parapluies* that one was rather daringly entitled. Stan could hardly have been more than twenty when he had taken it and, looking back, he could not help admiring himself for such clever and effective use of the French language.

The picture of the Jaguar was precisely as he had remembered. It was a good, powerful piece of photography that brought out the hard, masculine contours of the machine. But it was sad all the same because the driver looked so disarmingly, so heart-breakingly, young in it. It was hard to believe that the direct descendant of that sprightly bow-tied figure was the middle-aged man waiting in the lounge just below.

It was on the way downstairs that Stan decided to play a little trick on Cliff. He would hold the photograph up in front of him and, making the *vroomp-vroomp* noise of Cliff's present Jaguar, suddenly thrust the door open and burst in upon them. That was why he tiptoed so quietly down the last flight. He wanted the whole thing to be a surprise.

The door was no more than three-quarters shut. A tall, vertical slice of the room stood revealed to him. And, framed by the doorway, he could see Cliff and Beryl. They were seated side by side on the couch with their backs towards him. Cliff's arm was around her, and Beryl had her head down on Cliff's shoulder.

Stan stood there, the motor-car photograph in his hand. He was trying to catch what Beryl was saying. And it wasn't easy. Her face was too far snuggled-down for that. All that reached him were little snatches.

'. . . no proper holiday this year, either . . . not grumbling, just explaining . . . girl of Marleen's age got a right . . . do away with myself, I could really . . .'

There was more of it in the same vein. All unhappy, mumbled stuff. Then Cliff spoke.

'Always got me,' he reminded her.

Stan was leaning forward by now, listening intently. He heard Beryl give a long, deep sigh.

'. . . get up and walk out,' was the next little burst that he caught. Then there was a pause as though Beryl were reconsidering things. '. . . if it wasn't for little Marleen,' the words reached him. And this was followed by '. . . whatever would her teacher say?'

'You married the wrong man,' Stan heard Cliff say.

Beryl must have shifted her head. He could hear her quite distinctly this time; too distinctly, in fact. And what made it worse was that, in her own way, she was defending him.

'It's not Stan's fault,' she said. 'Not really, it isn't. Not Stan's. It's just that he's not up to it. Like not being made head of his department, I mean. Well, they couldn't have chosen Stan, could they? Not to be in charge like. He's not cut out for it. He'd still be the number two even if he was the only one there, Stan would.'

Stan put up his hand and coughed. It wasn't simply that he couldn't bear to hear anything more about himself. He was ashamed of himself for listening; eavesdropping, and on his own wife too, seemed a pretty despicable kind of thing to do.

At the sound of the cough, Beryl sprang away from Cliff and sat bolt upright. She was indignant.

'Oh, you gave me such a start,' she said. 'Coming in like that, indeed. I wondered whoever it could be standing there. Where *have* you been?'

'Fetching this,' Stan told her.

He handed Cliff the photograph.

'This remind you of anyone?' he asked.

It was no use, however. What he had just heard had knocked all the fun out of it. He didn't mind giving the print away. But he was in no mood for tricks. He simply hadn't got the heart to do the *vrooomp-vrooomp* bit as well.

It was because he couldn't sleep that he went back upstairs to his work-room. And he was careful to be very silent about it. He didn't want Beryl to open her door to find out what was going on, or have Marleen call out after him.

Once up there, with the door closed after him, he felt better. More secure. This was a part of his private world, the world where Beryl couldn't enter. This was where Stanley Pitts really came into his own and could do his dreaming.

Not that it was all dreaming. First, there was the register to correct, and he carefully deleted the reference to the photograph of Cliff's first Jaguar. Even if he had kept the negative, he wouldn't now have wanted to make another print of it.

And he didn't go straight back to bed again. He was far too wide awake for that. He pulled his dressing-gown around him and sat on thinking about the future. Beryl had been quite right about him. That was why it hurt so much. He'd never get to the top, never to one of the really upper rungs, not in the Civil Service, he wouldn't. With photography, however, it was different. There was nothing second-rate about him there. It was just that his choice of subject had been a bit too restricted. Character studies and nature pieces apparently weren't what the public wanted. But that was where his friend, Mr Karlin, came in. Mr Karlin knew what would sell and what wouldn't.

Up there in his private workroom, with Beryl and Marleen asleep in their beds one floor below, Stan made his big decision. In the morning – come to that it was early morning already – he would ring up and say that he had thought things over and was ready to have a go at the more saleable kind.

Chapter 18

In a recorded message it is difficult to sound eager, or even reasonably polite. But that is the way it had to be. Mr Karlin's agency seemed to be run entirely by remote control with the telephone answering service on duty for twenty-four hours a day. Stan resented the recorded voice as soon as he heard it, and he resented the fact that when his message eventually reached Mr Karlin that would be recorded, too.

What's more, he couldn't ask Mr Karlin to phone him back. The last thing he wanted was for calls to start coming through either to Frobisher House or to Kendal Terrace. That way his little secret would be out in no time; not that he need have worried. There was a naturally discreet side to Mr Karlin's nature. Stan felt sure that he would find some other way of getting in touch with him.

All the same, it was a restless and unsettled kind of week-end that he had. Beryl appeared to be avoiding him, and he couldn't help wondering whether she knew how much he had overheard. Marleen, too, was *incommunicado*. She had a part in the school play. It was only a small part, but Beryl was anxious that Marleen should make the most of it. She had helped her with the gestures, making her go through them over and over again in front of the mirror until they were quite perfect. It was the words, not the gestures, that were the trouble. Marleen was not a quick learner. With her pretty head bent over the book, she repeated them endlessly to herself, first with her eyes open and then with them shut. But, back in front of the mirror, her mind would go as blank as when she had started. More than once she had burst into tears at the sheer disappointment of not being able to remember. And because she never liked people to see her when she had been crying she stayed up in her room, and sulked.

Stan, too, was unsettled. The realization of what his decision meant kept coming back to him, and he wondered whether he could go on. He was afraid that at the last moment, he might funk it; simply turn tail and run, or be too embarrassed to focus properly. Then he recalled his own high status as a photographer, and that comforted him. It would be his sheer professionalism that would carry him through. So long as the lighting was right and the pose appealed to him, it would not make the slightest difference to him whether the girl was dressed or undressed. She was not really a girl at all, he kept telling himself; just a model, as much a model as the subject of *Village Pump*, which had been one of his earlier outstanding successes.

Monday and Tuesday both passed with no word from Mr Karlin and, by Wednesday, Stan was beginning to wonder whether the agency's telephone answering service had broken down. Then, as his morning train drew into Cannon Street, there was Helga standing at the barrier.

She folded up the paper that she had been reading, and came forward.

'Mr Peets,' she said. 'You remember me?'

As she smiled, Stan noticed again how white her teeth were. Very small and very white. It was the darkness of the lipstick that showed them up.

Stan held out his hand.

'It's Helga, isn't it?' He paused. Perhaps he was being over-familiar. 'I'm afraid I don't know your other name.'

She smiled again.

'Everyone calls me Helga,' she said. 'I have no other name.'

Stan glanced up at the station clock for a moment and then checked his watch by it. Helga saw the watch and patted it.

'You are wearing it. That's good,' she told him. 'Mr Karlin will be pleased.' Then she gave a little start. 'Oh, but I make you late. I go along to the Underground with you. I give you my message while walking.'

She had taken his arm as she said it. And, now that she was close beside him, he was aware once more of that strange, rather heady scent that she was wearing.

'What is the message?' he asked.

Helga's fingers tightened on his arm for a moment.

'That he will be very happy to see you. Tonight, if you like. If not, tomorrow.'

Stan pretended to be working out the run of his evening engagements.

'I think I could do tonight. Usual place?'

Helga shook her head.

'Mr Karlin says he is in the West End all day. He suggests a wine bar. Would the one in Swallow Street be all right? I expect you know it. Greco's. It is on the corner.'

'Six o'clock?'

He mentioned six o'clock because that meant that he could get back to Cannon Street in time to catch the seven-two. Then he would be back in time for a meal at eight. Anything later than eight o'clock would cut across Marleen's bedtime. And Beryl more than once had made it quite clear to him that she wasn't going to have office overtime, sessions of the Photographic Club, or rail strikes for that matter, cutting across her little Marleen's precious sleepy time.

Greco's was just the sort of place which Stan would have expected Mr Karlin to frequent. From the moment you stepped inside and saw the long row of polished casks, all with bung-taps and little copper drip buckets under them, you could tell that it had class. It was a sort of elegant ground-floor cellar. Even the barmen in their green baize aprons were dressed up like cellarmen, too.

The only thing that was missing was Mr Karlin. This was a distinct setback. It was getting near to the end of the month and Stan was keeping a tight hold on his personal expenses. After paying for lunch he only had two-and-fourpence left on him. The drinks that the cellarmen were serving all looked the expensive kind, and he didn't want to start sipping something and then find that he couldn't afford to finish it. After looking round, he decided to wait in the doorway.

When he had been waiting for nearly ten minutes he decided to stroll up and down on the pavement outside, as far as Piccadilly in one direction and as far as Regent Street in the other. That was when he saw Helga. She was not hurrying. In fact, she seemed rather to be killing time, going slowly from one shop window to another, sometimes pausing in between for a second look. As soon as she saw Stan she broke into that quick, revealing smile of hers.

'It is good that I have met you,' she said. 'Now we can go straight in. They do not serve single ladies. They think that they are tarts.'

'You don't look like a . . .' Stan began.

But Helga was already speaking.

'Poor girls. They cannot help how they look. It is their occupation.'

As they sat down, it occurred to Stan that things were a good deal worse than when he had just come in alone. Then he'd had only himself to pay for. Now he had Helga as well. Helga did not look a soft-drink-or-glass-of-water kind of girl.

It was almost as if she had read his mind.

'Order whatever you like,' she said. 'When Mr Karlin comes he will pay.'

It was a glass of hock that Helga ordered and Stan said that he would have the same. Really, he would have preferred a gin-and-tonic or even a half-pint of bitter but Greco's didn't seem to be cut out for that kind of thing.

After the first sip he turned to Helga and put a question to her. The answer had been worrying him for some time.

'How did you know what train I'd be coming on this morning?' he asked.

Helga's eyes opened wide, and then wider, at so extraordinarily simple a question.

'Mr Karlin told me. He said it must be either the 8.10 or the 8.19. Otherwise you would be late at your office. Mr Karlin said you were the kind that would never be late.' She gave a little sigh. 'It is very early to be at a railway station.'

'Mr Karlin seems to know a lot about me.'

Helga inclined her head.

'Mr Karlin is very thorough. That is why he is such a good agent.'

Stan raised his glass.

'Cheers,' he said.

Helga lifted her glass, and chinked it against his.

'Sold any of my pictures yet?' Stan asked.

Helga put out her hand and rested it on his arm.

'Not to be impatient,' she told him. 'Pictures like that are not news. They do not have to appear tomorrow. There is one publisher who is very interested. He is serious. He prints calendars.'

It was six-thirty when Mr Karlin arrived. By then Stan had got to know Helga pretty well, and she had told him her life story. It was lurid; also, in its way, classical. She had become orphaned at the age of three. An aunt had brought her up in Vienna, and been cruel to her. She had run away, penniless. In turn skivvy, waitress, usherette, chorus girl, air hostess, wife, model and divorcée. At the recollection of her past struggles, she had to wipe away a tear. Stan wanted to take her in his arms and comfort her.

They were both on their second glass of hock when Mr Karlin arrived. And it was the authentic Mr Karlin, all right. Large, smiling and good-humoured, he seemed to bring his own envelope of warmth along with him; and it was large enough to enclose all three of them. Champagne on draught was what he was going to have, he said, and he seemed surprised that the others should have contented themselves with ordinary hock.

Helga let Mr Karlin take his first sip before disturbing him. Then she leant forward and pulled up Stan's sleeve.

'He's wearing it, you see.'

Mr Karlin nodded in approval.

'Looks good on him, doesn't it? Got the right sort of wrist for it.' He slid back his cuff to show the duplicate watch on his own wrist. 'Nice piece of workmanship. I thought you'd like it as soon as you got used to it.'

Stan remembered Cliff's interest in getting hold of the agency for the wrist-watches, and he asked Mr Karlin about it. But it was no use. Mr Karlin merely shrugged his shoulders.

'Can't remember,' he said. 'I'm in pictures, not watches. Don't know where they got them. Japanese probably. Most things are these days.'

He lit one of the small Dutch cigars that he was always smoking, and sat back in his chair.

'Helga found you any nice models yet?'

It was Helga herself who answered the question.

'We have not talked any business,' she said. 'We have been speaking other things.'

Mr Karlin seemed disappointed.

'Can't keep the public waiting,' he told her. 'When can you fix up something?'

Helga was playing with her glass, twisting the tall stem round and round between her fingers.

'It is already fixed.'

Despite the hock, Stan felt the inside of his mouth go dry.

'What is?' he asked.

'The studio.'

Stan tried to appear casual and unconcerned.

'When for?'

'Tomorrow night. Six o'clock. For as long as you like. I have arranged for more than one model. You can make your choice.'

Mr Karlin caught Stan's eye.

'O.K. by you?'

Stan swallowed hard.

'O.K.,' he told him.

Mr Karlin was smiling.

'Don't know what I should do without Helga,' he said.

Stan turned towards her again.

'Where is it?' he asked.

She opened her bag.

'I have written it down for you.'

The piece of paper showed the address 27 Cremorne Crescent, Praed Street. Helga had used a thick felt pen to write it down. It was all in large capital letters.

'I shall be there. To introduce you. They are good friends of mine. You will find them sincere and obliging.'

'Your first time, isn't it?' It was Mr Karlin who was speaking, and he nodded his head approvingly. 'Fresh approach. That's what's needed. You've got the artist's touch, you have. I'm looking forward.' He broke off suddenly and thrust his hand into his breast pocket. 'Mustn't forget this, must we?' he said. This time the bundle of notes wasn't even in an envelope. It simply had a rubber band round it. Mr Karlin thrust it into Stan's hand. 'Same as before,' he told him. 'Don't bother to count. It's all there.'

Stan thanked him. He was still playing it cool. Cool and professional.

'Don't know that I've earned it yet,' he said. 'Do my best though. Just have to see what it comes out like, won't we?'

As he spoke, he felt his self-confidence returning to him. It was the bundle of notes in his pocket that was doing it. Held in by his ball-point and his pocket comb, it bulged there right over his heart with the pressure of a reassuring hand.

'And this, if you don't mind.' Mr Karlin was holding out a piece of paper. 'Just a receipt,' he said. 'Not for me. I don't understand money. It's for our auditor. He's the one who's particular.'

Stan disentangled the clip of the ball-point from the bank-notes, and signed.

Chapter 19

27 Cremorne Crescent turned out to be a perfectly ordinary-looking camera shop set between a newsagent's and a liquor store. Ordinary-looking, that is, in terms of camera shops. Everything on display was marked with a small orange-coloured ticket announcing the amount of the discount. 'Maker's Price' and 'Our Price' was how the little notices read, and the difference was sensational. But by no means out of place. The whole of this part of Praed Street and the Edgware Road was crowded with cut-price shops, all apparently bent on their own retail destruction, busily selling record-players, tape recorders, television sets, refrigerators, electric mixers, even complete suites of bedroom furniture, for less than it had cost the wholesaler to supply or the maker to manufacture them. It was a self-contained wasteland of crazy capitalism, a rather sleazy oasis where bad cost-accountancy, over-production and the eventual inevitable bankruptcy had at last all come to rest. The ghost of Karl Marx brooded over the place.

All the same, there was nothing in the window of number twenty-seven for the keen amateur to complain about. Stan paused for a moment wondering whether, if things went well, he would go for a Rollei, a Canon, a Minolta, another Pentax or a Praktica. He'd never before imagined himself able to afford any one of them. But a combination of Mr Karlin's advances and the special discount offers made almost anything seem possible.

By comparison his own camera seemed ridiculously old-fashioned. It was the sort of thing that an industrious schoolboy might expect for a birthday present. Mounted on a tripod in the middle of a well-equipped, modern studio it would hardly be calculated to persuade any self-respecting model that she was sitting in the nude for one of England's top-notch photographers.

The door of number twenty-seven opened with a little *ping*, and Stan found himself facing a display case of exposure meters, flash bulbs, telephoto lenses and magazine-projectors. He would have liked to stay to examine them. Indeed, the proprietor recognized a potentially serious customer as soon as he saw him. He was an excellent judge of class and summed Stan up immediately, putting him in the twenty-five-to-thirty-pound bracket with an exchange deal thrown in. He was therefore surprised when Stan enquired about the studio. It seemed somehow out of character.

'Are you the Agency booking?' he asked.

Stan nodded.

'Through here.' He pulled back the red velvet curtain behind him as he was speaking, and stood to one side to let Stan go past. 'They're all ready for you,' he said.

The studio stood at the end of a short corridor. The door was open and he could hear voices. His feeling of nervousness returned to him. For a moment he wondered if he was up to it. Then he braced himself. He wasn't going to turn back now. He intended to show how much at ease he was, to demonstrate that to him nude models were just part of his regular photographic equipment.

'Evening all,' he said as he stepped inside.

Helga came forward to meet him. She was smiling that charming smile of hers.

'It is good,' she said. 'We are all punctual. I will introduce you. Soon we can begin.'

'I'm ready,' Stan told her.

Helga turned away from him.

'This is Mandy,' she said. 'She has only just got here. There is Denise, too. She is in there, undressing. She, too, is well-built like Mandy.'

Helga was certainly right about her being well-built, Stan thought. In her tight-fitting woollen jumper she looked enormous. Enormous, and strangely bovine. With her wide, dark eyes set rather far apart and her deep, Mediterranean complexion she had an air of authentic farm-yard tranquillity. The hand that she held out to him was soft and dampish. And, when she said 'Hullo', he noticed that her voice was throaty like a man's.

'It is for studies of the bust that she is most excellent,' Helga assured him as though Mandy were not there. 'She has fullness.'

'I can see that,' he said.

For a moment he stood there regarding her. It was then that he realized why her voice was so thick, so contralto-ish. It was because she was chewing something. Whatever it was, it had got stuck round one of her teeth and with a red-nailed finger she patiently prised it free. Then she resumed her chewing.

'She is not yet eighteen,' Helga announced proudly. 'Denise is one year older.'

Stan wasn't thinking about Denise, however. He was thinking about the portable lighting console over in the corner. Up to now he had only read about lighting consoles, seen advertisements for them in photographic periodicals, heard them mentioned at camera club sessions. And this evening he was actually going to use one. With the lighting console up against his tripod he would, without moving, be able to control every lamp in the studio. The prospect pleased him, and he found himself feeling glad that he had come. He was, in fact, still fiddling with the console when the door at the far end opened and Denise emerged.

She was wearing nothing but a long bath-wrap and the folds fell apart as she shook hands with him. Stan tried not to look. Not that he need have bothered. For a nineteen-year-old, Denise seemed a remarkably self-possessed young lady.

She shot a quick smile at him. It was a strictly professional smile, produced and put away again all in a single instant.

'Got a cigarette?' she asked.

Because Stan did not smoke, it had to be Helga who gave her one. She did so disapprovingly.

'You smoke too much,' she said. 'Smoking darkens the teeth.' She put her hand on Mandy's arm. 'The changing-room is now free,' she said. 'Please to get ready.'

Excessive smoking, Stan discovered, was not Denise's only shortcoming. She seemed also excessively short of sleep. She had perched herself on one of the studio stools and, with the ash from the cigarette dropping onto her bath-wrap, she put back her head and yawned. All in all, she seemed to be pretty much at home in the studio.

That was evident when Stan started to pull one of the lamps into position.

'No good,' she said. 'It's fused. They haven't fixed it.'

Stan thanked her.

'You know this place well?' he asked.

'Should do. I'm the regular.'

'Keep you busy?'

'Keep *them* busy.'

The console was working perfectly, and there was now a pool of light spread out there in front of him. At his command, he could make it intense, suffused, dim, reflected, even shadowy. And already he could see the picture forming before him. He would bring over two of the white papiermâché columns, and have the model standing in between. She would be partly in the light and partly in the shadow. Her hand would be up to her forehead as though she were in thought and her left foot would be thrust out at an angle as in ballet.

Stan straightened himself.

'O.K. then,' he said. 'Shall we begin?'

Denise slid out of the bath-wrap, and wiped her eye on the sleeve.

'It's these lights,' she told him. 'They're murder.'

As she stood there in front of him, Stan realized that he had never really looked at anyone in the nude before. He'd seen Beryl undressed, of course. But only in glimpses. Beryl had a very keen sense of what was nice and what wasn't, whereas Denise seemed entirely unaware of any difference.

'How do you want me?' she asked.

Stan walked over to the papiermâché columns. The lighting was excellent, real brilliance on one side and a deep rich darkness on the other. The picture in Stan's mind was becoming clearer. He showed Denise very carefully where he wanted her to stand.

'You'll have to position me,' she told him.

He didn't like actually touching her. For a start, her skin felt colder than he had expected. And now that she was close to him he could see that her shoulders were covered in a fine, white down. It was the side lamps that showed it up. With ordinary overhead lighting he doubted whether he would have noticed. But it gave him an idea. When he had finished the thoughtful study, he would bring the camera right in and shoot deliberately along the shoulder line. He might even ask her to powder up a bit. All in all, he was beginning to discover that figure photography could make a rather exciting pastime. And meanwhile, the pure classical nature of his composition delighted him. He was beginning to think of possible titles for it. *Temple Gateway* seemed appropriate.

Helga's voice broke in on him.

'She is excellent also for *lingerie*,' she said. 'So, too, is Mandy. They will show you.'

Stan had finished the Temple Gateway study and was busy photographing the down on Denise's shoulder-blades when Mandy emerged from the changing-room. She was still chewing. Holding a rather creased kimono around her she sat down at the back of the studio and munched away contentedly.

It was Helga who was not content. It seemed that the agent and the salesgirl were at work within her. She got up and went over to Stan.

'Not to forget the full frontal,' she said. 'For centre-spread purposes.'

It was getting hot in the studio. Stan took his coat off.

Helga noticed immediately.

'The great heat is for the models,' she observed. 'Otherwise they go goose-pimply. It would not look pleasant.' She reached out and touched his arm. 'But you are tired,' she said. 'It is not good for the pictures. First, you rest. Then Mandy. After that, lingerie. And last of all, twosomes.'

'Twosomes?'

'Both models together. Classical and fun-shots. Both are saleable. The market is quite international.'

The session with Mandy was placid and without incident. She appeared somehow to have lost interest. Not that it was immediately apparent that she had ever had any. She merely chewed, posed and then started chewing again. Hands laced behind the neck and leaning slightly forward was the pose that Helga specially recommended. Taken from the side it was good for the fullness, she explained. She even went through to the shop for more film so that Stan wouldn't have to stint himself.

It was the lingerie studies with Denise that held things up. The lingerie was lacy, transparent and jet black. But he saw at once what could be made of it. With a little more of the lingerie and a little less of Denise, the effect could, he reckoned, be quite interesting. And with the captions all ready-made, too. *Toilette de la Duchesse*, for example, would do nicely for a back view of Denise gazing into a mirror with her hair drawn down over one shoulder and her quite remarkable bosom seen only in reflection. If, on the other hand, he turned her round so that she was facing him, smile and all, and got her to hold her hair on the top of her head like a crown, *Naughty Nineties* would seem just about right to catch the spirit of the piece.

Again, when it came to the twosomes, it was Stan's literary sense that saved him. What otherwise would have been simply another example of the sort of nude photography of which he disapproved was rendered harmless, even rather beautiful, when entitled *Turkish Harem* or *Arabian Nights*. Because Stan was naturally a rather slow worker he did not get beyond the classical studies. *Zenana Maidens, Odalisques Reclining, The Seraglio* – one after another he set them up, re-lit them, asked Mandy to stop chewing and pressed the little button. By then it was too late even to attempt the fun-shots that Helga wanted.

Not that Helga really minded. She was so eager to get her hands on what Stan had already taken that it was all that she cared about. To save time she offered to take the negatives back with her and have them developed at the agency. That, however, was something that Stan could not allow. He always did his own printing and developing and had strong views on the subject. His twenty-minute, illustrated talk on 'The Darkroom, its Use and Misuse' had been much admired by every camera club audience to which he had addressed it.

And Stan refused to be rushed. He didn't want to see all that hard work wasted through over-hastiness. That was why he insisted on having the whole week-end to make a good job of it. Reluctantly, Helga had to agree. They would meet next Monday night, she suggested, at six o'clock as usual. Only this time it wouldn't be at Greco's. The Clansman in Charing Cross Road would, if Stan didn't mind, be more convenient. Naturally, Mr Karlin would come too, she added, if he happened to be free.

By then it was nearly nine o'clock. Mandy and Denise had put their clothes on again and gone home. Helga stayed behind to settle up with the proprietor and Stan started to walk to the station. It had been hot under the studio lamps and the evening air felt chilly.

By the time he had reached Praed Street, he was shivering.

Chapter 20

As it turned out, Mr Karlin couldn't manage it. It was Helga alone whom Stan met in the rather brassy lounge of The Clansman. Distinctly further down the scale than Greco's, The Clansman did not appear to mind how many unaccompanied ladies there were sitting around on the premises.

Looking round him, Stan thought at once how out of place Helga looked. There was a freshness about her, almost an air of innocence, that did not seem to belong anywhere at that end of Charing Cross Road. And certainly not in The Clansman. The clientele of The Clansman was mostly middle-aged and a bit faded, the men fatter than was good for them and the women with hair that looked younger than their faces. Helga belonged to a different world altogether.

And she was certainly very encouraging.

'You are exactly what Mr Karlin has been looking for,' she told him. 'With the right models and with your artistic sense it cannot go wrong. The royalty payments will be most satisfactory. I am sorry about Denise and Mandy. They have now grown too fat. I will find you new ones.'

He had given her the envelope of prints that he had brought with him, and she was stroking it lovingly.

'I know these will be good,' she told him. 'I can feel it. They will start earning money immediately.'

'Any luck with the others yet?'

Helga shook her head.

'But do not worry about them. They are not important. It is with this kind that you will make your fortune.'

And again she stroked the envelope that she was holding.

Her eyes were fixed on him as she said it. Stan thought that they were the frankest, most honest eyes that he had ever seen. He couldn't bear to mislead her.

'But don't count on me,' he said. 'Not really my cuppa tea. I'm more landscape and costume. And nature, of course. Like my swans.'

Helga put out her hand, and rested it on his forearm. It was a small, delicate hand, blue-veined and practically weightless.

'Not to worry.' Her eyes were still looking into his, and she was smiling. 'See what Mr Karlin says. Mr Karlin can make you a rich man.' She paused. 'You are all right for money now?' she asked. 'Mr Karlin said I was particularly to enquire.'

Stan did not reply immediately.

'I'm all right,' he told her.

Helga gave his arm a little squeeze.

'Then we must arrange to talk to Mr Karlin,' she said. 'Next Saturday. Six o'clock. How about it?'

Stan thought about Beryl and Marleen, and odd jobs about the house and going round to the newsagent's for the evening paper that Beryl always liked to have.

'I'd rather a weekday.'

Helga shook her head.

'Mr Karlin does not get back until Saturday. You are his first appointment. He is returning early specially to see you. It is most important.'

Put like that, Stan did not see what he could do about it.

'O.K.,' he said.

'Then let us meet at the New Mexico in Southampton Row. It is very modern. The Sunset Suite would be best. And to be punctual, please. Perhaps I may keep you waiting. If Mr Karlin is late, too, it will not be intended.'

It seemed strange to Stan that Helga never suggested that they should meet twice in the same place.

'Why go there?' he asked.

Helga removed her hand. She was frowning.

'For Mr Karlin's sake,' she explained. 'It will be more convenient for him. He has so many engagements.'

She got up as she said it, and tucked the envelope of photographs under her arm.

'Now I must leave you,' she said. 'I have much work to do. It cannot be allowed to wait.'

'You won't have another drink?'

'I always have only one drink. More is not good for me.'

Her face was turned up to him as she was speaking and rather to his own surprise he bent forward and kissed her. Helga did not seem in the least surprised.

'I shall look forward to Saturday,' she said. 'Then I shall have more time.'

The New Mexico was certainly new. And Mexican. Any aboriginal from Yucatan would at once have felt at home there. Aztec and Mayan symbols were everywhere, and Stan found himself thinking about Beryl's housecoat. Large fibre-glass statues of the Sun God flanked the main elevator concourse, and the décor was all of gold and green stone with some plastic feather decorations ingeniously worked in.

The chain to which the hotel belonged was an international one, but the clientele appeared to be mostly down from the North; Leeds or Huddersfield, probably. To put these foreign tourists at their ease and make them feel at home, the management had opened a Shakespeare Head Inn down in the basement. Because Stan was early he strolled down and inspected it.

Stan wished straight away that it had been the Shakespeare Head that Helga had chosen for their meeting. But when he took the lift up to the Sunset Suite, he saw at once how right she had been. There you stepped straight out of the lift into the tropics. There were palm trees, singing birds in cages, zither music, coconut matting on the floor and a lighting system which allowed for an endless cycle from the clear, pale sunlight of a Central American dawn to full noontide splendour and on to dusk and twilight, finally arriving at night with a sickle moon and a myriad electric stars gleaming down from the ceiling. It stayed like that for about ten minutes of romantic, velvety gloom and then the whole thing started up again. Up in the Sunset Suite, the earth went round the sun punctually once every half-hour.

Helga had been quite right to warn him that she might be late. She was very late. It was six-twenty, and already darkening twilight, Sunset Suite time, when she arrived. But it was not so dark that he could not see that she was apprehensive about something. Stan wondered why. He himself had been sitting at the round bamboo table since five to six, and he had already drunk two of the Trader Vick Specials. In consequence, he felt slightly sick but strangely confident.

'Anything wrong?' he asked.

Helga did not reply immediately. Instead, she stood there simply looking at him.

'I will have a drink,' she said at last. 'I will have a whisky.'

There was just a suggestion of a 'v' rather than of a 'w' when she said 'whisky'. Stan found it irresistible. It showed how Continental she was.

When Helga had been brought her whisky, she sipped it thoughtfully without actually saying anything, simply lifting her glass, taking a tiny gulp and then putting the glass down on the bamboo table-top again.

Quite suddenly she turned towards him.

'Will you promise me something?' she asked.

At least for the time being, all sensation of sickness had passed. It was only the feeling of confidence that remained.

'Promise you anything,' he told her.

'Then do whatever Mr Karlin asks,' she said. 'For my sake, please do it.'

Her hand was on his arm again, and she was looking up at him with those dark brown appealing eyes of hers. Then she glanced down at her watch.

'By now Mr Karlin should soon be here,' she said. 'We will go find him.'

Helga seemed to know her way about the New Mexico. She stopped the lift on the fifth floor and turned right where the sign read '550–599'. Up here above the main temple area, the architecture was less strikingly Aztec. The last of the Montezumas would hardly have recognized it. The whole prospect was simply one of bedroom doors, service areas and fire notices. Outside number 561 Helga stopped, and turned towards him.

'This is where I say good-bye.'

Her voice sounded husky and breathless, almost as if she had been running.

'Then you're not coming in?'

'I tell you. This is where I say good-bye.'

Her hand was on his arm again, only this time it was trembling.

'Remember what I have said. Do what Mr Karlin tells you. Then you will be all right. It will be most profitable.'

Then, without warning, she kissed him.

'So good-bye it is.'

She had reached out her hand and pressed the push-button beside the door while her lips were still up against his cheek.

'They are expecting you,' she said.

'They?' he asked.

But it was no use. Helga had turned her back on him and was walking away down the corridor.

The door of number 561 opened, and Mr Karlin stood there. In the room behind him the radio was playing.

Mr Karlin looked down the corridor after Helga. She was nearly out of sight by now. Mr Karlin spread out his hands in disappointment.

'I asked her to stay,' he said, 'but she couldn't.' Then he stepped to one side. 'Come in. There's someone here wants to meet you.'

The private suites in the New Mexico were modern and impersonal, like the corridor outside. Just a two-seater couch, an easy chair, an upright armchair, a round table with some glasses on top, a small writing desk, a television set and an indefinite, Impressionistic-looking sort of picture on the main wall. The refrigerator was in the little alcove on the way through to the bathroom.

The easy chair was the one that was occupied. The man who sat there filled it entirely, even overlapping the sides a little. Mr Karlin led Stan up to him.

'Meet Mr Svenstrom,' he said. 'Mr Svenstrom, this is Mr Pitts.'

There was, Stan noticed, a note of pride in Mr Karlin's voice as he said it. Stan felt flattered.

But Mr Svenstrom did not get up. All that he did was to point towards the couch.

'Come and sit down,' he said. 'We've been waiting for you.'

Stan sat down, and Mr Karlin's hand descended on his shoulder.

'It's whisky, isn't it?' he asked. 'You're the one who doesn't like soda, I remember. You're the whisky-and-water man.'

While Mr Karlin had gone off to get the water, Stan found himself left there, staring at Mr Svenstrom. Mr Svenstrom was an unusually neatly-turned-out sort of man. His blue suit was the sort that dummies wear in the windows of multiple tailors' shops. His shirt was white and his tie was striped. He sat cross-legged and Stan could see over the tops of his beautifully polished shoes that his socks were striped, too. What was disconcerting, however, was that Mr Svenstrom was staring back at him. And it was purely a one-way traffic. Mr Svenstrom was wearing dark glasses.

There was a glass of whisky already on the table. It stood beside the ashtray where Mr Karlin had left his cigarette burning. Over on Mr Svenstrom's side there was no glass and no ashtray. It was evident that Mr Svenstrom was not of the self-indulgent kind.

'Mr Karlin tells me that you are very reliable.'

159

Stan rubbed the toe of his right foot up against his left ankle. This was not the sort of thing that he had expected the man in dark glasses to say.

'I do my best,' he told him.

'And that you have an expensive family.'

Stan did not know quite how to take that last remark. In one sense it was certainly true. Otherwise he wouldn't have needed those advances from Mr Karlin. All the same it was misleading, and there was an implied criticism of Beryl. That was something that Stan wasn't going to take from anyone.

'They're not so bad,' he said.

Mr Svenstrom did not move. His hands were clasped, and it was by no means obvious that he had even heard.

'But you like money?' he asked.

'I do when I've earned it.'

Mr Svenstrom gave just the slightest inclination of his head.

'And would you like to earn some more?'

It was Mr Karlin who interrupted them. He had come back with a plastic tooth-mug in his hand.

'Water,' he explained. 'Nothing else to put it in.'

He poured out something larger than a double whisky and slopped a little of the water on top of it.

'Sorry to have kept you waiting,' he said.

Then he raised his own glass.

'Cheers. Cheers and good luck.'

Mr Svenstrom turned to Mr Karlin.

'I was asking Mr Pitts if he would like to earn some more money,' he said.

Mr Karlin nodded understandingly.

'And would he?'

Mr Svenstrom shrugged his shoulders.

'I do not know. I am waiting for his reply.'

Stan was aware that by now they had both swung round and were looking at him. Mr Karlin could not have looked friendlier, or more encouraging; he seemed to be urging him on to say 'Yes'. And Stan knew why. It was what Mr Karlin had kept hinting at when he had told Stan about the sort of money that top stringers could make. This was the big chance that Mr Karlin had been setting up for him.

Stan cleared his throat.

'Yes, I would,' he said. 'I could do with it.' And, with the whisky, his confidence had now returned. 'I'm not cheap,' he added. 'Not cheap. But, like you said, reliable.'

Mr Svenstrom sat back in his chair.

'Nobody wants what is cheap,' he said. 'This is going to be very expensive. For somebody, it is going to cost a lot.'

Mr Karlin leant over and put his hand on Stan's knee.

'That's what you want to hear,' he told him. 'I'm only editorial. Mr Svenstrom's finance.'

Mr Svenstrom ignored Mr Karlin. His dark glasses were turned towards Stan.

'Are you a talker?' he asked.

'I . . . I don't quite follow you.'

'Can you keep your mouth shut?'

Stan was beginning to feel offended again.

'I suppose so. When I have to.'

'When your bread is buttered.'

Mr Svenstrom had so nearly got the saying right that it astonished Stan that it should go wrong at all. With an accent as perfect as Mr Svenstrom's it was hard to believe that the man was from somewhere the other side of the North Sea. If he were to change his name, Stan reflected, and wear suits that were not quite so carefully cut he would have passed for English anywhere; that is, if he put away his dark glasses.

'We are not a small agency,' Mr Svenstrom continued. 'We are a big one. Mr Karlin deals in both pictures and stories. Important pictures and important stories. We want to know if you will work for us.'

This was more than Stan had expected. And the thought attracted him. It would put Mr Parker in his place when Stan handed in his letter of resignation. And the letter was going to be a good one, too. Stan could feel the sentences forming inside him like a caption for one of the photographs. 'Having been offered a post at a higher salary and with better prospects . . . Desirous as I am of improving my position . . . in the absence of suitable advancement with the Service . . . resignation to become effective at earliest possible convenience . . .' In the morning he would just saunter in, quite casually, and drop the little bombshell into Mr Parker's in-tray, dusting the whole department off his hands as he walked away. But in the meantime he wanted to be certain.

'You mean give up my job?' he asked.

Mr Karlin and Mr Svenstrom exchanged glances.

'I mean stay where you are,' Mr Svenstrom told him. 'Stay where you are and work for us.'

'Part time? In the evenings, that sort of thing?'

Mr Svenstrom was shaking his head slowly from side to side.

'No,' he said. 'Full time. All day long. And in the evenings, too.'

Stan started to scrape the toe of his shoe up and down his ankle.

'I don't get it,' he said.

Mr Svenstrom's hands went up in a tiny gesture of despair. He turned towards Mr Karlin.

'He is your friend,' he said. 'You explain.'

As Mr Svenstrom turned his head, the light played a trick on him. For an instant, Stan saw himself reflected in the dark glasses. There he was – or rather, there two of him were – staring back at him out of the centre of Mr Svenstrom's face. He could even see the quiff of hair in front that always rose up again no matter how much he brushed it down. Then Mr Svenstrom leant back, and the dark glasses became simply dark glasses again.

Mr Karlin had edged in closer. He placed his hand on Stan's knee. It was a large hand and it cupped Stan's knee-cap as though it were grasping the bottom knob on a flight of banisters. Only it was more personal than that; as he talked, Mr Karlin kept giving Stan's knee a little squeeze.

'What Mr Svenstrom is saying,' he explained, 'is that you hold a very responsible position.'

Stan nodded.

'That's right,' he said.

'And you're proud of it, aren't you?'

'I suppose I am, rather.'

'So you should be. That's why it's all wrong.'

'What is?'

'Not giving you the top job. You deserved it.'

It wasn't something that Stan wanted to discuss. It was all too painful.

'Can't be helped,' he said. 'That's all over and done with.'

'But there's the money side to it,' Mr Karlin went on. 'They're under-paying you.'

'I can manage.'

Whenever the subject came up, Stan always made a point of defending the Civil Service. Anything else would have seemed disloyal. It was only to himself that he admitted feeling badly about it.

'But Mr Svenstrom doesn't want you just to manage,' Mr Karlin said. 'Mr Svenstrom wants you to be comfortable. And you can be if you do what Mr Svenstrom says.'

'What's that?'

'Combine business with pleasure. There's a lot of stuff stored away in those records of yours that would hit the headlines if only we could get the sight of it. That'd be worth paying money for.'

Mr Karlin's hand was still resting on Stan's knee. Stan pushed the hand aside.

'If you're suggesting what I think you're suggesting,' he said, 'I'm not having anything to do with it.'

Mr Karlin looked surprised. Surprised and possibly a little hurt.

'Pity,' he said.

'What's more,' Stan told him, 'it will be my duty to report this conversation. That's what the Official Secrets' Act says.'

'Does it now?' Mr Karlin asked. 'Does it really. But you wouldn't go and do anything like that, would you?'

'Why wouldn't I?'

Stan felt rather proud of himself as he said it. He'd never imagined that he'd have the opportunity to say anything like that, and he only wished that Commander Hackett of Security could have been there to hear him say it.

But Mr Karlin didn't seem very much impressed.

'Because it wouldn't be good for you,' he said. 'Because you wouldn't like what would happen.'

'Are you threatening me?' Stan asked.

Mr Karlin gave a little laugh.

'No,' he replied. 'I'm protecting you.'

'What from?'

Mr Svenstrom brought his hand down with a slap on the glass table-top.

'Show him the photographs,' he said.

'O.K., if you think he's ready.'

'He's ready,' Mr Svenstrom told him.

The photographs were in Mr Karlin's pocket. He pulled out an envelope and held it up for Stan to take.

'Take a look at these,' he said.

'Why should I?'

'Because you're in them. In every single one of them. Right up to your little neck, you are.'

Stan wished now that he had cut Mr Karlin short, hadn't allowed him to go on talking. It would have been better if he'd walked straight out of the room as soon as Mr Karlin had mentioned that bit about the headlines. All the same, he thought that perhaps it would be as well to see what it was that Mr Karlin was trying so hard to show him.

As he opened the envelope, one of the photographs slid out and fell down onto the floor. When he picked it up, Stan saw at once what it was. It had been taken in the little studio over by Praed Street. The twin columns of *Temple Gateway* showed up in the background and, in front, there he was standing talking to Mandy. It was like one of the conversation pictures in the society columns of the weeklies, only in this conversation Mandy hadn't got any clothes on.

'Where d'you get this?' he remarked.

Mr Karlin was wearing his smile again.

'Helga took it,' he said. 'She's good, isn't she? Helga took all this lot.'

Stan opened up the envelope and glanced inside. Then he dropped the photograph of him and Mandy in along with all the others. He'd seen all that he wanted to see.

'Well, what d'you want me to do with them?' he asked.

Mr Karlin's smile widened, it now reached right across his face.

'Oh, they're not for you,' he said. 'They're for the family. For the family and friends. One set for Beryl. And one set for Marleen's schoolteacher. And one set for the bank manager. And one set for Mr Parker . . .' It was evident that Mr Karlin knew everything about him.

Stan felt his stomach suddenly go cold and empty. He was afraid that he might be on the verge of being sick. But he wasn't going to let Mr Karlin know how he was feeling. He was determined to fight back.

'You know what this is,' he said. 'It's blackmail.'

Mr Karlin merely nodded.

'You're too right it is,' he said.

'Then I'm going to the Police,' Stan told him.

Mr Karlin, however, did not seem to think that was a good idea, either.

'Take a look at these,' he said. 'They're different.'

The photographs in the second envelope that he passed across were, in Stan's opinion, technically pretty poor; just bad amateur stuff. And nothing much to worry about there. They were simply shots of Stan in the bar of that run-down hotel in Bayswater. A few included Mr Karlin, smiling and benevolent-looking, thoughtfully running his thumbnail across the wad of bank-notes. But, mostly, they were of him talking to Mr Karlin's assistant, the young man who had been so polite and attentive. One of the photographs showed Stan himself flicking through that same bundle of five-pound notes.

'Helga never took that,' he suddenly blurted out. 'Helga wasn't there.'

Mr Karlin gave a little sigh.

'You're smart,' he said. 'You notice things. That's my work. That's the one I took.'

'Well, what about them?' Stan asked.

'D'you know who that is?'

Mr Karlin was pointing to the young man, and he was smiling again.

'Your assistant,' Stan told him.

Mr Karlin shook his head.

'Not any longer,' he said. 'He's left the country. MI5 were on to him. Suspected a spy-ring or something. Couldn't have anything like that in the agency. Had to get rid of him.'

Mr Karlin paused, and shook his head again.

'Wouldn't look good, you know,' he reminded Stan, 'you turning up in the photograph with a wanted man. Not with all that money in your hands. Whatever would Security start thinking?'

Mr Karlin had momentarily stopped smiling; instead, he was shaking his head sadly at the prospect.

Stan did not attempt to reply. The feeling of sickness was too much for him; and he had started to sweat.

'Can I use your toilet?' he asked.

Mr Karlin pointed towards the corridor.

'Second door on the right,' he said. 'Can't miss it.'

It was nearly ten minutes later when Stan came back. His shirt-collar was still undone, and he was shivering.

'You look terrible,' Mr Karlin told him. 'Mr Svenstrom was just saying so. Think it over. There's no hurry. Give me a ring when you're ready. Then we'll arrange something.'

Stan steadied himself.

'I think I will go home,' he said.

Mr Karlin seemed pleased.

'Best thing you could do. Best thing in the world. Go back home and have a good night's rest.'

He got up and put his arm round Stan's shoulders. Stan felt too weak to push it away again. Then, suddenly, Mr Karlin remembered something.

'Just a moment.'

He went through to the inner room and came back carrying a large brown-paper parcel.

'Your album,' he said. 'Better have it back. You may need it. I never opened it. Not our line really. Not that sort of photograph. We're technical.'

Chapter 21

It was what Mr Karlin had said about the unopened photograph album that hurt most. Compiling it, re-printing all those old award-winners and trimming down the mounts had meant a great deal to him; the whole operation had shown that life as he had lived it had, after all, been worth the living. Or, rather, so it had seemed at the time. And, at the thought that really it had meant nothing, just nothing at all, Stan sat on the edge of the bed in that single room of his at the end of the landing in number sixteen, and wept.

On the whole, it was just as well that this was one of those periods when Stan and Beryl were not sleeping together. Not that there had been any unpleasantness about the arrangement. It was simply that she hadn't been feeling like it, Beryl explained; and she was awake such a lot too, she added, tossing and turning all night like. If Stan had been there alongside her she didn't see how he could have been expected to get a wink either.

As it was, Stan's crying had come on quite suddenly. At one moment, he had simply been sitting there, perched on the bed end, feeling sick and frightened. Then, without warning, something inside him had snapped. He was no longer Stanley Pitts, civil servant, aged thirty-six. He wasn't even young Stan, Boy Scout, aged nine. He was Little Stan, hope of the family and aged about six. The corners of his mouth went down, his shoulders started heaving and he threw himself full-length on the bed and sobbed into the pillow, pulling it close up round his face so that the others shouldn't hear him.

And, all the time, he kept thinking about those dreadful pictures of himself and Mandy. More than that, too. He kept thinking about those dreadful pictures being looked at by someone else. By Mr Winters. Or by Marleen's schoolteacher. Or by Mr Parker. Or, worst of all, by Beryl.

At the thought of Beryl with those pictures in her hand, his heart gave a great bump and he found himself gasping for breath as though he had just dived into icy water. He sat up in bed. He turned the light on. He tried to read. He couldn't concentrate. He put the book away. He lay down. He turned the light off. He pulled the bedclothes up round him. He pushed them down again. By turns he was too hot and too cold. He shivered and he sweated. And he thought of ending it all.

When dawn came lighting up the fancy brickwork of the houses on the other side of Kendal Terrace, he was still awake. By then, he was not sobbing into his pillow any longer. There was no more cry-baby stuff. He was lying on his back, staring straight up at the ceiling, being brave. The eiderdown had got itself rolled up into a bundle and he was clasping it. It had become his Teddy-bear: Stanley Pitts was little Stannie again.

And what was so unnerving, so catastrophic, was the way the realization of the situation kept coming back to him all the next week. In the middle of routine filing, or merely when sitting in the canteen, or while washing his hands in the staff lavatory, he would, without warning, find himself abruptly and mercilessly launched into the appalling future.

It was at those moments that he would begin to tremble. It would start in his fingers, spread up to his elbows, move onwards to his shoulders, attack his knees and set his feet twitching.

He had one of those sudden spasms while quietly finishing his fish-fingers and frozen peas in the dinerette alcove on the Wednesday night. No danger signals, either. Not a hint of the impending panic. He was fond of fish-fingers and Beryl had cooked these to perfection. The frozen peas, too, were delicious, garden-fresh and faintly minty. He was still chewing away when, from nowhere, the full nightmarish awareness of things broke over him. He saw himself sent for by the Head of Personnel, and he knew just how it would be. Mr Parker would be standing on one side of him and, on the other, Commander Hackett from Security. Behind would be two strangers, large men with large red hands. At a nod from the Head of Personnel they would come forward. One of them would be holding something behind his back. Stan could feel the cold of the steel as, with a click of the lock, they snapped the handcuffs on.

Beryl couldn't help noticing. He must have got a chill, she told him, and he ought to go to bed. There was only one thing, she added: if he went up to bed as early as this it was to keep warm and go to sleep. There was no point in lying there, reading. It was just wasting electricity. She'd had to go along to the bathroom the other night, she said, and she'd noticed that his light was still full on.

That was the night when Stan had lain there, contemplating suicide if only she had known. Nor did the prospect any longer alarm him. Instead, he could see a sort of comfort in it, an end to all anxiety. It would spare Beryl and Marleen the shame that was stored up ready to descend upon them; it would show Mr Karlin that Stan wasn't just the puppet that Mr Karlin thought he was; and it might even make Helga feel sorry for what she had done to him. He minded a lot about Helga.

It was only the method that remained to be decided and, when you came to it, there wasn't really very much choice. To get hold of poison it was necessary to sign a register at the chemist's. And he couldn't blow his brains out because he hadn't got a shotgun. Besides, insurance companies could be very awkward about suicides, and Stan certainly didn't want to risk anything going wrong with the insurance. That would have been letting Beryl down instead of helping her.

Drowning was one possibility. But Stan had always been a rather good swimmer. Eight lengths of the baths breast-stroke; that sort of stuff. And he was afraid that if, say, he took a header off Hammersmith Bridge, he would turn the whole thing into a quite presentable swallow-dive and then instinctively strike out smartly for the Barnes waterworks when he came up again.

So he could see that it was a dry end that he would have to prepare for himself. But falling out of a window at Frobisher House wouldn't do, either, because his own office was stuck away down there in the basement: it would inevitably look suspicious if he took a lift up to Medical and Welfare on the top floor, only to come crashing down again into the forecourt a few minutes later.

By now, he was perfectly calm about it all; calm and resigned and determined. There was no other way for it. And he saw that the eight-ten was the answer. It was *his* eight-ten, that train that he had caught every weekday morning for the past fourteen years. There wasn't going to be any difference in the arrangement either; it was simply that this Friday he would be there on the platform waiting for it for the last time.

The whole episode was as clear to him as if it had already happened, and he were merely recollecting it – his usual cheery greeting to the other regulars, the quick glance at the headlines while the paper was still folded up bookstall-fashion, the over-the-shoulder check to see if the train was coming. Then, just as it was drawing level – hand up to forehead, a little gasp as though he were in pain, limp at the knees, weight of the body well forward – and so down on to the line. He had frequently remarked on the speed at which the train came into the station, and was in no doubt that the end would be quite painless.

Simply because there were a few personal details, like the gas bill and the television licence, that he wanted to check up on he decided to give himself just one more day to get ready. Eight-ten on Friday morning was to be the time.

In consequence, the whole of the Thursday was marred by the recurrent thought that everything that he did was being done for the last time – after eight-ten, of course, that is. As he woke to a pleasant and sunny morning, he saw the remainder of his life spread out in front of him. It was as unremarkable as it was brief: two more visits to the bathroom, two more breakfasts, two more good-byes on the doorstep, two more walks to the station, two more morning papers, two more arrivals of the train. But only one departure with him there in his favourite seat in the corner of the compartment. After that, of course, only one more of everything else, until the same time on Friday when there would be no more of anything.

He managed his cup of morning coffee, but he couldn't face up to the staff canteen at lunchtime. It would have been too poignant. Too many old friends and too many unsaid good-byes. Instead, when one o'clock came round he walked out of Frobisher House and allowed himself a half-pint of bitter and a ham sandwich in the saloon bar of the Lord Ramsay. In the ordinary way he enjoyed going round to the Lord Ramsay. It was one of the few public houses he knew where, if you wanted a ham sandwich, it wasn't made until you asked for it. And then, when you did, the thin, razor-sharp knife would be drawn through the thickest, tenderest, pinkest part of the joint, the fat would be cut off like frilling; just the right amount of mustard would be smeared across the meat; and it would be crusts-on or crusts-off according to how you wanted it.

But today he was not interested. It had been a mistake even to think about ham sandwiches, and he left his half-eaten. There was too much on his mind. He was, in fact, composing his farewell letter to Beryl. It did not in the least matter that he knew that, because of the insurance company, he could never send it. There was still the relief that came from saying, even though it was only to himself, all those things that, deep in his heart, he knew that he should have said long ago.

The letter, he reckoned, ought to go more or less along these lines.

First, he would apologize for having all through their marriage kept her so short of housekeeping money, simply because he had never really earned enough to do any better. And the same went for theatres, foreign travel, jewellery and a small car. He would apologize also for the fact that his photography had taken up so much of his time, both outdoors and in the darkroom, when he should have been playing the part of the family man, first alongside Beryl, and then when Marleen came, alongside the two of them. But it wouldn't be just one long string of apologies, the letter. He would say thank-you to Beryl for having always looked so beautiful and so distinguished, and tell her how proud it had made him merely to be seen about with her. He would admit, quite openly, that he had always known perfectly well that he had never really been up to her class socially. Or physically, for that matter. He might even add that was why, with him out of the way, Beryl should marry Cliff. And, last of all, he would ask her to keep the unopened album of photographs, and give it to Marleen as a twenty-first birthday present when she would be old enough to appreciate it properly.

A glance at the oversize chronometer that Mr Karlin had given him showed that it was two o'clock already. Frobisher House was all of half a mile away, and he hoped that if he set off immediately he might just be able to get back to his desk before Mr Parker had noticed that he was missing.

And then the thought came to him that it didn't matter any more. If Contracts (Filing) was never going to see him again after he had left the office at five-thirty that evening, a few minutes either way couldn't make very much difference.

It wasn't even that the work he was engaged in was very urgent. There was really nothing to it. It amounted simply to clearing out the old files of projects long since cancelled to make way for files of new projects, all fresh-looking and promising, half of which like their predecessors in due course would be cancelled too.

The files of the Leviathan project were as good an example as any. In their buff cardboard covers they stretched, yard after yard of them, along the steel shelves in section D/127/A. That was the Top Secret section. And with good reason. If Leviathan had not been turned down by the Government, NATO would by now – or, at least, so the Opposition contended – have been in a position to impose its will on Moscow. The project had been the subject of one of the most vituperative debates of the century. The thousand million pounds that was involved was regarded, according to which side of the House was speaking, as an extremely modest price to pay for peace and security, or the spendthrift gamble of a bankrupt and panic-stricken administration.

Clearing out was, as it happened, work that Stan had always particularly disliked. It was tedious rather than exacting. Every cardboard folder had to be taken out, checked with the reference number in Central Registry and loaded onto the electric truck ready for transport down into the Morgue. The Morgue was what the lower vaults were called. If the folder appeared to be in really bad condition, the contents had to be taken out, examined for possible loss and then re-packed in an entirely new folder. More than once Stan had considered making a special application for transfer just so that he could escape the endless monotony. But not today. He kept remembering the lastness of it all and wished, instead, that the clearing out could go on for ever.

It was this awareness of the last time for everything that made the whole afternoon so painful. The sudden desire came over him to go round saying a cordial good-bye to people. He wanted to thank the tea-lady and give her a loving hug. He would have liked to make a small presentation – a bunch of violets, or a half-pound box of chocolates – to the girl who kept the In-and-Out Book. He wished that he could have found a plausible excuse for going along to PBX to tell the supervisor how grateful he was to her for all the calls that, over the years, she had put through to him. He even felt for once like wishing Mr Parker a friendly and polite good-night.

The actual moment of leaving the building was the worst. As he walked across the worn marble flooring of the entrance, past the security screen with the strip of woodwork across it that had never been painted quite the same colour as the base, he thought that he had never seen anything quite so beautiful. He knew that once outside, he would not dare to look back for fear of breaking down completely.

In short, Stanley Pitts and the British Admiralty were saying their last farewell.

The return home had the same sense of pain and finality about it. Even inserting the Yale key into the lock was in its way an ordeal: it carried too many memories of the snugness, the sweetness of life, as lived in number sixteen. For a moment, he found himself envying the three gnomes gathered round the small concrete fish-pond: not one of their little concrete hearts was breaking.

When he got inside, it was really just as well that Marleen happened to be sulking about something and that Beryl, in consequence, was a bit short with both of them. It served to take the edge off the anguish.

The night that followed was an entirely sleepless one. And, therefore, seemingly endless. He did not even attempt to lie down. Instead, he simply changed into his pyjamas, cleaned his teeth at the exceptionally small handbasin that Beryl had installed for him, and propped himself up in bed. The bed itself was in the corner, and Stan found it surprisingly comfortable with the angle of the two walls to support him.

He thought of many strange things that night; things of the past that had been long since forgotten. He remembered the bunch of flowers – pink and white carnations – that he had taken round to the nursing-home the evening Marleen had been born. Then there came a clear picture of himself passing his Test for the Civil Service, and being congratulated on the neatness of his rather small handwriting. Next, he was standing in front of the desk in the Headmaster's room at the Crocketts Green County Secondary School to be told that he was going to be made a prefect next term. And, again, he was on a bus: it was a hot day, and he was sticky and excited and going to the Zoo; he could smell the strong, tobacco-y odour of his father beside him. Everything was all jumbled up and all going backwards. At this rate, by the time the eight-ten had drawn into the platform, he wouldn't even have been born.

In the small hours, he got up, tiptoed downstairs and made himself a cup of tea. In different surroundings, he began remembering different things. He began thinking about Helga and kept telling himself that she wasn't really bad like the rest of them but had somehow been trapped into it the way that he had been.

All those thoughts were still in his mind as he shaved before going down to breakfast. As it happened, it turned out to be a poor sort of meal. Beryl and Marleen had failed to settle their difference, and the silences were awkward and prolonged. Even saying good-bye, this good-bye of all good-byes, wasn't quite as Stan would have wished it. Beryl asked him to be careful and mind her hair and, when he bent over for his kiss, Marleen complained that he tasted all soapy and toothpasty.

Slamming the front door behind him for the last time was bad enough. But the ten minutes' walk to the station was far worse. It took him past so many old, familiar landmarks. But what was remarkable was that it seemed as though he had never properly noticed them before, that he was seeing them for the first time as they really were. And the thought that they would go on being there when he himself was gone made him feel sad, very sad indeed.

Indeed, as he bought his paper and made his way over the iron bridge onto the platform, there was little spirit left in him. He knew that what he was doing was inevitable. He had argued that out already, and he accepted that there was no other way. In consequence, he did not even mind. He had always tried to do what was best for Beryl and Marleen; and he knew now and for the last time that he was doing it.

His watch showed eight-nine, he knew exactly what he had to do: little gasp, hand up to forehead, knees limp, weight forward. And there, coming round the bend, just as he had foreseen it all, was the train bumping up and down as it went over the points.

Stan took a half-step nearer to the platform edge.

BOOK TWO

The Man with Two Wrist-Watches

Chapter 22

The train, as usual, pulled jerkily out of the station, gathering speed as it passed the little wooden, model-kit signal box. And, as usual, there was Stan in the first non-smoker compartment in the second coach.

He was sitting bolt upright, his knees close together and his arms folded, making a tightly-done-up parcel of himself. He had to sit like that because he was still trembling all over; trying to read the morning paper would have been impossible because he couldn't have held it still enough.

And he certainly didn't want anyone to notice the condition he was in. That, indeed, is the whole trouble with these regular commuter compartments. They are merely so many mobile versions of the old family fireside; same faces, same conversation and the same tendency to make comments if anything is the least bit out of place or unusual.

It was like that today. The man opposite – a solicitor's clerk who was giving up smoking and always popped a peppermint drop into his mouth as the train began to draw out of the platform – thrust his morning sweetmeat into the corner of his cheek and leant forward.

'Yewerite?' he asked.

Stan avoided catching his eye.

'Bitterver chill,' he told him.

The legal mind came into play, and the clerk nodded understandingly.

'Gotta be careful. Doanwanner risk anything.'

These early morning conversations were like that, brief and perfunctory. People weren't really awake yet; hadn't got going properly. But illness is always irresistible: it strikes a chord in everyone. Soon the whole carriageful was talking about aspirin, electric blankets, hot lemon laced with whisky, warm underwear.

Not that Stan was listening. Nor was he shivering any longer. Instead, in a calm, detached sort of way he was sitting back congratulating himself.

And only just in time, too. At the thought of how close it had been, another tremor ran through him starting up in his shoulders, twisting down through his stomach and ending somewhere around his knees.

177

But that was the last of them. Because he knew that he could relax now, that he didn't have to be afraid of Mr Karlin or Mr Svenstrom any more.

And it had been in that last minute on the platform edge that his plan had come to him; his beautiful, infallible and fool-proof plan. As soon as the eight-ten reached Cannon Street, Stan went straight over to the nearest telephone kiosk.

But it is always easier to dial than it is to get the number that you are wanting. First, Stan found himself talking to a surprised housewife in Neasden. Then he got the engaged signal. Then no dialling tone at all. Then another wrong number, a fishmonger's this time. Then the engaged signal again. He had already spent fourpence and wasted over five minutes. There was clearly nothing for it but to try again later.

He was just letting himself out of the telephone box when a young man who had been hanging around outside came up to him. Stan had seen him standing there, doing nothing apparently. And not particularly noticeable, either. Simply one more human being, aged anywhere between twenty-five and thirty-five, hatless, featureless, inconspicuously dressed and pale-looking; the sort of person whose views are heard for the first time when national opinion polls are conducted.

'You been trying to ring 003 0004?' the young man asked.

His voice was as flat and colourless as his appearance. It was a voice that would have gone unremembered in any company.

'Suppose I was,' Stan said.

He was being cautious, not giving anything away.

'No good,' the young man told him. 'It's not working.'

'How do you know?'

'They've moved. They're not on the phone yet. That's why Mr Karlin sent me.'

Stan paused. It made him feel uncomfortable to think that he was being watched and followed about and waited for.

'Well?'

'Said you were to go to the World-Clifton. Cromwell Road. Tonight. Six o'clock. Suite number 303. Booked in the name of Harper.'

All round them, the eight-thirty immigration rush was in full spate. Another train had come in and, from Platform 3, a fresh tributary was joining up, surging into the stream of people already pouring across the concourse ready to cascade down into the Underground.

Stan joined them, with the young man somewhere close behind him.

There was never any time to spare in getting to Frobisher House in the mornings, and Stan had wasted too much of it already, shut up in that telephone kiosk. He wanted to get on with things.

'Tell Mr Karlin I'll be there,' he said.

He had turned his head as he said it, looking over his shoulder for the young man. But the young man wasn't there any longer. He had been caught up somehow, swept away in one of the side eddies. There was no sign of him; not even a row of bubbles.

The World-Clifton in the Cromwell Road was like every other World-Clifton the whole world over. A World-Clifton patron setting out on his global tour could choose any of the great national capitals and be sure of feeling at home there: same wallpaper in the bedroom, same menu in the roof-top restaurant, same sanitized lavatory seat beside the same porcelain-finish bath-tub. If the brotherhood of man were ever to become a reality on earth, the World-Clifton courtesy card with advance booking facilities could claim a major part of the credit.

This particular one, the West London World-Clifton, was something that Stan had seen often enough. It stretched up and up into the sky like a whole postal district torn out of the map and arbitrarily stood on end. Along the top, where the streets came to an end, the flags of all nations were kept flying.

It was five to six when Stan got there. The foyer of the hotel was crowded, and exciting. Wherever you looked, there were people arriving, leaving, making reservations, paying their bills, meeting other people. Stan could tell at a glance that the World-Clifton was a whole cut above the New Mexico. In a different class altogether, in fact. It was all glossy and expensive-looking like life lived inside a travel brochure. And, secretly, Stan was rather proud of himself for having contrived to be in the midst of it. Just looking at the display of Continental and trans-Atlantic newspapers spread out there on the bookstall made him feel pleasantly superior and cosmopolitan. It was the sort of bookstall that Crocketts Green simply wouldn't have known existed.

The lift, with its Muzak and its feather-touch controls, was both swift and silent. Stan felt that he would have liked a long non-stop run in it. But it was no use. Suite 303 was only in the foothills. The lift door had opened again before he'd even had time to check his appearance in the side mirrors.

If it had been one of the lifts over in Frobisher House he'd have had comfortable time to take out his pocket comb, run it through his hair, clean it off on his handkerchief and put it away again before the steel cage had finally got him there.

The corridor, too, was better than the one in the New Mexico. Outside the lift there was a Louis Quinze sort of table with a vase of real flowers on it. By the time Stan had reached the door of No. 303 he was more pleased than ever to find himself visiting someone in that class of hotel.

But, for once, Mr Karlin did not seem pleased to see him. This time he wasn't smiling.

'You ran it pretty fine, didn't you?' he asked.

This surprised Stan. He looked down at his watch. It was the large watch that Mr Karlin had given him.

'It's only just six. Six o'clock exactly, like you said.'

'I didn't mean tonight,' Mr Karlin told him. 'I meant all this week.'

'Could put it like that,' Stan agreed with him. 'You said you wouldn't do anything till Saturday.'

Mr Karlin's smile returned for a moment, and then disappeared again.

'Well, I haven't, have I?' he said.

There was a pause; rather a long pause. Then it was Stan who spoke first.

'What exactly do you want me to do?' he asked.

Mr Karlin put his hand on Stan's shoulder, and suggested that they should both sit down. But he would get Stan a drink first, he said. Whisky with water and no ice it was, wasn't it? Funny thing was, he added, that ever since he'd been mixing it like that for Stan he'd got to like it himself that way too.

When he came back he turned the question round again.

'What are you prepared to do?' he asked. 'That's what matters.'

Stan did not answer immediately. Nor did he start to drink his whisky and water. He was determined to remain entirely clear-headed this evening. When Mr Karlin handed him his glass, he put it down on the table beside him giving it a little extra push just so that it would be out of reach if he were absent-mindedly to reach out for it.

It was time now for the speech that he had been getting ready and polishing up all day.

'Well, I've been thinking about what you and Mr Svenstrom said to me,' he began. 'And it makes a lot of sense. There's a whole gold mine of official secrets buried inside Central Filing. Only Admiralty, mind you. But it's all there.' He gave a little cough. 'Too much, in fact. I'd have to know what you were looking for, wouldn't I, before I could do anything about getting it for you?'

For a moment, Stan thought that Mr Karlin's smile had died away. But, an instant later, there it was again, bland and embracing as ever. It was only the eyes that seemed to belong to a different face altogether.

'That's where you're right again,' he said. 'No point in coming up with stuff the agency's got already. Who wants to print stale news? It's the big break we're after. Kind of thing Reuter's and the PA don't provide. Technical information. Electronic – and mechanical. Sonar, range-finders, anti-submarine devices, radar, mine-laying, rockets, nuclear fuel. That sort of stuff. And no good without the details. Specifications, blue-prints, test-charts, everything.'

Stan took a long, deep breath.

'I can get it for you,' he said.

Mr Karlin's eyes were still fixed on him.

'How?' he asked.

'I told you,' he replied. 'It's all there. I'm in charge of it. No difficulty. Get you what you want any time.'

Mr Karlin was smiling again. He broke off for a moment and began reaching down into his pocket.

'Ever seen one of these before?' he asked.

It was an oversize wrist-chronometer that he had placed on the table; a duplicate of the one that Stan was already wearing. Mr Karlin pushed it towards him.

'Take a good look at it,' he said.

'I don't have to,' he told him. 'You gave me one. I've got it on now.'

He slid back his shirt-cuff so that Mr Karlin could see.

But Mr Karlin did not seem to be impressed. He pushed the watch that was lying there on the table nearer still.

'Just to please me,' he said. 'Could be a different model, you know.'

Stan picked the watch up and examined it carefully. Then he placed it on his wrist alongside the other one.

'Same model,' he told him. 'No differences.'

This amused Mr Karlin.

'And I thought you were a bright one,' he observed. 'One of the really bright ones.'

He leant across and took the watch away from Stan. Then he held it up in front of him, dangling it there by the strap.

'One of the bright ones and he doesn't know a watch from a camera,' Mr Karlin went on. He was pointing at the watch on Stan's wrist as he was speaking. 'That watch tells the time,' he said. 'This watch' – here he joggled up and down the one that he was holding – 'takes pictures. Micro pictures. Get a lot of micro information into a watch that size.'

Stan reached out his hand. He wanted to take another look at the watch. But Mr Karlin only shook his head.

'All in good time,' he said. 'You'll be taking it home with you. And I want you to practise with it. Get used to it. Make it second nature. I don't want documents. I just want microfilm. And I want the best quality. You should find it easy. You're a photographer.'

By now Mr Karlin had strapped the watch onto his own wrist and was holding it face downwards over the evening newspaper.

'Make sure the light's O.K. Keep the camera face square with the paper. Six-inch focus.' He was speaking rapidly, almost as if he had been reading from the instruction handbook. 'Press the winder button and' – here Mr Karlin raised his tongue to his palate and brought it down again with the noise that children make when playing at horses – 'you've got your picture. Fifty-eight in each cartridge.'

It seemed to Stan that Mr Karlin had finished. But Mr Karlin had something else to say.

'And only one cartridge at a time,' he said. 'No spares. Wouldn't look good if they found one of these on you.'

Stan nodded understandingly.

'When d'you want me to start using it?' he asked.

'Up to you,' Mr Karlin told him. 'Depends on when you want to get paid. Cash on results from now on. No pictures, no payments.'

Stan was smiling back at Mr Karlin.

'You'll get your pictures all right.'

It gave Stan a pleasant sense of superiority to be able to talk to Mr Karlin in that way. That morning he'd still been frightened of him. Now it was almost a sense of pity that he felt.

He put out his hand to take the watch.

'Could I have another look at it, please?' he asked. 'I don't see how it works. Not with a lens that size. Not at six-inch focus, I mean.'

It was while Stan was re-examining it, that Mr Karlin took the opportunity to give him some good advice. He had become very friendly again, warm and considerate as Stan had first remembered him.

'And if you take a tip from me,' he said, 'you'll open a separate bank account. It's nobody's business but yours where the money comes from. But don't go spending it. Not all at once, I mean. It's the neighbours, you know. They notice things. They talk. Just play it quietly and you're onto a small fortune.'

As he said it, Mr Karlin began buttoning up his coat as though getting ready to go. Then he broke off for a moment.

'And remember which one of the watches you're wearing,' he said. 'Put the other one away. Out of sight somewhere. You don't want everyone to know that you're a man with two wrist-watches.'

Chapter 23

Even though Beryl hadn't liked Stan's late return on the Friday evening, the rest of the week-end turned out to be an unusually pleasant one.

There were two reasons for this. First, Marleen's teacher had given her a 'Good' for reading as well as for dancing; and, secondly, Beryl had decided to change her make-up. Brunette as she was, she had gone straight over from crushed loganberry to bright, shrieking geranium. And not just lipstick, either: her finger-nails were now pink and brilliant, too. And her powder was three shades lighter. But not her eye-shadow. By comparison, that looked darker still. Beryl had good eyes: they were naturally deepset. And, with the dark eye-shadow contrasting with the pale cheeks and with the two deep wings of ebony hair that framed her face, they appeared cavernous.

It was only perhaps that the contrast was too great. It gave her an astonished, rather startled expression; and she realized right from the start that she would have to be careful about what she wore. The Mexican housecoat was on its last legs anyhow. But, in the meantime, the effect of the bronze Sun-God buttons and the bright geranium of the make-up was certainly striking enough. Beryl herself was distinctly pleased with it.

It may have been because of the relaxed almost idyllic domestic atmosphere that Stan went out and bought the idiotic, drinking-bird novelty; and it was certainly impulse-buying of the most irresponsible kind. Every morning on his way to the station he had seen the ridiculous creature, with its overlong beak and its huge cluster of brightly-coloured tail feathers, standing in the window of Hodgett's, the news-agents. Scientifically automated, the bird would lean forward to take a sip from a wine-glass; then, having drunk its fill, it would fling its head back, steady itself, and return to a dignified upright position – only to be assailed a moment later by the same fierce, ungovernable thirst that made it drive its beak deep into the wine-glass again.

The price of three-and-sixpence seemed reasonable enough for what promised to be practically non-stop entertainment. Stan felt that it was exactly the sort of sum that he could afford to spend without alerting the neighbours; and, because for once he was in a carefree, playful mood, he set the bird up on the mantelshelf in the lounge, wine-glass within beak-reach, without saying anything about it to Beryl.

It was not until around five-thirty that the phone rang, and Beryl went through to answer it. Secretly, she was in dread of that phone. Too often it roused hopes, and then it dashed them. By now she had even taken to answering it in her Aim-aifraid-yew-muest-hev-ai-roeing-nember kind of voice. But tonight it was all right. It was Cliff. He was driving up from the coast, he said, and he had a friend with him. Could they please both drop in. Only for drinks, he explained. Not to go to any trouble.

Lovely, lovely, Beryl had told him. Just what she and Stan needed was to see someone. And then, as she hung up, the misery of her kind of life came back to her. There wasn't anything in No. 16 to offer anyone. If she and Stan had been card-carrying Rechabites, the house could not have been drier. She was very close to tears as she remembered the humiliation that she would feel when she had to admit to Cliff that there was nothing stronger than Nescafé that she could offer to him or to his friend.

That was why she was so surprised when Stan suggested that he should go out and buy something. And more than surprised; annoyed. She felt herself in need of telling Stan what, for a woman, it felt like not to be able even to invite a couple of friends in for a quiet drink. And, now that Stan had volunteered, she was left with a hungry, deprived feeling.

It was worse still when Stan returned. He hadn't just bought something: he had laid down the beginnings of a cellar. One by one he set out the exhibits on the table in the alcove. There was a bottle of medium sherry, half-a-bottle of Gordon's gin, half-a-bottle of Johnnie Walker, a heavily-stoppered bottle of soda water and half a dozen small bottles of Bitter Lemon.

'Everyone's drinking them nowadays,' he said, lifting the last of the Bitter Lemons out of the shopping-bag. 'Either with gin, or plain just as they are. They're quite the thing.'

For a moment Beryl became a mother again.

'Well, for goodness' sake, keep them out of Marleen's way,' she said. 'You know what happens to Marleen if she has anything fizzy. We don't want that sort of thing tonight, do we?'

Then Beryl remembered that it was really as a wife and not as a mother that she should be talking to him.

'I don't suppose you thought of buying anything to eat like, did you? Not some nuts or cheese straws or something?'

And once more Stan upset her. Slowly, as though deliberately being irritating, he reached into the pocket of his sports coat and brought out a flat cardboard box. 'Cocktail Savouries' it said on the lid. And there was a picture in colour of a whole happy family, grandparents, toddlers and all, busily munching away at them. 'Real cheese' the label said; and when he was buying it, Stan had found himself wondering what imitation cheese would taste like.

'These do?' he asked.

His voice sounded flat and casual. His mind wasn't even on the cheese biscuits at all. He was, in fact, still thinking how clever he had been to buy all that drink without drawing attention to himself. Bearing in mind what Mr Karlin had said, Stan had been careful to go from shop to shop, picking up the sherry at the International Stores, the half-bottle of Gordon's at the Red Lion off-licence, and the Johnnie Walker at the Victoria Wine shop: that way nobody could possibly think that they had suddenly come into a fortune round at No. 16 Kendal Terrace.

And paying for it all had been so easy. He'd merely had to extract four one-pound notes from the last wad that Mr Karlin had given him. He was glad now that he hadn't paid that lot into the bank along with the first advance; there was a pleasantly independent and privileged feeling about having ready cash always on the premises. Even so, he was careful. He didn't intend that the money should simply be frittered away. When he got back home from his round of shopping, he put the change – all eleven-and-sixpence of it – back into the envelope with the bank-notes.

Because it was to be kept easy and informal, Beryl decided that she would wear her other housecoat, the Mandarin one made of Chinese silk. It had come all the way from Hong Kong, but it somehow didn't *feel* like silk. More like nylon, really. It sent shudders right through you if you ran your nail along it the wrong way. All the same, she was fond of it. And, when she had it on, she made a point of sitting back in her chair with her wrists raised slightly upwards so that the big, floppy sleeves would gradually go sliding back all the way down to her elbows. No matter how miserable she might be about other things, she could always console herself by remembering that, thank God, her arms were still the shape they were when she had been a girl.

Together with her heel-less sandals with the embroidered fronts, the whole effect ought, she reckoned, to be about right for casual, Saturday-night entertaining. And she told Stan to go upstairs and change out of that awful old sports coat of his. Even so, the evening did not turn out to be quite the success for which she had been hoping. Of course, it was lovely having Cliff in the house again, and it had been sweet of him to want to come. But to bring a girl like that with him! It only went to show how desperate he must be, how frustrated for the real thing.

For a start, Beryl thought that it was nothing short of ridiculous of Cliff's friend to wear that sort of a costume for a day at the seaside. Even the chiffon scarf would have been too much. And for any girl with a really olive complexion – not just brunette like Beryl's but positively oily – the light make-up was simply wrong. It made her look common. The moment she saw her, Beryl knew that she wasn't going to like her. And she was only glad that, while she was getting ready, she had decided against the two wide, gold-looking bangles that she usually wore. Cliff's friend had on a pair exactly like them.

Her voice, too, annoyed Beryl. And the things that she said. She kept explaining that she'd no idea that Cliff had ever known Beryl so well, that he had never told her. Rubbing it in, Beryl thought it was. And she could not help noticing that, while she was talking, she kept glancing from one to the other, from her to Cliff, from Cliff to Stan and then back to Cliff again. She made it perfectly plain that in her mind there was something entirely incomprehensible about the whole arrangement.

Even the celluloid bird, endlessly swinging backwards and forwards on the mantelshelf, did nothing to add to the fun. If only Cliff had known, he said, he could have brought one along with him. Come to think of it, he could have brought a whole caseful: he had been distributing them for years. Cliff's girl-friend looked at him admiringly as he said it.

Considering the amount of drink that Stan had bought they got through very little of it. Cliff's girl didn't drink at all, she said, adding confidingly that Cliff didn't like girls who did. Beryl had a single glass of sherry. Cliff asked for his usual whisky-and-soda. And Stan, rather to Beryl's surprise, drank whisky-and-water.

It was only little Marleen who really availed herself. The Bitter Lemon, straight from the refrigerator, was ranged on the dresser ready to be carried through to the lounge. Feeling sure that it had been got in specially for her, she drank first one bottle of it and then another. In consequence, she had to leave the party quite suddenly. And, because Beryl had to go upstairs and stay with her for rather a long time, Stan found himself alone with the two of them.

Naturally, he did his best to keep things going. For Beryl's sake as much as for his own he wanted to show what a jolly, swinging sort of life went on in Kendal Terrace. But his heart wasn't really in it. He was thinking of other things; of the wad of one-pound notes and the small change stuffed behind the packets of matt-surface printing paper in the bottom drawer of his cabinet; and of being able to double his salary practically whenever he felt like it; and of the big bogus wrist-watch concealed in an old developer tin.

But most of all he was thinking about his plan. That wonderful water-tight plan of his that he was going to put into operation tomorrow. At lunchtime, to be exact. From one o'clock till two o'clock Stan was in sole charge of Central Filing.

In sole charge, and alone there.

Considering that he hadn't been able to use an exposure meter and that, even standing at a proper photographic bench, fixed-focus work always presents its own difficulties, the samples he produced were surprisingly good. Mr Karlin himself said so.

When he came to give that as his opinion, the two of them were sitting side by side on the couch in Mr Karlin's hotel suite. This time it was in Bloomsbury. The hotel itself was a small private one of the old-fashioned sort. It bore its name – the Bellcham – on a polished brass plate beside the bell-push; and, inside, a floral arrangement of artificial roses bloomed all the year round on a mahogany side-table. Not that Mr Karlin minded whether the hotel was in the top class or not. He was there only for one night, he said; Mr Karlin, it seemed, rarely occupied the same hotel bed for two nights running.

He leant forward as he was speaking and then passed the watch-maker's lens over to Stan. The tiny strip of micro-film lay on the pad set across his knees.

'They'll print up fine,' he said. 'They're real working drawings.'

Stan did not reply immediately. He was busy peering down through the lens. And it was exactly as Mr Karlin had said. 'INDUCTION NOZZLE RE-ENTRANT VALVE DETAIL', reference number 'B117/43/B2' and the overall identification 'ABG/3005/Y/474' stood out as clearly as if they had been newspaper headlines.

Stan could not help admiring the miniature camera that had taken these shots. There was no maker's name on it anywhere. Not even any hint of the country of origin. But it couldn't be German or American, Stan decided. All craftsmen leave their national signature plainly inscribed upon such work. There was no trace of Leipzig or Rochester, N.Y. on this one. The camera was Japanese, possibly. Or Czech. Or Russian. Russian most likely. Somewhere from behind the Iron Curtain anyhow.

But it wasn't only the camera that Stan was admiring. He was admiring himself; admiring himself for having thought up his plan. His beautiful, ingenious, irresistible plan; the master-plan that was going to fool Mr Karlin while making his informant rich; the plan that was calculated to confuse and deceive the enemy, expensively leading him further and still further astray.

Because 'ABG/3005/Y/474' was simply Central Filing's own identification number. No one outside the department, and even then no one without access to the Code Book, could have any idea of what it stood for. And that was the big joke that Stan had cooked up for them: 'ABG/3005/Y/474' was the internal identification number for Leviathan. And Leviathan was the nuclear-powered underwater rocket station that had been scrapped. What Mr Karlin was paying for was a complete set of drawings, blue-prints and all, for something that, one by one, the NATO powers had all rejected; something that nowadays raised a laugh in Parliament or in the music hall whenever anyone referred to it.

The inside of Stan's mouth felt dry, and he had to run his tongue across his lips before speaking.

'These are going to cost you something,' he said.

He was pleased with himself for putting it like that. The words were something that he had rehearsed to himself over and over again. Even single sentences like that were important to him. They were all part of the process of teaching himself to be a different kind of person.

And it was evident that Mr Karlin entirely approved. He was wearing his very broadest smile.

'They're worth it,' he said.

'A thousand pounds like?'

The smile faded and went out.

'Have you ever found me mean about money?'

Stan shook his head.

'Then why don't you just go on trusting me?' he asked.

He leant forward as he was speaking and gave Stan's arm a little squeeze.

'And how would you like it? It's up to you, remember. Entirely up to you. Once a month? On delivery? Something in advance? Quarterly settlement? Lump sum on completion? You tell me. I'm easy.'

Stan did not reply immediately. He was stroking his chin with his forefinger.

'End of the month,' he said at last. 'Then you'll know what you're getting.'

'As you please,' Mr Karlin told him. 'But what am I to do about this?' He removed his wallet from his pocket and let a thick Manila envelope slide out of it. 'Had to have it with me in case you said you'd like it that way. Why not take it now?'

Stan did not want to show weakness. But, on the other hand, he did not want to upset Mr Karlin.

'O.K.,' he said. 'I'll take it. Comes to the same thing, doesn't it? In the end, I mean.'

There was no time to waste, and Stan put his plan into operation straight away.

On the Monday morning Mr Parker, efficient as ever, returned refreshed and fit-looking after his week-end rest, and Stan tackled him as soon as he got there, hardly giving him time to prop his golf clubs up in the corner beside the hat-stand.

It was the condition of some of the files that was worrying him, Stan said. Ever since the time of the false alarm when the fire extinguishers in the ceiling had begun spraying, the state of some of the folders was really quite disgraceful. Stan wouldn't have minded so much, he explained, if it weren't for the ones that were due to be taken out of circulation and sent down to the Morgue. Then other eyes would be bound to see them and, naturally, people would begin wondering what things were really like in Central Filing.

Mr Parker saw the point at once; and, when Stan offered to undertake the renovation work in his own lunch hour, Mr Parker placed his hand on Stan's shoulder in the condescending way Stan didn't like, and told him that it wouldn't go unnoticed.

That was how it was that Stan was at work down there in the basement with a savoury roll and a cup of coffee beside him while everyone else in the department was up in the canteen, amid the piled-up trays and the plastic sugar sifters, going through all three courses like competitors in an eating contest.

But only on Mondays, of course. Stan had been very particular about that. Anything more would look like overdoing it, he felt. And the one thing that Stan wanted was not to draw attention to himself. Nowadays, he even made a special point of agreeing with whatever other people said to him, just so that he should avoid becoming conspicuously caught up in an argument.

Overall, the work could not have been proceeding more smoothly. Now that he knew the fixed focus of the camera, it was all so ridiculously easy. First, remove the file and sign for it in the 'Out' book. Then take it back to his desk hidden away behind the filing-cabinets in the corner, lay out the contents one by one on the blotting-pad and hold out his hand palm upwards with the watch pointing down. The beauty of the whole operation was that it was so simple and straightforward. If anyone, even anyone from Security, should come upon him they would merely assume that he was winding-up his watch or adjusting the wristband, or something of the sort.

Altogether there were one-hundred-and-eighty-six files for Leviathan. Stan had got it all worked out. Left to himself, even with Christmas and a fortnight in the summer and bank-holidays and the occasional bit of sick leave, he could get through the job quite comfortably. That is, except for the size of the cassette inside the chronometer. The cassette would only take fifty-eight exposures. And, at that rate, Stan could see himself down there in the basement with his savoury roll and his cup of coffee every Monday for about the next five years.

Mr Karlin, however, did not seem unduly worried. He was getting what he wanted, he said; and he didn't mind how long it took.

'You get on with the photography,' he said. 'And leave everything else to me. If you get searched, I don't want anyone getting hold of one of these.'

He held up the little pea-sized cassette as he was speaking, and jogged it thoughtfully up and down in the palm of his hand.

'The watch is different. You might get away with the watch. That is, if they didn't know what they were looking for.'

Stan felt one of his shudders pass through him as Mr Karlin said it. The possibility of his being searched seemed suddenly to have come so much nearer; he could feel the hands moving up and down, frisking him. But Mr Karlin soon put everything right again. He was smiling when he came across the room to him. Leaning over the arm of the chair, he bent forward and gave Stan's ear a little playful tweak.

'Don't think about it,' he told him. 'It won't ever happen. Not unless you start getting careless, that is. Just keep at it, and remember where the money comes from.'

Mr Karlin's smile widened still further. He straightened himself and began patting at his breast pocket.

'I was nearly forgetting,' he said. 'You'll be wanting this, won't you?'

It was another of those fat envelopes of rather dirty-looking, used bank-notes that he was holding out to him. Only this time, Mr Karlin was teasing him again: he kept drawing the envelope back every time Stan reached for it.

The room where they were closeted was in one of the small hotels near Victoria Station. It stood in a long row of other small hotels, all equally run-down and sad-looking. And all identical. Mr Karlin had never before suggested that Stan should meet him there. Not that there was anything very surprising in that. Mr Karlin was scarcely what might be called a regular; more one of the moving-on kind.

For most people who live in the suburbs, British Rail acts as the great healer. It is the journey home with the evening paper that serves to bind up the wounds inflicted during office hours, just as it is during the trip back to town next morning that the scars of last night's domestic discord are finally washed away.

But for once the cure wasn't working. At least not for Stan it wasn't. It had been around seven o'clock when he left the hotel in Victoria and, by the time he reached Cannon Street, the rush-hour was all over. The station looked large and empty. The ticket collectors were standing about in pairs, talking; and Southern Region had laid on a whole trainful of coaches for Stan to choose from. In his favourite seat – right-hand side, facing the engine – and with his feet up on the upholstery opposite he should have been satisfied. But tonight things weren't like that. He was still resenting the fact that Mr Karlin had tweaked his ear. It wasn't the physical contact that had upset him. It was Mr Karlin's attitude that he resented. Mr Karlin had treated him the way an indulgent dog-lover might treat a pet spaniel.

Then Stan remembered about the money. Indeed, with the bulge that the envelope of bank-notes made in his breast pocket, he could hardly forget about it: every time he bent forward there was a re-assuring creaking sound to remind him. And, so long as he was paying him, Mr Karlin was, he supposed, entitled to behave pretty much as he wanted. That, Stan recognized, is the sort of power that money gives people.

What's more, in the meantime, Mr Karlin's money was certainly helping to tide things over. He didn't mind it nowadays when Beryl turned on him; he felt that he could ignore it. Or even, like tonight, afford to be indulgent. As it happened, Beryl was particularly annoyed this evening. And not unreasonably. She had been experimenting with a family-size, economy pack of a genuine San Francisco delicacy, called Kow Wong's Take-Away Prawn and Bamboo Shoot, prepared according to a secret recipe of the Old Chinese Imperial Court. Twenty minutes, according to the directions, was all that was needed to bring out its unique Oriental flavour. And Beryl had put it on at five minutes to seven. By ten past eight when Stan got back, San Francisco, Kow Wong, and the Old Chinese Imperial Court might all as well have been forgotten because the unique Oriental flavour had gone up in steam long ago.

By then Marleen was sitting up in bed with a glass of hot milk and a dish of Marmite sandwiches beside her, and Beryl said that she herself just wasn't hungry like, at least not by now she wasn't.

'I don't know why I even bother,' she told him. 'There must be something wrong with me. Really there must. It isn't as though me and Marleen minded. Don't imagine that I'd been looking forward to it because I hadn't. It was only . . .'

As it happened, Stan hadn't been listening. He was doing sums in his head. They were nice, comfortable sums. They made him feel good as he thought of them. By July he would have six hundred pounds of Mr Karlin's money to his credit. And he had just got the arithmetic worked out. This summer they would be able to relax a bit. Take things easy. Nothing ostentatious, of course. Nothing showy. No Cunard cruises or trips to the Caribbean. Just a quiet fortnight somewhere on the South Coast, with Beryl in a deck chair and Marleen lying on the sand beside her; both of them safe and secure in each other's company, leaving him free for once to get on with his photography.

Beryl's eyes brought him up with a jerk. They were fixed on him, unsmilingly.

'Sorry, dear,' he said. 'I was thinking about something else.'

'You would be,' Beryl began again. 'That's what I complain of about you. I might just as well . . .'

The fact that he raised his finger to stop her came as a surprise. In the ordinary way, he would never have dared to do a thing like that. But what he was saying was even more surprising. She let him go on out of sheer astonishment.

'I'd been wondering what you'd like to do about holidays this year,' he told her. 'I reckon a couple of weeks at the seaside might do us all a bit of good.'

Stan was rather pleased with the way he'd brought up the matter of the summer holiday. He hadn't forgotten Mr Karlin's warning. But, after all, most families on his kind of income managed something of the sort. It was only that, for the last two years, Beryl's other plans had cut across it. Two summers ago they'd had the expense of all that crazy-paving to convert the top end of the lawn into a patio and, next time, there had been the installation of the American-type shower in the bathroom. This year, however, if Beryl were to think up something at the last minute even that wouldn't matter. And there would still be nothing to draw attention to himself if the family packed up and went quietly away to a small seaside hotel somewhere; not one of the two- or three-star French-cuisine-a-speciality sort. More the kind that says TV room, children welcomed.

That, however, was not quite the way Beryl saw things. She was a great reader of travel literature and was more inclined towards Majorca or Minorca; or even Ibiza, wherever that was; though, of course, there was always one of those 10-day tours of romantic Rhineland with its castles and cathedrals seen through the non-glare glass of a luxurious, Pullman-built, reclinable-seating, air-conditioned motor-coach, or a trip round the fjords and Northern Capitals in a ten-thousand-ton cruise-liner that combined big-ship comfort and amenities with the distinction and exclusiveness of a private yacht. On the other hand, the fly-one-way-and-return-by-sea package deals made a special appeal to her and she more than half wondered about Bermuda. Or Malta, or the Everglades, possibly.

In consequence, during the next few days, the Pilgrim Travel Agency next door to the Post Office saw a great deal of Beryl. The manager even said that he envied her the kind of trip that she was planning, really he did.

That was where Stan had to step in. And that was where Beryl lost her temper.

'First you say the seaside. And then you tell me not *that* seaside. How was I to know? After all the Mediterranean's still the sea, isn't it, even if it is over there?'

She paused, thinking what a disappointingly small-minded little man he was, and how silly it had been, after all these years, to have expected him to see her point of view.

'It's Marleen I'm thinking of, not me,' she told him. 'All the others in her form go abroad like. It breaks my heart to see the way her little face lights up when the holiday postcards start coming in. She keeps them in her treasure-box, you know; all of them.'

In the end it was a picture in one of the Sunday papers of Prince Philip, lean and classic-looking, silhouetted against the straining bosom of a spinnaker, that converted her. Cowes was where the picture had been taken and Cowes clearly seemed a distinct possibility – it was only that, after the talk about Ibiza and sea-and-air combined holidays, she felt that she could not face the man behind the desk at the Pilgrim Travel Agency to tell him so. This meant that she had to go all the way to Swallow Tours in Station Approach.

And, as it turned out, she could not have been more fortunate. The manager at Swallow Tours was himself an enthusiastic Isle of Wight man. He knew it like the back of his hand, he said, and could recommend it whole-heartedly. But not Cowes. Not for children, that is. And not unless you intended to spend most of your time afloat. Somewhere more like Ventnor or Sandown or Shanklin, he suggèsted. Or Bembridge, perhaps, or Seaview or Freshwater – the places came tripping off his tongue like names in the Old Testament.

And not to forget about holiday camps – the better ones, of course – he reminded her. There was something about a good holiday camp with its free entertainment and its sense of companionship that even the best of the hotels could not begin to offer. Personally, he would go for the one at Blackgang, with the Swiss carillon and the illuminated water-chute, he said.

But here he had made his mistake. He was wasting his time, Beryl told him. She regarded all holiday camps as vulgar, and felt certain that they would be full of families with the sort of boys of Marleen's age that Beryl particularly wouldn't want Marleen to meet. Also, she did not in the least like the idea of being called in the morning by a bugle blown by the resident camp-master in a red blazer.

The manager, however, told her that it was not like that nowadays. Not in the upper price bracket, that is. Take Pineland Colony, for example, he suggested. Just a score of little detached chalets, more like log cabins really, all with their own TVs and individual fridges, set in isolation on a hill-top near Yarmouth, with a pool and a Trading Post and a Frontier Inn and a ranch for ponies in the middle of the clearing and an eight-foot stockade running right round the place to keep it private; film stars and radio announcers and people like that frequently stayed there, he told her.

The brochure was certainly an attractive one. Printed on very shiny paper, it was copiously illustrated with scenes of camp life showing the Beaver Pool diving board, the pony paddock, the Trading Post Boutique, the flood-lit reception area and, in close-up, one of the Frontier Inn's special prawn salads with real, Isle of Wight King-size Prawns.

All in all, Beryl could imagine herself being very happy there. Even with Marleen at half-price, however, the rates charged to the incoming summer trappers and prospectors still seemed to be exorbitant. Beryl pointed out that she could have done Corsica and back for less. But not in such style, not in such exclusive company, the manager assured her. And, when she showed the Pineland Colony brochure to Stan, she was taken aback to find that he didn't seem in the least put out. Nor was he. After all, it was Mr Karlin who was paying.

'It's only once a year,' he said. 'Let's give our Marleen something she'll remember.'

What with the surprise present of the yellow plastic bird that continued to take sips out of the glass in front of it provided you remembered to keep up the level of the water in the wine-glass, and the prospect of a fortnight at Pineland Colony, it promised to be the best summer that Beryl had known since her childhood. And the cheerfullest. It had been such a different Stan who suddenly hadn't minded about spending all that money on her and on little Marleen. She found herself somehow admiring him; even loving him a little.

And, in the meantime, there was certainly plenty to do. Like getting a complete three-piece suite of light-weight matching luggage and a brightly-coloured beach bag to go with it; and a few suitable clothes, ranch-style for daytime wear and something long and swirly for the evenings; with, of course, the right kind of bathing costume – she was too full-bosomed for a bikini – and above all, the sort of wrap that would go with a decent pair of sandals and one or two pieces of good costume jewellery.

Beryl liked bathing pools, liked everything about them – the bright greeny-bluey colour of the water, the clean chloriney smell, the sound of splashing and of laughter, the little tables under their coloured sunshades, the open-airness of it all. Everything, that is, except the actual swimming. It wasn't that she couldn't swim and was afraid of the water. At school she had been first in the form team, then in the house team and finally in the school team of St Hilda's High. It was simply on account of her hair. If she attempted to wear a cap her whole hair-do would have been crushed flat and she would have to go straight back to be scolded by M. Louis, and, if she went in without one, she would come out looking all Afro. In consequence, though a regular pool-goer, she remained untouched by pool-water from one summer to another – which reminded her that she really ought to do something about getting Marleen some extra swimming lessons now, before it mattered about her hair, too.

There was something else, too, that was nice about life the way it was at the moment. Cliff had taken to coming out to Crocketts Green almost every week-end the way he always used to do. And sometimes on weekday evenings as well. That meant that he was midway in between girl-friends, with no one very compelling even yet in sight. Not that he seemed to mind, Beryl kept telling herself. And no wonder. She was the only one he had ever really cared for, she was the only one who brought out the best in him. It was nothing short of heart-breaking the way he still wanted, *needed*, to be with her. Nothing could ever alter that. She kept remembering it all the time. She was remembering it now.

If she hadn't also been remembering Pineland Colony, she would probably have cried.

And then, when life at last seemed to be opening up for both of them, it was Stan who came in for a very nasty shock.

It occurred on one of his Mondays. With his savoury roll and his cup of coffee beside him, he was down there in the basement with the Leviathan file spread open on the blotter, and the desk lamp shining full onto it. By now he'd really got the knack of Mr Karlin's camera-chronometer. Even the six-inch fixed focus no longer bothered him. It was no trouble at all to twist the watch round to the inside of his wrist and press the winder-key. That was all there was to it, and Mr Karlin continued to say that the photographs were some of the best he'd ever seen.

This time, Stan had just taken his overall identification picture – the ABG/3005/Y/474 bit – and was moving on to the page with the reference number B/124/43/B2 when he thought that he heard something. It was faint; very faint. Hardly audible at all, in fact. Just a ripple in the air that reached him from nowhere and passed on leaving nothing behind it.

But Stan was taking no chances. He realized immediately that it was possible that he was being watched. That was why he held up his watch and shook it to make it seem that he suspected that his watch might have stopped. Next he held the watch up close against his ear as though he were listening for the tick.

Then, slowly and deliberately, he unwound the roll of Sellotape and set about repairing the frayed edge of the binder. It was a thoroughly neat, professional-looking job that he was making of it; real book-binder's stuff. The strips of Sellotape were all exactly parallel and, when he had snipped off the ends with a pair of office scissors, it was hard to believe that the manufacturing stationer had ever intended the binder to be finished in any other style. For a moment, Stan just sat there admiring the result.

Then he heard the sound again; faint and whispering as ever. It came, went away and, just as definitely, returned. Stan kept his head down and went on Sellotaping. The inside of his mouth had gone dry and he could hear his heart-beats. He knew the symptoms only too well. Any moment now the trembling might begin. And that would be fatal. It would give the whole game away if he were discovered sitting there at his desk fairly shaking all over with fear when he was supposed simply to be doing a spot of lunch-hour overtime.

But, by now, there was complete silence once more, the thick blankety silence of all basements. Stan began to tell himself that he must have been mistaken. And, as he did so, there it was, close beside him, the mere shadow of a sound, but present and distinct; and familiar. It was the sound of breathing.

This was when Stan told himself that he would have to act. Even if he weren't the one who was being spied on, it wouldn't do any good to his reputation within the department if there really happened to be a snooper down there in the Classified and Top Secret bay, and he had just failed to notice him.

He got up.

'Looking for me?' he asked.

And it was just as well that he had decided to play it that way, all brisk and open and business-like. Because, almost at once, there was the sound of a heel turning on the polished linoleum and then, round the corner of the end cabinet, head thrust forward, appeared the weather-beaten face of Commander Hackett.

And the Commander himself could not have been nicer. He had heard that Stan was doing a bit of tidying-up, he said, and had thought that he might just drop in for a moment to see how he was getting on. Locked doors and security screens meant nothing to Commander Hackett because he had a pass-key for all of them. It was, as a matter of fact, he confessed, the first time he had ever been down to Stan's particular little cubby-hole. And, he added, he couldn't help envying him because it was all so snug and cosy.

There was a rather coarse, nautical side to Commander Hackett, and he gave Stan a wink as he said it. The junior filing clerks (female) were what he had in mind, he gave Stan to understand; Stan could get up to anything inside that little alcove of his and nobody on the floors above would ever be any the wiser.

Altogether he was down there with Stan for upwards of quarter of an hour, gossiping about this and that. And, when he came to go, he seemed surprised to find how late it was. He looked at his watch with real dismay.

Then he turned to Stan.

'What time d'you make it?' he asked.

'Ten to two,' Stan told him.

Commander Hackett's eyes were still turned towards him.

'Nice watch you've got.'

Stan made no attempt to conceal it.

'Japanese,' he said. 'Cost a bomb if it was Swiss.'

Commander Hackett nodded.

'Clever devils, those Nips. That's why you've got to keep an eye on 'em.'

And that was all there was to it. Commander Hackett's face creased itself into the most casual of farewell smiles, and he was gone.

It was a full minute, however, before Stan felt able to move. His heart had stopped pounding, and he was breathing normally again. But the trembling had started up, and his stomach suddenly felt strangely cold and empty. What's more, he was sweating. Back, neck and hands, he was clammy all over. That meant that there was nothing for it but to go along to the lavatory and stand up in one of the cubicles until he felt better.

Ten minutes later he was back at work again. All the same, he was disappointed in himself. Not that there had been anything wrong with his behaviour in front of Commander Hackett. He'd carried that off all right. It was his nerves that had let him down. And, on the way back home in the train that night, he went over the whole business again, silently talking to himself as he did so. Talking to himself, addressing remarks as though to a comparative stranger, had become rather a habit to him lately. Without moving his lips he carried on long, rambling conversations, full of good advice and sound counsel.

'You've got to get a grip on yourself,' he kept saying. 'That's what you've got to do. You're not a small-timer any longer, you're in the big league now. You're playing with the blue chips, remember. There's money on the table. It's stacked there, waiting for you. So ask yourself one simple question. Just one. Are you serious? Do you want it, or don't you?'

Playing games like that, pretending that he was someone in a casino, always made Stan feel better, because he was always the superior one in the game, the old hand; the kind the croupiers nodded to. And turning it all into a game made what he was really doing seem somehow so much less frightening.

Cliff had switched over to a Mustang. Not that he had anything against Jaguars. Not against E-types, that is. They could certainly show their heels to most other makes, Italian sports cars included. But they had become too popular. In some circles, even common, in fact. Only last week-end he had taken a girl-friend down to a country club in Surrey, and that had made three of them: three E-types, all black with red upholstery, all with an extra bar for the Continental motoring badges, and all with an off-duty air hostess in a flowered headscarf sitting next to the driver.

Whereas, with a Mustang you were singular. And dominant. There was something about the whole frontal grille that was male and challenging and aggressive. You took on the other traffic rather than just slipped past it. Mustard-colour, too, made a nice change from all-black, and the louvred discs set off the white-wall tyres to perfection. Cliff felt himself spiritually and physically renewed every time he got into the car. Trans-Atlantic it might be, but it undeniably had class.

And class was precisely what Cliff was in need of. That was because he was in process of re-making his life. Not his private life; at least, not for the time being; a new girl, Jeannie, from British Caledonian, was helping there. It was his business life that needed renovation. And Armed Services catering was what he was working to get into.

Admittedly, professional opinion was against it; too much of a closed shop, all his friends told him. But Cliff had gone against professional advice before – and profited. He had also broken other closed trade circles – watches, garden furniture, reproduction antiques; and very remunerative he had found them, too. But nothing like the prospects of Services catering, and Naval catering in particular. Down there at Chatham there was, he felt confident, a whole rich living to be picked up by as little as a-penny-in-the-pound taken off this and that, and added on again somewhere else to that and this. A Mustang was, in the circumstances, exactly the kind of car he needed to show that any tender that he put in was likely to be a bit out of the ordinary.

Kendal Terrace was exactly the sort of neutral background against which the Mustang really did show up; there had, in fact, never been a Mustang parked in Kendal Terrace before. And Beryl, looking out of the window, was pleased to see the way that passers-by – total strangers some of them – paused instinctively to take in the full effect.

Naturally Cliff wanted to take them out for a ride, and naturally Beryl wanted to go. It was Marleen that was the trouble. This time Cliff hadn't told them that he was coming, had simply dropped in without warning. And long after Marleen's bedtime at that. Her good-night biscuit, her beaker of Ribena and her Enid Blyton had all been finished before Cliff had even got there. And Marleen herself, with wisps of her pretty silvery-gold hair straying over the pillow, was now lying there, her eyes closed, happily exhibition-dancing in her sleep.

What's more, Beryl wouldn't hear of waking her. Not with school tomorrow, she wouldn't. Cliff was secretly not sorry; he had known Marleen from birth and had disliked her all the way. The very last thing he wanted was to have Marleen in the car asking what all the switches were there for.

In the end, it was Stan himself who provided the answer. If Marleen couldn't be left alone he was quite ready to stay behind, he said. As a matter of fact he would, he added, even rather welcome it: being on his own for a bit would give him a chance to get some of his old photographs properly sorted out.

And, standing there on the kerb, waving good-bye to the bright, receding rear lamps of the Mustang, Stan let out a long, grateful sigh of sheer relief. This was one of those moments that he found himself so much in need of nowadays. To be alone, that was the thing. To be able to bask in his own uninterrupted presence, and to have the opportunity of carrying on another of those highly personal two-way conversations with himself. He walked back indoors, past the sunken pool with the little fishing gnome and his companions, and closed the Spanish grille of the front door behind him.

He was sorry that there was no whisky in the house. Ever since he had taken to going round with Mr Karlin he had found that whisky served a very useful purpose. It detached you. There you would be one minute, all humdrum and ordinary. And a couple of whisky-and-waters later you could be up in the clouds with your own private firework display going on all round you. He wouldn't have minded in the least forgetting all about his own photographs and simply sitting down with a glass beside him, planning that wonderful big new studio of his, thinking of the look on Mr Parker's face when he handed in his resignation, even just closing his eyes and trying to remember what Helga's voice sounded like.

As it was, he went through to the kitchen and made himself a cup of Nescafé in one of the new earthenware breakfast beakers that Beryl had bought on special offer at the Supermarket. On the way upstairs, holding the beaker carefully to avoid any drops on the carpet – pottery of that kind apparently didn't have saucers to go with it – he paused at the door of Marleen's room, and stood there looking down at her. She was certainly beautiful and, in her delicate, pale gold way, not really like either of them. *Fairy Child* was what he had called the best-known of his nursery studies of her, and it had appeared in reproduction both in 'Home Photography' and on the woman's page of a South London local paper. *Ice Princess*, he reckoned, was what he would call the picture if he were to make another study of her now.

For a moment, the thought passed through his mind of opening up his equipment case and taking a flash portrait of her there and then. But he checked himself. He had used the flash once before in Marleen's bedroom while she had been asleep, and Beryl had been furious. It might have blinded the child, she said. Or set fire to the bedclothes. Either way, it seemed, the risk was disproportionate.

Sipping his Nescafé up there in the quiet of his darkroom and with no double Scotches to brighten things up, Stan's thoughts turned exclusively to money. He checked and re-checked his calculations on the number of Leviathan files and compared it with Mr Karlin's scale of payment. He added up the interest on the money in his number two bank account and hoped that he was right in supposing that, if he didn't say anything about it, the Income Tax would never notice.

He even wondered whether Mr Karlin with his excellent international connections could not perhaps pay some of the money into a foreign account; in Switzerland, for instance, and a numbered one at that. About three thousand pounds in all was what Stan made it. And that was where he told himself it would be wise to stop. Three thousand pounds was enough to get Beryl and Marleen everything they needed.

That is, coming on top of his Civil Service pay, of course.

In a leafy, Surrey side-lane, the mustard-coloured Mustang was now parked. The lights had been turned off and the driving-seat and the front passenger-seat were both empty. In the back – Mustangs are fast rather than roomy – two figures were huddled close together.

It was the one with the elaborate hair-do who was speaking. And there was a little catch in her voice as she said the words.

'No, not now,' she was saying. 'It wouldn't be right. Not with Stan staying behind to look after Marleen, it wouldn't. Besides, I don't feel like it. Not out here in the road, I don't. Somebody might come.' She paused long enough to run her fingers along the back of Cliff's hand. 'Some other time, perhaps. But not tonight. So just don't go on about it.' Her head was on his shoulder and she slid down lower into the seat beside him. 'Why not come down to the Isle of Wight with us?' she added, breathlessly. 'Stan's bound to be out photographing once we get there. And Marleen'll be playing table tennis or something. Then we can be together like.'

Cliff was bending over her and his lips were close to hers. Beryl, however, had not quite finished.

'But not every night,' she said firmly. 'Just once. Only just once.'

203

Chapter 24

Oddly enough, it was Beryl and not Stan who began to be haunted by suspicions of infidelity.

It came to her in a flash, and she knew instantly that the facts were too stark and too compelling for her to be able to ignore them. There were those frequent, mysterious late nights of his; and the unexpected gifts, like that of the perpetual drinking duck; and his new carefree attitude towards money. Some other woman, she realized, must have taught him how to begin spending it. It all added up: it was part of one big, sinister pattern.

In consequence, she began taking stock of him, casting sideways glances at meal-times, wondering what on earth it could be that this other woman, whoever she was, could possibly see in him. It must be something to do with his manner, she supposed, because that was precisely where the greatest change had occurred. He was so much more self-assured nowadays. More positive. More easy-going. Yet, at the same time, more withdrawn, more secretive. And slowly the alarming truth began to dawn upon her. This wasn't one of those trivial everyday affairs between a man in his late thirties and some little common chit of a typist. This had the authentic hallmark of something far more serious.

And now it was not only every Tuesday evening that Stan was out, but most Saturday mornings as well. Practically desertion, she called it. Beryl had already decided that, if things hadn't changed by the time she got back from their holidays, she would consult a solicitor. And it wouldn't be legal separation either that she was after. This would be the real thing. Divorce; divorce, with alimony; divorce with alimony and with Cliff thrown in as well, she wouldn't wonder.

In the meantime, it was the Saturday mornings that annoyed her most. Stan had always been such an excellent shopper – quick, thorough and willing. He never seemed to mind how long he queued up to pay for things at the Supermarket, or how much he carried home afterwards.

That was why it was nothing less than infuriating nowadays the way he would set off on Saturdays, all smug and superior, to catch his usual train, saying in an indifferent, off-hand manner that he was just putting in a little bit of extra overtime.

Naturally, she didn't believe him. That was why she began going through his pockets to see if she could find anything incriminating. Not that the search yielded very much; receipts from Kodak mostly, an odd voucher for an office raffle, a paper clip or two and a screwed-up toffee paper; that sort of thing.

Nor need she have bothered. Stan's Saturday mornings were not a part of any permanent pattern in his life; just a passing and impulsive phase. At the very moment when Beryl was searching, Stan was in a first-floor front room in Earls Court. And the girl – a young and rather pretty one – was showing herself every bit as understanding as her calling demanded.

'I'm sorry if I did anything wrong,' Stan told her. 'Perhaps I did go a bit too far.'

'Oh, I don't know,' she replied. 'It's what you came for, wasn't it?'

'Not really. Not right at the end, I mean. It's just that I didn't seem able to stop.'

She smiled back at him.

'That's what they all say. But don't tell the policeman. He mightn't believe you. Anyhow, better luck next time.'

And, so far, Stan had certainly been having it. He had pulled away from the kerb satisfactorily, he had braked at the pedestrian crossing giving due notice of his intention, and now he was edging gingerly into the outside lane before making a right-hand turn. The instructor no longer even seemed unduly worried about him. He merely sat there, relaxed and reconciled, wondering how he could get a bit more spirit into his pupil.

'You're only doing eighteen miles an hour,' he had kept reminding him when the motorists behind had started to object. 'Step on it a bit, sir, keep moving.' Indeed, so long as he had been on the staff of the motoring school, he had never known a learner so polite, so unimpulsive. Running into the back of the milk float last week had, he felt sure, been no more than a minor misadventure, the sort of thing that might happen to anyone. Star quality, he was sure, was what he had sitting beside him if only he could really get him going.

Stan himself was determined that his driving should be nothing less than perfect. To begin with, there would be the full course of twelve lessons; next, he would pass triumphantly through the driving test;

and then, a whole month's more Saturday morning practice motoring with someone from the school as a back-seat passenger. By the time he took Beryl and Marleen out with him for the first time he was determined that he should be an experienced motorist with quite a few hundred on the clock; even something of a veteran driver, in fact.

And there was more to do than that. It all had to come as a surprise to Beryl. That much was essential. And more than a surprise, it had to be kept entirely secret. Taking driving lessons was precisely the kind of thing that Mr Karlin had warned him against. It was the kind of indiscretion that might hint at a sudden improvement in living standards. And that, Mr Karlin kept stressing, amounted practically to a signed confession.

In consequence it was under an assumed name on his driving licence that Stan sat himself down every time behind the wheel of the motoring school's Morris 1100. What's more, it had taken a bit of organizing to arrange about the false licence. Here Stan had been extra careful. For a start, he hadn't wanted to risk giving the accommodation address of the newsagent's in Putney from which he had opened his second banking account. And he certainly hadn't wanted to give the same name. His number two account had been opened in the name of a Mr Arthur E. Edwards of Wimbledon, whereas his driving licence was for someone called P. F. Richardson, living at another accommodation address in Notting Hill.

It was the spy-stories that Stan kept reading nowadays that had first given him the idea of using the various aliases; and it was his relationship with Mr Karlin that had first given him the idea of reading spy-stories. Even there, however, he had been cautious. They were paperbacks mostly that he bought, or cheap, pulp-trade American crime magazines. For him to be found with a whole library of such literature would, he knew, be nothing less than incriminating. He therefore made a point of throwing them away as soon as he had finished reading them; and, even then, never in the same place, never to establish any kind of pattern, simply thrusting them into station waste-baskets, dropping them into Corporation litter-bins, leaving them about on the upstairs seats of buses.

It was his own workroom back in Kendal Terrace that still worried him. If Security ever did begin to get suspicious that was the first place they would start looking. And with the watch and false driving licence and the extra cheque book staring up at them from one of the drawers it would be all up straight away. He had thought of dislodging one of the floor boards and constructing a hiding-place beneath or going up into the loft and hollowing out a space above the rafters. But he dismissed both ideas. The spy-stories and the crime magazines were full of descriptions of searches by MI6 where even the upholstery had been slashed open.

In the end, he decided on one of the safe deposit boxes in the bank at Wimbledon. That made things practically fool-proof. In the first place, there was nothing to connect Stanley Pitts of Kendal Terrace with the bank in Wimbledon. And secondly, if the safe deposit box ever should come to be opened, the trail would lead back only as far as the news-agent's in Putney. And the masterstroke of the plan was that he had already posted the key of the safe deposit addressed to himself at the self-same newsagent's. For as little as sixpence a week it could rest there safely. And once a month or so, just to keep up the pretence, he could take it out, go along to the Post Office, buy one of their ready-stamped envelopes and mail it back again. 'Snake-eating-its-own-tail' was what such an arrangement was called in Secret Service circles; and, according to 'True Spy Stories', there was always a lot of it going on.

That isn't to say that even now Stan's mind was ever completely at ease. It isn't possible to live two different lives both at the same time without experiencing a certain sense of strain. But the anxiety, the jumpiness, were made up for by quite a different feeling; and it wasn't simply a matter of the money. It went deeper than that. Self-congratulation was at the core of it. Stan was conscious of being aloof and superior to everybody.

Inside himself he was smiling.

'I've pulled it off, that's what I've done,' he kept repeating. 'I've got 'em all guessing. This isn't just feeding *false* information – all that's been done before. This is *real* information. They can check it. It's real. But it's the wrong kind. It's out-of-date. It's useless. And they don't know it. That's the big joke. It's useless. They've been taken for a ride, they have. And I'm the one who's been taking them. If people knew about me, I'd be famous. I'm Unknown Public Hero Number One, I am.'

In the meantime, the most important thing in his life was, Stan re-cognized, to go on being unknown. That was why he had to be so careful about his driving lessons, and about his eventual possession of a car.

It was the use – not necessarily the ownership – of a car that he was working up to; and this was all-important. Because if anyone should ever get to hear that he was by way of being a motorist he wanted it to be clearly understood right from the start that it was not an extravagance but an economy.

Accordingly, whenever he saw the chance, he kept raising the matter of domestic railway fares, bringing the conversation round to it in the most casual and disarming manner. That very day, over lunch in the canteen, he managed to establish the point most neatly. A Mr Holdsworthy from Sickness and Claims had mentioned that he and his wife were off on a charter flight to Morocco. Stan let him ramble on about seeing foreign places before you were too old before he interrupted him.

'D'you know,' he said as though the thought had only just occurred to him, 'that, mile for mile, it's cheaper nowadays to fly than it is to go by rail?'

Mr Holdsworthy demurred, just as Stan had expected him to do. And he was ready for it.

'Well, I can tell you one thing,' was how he finally wound up as two o'clock came round and the lunch-break was nearly over. 'I'm thinking of hiring a Mini this year. Quite big enough really. There's only the three of us. And think of what you save. No taxi to the station. No porters to tip. No hanging about waiting for trains. Just slam the door and off you go.'

Back at his desk down below in the basement Stan picked up his ruler and, raising it to eye-level, looked down the length of it as though it were a shotgun. It was an old habit of his; something left over from quite early childhood. But nowadays he did it only when he was thinking about something. And this time he was thinking about how clever he had been.

Of course, he knew perfectly well that two Second Class returns and a Child's was cheaper than hiring a Mini. It stood to reason. But it also stood to reason that he had to cover up for himself. He was only sorry that Mr Karlin hadn't been there to watch him do it. If Mr Karlin had been sitting at the table with the rest of them, he would very soon have realized that Stan wasn't just the raw, untrained amateur that he sometimes seemed to take him for.

Then, just when everything seemed to be proceeding so smoothly and the whole family future looked happy and secure, there came the disturbing incident of the man from the Electricity.

On the face of it, there was nothing to it. Merely the most ordinary of routine visits. It had certainly not alarmed Beryl in the slightest. She had merely mentioned it casually over supper by way of illustration of the kind of petty annoyances to which housewives are nowadays subjected by the nationalized industries; and that sort of thing was, she had added, getting worse all the time, not better.

Apparently, in the middle of the morning, the Board had sent someone along to read the meter. So far, there had been nothing remotely unusual in that; and, she had felt forced to admit, the man had shown himself to be thoroughly nice, polite and considerate. Actually on her side, as he had kept telling her. Because the fault that he had detected as soon as he could reach the box was something that could, he said, have cost the consumer as much as an extra ten or even fifteen pounds a quarter. For, with everything in the house securely switched off as it seemed, the meter under the stairs was quietly ticking away all the time, the little dials busily turning, adding kilowatts to the invoice; in short, defrauding the householder.

And, being the honest servant of the Board that he was, that man had insisted on going all over the house to find out why. In the result, he had checked lamp-sockets, power points, the fridge, the washing-up machine, the boiler, the Hoover and the spin-drier. He had even, at some cost to his neat blue trousering, clambered up into the loft to check the thermostat.

At first, Stan had been rather impressed. Distinctly grateful, too, if it all meant that the bills were going to be smaller. Then – and it came like a bomb-blast – he suddenly realized that it might mean that They – the dreaded, ever-watchful They – were on to him, and that this was one of those classic income-standard v. living-standard comparisons that MI6 were always conducting.

Then an even more intense alarm came over him. Alone and un-attended, the prowler had been left free to pry into the secrets of his darkroom, switching on his enlarger; playing with the red lamp over the developing dish; opening up boxes and drawers too, he wouldn't wonder.

In consequence, Stan panicked. Forgetting everything that Mr Karlin had told him, he made a complete ass of himself. Overnight, he became conspicuous.

It all began with the complaint that he telephoned during the coffee-break on the Tuesday morning. Making private calls within office hours was not easy. The Civil Service is very strict about the use of office telephones, and Stan was compelled to go along as far as the two kiosks in the corridor outside the staff canteen.

That was when he discovered that Beryl had been entirely right in her opinion of nationalized industries. They were not only intolerable, they were also impregnable. Trying to telephone to one of them was as forlorn as dialling Vatican City and asking to be put through to the Pope. The girl on the switchboard at the other end was calm and evasive. She transferred him to extensions that did not answer, and then passed him on to internal numbers that disclaimed all interest. Through her he made the rounds of Accounts, Engineering, Applications, Emergencies and, inadvertently, a display showroom somewhere out in Balham. By then, the office break was over and Stan had run out of small change.

That was why he put his complaint in writing. It was a good strong letter, full of words like 'privacy' and 'intrusion' and, as soon as it was posted, he regretted having written it. But by then it was too late. There was nothing to do but wait for an answer. And, when the answer came it made him go clammy all over from sheer fright and started up another of his trembling fits.

That was because one of the top men from the Electricity Board rang him up at his own desk in Frobisher House in the middle of a normal working morning. And, in a flash, Stan realized that it meant they knew everything about him – his name, his address, the secret nature of his employment, the tension of his life, his guilty anxiety. When he heard who was calling him he nearly dropped the receiver because, naturally, he had been careful not to write on official note-paper. Instead he had written on the thick, faintly mauve stationery that Beryl always used; the one with the name of the telephone exchange in Gothic lettering set sideways up in the top left-hand corner. And, of course, that was the number that the Electricity trouble-shooter had rung up.

Beryl had, in point of fact, been rather pleased to speak to him. That was because, week in and week out, so few people ever rang her up at all. And, after the ordinary preliminary courtesies she had been more than delighted to say, using the old elocution accent that came back to her so easily at such moments: 'Way not tray may husband at his erfice? It's the Edmeralty, you know. Aim sure he'd be heppy to speak to you. That is unless he's in cernference, of course. Thenk you so much. Good-bay.'

The fact that the man from the Electricity was so suave and conciliatory did not make it any better. Rather worse, in fact, because he didn't sound to Stan like a nationalized employee at all. The voice was altogether too smooth and too ingratiating. More like the voice of someone with a public-school background who, after Sandhurst, had gone into Intelligence.

Momentarily, it gave Stan a pleasant sense of inner keenness and intelligence to think that he should have been able to recognize the whole thing for the ruse that it undoubtedly was. He even asked the caller his name so that he would be able to ring back and see if the switchboard at the Electricity had ever heard of him.

But by then he was trembling so much that he could not even write it down. He sat back limply in his chair and heard the unknown voice explaining that it was really just as well that their representative had been so thorough because the fault was there all right, actually inside the Board's own meter; it was the customer's interest that they were protecting, the voice had gone on, and they had made a note to keep a special check on Number Sixteen Kendal Terrace in future.

There was quite a bit more of it all in the same vein and, on the surface, all pat and reassuring in a slick Public Relations kind of way. Stan, however, was not listening. Things with him had gone past the clammy, trembling stage. And it was always the same. First, the shakes and then his tummy. At any moment, he would simply have to hang up and make a dash for it. Quite a dash it was, too, from the Lower Basement where he was working, up one flight of stairs, and then all the way down the corridor from the Hammersmith end practically as far as Putney.

That is, if he could make it.

Chapter 25

Two months later and two hundred pounds the richer – Mr Karlin was always painstakingly punctual with his payments – Stan had all but forgotten about the man from the Electricity.

Admittedly they had been exceptionally busy months. For a start, Mr Karlin had begun putting on the pressure. He now wanted two photographic sessions a week from Stan instead of only one. And, come to that, he appeared to be under some kind of pressure himself. Instead, nowadays, of arranging their meetings in hotel bedrooms, he had taken to suggesting open-air encounters in places like Queen Mary's Rose Garden in Regent's Park or the Embankment terrace outside the Festival Hall.

On one occasion, there had even been a quite startlingly ingenious variant. It had all been fixed up on the platform of Cannon Street Underground station. A young man of average height, with medium-brown hair and wearing perfectly ordinary clothes – in short, entirely nondescript – had come up close beside Stan and had said out of the corner of his mouth: 'Your friend would like to see you tonight if you can manage it. He asked me to give you this.' And as he was speaking, he was passing over, sliding as it were, an envelope into Stan's hand. 'It's the six-thirty performance. Not the late one, remember.'

Just then the train had come in, and Stan had instinctively battled his way onto it. But by then, there was no further sign of the young man. Mr Karlin's friends, Stan remembered, had a habit of emerging, unannounced, on railway platforms and then suddenly disappearing again. Either the young man had been left behind by accident, or had simply turned on his heel and walked away. Probably the latter, Stan thought; and he didn't like that kind of thing. In particular, he didn't like being perfectly easily singled out in a crowd by someone he didn't know, and wouldn't recognize if he should happen ever to run into him again.

The envelope had contained a single ticket, for Seat 6, Row 'N', at the Leicester Square Odeon; and, all day, Stan was conscious of the ticket sitting there in his pocket. When six-thirty came, he was punctual and on duty. And sure enough, within ten minutes of the start, there was

Mr Karlin sitting down beside him. He didn't, however, even say a word as he handed Stan his wages; just quietly passed the packet across under cover of the evening paper that he was carrying. And, even though it was, Stan thought, quite a good film, an epic, that they were showing, Mr Karlin had quietly stepped out in the interval and not bothered to come back again. Stan himself had sat on right to the very end because he had been rather enjoying the photography.

What was more, with his mind comparatively at rest, Stan was taking up his own artistic photography again. Had driven himself to it, in fact, because he knew that any change in behaviour pattern was exactly the kind of thing that MI6 would be on the look-out for. And, like the true professional that he was, he found top form almost immediately. On the very first week-end he took two potential prize-winners. The first, entitled *Sun and Shade* – subsequently re-named *Sunlight and Shadow* because he found that he had another *Sun and Shade* already in his collection – was a classically formal study of the poplar avenue in the local Corporation cemetery; the other, simply called *Wheels*, was a daring knee-height shot taken in the Station car park. And it had a genuine International Salon quality to it. Even while it was still in the developing dish he could see distinct reproduction possibilities coming up at him.

All in all, they were turning out to be a couple of tranquil, rather happy months for Stan.

That was because, with Mr Karlin's money coming in so regularly, he had felt able to allow himself to become more indulgent towards the family. Only in small ways, of course. Nothing ostentatious, or expensive-looking: nothing that would betray his private and new-found prosperity. Just simple little things, like an eight-inch toy model of a horse in real leather that Marleen had suddenly set her heart on; and a Ronson table lighter, Regency style, to stand along with the electric clock and the room thermometer on the walnut bureau in the lounge.

He had even, on impulse, gone so far as to buy himself a new ball-point, a Paper Mate this time, to replace his old red one of unknown make which just lately had taken to springing back into its scabbard as soon as you pressed down on it to write anything.

As for Beryl, she confessed to feeling a different woman; and not only because of the Ronson table lighter. It was because of her dress plans for the Pineland Colony holiday. Some women, she knew, didn't mind how they looked; their friends didn't expect anything of them. But, with her, it was different. She had a reputation for being a good-looker; and, as she kept reminding herself, she could hardly be expected to carry the whole show simply on the strength of an expensive hair-do.

And, with the staff dance only six weeks away, there was also the urgent question of what to wear for that. Stan being Stan had not given it a thought and, in the end, she was forced to raise the matter with him.

'Not that I mind if you don't,' she said to him. 'Nobody's going to look at me. Not any longer, they're not. It's only – if anybody does . . .' Here her voice went all flat and chokey, and Stan was able to catch only stray phrases: '. . . nearly four years old . . . just a mess . . . been taken in twice before . . . all this dieting . . . nothing left of me round here.' Then sobs had obliterated the rest.

The whole scene upset Stan considerably. And not least because it was so unnecessary. With Mr Karlin's money coming in the way it was, Beryl could have had a whole new wardrobe provided she didn't make herself conspicuous. All the same, she was a bit taken aback by the way in which he agreed so readily, and realized that he must have been promoted even higher in the Civil Service than she had supposed.

With the way ahead now clear, Beryl was certainly nothing if not thorough. She bought the month's new fashion magazines. She listened to talks in Woman's Hour. She toured the Model Gown departments. Selfridges, Bourne and Hollingsworth, C & A, Peter Robinson, Swan and Edgar – one by one they all got to know this handsome, rather imposing woman with the white hair-streak who could not make up her mind between pale oyster satin and deep crimson velvet; who tried everything on; who made enquiries about alterations; who went away, came back and went away again. And all to no purpose. Because in the end, she decided that she would get something made. It was, she knew, a gamble. But, if the big stores for some reason weren't up to it, she saw that there was nothing else that she could do. And it was Madame Desmonde that she chose. Beryl had been to her before; had, indeed, known her ever since she had been plain, anxious Mrs Desmond over in the Council flats furtively trying to make a little, undisclosed money on the side because of that poor, sick husband of hers.

Mr Desmond, however, was dead by now and his widow had blossomed. She had premises just off the High Street, with a sewing room and a cubicle with mirrors and her own cardboard delivery boxes. In short, Madame Desmonde had class. But even she was a bit overwhelmed when she found out what it was that Beryl wanted. It wasn't anything simple or straightforward out of a pattern book; not even an advertisement torn from the pages of *Vogue* or *Harper's*. It was an artist's illustration to an article in one of the Sunday supplements: 'Edwardian Elegance re-captures Mayfair' was what the piece was called, and it showed a lady of very much Beryl's proportions against an opulent background of white waistcoats, chandeliers and potted palms. What unnerved Madame Desmonde, however, was the fact that the dress in the illustration had a bustle. Madame Desmonde had never tackled a bustle before.

But Beryl was determined. And insistent. It was the corsage that concerned her most. That was why her instructions were so detailed, so explicit.

'I mean I'm not so big up there as that lady, am I?' she asked, pointing with her forefinger at the top half of the illustration in Madame Desmonde's hand. 'Full, but not big like. So the dress wouldn't have to be so low as in the picture, would it? Not with me the way I am.' She paused. 'But I don't want that sort of all-covered-up feeling. After all, I'm the one who'll be wearing it. You've got to show something these days, haven't you? And if it's Edwardian what's it matter? I mean it's what they were like, isn't it?'

It all came out a lot more expensive than she had intended. But, she kept reminding herself, if you divided the price by three because by the time of the dance it would be four years since she'd had a new one, even Stan would have to agree it was remarkably reasonable. There were still, of course, the bits and pieces. As it was, her shoes were wrong. Her stockings were wrong. Her evening bag was wrong. Her gloves were wrong. And until now she had never even so much as thought of owning a sticking-up sort of hair ornament like the one that the lady in the illustration was wearing.

In the result, it was touch and go whether or not the replica Edwardian ball-dress would be ready in time. But Madame Desmonde, reliable as her old, desperate Mrs Desmond days had taught her to be, came up on the deadline. It was getting on for three o'clock on the afternoon of the dance when Madame Desmonde herself, in one of the Station taxis, delivered the three distinctive boxes; one for the dress, one for the foundation garment, and one for the accessories. Caught up by Beryl's inevitable enthusiasm, Madame Desmonde had volunteered to make the hair ornament herself. Fan-shaped and mounted on a comb, it stood nearly three inches high, and bobbed up and down most engagingly with every movement of the head.

Being so short on time, Beryl had arranged everything strictly on schedule. By four-thirty, Marleen had been parked with the Ebbutts next door to be picked up the following morning before breakfast so that they wouldn't feel that they were being expected to support the child; and by four-thirty-five Beryl was in her bath wearing her transparent plastic head-shield that was more diving-helmet than merely bathing cap. It was while lying back, letting the foamy bubbles drift over her body, that it was suddenly borne upon her how fond she was of Stan. Not fond, of course, in the way she was fond of Cliff; not excitingly fond, that is. More sorry fond. But fond enough to recognize how pathetically faithful it was of him to try to make up for all those wasted years – her awful time, as she thought of it – when he had kept her so pitifully short of money. Nothing, she knew in her heart, could ever quite make up for that; but it was touching all the same that Stan should now seem so desperately to be trying.

By seven-thirty precisely she was ready. She had intended to be sitting downstairs in the lounge in the Parker-Knoll chair over by the television set so that Stan could get the whole effect as soon as he came in. But the bustle had clearly not been designed with sitting down in mind; and, after the second attempt, she decided to remain standing, her arm on the corner of the mantelshelf – rather in the posture of the Edwardian lady in the illustration, in fact.

Outside it had come on to rain. Not ordinary rain, either. Real, automatic-car-wash stuff. Even from indoors, she could hear it lashing down into the gnomes' fishing pool, battering against the heavily speckled toadstool.

When he finally reached Crocketts Green, Stan saw that he would have to make a dash for it. And tonight of all nights he was in no condition for dashing. A slight headache early on and a touch of huskiness had developed into a steady nagging pain in both temples and a real sore throat. Also, throughout the day Mr Parker had been at his most impossible; arrogant, carping, contemptuous. He had even questioned Stan's knowledge of the new filing system and had then failed to apologize when he himself had been shown to be wrong. By

the time the office had closed, Stan felt that he'd had enough of it;
enough of everything, in fact. Going home, propped up in his corner
seat on the six-forty-two, and swallowing hard because his throat kept
hurting him, he had wondered more than once whether he could pluck
up the courage to ask Beryl if she would be prepared to call the whole
thing off.

By the time he reached Kendal Terrace the rain seemed, if anything,
to be coming down even harder. Even sheltered as it was under the over-
hanging canopy of the porch, the illuminated bell-push had a stream of
little droplets running down from it. Stan shuddered. He recognized
this for one of those nights when Beryl would expect him to take his
shoes off while standing on the door-mat so as to avoid leaving a trail
of dirty footprints across the Wilton. He had just got the left shoe off, and
had bent forward, balancing himself on one leg to remove the other,
when he caught sight of Beryl.

Remember that Stan was ill and tired as well as wet through. Otherwise he could not have behaved so badly. But the sight of her with the
bustle and the puff sleeves and the revealingly low-cut corsage was too
much for him. Or perhaps it was the bobbing-up-and-down hair
ornament that did it. Whatever it was, he temporarily lost control of
himself. For a moment he stood there simply staring. Then he spoke.

'You're not going to wear that thing tonight, are you?' he asked.

In his voice there was a mixture of fear, anxiety, pleading and sheer
incredulity.

It is to Beryl's credit that she, too, did not lose control. Not that she
was by any means wholly unprepared. Standing in front of the cheval-
glass in her bedroom she had thought that perhaps it was all a bit
much herself.

'Now you go upstairs and get changed,' was all she said. 'What you
need's a hot bath. We don't want you with one of your chests, do we?'

Because sitting down was impossible, she remained standing over by
the mantelshelf even after she had got rid of him. Then a happy idea
came to her. With the weather the way it was, Stan would have to
agree to the hire-car to get them there. And, using her other voice – the
carefully-modulated one – she went over to the side-table and rang up
the Reliance Garage in the Parade.

It may have been because they didn't know each other or, because
from Beryl's accent the night manager assumed that this was some kind
of a high-class emergency, that he sent the wrong car. The choice lay

between a Morris 1100 and the big Daimler; and he sent the big Daimler. It was not a new car. It had done its share of weddings and funerals in its time. But never a dance date; that is, not unless a whole party of revellers had all been setting off together somewhere.

By then, however, it was already nearly half past seven. There was nothing that Stan or anybody else could do about it. The thing was there, like a berthed liner, making all the other parked cars in Kendal Terrace look like so many abandoned dinghies. Holding his umbrella over Beryl, Stan stumbled into it, too stunned to say anything. It was everything that Mr Karlin had warned him against; and more. Sitting silent beside Beryl, one hand upon the wide central armrest, the other toying with the let-in cigarette lighter, he wondered how they could slip quietly in, and then out again, secretly and unnoticed.

After a moment, Stan became aware that every time they passed a street lamp, Beryl turned to take a look at him. Then, after a bit of twiddling, she found the switch that turned on the roof light.

'That dinner jacket's terrible,' she said. 'And that tie. I don't know what you look like. I don't really.'

The Maybury Rooms in Earls Court where the Frobisher House dances were held was part of the West London Establishment. You could live North or East or South, in places like Barnet or Ilford or Beckenham without necessarily ever having heard of it. But in the western quarter all the way from Paddington to Richmond, it was where everything of any importance went on. The Frobisher House dances had been taking place there for years; ever since Frobisher House had been built way back in the twenties, in fact.

One of the special features of the place was the car park in front. Mr Parker, in his own little Fiat, was just turning into it when the big Daimler made him brake hard while it cut in ahead of him. But the Daimler wasn't making for the car park. The Daimler was making for the main door under the flood-lit canopy. And this was unfortunate because, having discovered how the roof light in the Daimler went on, Beryl had left it that way. In consequence, when Stan and Beryl swept past Mr Parker practically at arm's length they could not have been more conspicuous if they had been in a display case.

For her part, Beryl was rather pleased with the driver. He had made the whole journey in under forty minutes and, once there, that gave her nice time in which to tidy up inside the door marked 'Powder Room'.

As the minutes ticked by one by one on the Maybury Rooms clock above his head, Stan stood there rocking backwards and forwards on his heels, wearing the deliberately blank, unworldly expression of all husbands waiting for their wives outside Ladies' Cloakrooms. And, when she emerged, it was even worse than Stan had feared. She was carrying a long, silver-looking evening bag. He had noticed it in the car, and had wondered gloomily how much it had cost. But what he had not known was what it was that it contained. And, as he looked, she produced a tortoiseshell fan and shook it open with a loud and challenging *frou-frou*.

It was entirely Beryl's idea that she and Stan should take up their places just inside the door ready to receive the guests. When Stan objected, she smiled that same superior smile of hers and told him not to be silly. Now that he'd been promoted it was, she reminded him, only what would be expected of them.

The person who was most surprised was the Honorary Secretary. But with him it was the other way round. Only last year he had complained to his wife that she wasn't taking sufficient advantage of his position. But, at the back of his mind, he had known all the time that it was quite hopeless. Neither he nor his wife had presence or charisma. Even if he had stationed himself in the very centre of the doorway with his spouse beside him, the couples would have walked straight past without even noticing either of them.

Whereas, with Beryl that was impossible: she did not merely welcome, she loomed. The handshakes were compulsory; and a bit intimidating. There was something about the way she came forward – long white gloves, bosom, smile, mobile hair ornament and all – that tended to alarm people. From sheer nervousness some of the juniors actually giggled. As for Stan, he stood as far back as possible; as nearly out of sight as he could make it, but still close enough to be able to warn Beryl when necessary. One such warning was just coming up. He had observed Mr Parker on the stairway, and he edged forward immediately.

'Just say "good evening",' he told her, keeping his voice low and speaking through clenched teeth like a ventriloquist. 'Just say "good evening" and nothing else. Don't make a thing of it.'

But it was too late. Mr Parker made a point of keeping himself in training. He took the hallway steps at the double and made straight for the dance floor. In that instant, Beryl was upon him. She was inescapable.

'Aim so gled you could come,' Stan heard her saying. 'Such a frateful nate, isn't it?'

Because he had got drenched coming in from the car park, all that Mr Parker wanted was to find a place somewhere over by the radiator where he could dry off the bottoms of his trousers. It was only after he had shaken hands and gone inside that he wondered who on earth the large woman with the fan could possibly be, and why Stanley Pitts, his Number Two, should be hanging round her in that way.

By then, Beryl was in her full rhythm. No one got past her. One and all, male and female alike, received the handshake, the smile, the remark about the weather. Even the drinks waiter, who had seen a lot of receiving done in his time, had to admit that he had never seen it done better. He summed up the situation and came across and whispered in Beryl's ear. In case she needed it, there was a gin-and-tonic, he told her, tucked in beside the vase of flowers on the side-table. From long experience, he knew that his tip at the end of the evening depended very largely on little remembered courtesies like that.

For her part, Beryl did not flinch. She stood at the top of the empty stairway until nearly nine-thirty in case there were any late-comers to be greeted. Then, and only then, was she ready to mingle and relax. She left her post and came forward, fan fluttering, to make the complete round of the Maybury Rooms.

Stan followed half a pace behind; too far behind, it seemed, for Beryl's liking. She turned towards him.

'Well, you might at least behave as though we were together,' she said. 'I don't know what's the matter with you. Really I don't. You've been like it all the evening. I'm only doing it for your sake, remember. Don't imagine I . . .'

She was interrupted by the approach of Mr Hunter-Smith. White-haired and courtly – he might, it seemed, have been supplied along with her dress – he advanced towards her, and asked if she would dance with him.

The invitation had come so early on her round – practically as soon as she had left the reception position – that naturally Beryl felt flattered. But sad, too, at the same time. It was, indeed, what she had always dreaded: it must mean, she realized, that though she was still as attractive as ever, in a mature, sophisticated way, only distinctly elderly men could nowadays pluck up the courage to approach her.

All the same, she liked the style of his dancing. It was dreamy. After so much standing about and so many of those gins-and-tonic that the wine waiter had kept putting down on the side-table at her elbow, she felt strangely relaxed and unanxious. If, then and there, she were to fall asleep in Mr Hunter-Smith's arms, she had every confidence that somehow or other he would be able to steer her through the maze of dancing couples and onto a safe seat on one of the settees.

By the time he did so, however, she was fully recovered; quite wide-awake and talkative, in fact. She invited him to tell her all about himself and, when he said that he was in charge of Appointments, she reminded him with a laugh that in that case he must know all about that husband of hers. Mr Hunter-Smith said he did, and let the matter rest there.

Stan, meanwhile, had been talking to no one. All by himself at the end of the Tudor Bar he was drinking a small whisky-and-water and staring down glumly at his feet. Even if someone had addressed him he would have been unaware of it.

'Stan, my boy, you're finished,' he was telling himself. 'Done for, washed-up and good as buried. You might just as well pack it in now, and call it a day. After this, they'll be on to you. They'll be watching. You're a marked man, Stanley Pitts. You're a Number One suspect . . .'

He broke off because he was suddenly aware that the band had stopped playing. Under the terms of their engagement they were allowing themselves the tea-break to which they were entitled, and already the Tudor Bar was beginning to fill up. Even at the far end where he was standing there was someone who wanted Stan's place so that he could catch the barman's eye and order the vodka-and-pineapple-juice for the young lady whom he had brought along with him.

Not that Stan minded having to gulp down his own drink. Something told him that it was high time for him to see what Beryl was up to. In the last glimpse that he had caught of her she had been playfully poking Mr Hunter-Smith in the ribs with her rolled-up fan. That was when he had gone hurriedly through to the bar to order himself his glass of whisky.

By now, however, Beryl was nowhere to be found. The fact that she was not in the bar did not surprise him in the least because he remembered that right back in their young days together, she had always regarded bars as somehow rather common and vulgar. The dance floor itself was deserted. And there was no sign of her in the lounge where he had more than half expected to find her: the small, separate tables there and the waiter service were so much more in Beryl's style.

When he did finally come upon her she was tucked away in a corner, and was whispering something to Commander Hackett of Security. And the Commander was eagerly leaning forward to hear more. From the expression on his face – one of simple, startled wonderment – it might have been her secret life story that she was telling.

That was when Stan went back to the bar for the second time. And this time he regretted it. Everyone else appeared to be having a thoroughly good time. He alone was on his own; and, either it was really happening or he was just imagining it, people seemed to be nudging each other as he passed.

What could not be entirely in his imagination, however, was a snatch of conversation that he overheard just as he had managed once again to elbow his way back up to the bar counter. There were four of them in the group, all juniors; and all with their backs towards him. It was the youngest of the four, a little copy-typist who looked as though it was already past her bedtime, who was speaking. 'She can't be,' were the words Stan heard. 'Not *his* wife. I don't believe it. I nearly burst out laughing. How could she?'

After that, Stan did not feel like waiting around any longer for his drink. He simply wanted to get away. And he wanted to get Beryl away, too; right away, somewhere little copy-typists wouldn't be making fun of her.

But it was not so easy as all that. Beryl was back on the dance floor again. And she had changed her partner. This time it was Mr Parker who had her in his arms. They were going through a rather stylish turn together, and the near-by couples were glancing admiringly across at them. Beryl's eyes were half-closed. Mr Parker's, however, were wide open. They were fixed hard upon her. And Stan could hardly believe it. On Mr Parker's face was a look of sheer doting and devotion.

Not that this was altogether surprising. After all, Beryl was by any standards a strikingly good-looking woman; and, at this moment, conscious of the success that she was enjoying, she was radiant. She glowed. The bobbing-up-and-down hair ornament had come off some time during the last dance and was now crammed away at the bottom of her evening bag. But Beryl did not care. She knew instinctively that it was her night, and she was happy. Everything had, at last, turned perfect. She liked dancing. She liked the dress that Madame Desmonde had nearly killed herself to finish off in time. And, best of all, she liked

Mr Parker. More than once, as she had felt his strong, athletic hand in the small of her back or had caught the rich, Fifth-Avenue odour of his after-shave lotion, she had thought how lucky Stan was to have nice, presentable young men like that working for him. There must, she supposed, be more to Stan than she had ever realized.

Oddly enough, that was what Mr Parker in his own way was thinking, too. Bachelor as he was, he harboured no hostile feelings towards women, no animosities. It was merely that he was frightened of them; frightened, but not uninterested. All that fitness-cult of his – the running round the streets in a track-suit, the twelve lengths in the swimming bath, the two rounds of golf at the week-ends – was simply his way of being manly without involving anyone who was likely to be womanly. He secretly envied those dull, ordinary men who solved it all just by getting married; and apparently Stan was one of them. What for the life of him, however, he could not imagine was how Stan could ever have mustered sufficient courage to propose to so magnificent a human being as Beryl; or, for that matter, how Beryl could ever have consented to throw herself away on anything so insignificant as Stan.

This time when the dance was over Mr Parker insisted on ordering champagne. It was only a half-bottle that he asked for but, because the waiter knew his job and brought it in a bucket, it gave their little table just the look of distinction that Beryl liked. Nor did she forget her role as hostess. In between sips and smiling across at Mr Parker, she kept lifting her glass to anyone who passed by or even happened to glance in her direction.

Stan was not among them. He had found his way up to the gallery that ran round the dance floor. Compared with all the fun and merriment going on below, it was a desolate, unfestive sort of place up there, with just the tops of the painted metal columns that supported the roof, and a row of tip-up seats that were used only on spectator nights. Stan chose for himself the end seat in the furthest row. From there he could keep an eye on Beryl and Mr Parker.

And what he saw appalled him. They had reached the physical contact stage. At the end of any remark made by Mr Parker he would place his hand lightly on Beryl's arm; and Beryl in return would let her fingers rest equally lightly on the cuff of Mr Parker's sleeve. All in all, amidst the hurly-burly of the dance, it seemed to be a secret seance that the two of them were having, a new and rapidly growing friendship, carried on in a kind of romantic Braille. When Stan allowed himself the

223

liberty of leaning over the balcony-rail to observe them more closely, he was amazed to see on Mr Parker's face an expression of sheer human yearning.

That was why Stan came downstairs again to say that it was time to leave.

The ride home in the enormous Daimler was quiet and uneventful. Conscious of her success, revelling in the part which she had played to make the party go, Beryl dozed. Like a happy child, she rested her head up against the hired car's upholstery and dreamt her own way home.

Stan himself was not dreaming. He was thinking of the consequences. And not only of what MI6 might make of it. He was thinking of the fact that, over and above the cost of the hired Daimler, he had a perfectly good season ticket that had been left unused, and that he hadn't got any spare change with which to tip the driver. Stone sober and despondent, he stared blankly out past the driver and wondered how he was going to be able to face Mr Parker tomorrow.

Or, for that matter, how Mr Parker was going to be able to face him.

Chapter 26

Things usually look a bit different, however, on the morning after, and Mr Parker showed no sign of any embarrassment whatsoever when he came down to see Stan next day.

All that was worrying Mr Parker were the holiday arrangements to fill in for Stan while he was away. An elderly and rather morose-looking senior clerk, the sort of distant half-forgotten cousin who turns up only at Christmas parties, was the best that Personnel had been able to promise, and Mr Parker saw himself having to dash up and down every half-hour just to make sure that the department wasn't getting itself a bad name. A fortnight may not seem a long time, but fourteen days of slipshod filing can leave a hurricane trail of chaos and confusion in their wake; something that may take months, even years, to clear up.

But, for the first time in his life, Stan realized that he didn't care. Just didn't care. If he had been Head of the Department that, of course, would have been different: he might even have had second thoughts about going away at all. But he wasn't Head. They – that remote, self-perpetuating, mysterious They – had decided to pass him by. And it was now up to Them to take the blame for anything that went missing, or got itself mislaid, or couldn't be found, or had to be returned because it was the wrong one when eventually it did reach its destination.

Stan, in fact, wasn't thinking about the department at all. What he was thinking about were things like a pair of blue canvas shoes with thick crêpe soles; and a couple of open-necked shirts with short sleeves; and a dark, preferably nautical-looking jacket with gilt buttons that he could wear beside the pool after dinner when Beryl was in her semi-evening; and a hat with a brim – straw or canvas, he didn't mind which – in case there should be a heat-wave.

'Everything in order for while you're away?' Mr Parker had asked in that clipped, CO-ish voice of his.

Stan, however, had just remembered that he needed a new toothbrush and a bottle of insect repellent in case the midges should prove troublesome. That was why he was a trifle slow in answering. But he pulled himself together before Mr Parker could say anything, and even managed to pass it off with a bit of a joke.

'Everything except old Boanerges.'

Boanerges was a code-name left over from World War I. It had been used to conceal the invention of a radio-controlled torpedo. The missile had, however, never worked properly. It had, indeed, exhibited extremely alarming homing tendencies. And when, in 1920, Designs Development Department called for the files to see if anything could be learnt from the mistakes of the already defunct inventor, it was discovered that everything about it had disappeared – description, specifications, blue-prints, everything. It was as though Boanerges had never for a single moment existed. There had been an Enquiry, a court martial, a couple of suspensions on half-pay and a dismissal. Not a trace of the missing papers was ever found. Nor did it appear to matter.

Even so, it was generally recognized as not in the best of good taste ever to refer to Boanerges at all; and certainly not to Mr Parker who did not like to be reminded how much of a new-comer he was.

As it turned out, Stan need not have worried about what Beryl might have said to Commander Hackett at the staff ball or, for that matter, to Mr Hunter-Smith either. They did not come near him.

When the pressure did begin to build up, it came from quite a different quarter: it came from Mr Karlin. He, apparently, was being got at from above. Results were all that he was interested in, he kept saying. He even went so far as to make the offer that, if Stan could double his output of pictures he, for his part, would be ready to double up on the money.

The last conversation between the two of them took place in the rear seat on the top deck of a No. 73 bus going to Hounslow. It was not a route – not in that direction, at least – with which Stan was at all familiar. All that he knew was the No. 73 passed regularly through Hammersmith nosing its way to places like Richmond, in search of its ultimate, late-night resting place, the depot.

And, the way things were, the assignation could not have proved a more inconvenient or unsatisfactory one. Stan had received a message asking him to be at the Hammersmith bus stop by six-ten. And at six-forty-five he was still standing there. Then, just when he was on the point of calling it a day and packing it in, Mr Karlin came sidling up, with no suggestion of an apology, not even so much as a hint of re-cognition; merely absent one moment and there, present in the bus queue beside him, at the next.

It was not until they sat down together, with the whole of the half-deserted top deck of the bus stretching out before them, that Mr Karlin said anything. And, when he did so, he shielded his mouth with his hand, keeping his voice so low that Stan had to tilt his head over to hear him.

It was then that Stan noticed how nervous, how unusually appre-hensive Mr Karlin seemed to be. One by one he eyed the other passen-gers as they came up the stairs after him; and then, when the conductor came along for the fare, he kept his chin buried in between the flaps of his raincoat with the brim of his grey trilby entirely covering up his face as he held out the money.

The awaited transaction was equally furtive. Mr Karlin produced a plastic carrier with 'Express Dairy' stamped on the outside, and put it half-open in Stan's lap. Stan had known what to expect. The bulge in the carrier that made a deep wrinkle in the word 'Dairy' was caused by a neatly stacked-up wad of one-pound notes. Stan slid them out and thrust them down inside his own overcoat pocket. A moment later, he dropped his own cassette of microfilm back into the empty bag, and that was that.

Then, something occurred that had left Stan really on edge. The No. 73 was trundling placidly along between the bus stops, with the rows of small, identical suburban villas sliding by on either side, when it drew up at one of the Request signs. A large, overcoated man got on and came up the stairs. Once on the top deck, he glanced round and then, finding that the rear seat was occupied, sat down one row in front.

That was enough for Mr Karlin. Without a word, he slid out of his place and went down the stairs at the double. The bus was well under way again by then. But Mr Karlin had not paused. Out of the side window, Stan saw it all happen. Mr Karlin jumped, landed, stumbled and recovered himself. Then, without even looking up, he turned into a side road on the left and, half walking, half running, disappeared rapidly away along it.

The man in the overcoat had not seemed even to have noticed. He unfolded an evening paper and was busy reading. But Stan was sitting bolt upright. He had gone clammy. He could feel the sweat breaking out along the backs of his hands, and knew that any moment now he was due to begin feeling sick; then the tremblings would be sure to start up, too.

There he was, all jumpy and alone and miserable, with his handkerchief pressed against his mouth just in case, on a No. 73 being whisked away into the night to an unfamiliar, unwanted destination.

The whole incident had upset Stan more than he realized; more even than that unannounced visit of the man from the Electricity.

A couple of weeks later it still kept coming back to him – Mr Karlin's abrupt departure, his flying leap off the moving bus, his stumble. And it was the stumble that disturbed him most, because Mr Karlin had gone right down on one knee and a sprawling, outstretched hand. Stan had never seen Mr Karlin at a disadvantage before. Behind that steady smile of his he had always seemed so calm, so quietly sure of himself. There was something strangely unnerving in the thought that Mr Karlin for once had been unnerved, too.

Mercifully, however, there was plenty going on at home to take Stan's mind off such things. The travel agent's reservations for Pineland Colony, together with another copy of the illustrated brochure, were already in the drawer of Beryl's desk; and the holiday itself was now only ten days off.

In consequence, Beryl had been kept unusually busy; busier than most women would have been, she kept explaining, because it was so long since they'd had a real holiday that she hadn't got any of the proper things.

To begin with, there was the matching luggage. Matching luggage was something which she had always set her heart on, and she made it perfectly clear that she would rather die, she would really, than turn up at the Colony's stockade gates with her two pale blue suitcases with the soft tops, Marleen's hard fibre one and Stan's old leather thing with the faulty clasp and the strap round the middle of it.

Even here Stan did not deter her. Indeed, he actually encouraged Beryl to take up the special offer of a complete set – four pieces in all – of light-weight, Jetset Executive air baggage that she had seen advertised in the Tourism Supplement of one of the Sunday papers. He knew that it was unwise of him; knew that it would be drawing attention unnecessarily to the family. But he felt that somehow he deserved it. To be able to let Beryl spend money like that, to watch her almost childlike happiness at being given new things, was at least some compensation for his own sleepless nights. Just lately he had spent rather a lot of the darkness hours staring up at the ceiling, thinking things over; things like lightning Security checks, and about being kept for months on end under observation without knowing it, and about plain-clothes men calling at the house; and about Mr Karlin and how he had failed to keep his balance that time he hit the pavement somewhere over Roehampton way.

Inevitably, too, Stan was beginning to show signs of the strain that he was under. Never freshly-coloured, he now looked washed-out and pallid; and there were conspicuous dark circles beneath his eyes. What was more, he was losing weight. Over the past few months he had shrunk visibly. Even his old shirts, the ones with the collars that had been too tight, suddenly fitted him perfectly again. And, when he was sitting down with his jacket open, there was a quite noticeable gap between him and his trouser-band.

Beryl herself had observed it. She was glad for his sake that the holiday was coming so soon. Indeed, more than once, she had half wondered whether in suggesting it he hadn't perhaps been thinking as much about himself as about herself and little Marleen. Not that Stan was selfish, that was the one thing that you certainly couldn't call him; and there couldn't really be anything the matter with him or he would have gone to see a doctor. All the same it was strange somehow, remembering her own headaches over all those years, her faintnesses, that awful I-can't-go-on-any-longer feeling, that when he was the one who wasn't well he had been so quick in making sure that they all did something about it.

Even so, when the day came and they were all due to set off, it was Stan who proved to be the one who wasn't ready.

As for Beryl, everything had been planned with remorseless and military precision. An early bedtime wearing the nightie she had worn since Monday – and all that she would have to do on getting up would be to pop a few things – toothbrush, face flannel and so forth – into the new waterproof toilet bag that she had bought specially for the occasion, and they could be away. Even the slept-in nightie had been provided for; it would be going into the laundry-box to be left next door with the Ebbutts, and delivered while its owner was away relaxing somewhere beneath the island pines.

Nor had Marleen been forgotten. In particular, knowing how

delicate Marleen's little stomach was and how even the smallest things upset her, Beryl had armed herself with everything that the local chemist could think of. He had even suggested that she should take along a bottle or two of pure Malvern water, and had been rather surprised to find that it was only as far as the Isle of Wight that they were going.

Stan himself, however, had done precisely nothing. He had been too jumpy. After all, going round in perpetual fear of having a policeman's hand laid upon your shoulder doesn't exactly put you in the mood for buying short-sleeved sports shirts and fancy blazers. In consequence, Beryl was furious with him. If he expected her to feel comfortable, let alone enjoy herself, she told him, with him in his tweed jacket with the leather patches on the elbows and those terrible old trousers that he always wore with it, then it just showed how little he knew about her; or cared.

But Stan wasn't really listening. He was looking at his watch. It was the first of the watches, the simple chronometer, that Mr Karlin had given him. The other one, the camera-watch, was wrapped up in an old duster and stowed away in the drawer in his developer cabinet. And it had been with a welcome feeling of relief that he had made the change-over. It was something to be looking forward to a whole fortnight without any of those secret photographic sessions at lunchtime, those cassettes of microfilm temporarily hidden away in his darkroom, those furtive encounters when they could be handed over. Stan felt himself beginning to relax already.

It was, indeed, this apparent lack of any sense of urgency that upset Beryl. Her two cases were packed and waiting; so, too, was Marleen's. All that they needed was to be locked and brought downstairs. Even Stan's, she imagined, would at least by now be ready.

Finally, she could bear it no longer.

'Well, if we're catching the mid-day ferry, hadn't you better phone up for a taxi or something?' she asked. 'You're not expecting us to walk like, are you?'

Secretly, Stan was rather pleased: it was all working out exactly as he had intended. Standing by for him at the U-Drive branch in Station Approach was a nearly new 1100. And he had attended to the formalities on the previous evening; all that he had to do this morning was to walk round, get in and drive it back.

Marleen, however, could not have been expected to know this. All keyed-up as she was after an over-excited, tossing-about kind of night, she suddenly saw the whole holiday at risk. They would never even get to the Isle of Wight at all, she feared. The other girls would think that she had simply been boasting about the promised luxury chalet within a stockaded enclosure, and she would become a laughing-stock. Unable to bear the strain any longer, she thrust her bowl of half-eaten Weetabix from her, and burst into tears.

What made it all so much worse was it took Stan rather longer than he had planned to collect the car. That was because he was taking no risks. Indeed, he made a special point of driving round for a bit – out as far as Edgerley roundabout in one direction and then back through Keston and Ilworth – just to get the feel of the thing. Not that he need have bothered; the little Morris was running beautifully.

And, as it happened, it proved to be another mistake of his to spring his little surprise on them quite so jauntily. They were not in the mood for it. When he threw open the front door and called out 'Any more for the Skylark?', Beryl told Marleen not to answer. She would deal with him outside by herself, she said.

Fortunately, however, the morning was a fine one. And it was still quite early; not yet nine o'clock, in fact. The feel of summer was in the air; and, though it was as yet no more than pleasantly warm, it promised to be really hot later on; probably baking by the time they were over on the other side of the Solent, Stan kept assuring them.

In England, going away by car is always a pretty serious affair. The grim, slit-eyed faces of the drivers, and the sagging, often unconscious bodies of their passengers are proof enough of that. There is something of universal panic, of sudden flight, of enforced expulsion about it all. The notion that it could all be voluntary seems somehow improbable.

The police have certainly got the measure of it. On foot, in cars, on motorcycles, in helicopters, they assume command of this annual retreat. Recce parties are sent out, and fresh trails marked across unmapped terrain and then sign-posted so that the vanguard may get away before fresh waves of refugees bear down upon them from the rear. Local control posts are established and emergency First Aid Stations set up. Even then, without the help of mobile radio this whole vast movement of peoples would become a rout, a stampede, a shambles.

And, though it was still only early June, the Portsmouth Road, when

Stan got there, was already full of other holiday-makers, all in small cars, all with children, all with just a little more luggage than the boot would take, some with roof-racks, even one or two with trailers; and all flat-out for the seaside and salvation.

Meanwhile, it had become more than ever apparent that Stan's plan of keeping the hire car a secret had not been a good one. At least, not nearly as good as he had hoped. For a start, Beryl resented it. Her opening remark after they left Kendal Terrace had begun with the words, 'I think you might have . . .', and miles later, right on in a different county in fact, she was still starting up the conversation with phrases like 'Why couldn't you have . . .?' and 'What was the idea of . . .?'

What was more, it seemed to Beryl that Stan had somehow deliberately contrived to spoil things for her. There was nothing that she would have enjoyed more than letting it be known locally that they were setting off by car.

She even knew how she would have explained it: 'One of those small saloons, you know,' the words would have been. 'Self-drive, of course. Actually, my husband finds driving rather relaxing like. But only for holidays, of course. He wouldn't dream of driving up every day just to go to the Admiralty. That's why we've never bothered to buy one.'

It was while she was silently rehearsing the speech to herself that a sound from the rear seat like a half-suppressed cough interrupted her thoughts. Beryl knew that cough, and ordered Stan to pull up immediately. From early infancy car travel had tended to upset Marleen. And Beryl was taking no risks.

'Not in this car, you don't,' she told her. 'You come with me.'

While Beryl and Marleen went along together to the split-pine toilet cabin which stood at the end of the lay-by, Stan pushed the driving seat back as far as it would go, took out one of the assorted toffees that he had bought specially for the journey and opened up his newspaper. He had been carrying it about with him, neatly folded in the side pocket of his jacket, ever since they had left home, and he was looking forward to it. He had already listened to the nine o'clock bulletin on the car radio. But that wasn't the same, somehow. He liked his news in black-and-white and, in the ordinary way, it was the read in the train going up in the morning that served to keep him abreast of things.

Not that there was very much in the paper when he did at last get down to it. Not much that was new, that is. It might have been yesterday's paper, or last week's, or last year's, or the paper of the year before that, simply with the names changed and the times and places altered. Otherwise, it was just the same: same murders, same divorces, same sports results, same scandals, same political uproars. And of these it was the last that, on the whole, promised to be the most interesting. On the last three nights in succession, the House had sat on until after breakfast time; and there was even talk of a Government defeat.

What particularly distressed him was the thought of the lady members. On this point he was at one with Beryl because neither of them believed that women should really be in Parliament at all. It was, he supposed, all right for men if they wanted to sit around, yawning and unshaven, into the small hours. But he could not bring himself to accept the idea of sleepy, dishevelled females. Beryl, throughout the whole of her married life, had always kept up a very high standard of appearance, and it was not nice to think that those chosen by the nation to direct our affairs were prepared to sink to a lower one.

His thoughts were interrupted by the return of Beryl and Marleen. Beryl looked all right to him but Marleen, he was forced to admit, still seemed pretty shaky. This appeared to be Beryl's view, too. Shut up with Marleen inside that split-pine County Council convenience she had become fiercely maternal and protective.

'And don't drive so fast,' she told him as soon as she was seated beside him again. 'You don't have to kill us all just to get us there.' She turned with difficulty because her seat belt was too tight. 'You all right, darling?' she asked. 'Not feeling sicky-wicky any more?'

Beryl had managed to wriggle round by now, and Stan heard the sound of a smart slap behind him. He knew at once what it was. It meant that Marleen had been sitting cross-legged again. For months now Beryl had been trying to break her of the habit. No nicely-brought up girl – if she had told her once she had told her so a hundred times – ever crossed her legs higher up than round the ankles. It was just one of those things, like not having the butter-dish on the table at tea-time, and remembering to say 'Pardon?' instead of 'What?' when you hadn't been listening.

Because of the delay and the enforced speed limit, in the end it was a later ferry that they had to take. And even then Stan doubted whether they would have got on it if Beryl hadn't insisted on the grounds that Marleen was an invalid. The Ferry Supervisor, however, was not easily impressed. He came over himself to have a look inside the car. But he could have saved himself the trouble. Marleen was not an unintelligent child. She had been listening to the dispute throughout. By the time the Supervisor arrived she was lying flat out, one arm trailing listlessly on the floor, eyes shut, her breathing imperceptible.

Not wanting any trouble at his end, the Supervisor waved them forward immediately. With the landing-ramp of the ferry all ready, Stan's little Morris was first on.

The rest of the trip was perfect. With the sea breeze playing on her face, Marleen made a quick recovery. Gripping the ship's rail in sheer happiness as the mainland fell away astern and the hills and forests of the Island came in view, she finished up the toffees and said that she felt hungry. But Beryl was taking no risks. Nothing more until they got there, she said.

She did, however, make an exception for Stan's sake. If he wanted to go down to the bar for a drink he was free to do so, she told him; but only one, she added, because he was driving.

She would not even have suggested the single drink if she had not, quite suddenly, again felt sorry for him. He was so obviously trying to be nice. Otherwise he wouldn't have gone to the trouble of learning to drive a car so that he could take them all away in a hired one, or buying the toffees for the journey, let alone booking them into somewhere exclusive like Pineland for a whole fortnight.

Being sorry for him did not, however, mean for a moment that she was actually pleased with him. Indeed, she didn't see how she could be expected to be. For a start, his whole appearance was so much against him. As he walked away from them in the direction of the bar, she winced: if he had been wearing bicycle-clips the whole aspect could hardly have been worse, and she found it hard to believe that the figure in the worn sports jacket and the thin, baggy-looking flannels really could be that of her husband. She herself had on a light blue Crimplene travel coat and a white headscarf. Her large, shoulder-strap bag – an extra in the Jetset Executive range – was pure white, too.

But Beryl was not really bothering herself about Stan. It was Cliff of whom she was thinking. That breathless, half-suppressed promise that had been forced out of her in the back of the Mustang, parked in one of the leafiest lanes in all Surrey, kept coming back to her. By this time tomorrow Cliff would be there in the Colony with her; next door, for all she knew.

The poignancy of it all proved too much and, putting out her arms, she drew Marleen closely to her. It seemed so dreadful somehow to think that Marleen, too, was a woman – or, rather, would be one day – and might find herself perplexed and agonized like this.

The sadness, the overwhelming sense of tragedy, brought tears to her eyes. Try as she might, they still came. But she was determined not to make an exhibition of herself, not up there on the boat deck of the Lymington-Yarmouth car ferry. Plunging her arm down into the white, outsize shoulder-strap bag, she found her handkerchief. And even those on the seat alongside her can never have known the real reason. Because hugging Marleen so tightly had been a mistake. There was now a long toffee-covered smudge on the light blue Crimplene where Marleen's little face had rested.

Spitting discreetly into the handkerchief, Beryl proceeded to get it off.

Tucked away as it was behind two other holiday camps, Pineland Colony was a bit difficult to find. But as soon as Beryl saw it she could tell that the young man at Swallow Tours had not been wrong. The brightly-coloured gates set in the high stockade, and the Colony's flagstaff with the Colony's flag – the letters 'PC' surmounted by a feathered head-dress – were proof enough of that.

And inside it was even better. The place had atmosphere. In the centre of the compound stood a totem pole that was also a signpost. And, because the language of the place was White Man's talk, the roughly-hewn wooden arms pointed the various ways to 'Trading Post', 'Beaver Pool', 'Scalps', 'Pipe of Peace Bar', 'Medicine Man', 'Smoke Signals', 'Trapper's Lodge' and, discreetly, 'Squaws' and 'Braves'. The shallow end of the Beaver Pool, the one away from the chute and the diving board, was labelled 'Papooses only'.

Beryl was pleased, too, with the accommodation that Head Trapper, the Colony's resident superintendent, had allotted to them. Admittedly, there was only a shower in the bathroom, but there was pink bed-linen, and a small fridge as well as a tea-maker in the living area. The name of the cabin was 'Hiawatha', and Beryl saw this as a good omen because Marleen had been learning the poem at school. There was only one thing that worried her. Marleen had a memory like a computer, and Beryl was more than half afraid that the inscription over the front door might trigger something off.

Stan, for his part, was entirely contented. He was giving the family just the kind of holiday that he had planned for them. For the first time in years he felt adequate. A feeling of immense relief and well-being kept breaking over him in waves, and he more than half wished that Mr Karlin could have been there to see what a difference that bit of extra money had made to things. When he had carried in the bags and moved Marleen's bed away from the wall out of reach of spiders, he sauntered round the place, his camera slung over his shoulders, whistling to himself as he strolled along.

Down here in the Isle of Wight, the afternoon sunlight seemed somehow brighter than in Crocketts Green, and the colours that much stronger. The sun-umbrellas round the pool shone back at him like variegated rainbows as he walked past them. It was then that Stan realized what it was that had been lacking in even his best work. *Hoar Frost on Wimbledon Common* and *In Winter's Grip* might be all right for black-and-white work around Christmas time, but they were not by any means the whole of the art. With Daylight Colour and the correct ASA setting, Stan suddenly saw himself as the new Van Gogh of Koda-chrome. The prospect overwhelmed him and he stood transfixed. Indeed, he stood so long in front of one of the multi-coloured parasols that the woman underneath it finally got restless and demanded to know if he wanted something.

Because it was their first evening there, Beryl decided that she should wear something simple, informal almost, and she made Marleen do the same. It was only Stan that she couldn't do anything about. The trouble with him was that everything he'd got was simple. Even when he'd had a shower and changed out of that terrible sports jacket, he still showed up as plain ordinary. From the look of him, he might have been setting off to catch the 8.10 as usual instead of wending his way through Wolf Wood, already lit by dangling storm lanterns, on his way to the Pipe of Peace Bar, with squaw and papoose following, to taste his first mouthful of fire-water since the three of them had reached the clearing.

Dinner was served by waitresses all in Quaker costume. At nightfall the hungry settlers gathered together in Trapper's Lodge and sat round a big open fireplace exactly as it was shown in the brochure; in the background, too, Muzak was playing softly. It was at once restful and warm; and Beryl was amused to see that all the other dresses were even simpler than her own. She was, in truth, rather looking forward later on in the week to showing the rest of them how a nicely-turned-out woman looked in the evening when on camping holidays like this one; women with a natural dress-sense, that is.

With all the food and the heat and the soft music, Stan found himself growing drowsy. Drowsy and contented, he felt that he could go on drifting through life like this forever. It was the BBC's nine o'clock news that woke him up. Stan and Beryl had by then moved along to the Tomahawk Lounge at the back of the cabin. That was where the TV was. Marleen had been allowed to go down rather earlier while the big Western was still on. And now they were all together again, one happy and compact family unit, with shared tastes and not a care in the world.

At least, that was how it was until one of the two news readers – the handsome, superior-looking one – suddenly spoilt it for them; and the casual, off-hand way in which he did it seemed somehow to make it so much worse. The Leader of the Opposition, he said, speaking out of the corner of his mouth as though the words were hardly worth uttering, had been denouncing the cancellation of the Leviathan project and was demanding a fresh debate. MPs of both Parties, he added, were in support of the motion.

It was the nervous start that Stan gave that betrayed him. Beryl felt the sharp, unexpected jab and asked him what was the matter. Stan did not reply immediately because he was listening too hard. As it was, he nearly missed the bit that the young man was telling them – still as though it didn't really matter – about how the Speaker had refused to let them have their way, and had reminded the House of all the other urgent business which it had on hand.

Beryl repeated her question.

Even then, however, Stan paused. He knew that he had to be careful and play it just right, not giving anything away but not, on the other hand, appearing to have something to conceal. It was with a little laugh when he did eventually answer her.

'Oh, just funny to hear him talking about it,' he said. 'They all come under me, you know – Leviathan, Sting Ray, B24, Cat's Paw. The lot. Might be back in the office again. Makes me feel at home some-how.'

The bit about Stan's feeling at home when in the office did not please Beryl. On reflection, she resented it.

'That's the trouble with you,' she told him. 'It's office, office, office all the time. It's all you ever think about when it isn't your photography.

I believe you'd rather be back there at this very moment than down here on the Island with me and Marleen, I do really.'

She had raised her voice a trifle while she was speaking, and the couple next to them had turned to look in her direction; Stan decided that this would be the moment for him to slip away.

'Just going for a breath of air,' he said. 'Shan't be long. Don't let Marleen sit up too late.'

Outside, the night was warm and beautiful. Stan felt pleasantly luxurious to be alone in it. He began another of his one-way conversations.

'You're doing all right,' he told himself. 'Just keep on as you are, and stop worrying. Don't let little things upset you. Play it cool and take it easy. You deliver the goods. That's all you've got to do. You deliver the goods, and leave the rest to Mr Karlin.' The flicker of a smile passed across his face as he remembered his cleverness, his own downright cunning, and he wondered vaguely what would become of Mr Karlin when the deception was at last found out. But already his thoughts were running ahead of him again. 'Only six more months of it if I really speed up. Thursdays as well as Mondays from now on. Last batch on the first of December. Then you can sign off forever.' He'd had the timetable all worked out from the very start; knew exactly the number of lunch-hour sessions he would have to put in to finish off the job. 'Free man by Christmas,' he went on. 'Don't forget to have your resignation ready. Cash in and clear out. Better start straight away looking round for that new studio of yours. Can't afford to keep them waiting.'

Then the old recurrent fear came over him. Suppose Mr Karlin didn't keep his word, suppose he blackmailed him into going on copying Top Secret things for ever? The threat was so sudden and unexpected that he felt his whole stomach go cold and the palms of his hands become clammy. They were the bad signs, the familiar ones; at any moment now his tremblings might begin. But he managed to control himself. 'Cool and easy,' he kept saying, over and over again. 'Cool and easy. Stop worrying. Don't let little things upset you. Just play it cool and take it easy.' And the treatment worked. Little by little he could feel himself relaxing and this time when he had wiped his hands down the seams of his trousers they did not mist up again.

He remained out there in the night air for some minutes longer. Through the trees a tiny chink of the Solent was showing, and there was moonlight on it. He stood quite still, looking on and admiring. He was calm now; and thinking about what he had already been able to do for Beryl and Marleen, and what he would be able to do for them in the future, he returned to Hiawatha peacefully, and at rest.

Beryl was already in bed when he got back there, and he decided to make his peace with her, too. Something like 'Sorry, I'm-always-talking-about-that-silly-old-office' was what he felt was needed. Not wanting to put the light on and being careful not to bump into anything, he slid his shoes off and tiptoed over to the bedside. He had just bent over and kissed her gently on the forehead when Beryl sprang up and pushed him away from her.

'What's the matter with you?' she asked. 'You gone mad, or something? You know Marleen's just in through there. She'd hear everything.' She was sitting bolt upright by now, and it was her other voice that she was using, her motherly one. 'You all right, darling?' she enquired. 'Mummy's here if you want anything.'

The door of the inner room was only some six feet away and the door itself was more than half ajar. Even so, there was silence, complete, stilly silence.

Beryl turned back to him.

'And you go off to sleep at once,' she told him. 'The very idea. I never heard anything like it. That's the trouble with you men: you think it's all women are made for.'

She slumped down onto the pillow again, and pulled the bedclothes slowly up round her. Stan could just make out that, from beneath the folds, she was telling him that she would go off on holiday by herself next time, she would really.

This was only partially true. But it was understandable. Beryl had been almost asleep when he had gone up to her; almost, but not quite. She had been in that limbo between sleep and waking when dreams have not entirely taken over and thoughts can still become dreamlike. Already in her dream it was tomorrow. Cliff had arrived in his Mustang some time before lunch, looking just as she always saw him in her mind – well-dressed, well-groomed and sauna-fresh. It had been distinctly gratifying as they had walked together arm-in-arm beside the pool to see how all the other women had eyed him; openly, unconcealedly envious of her. And now the long sunny day had drawn to a close and evening – tomorrow's evening – had come at last. Marleen was over in the lounge watching television, and Stan was away on the other side of the Island – photographing something or other. For the first time that day, she and Cliff were alone together. Almost by accident, as it were, they had reached his wigwam. Cliff had one hand resting lightly on her shoulder and, in the other, he was dangling the front-door key. The reminder of her promise had been no more than whispered to her, and her reply had been silently to nod her head . . . That was the moment when, without warning, she had felt Stan's breath upon her cheek and had found him bending over her.

After that, it was no wonder that she could not go to sleep again. She lay there, all tensed-up and rigid, listening to the sound of Stan's regular breathing in the bed alongside hers, and wished more than ever that she had insisted on single rooms. His very presence was an insult. It served to remind her that, if it hadn't been for that sudden interruption, she might at this very moment have found herself being unfaithful with Cliff.

A faint sound like the creaking of a mattress reached her from the inner room. Immediately she sat up again.

'That you, Marleen?' she asked.

There was no reply. Marleen was tired, too. Ever since Stan had come in and taken his shoes off she had been sitting, propped up on one elbow, listening to see if Mummy and Daddy had anything else interesting to say to each other. But all that, she decided, was over for the night. Sleep was now what she most wanted.

Silken gold hair streaming across the pretty pink pillowcase, she was already snuggled down, and really dreaming.

Chapter 27

Beryl was not the only one who had been thinking about Cliff's arrival. Stan had it in mind, too, and he had decided that he had better do something about it.

There was, he had noticed, an excellent Men's Wear section in the Trading Post; and, if his present sports jacket upset Beryl as much as she said it did, he had decided that he would go along and buy himself a new one. Double-breasted blazer style in blue with brass buttons was what he still wanted, but he was prepared to consider anything that was his size and looked suitably jaunty and holiday-ish. Nor was there any difficulty about seeing whether they would take a cheque. Before he had come away he had drawn a whole hundred pounds in cash from that second bank account of his – the one in an assumed name using the accommodation address in Putney. That was one piece of advice of Mr Karlin's that he had not forgotten: never write a cheque when cash will do, and never let your real bank manager know by how much your personal expenses have suddenly gone up.

The Post, however, had nothing in navy blue. It was check, the assistant said, that everyone was wearing this year; bright check, American-cut and in reds and russets mostly. In the end, Stan chose a russet one, with a pattern of broad yellow and magenta stripes criss-crossing it. That was his mistake. The yellow and magenta stripes clashed distressingly with the pale green shirt that he was wearing and the assistant suggested a new shirt altogether; something in orange, perhaps. After some hesitation, Stan agreed with him.

There was no hesitation at all, however, when it came to the trousers. He had to admit straight away that, below an orange-coloured shirt and a russet check sports jacket, baggy grey flannels with the nap long since worn off looked simply incongruous: they might have been something picked up in one of the smaller Oxfam shops. Pale fawn he finally settled for, and a pair of toe-strap sandals to go with them.

Thirty-seven ten was what the whole lot came to, and he changed then and there in the small, curtained fitting-room at the back of the shop. Surrounded as he was by tall mirrors, the effect was remarkable.

He hardly recognized himself. And already the new outfit had done something to him. He felt a new zest for life come over him. Before he left the shop he bought himself a white floppy linen hat that came down rather low over the ears, and – by now for the sheer devilment of it – a pair of dark glasses. By the time he stepped out into the sunlight again he was a different man, a stranger. With the Trading Post shopping bag containing his everyday clothes slung over his arm, if he had met Beryl face to face she would not have known him.

Nor did she. When, unannounced, he slid into the deck chair next to hers and attempted to put his arm round her shoulders she let out a little scream; and she could not find it in her to forgive him very easily. It was not funny, she said, to come up from nowhere and startle people like that: if she'd had a weak heart or something she didn't like to think what might have happened.

She didn't like what he was wearing, either. The best thing he could do, she told him, was to take the whole lot back where they came from and try to get something sensible for once. She even called Marleen over to back up her opinion. Marleen, however, could only spare a moment. She was busy watching a tall young man in black trunks swimming a very splashy butterfly-stroke down the length of the Beaver Pool.

'Oh, Dad, really,' was all she said, and turned away again to go on watching the tall, energetic young man. With Marleen, Beryl had noticed, horses already seemed to be on the way out and rather leggy young men definitely on the way in.

By midday, when Cliff did arrive, he was wearing just the kind of blue blazer that Stan himself had wanted. It looked very well on him, too, with the spotted yellow foulard, worn cravat-fashion, and the open-necked shirt.

It was purely by accident, mere coincidence as it were, that Beryl was there at the entrance gates to meet him. All morning she had been restless and unsettled. Twice she had tried sitting down by the Pool, but each time she had got up and begun walking about again; she had been along to the Store where Stan had bought that ridiculous outfit of his, not buying anything, just looking; she had made a hair appointment; she had been back to the Pool again to keep an eye on Marleen; she had washed out a pair of nylons in the little private shower-room of their cabin.

Then around twelve o'clock, when Cliff had told her to expect him, she had strolled idly along in the direction of the front gates, more to kill time than for any other reason. And there sure enough he was, just as he'd said he would be: it caused quite a stir when she jumped into the Mustang beside him and they *veroom-veroomed* together down the side lane that led to the bachelor quarters. 'Powhattan' was what Cliff's was called.

It was just as well that Cliff had arrived because Stan didn't show up very much; he was much too preoccupied. From breakfast-time onwards, he had been wandering around, light meter in hand, and as soon as lunch was over he wanted to get back to the job. Indeed, he was so intent upon his work that he didn't even bother to listen when Cliff began making remarks about his russet sports jacket with the yellow and magenta stripes. Stan had more than that on his mind. He had just come to one of his big decisions: *Sunshine in Summerland* was what his new album was going to be called, and every study in it would be rainbow-bright and blooming.

When Marleen said that she wanted to go back down to the Pool, Beryl raised no objections. She had just seen the tall young man who swam butterfly-stroke go off in the opposite direction and, in any case, she wanted to get Marleen out of the way for a bit. Stan himself was just setting off. He had loaded himself up with his large equipment case that seemed too big for him; and, as they looked at the retreating figure in his strange holiday clothing with the white linen hat on top, Cliff and Beryl raised their eyebrows and smiled understandingly at each other.

'It's what he likes doing,' Beryl said. 'It's all he ever thinks about.'

Cliff let his strong, masculine hand rest for a moment on Beryl's slim, pale one.

'Suits me,' he said. He took out a cigarette and lit it slowly, deliberately. 'Thinking of coming over to my place?' he asked.

Beryl knew that was what he was going to say, and she was ready for it. She gave his free hand a little slap, not hard enough to hurt but just sufficient to show that she disapproved.

'Not yet,' she said. 'Later on perhaps. We'll see.'

Her voice had a distinct tremor in it. It was by no means the calm, matter-of-fact voice that she had intended to use.

It was Cliff who made everything all right for her, the way he always did. His big, muscular hand came down on top of hers again, only this time he left it there. And the little squeeze that he gave showed that he knew that everything was going to be all right.

For a while they sat on together in silence, happy in each other's company; and then, when they did speak, it was about Cliff himself mostly. That was because he was so pleased with the way his business enterprises were going that he couldn't keep quiet about it. He had to tell someone; Beryl preferably. He was, she learned, by now reasonably confident – practically certain, in fact – that he had broken into the magic circle of Service contracts. It was still too early to go into details, and he'd had to agree to go into a syndicate. That, he admitted, was a minus. But there was also a plus. Because his side of it was Disposables – plastic cups, plastic cutlery, cleaning tissues, toilet paper, that kind of thing. And the great thing about Disposables, as he kept explaining to her, was that by their very nature the customer was always coming back for more. He even went so far as to say that it looked as if his whole future – and hers, too, if she cared to have it that way – was now set fair. There were still bigger things on the horizon; and, after that, who knows, who cares, he added.

Naturally, as she listened she couldn't help admiring him. He was so sure of himself, so positive; and she couldn't help feeling flattered, too, with so much that he'd got already, she herself was what he wanted most. Just thinking about it, remembering how it all might have been, brought a lump into her throat and made her want to cry. The one thing she longed for was to have his arms around her; and, when at last he bent over her and whispered 'What about it?' she got up obediently, to go down with him to Bachelors' Row.

Destiny, she had read somewhere, is what happens when it comes to you.

Oddly enough Stan, too, had been thinking about destiny. From two-thirty onwards he had been down at Yarmouth harbour going round the yacht moorings; and, in all that time, nothing had seemed to go quite right – just sunlight and seagulls and fleecy clouds and mast-heads, but no colour; or sunlight and blue sails, fleecy clouds and mast-heads, but not a single seagull in the right place.

Then, magically, it all fell into place as though some divine director had been arranging it: same sunlight, same fleecy clouds, same mast-heads, same seagulls and, down on the water, blue sails, white sails and a tiny dinghy with red, all grouped, prize-fashion, around a single floating swan. The effect was so beautiful, so overwhelming, that he held his breath the whole time he was taking the picture – one twenty-fifth of a second at f.8, he gave it – lest the least movement on his part should somehow shatter the bright image.

It was getting on for five-thirty by then, and Stan suddenly realized how tired he was; physically, mentally and emotionally worn out; even if the swan had managed to get the boats to cluster around again, he would not have had the strength to take another picture. But that's the way it always is with serious photography: Stan knew from experience how one really successful shot can leave you knocked out for hours.

It was because he felt so pleasantly exhausted that he went into the bar of the George to give himself a drink. It was not something that normally he would have dreamed of doing; in the ordinary way, he would have hurried back to Pineland to see if Beryl wanted anything. But tonight he just didn't feel strong enough to laugh at any of Cliff's jokes, even when they were not in a roundabout way more or less deliberately directed against him.

After his second whisky-and-water, Stan felt better; more at one with the place. Quite nautical, in fact. It was as though all his life he had mixed with bronzed young men wearing gum boots and thick guernseys. They seemed such a happy, wholesome breed that he found himself rather envious. But, at the same time, sorry for them, because their day at sea was already over, and night would so soon be upon them. Whereas in a single frame in the camera inside his equipment case, that swan and those boats of his would go on gleaming in celluloid sunlight until the end of time.

So as not to get in anyone's way he tried to keep his equipment case tucked in neatly between his legs. But it was a large case, and people still kept falling over it; that was why he took up his drink and moved out onto the terrace. It was cooler there, with a breeze that had come in straight past the Needles from the open sea. Someone had left a folded-up newspaper on one of the seats, and Stan was grateful for it. Because of all the excitement about Cliff's arrival he'd missed the radio all day; simply hadn't heard a word of news, in fact. He opened up the paper and began to read.

That was when anyone sitting near him would have noticed that he had suddenly gone very pale; pale and frozen. He just sat there, motionless, staring down at the sheet of newsprint.

Apparently, under pressure, the Speaker had given way and agreed to an emergency debate. That had been yesterday; and, by midnight, the whole issue had been decided. 'LEVIATHAN REPRIEVED' was what the headline said.

His hand began to shake. They were just little tremblings at first, but soon there were great big jerks, too, and twitches as well in the midst of them. Holding a glass was entirely out of the question: he had already realized this, and had hurriedly put it down; so hurriedly, in fact, that he had to let go too soon. The glass balanced itself for a moment on the edge of the round metal table, then tilted over and fell off onto the stone paving with a crash. People were beginning to look at him by now.

But Stan didn't care about other people. There was only one thing on his mind, and that was to get to a telephone before it was too late. It was his duty to warn somebody; somebody important. The Prime Minister preferably.

The telephone in the hall was already in use when he got to it, and there was nothing for it but to try one of the kiosks on the quay outside. Pushing his way past a party of visitors who were just coming into the hotel, and not stopping to apologize even when his equipment case banged into them, he set off at the double. But it was hopeless; quite hopeless. There was frustration lurking round every corner. The first kiosk was a wreck, freshly vandalized and without even a mouthpiece to speak into; the one next to it had someone in it, and an impatient-looking woman already standing by outside. It was when Stan tried the third kiosk that he knew why she was there; even though everything in there looked perfectly normal and in good order, all that you got when you lifted the receiver was a low whirring sound like birds twittering.

By now, Stan was beginning to get desperate. He stopped the first person he could see and asked the way to the Post Office. But he had picked the wrong man, an idle holiday-maker, someone who was a total stranger to the place. Stan set off himself to look, still half running, his equipment case bumping up and down with every step he took. When at last he did find it, the front door was already closed. There was a GPO notice pasted on the glass panel. It was there to direct people to the nearest public telephones: they were the ones that he had just come from on the quayside.

It was while he was standing there, breathless, that he looked up the road and saw the blue lamp of the Police Station. Stan did not hesitate. With the coins that he had been holding in his hand all ready to feed into any telephone that was working properly, he grabbed at the strap of his equipment case and set off for the Station.

He was so sure that what he was doing was right that, once inside, he tended to be a bit brusque and peremptory. He simply walked straight up to the desk and asked if he could put through an urgent call to London. If he had been talking to a switchboard operator he could not have been more matter-of-fact about it.

'I'll pay for it if you tell me what it comes to,' he added, just to show that he wasn't trying to get away with anything.

The relief constable behind the desk did not move. He was a lethargic, heavily-built man with large hands.

'I'm sorry, sir,' he said, 'this telephone is not for use by the public. It's a police telephone.'

The remark annoyed Stan: it was precisely because it *was* a police telephone that he had gone there in the first place.

'It's very urgent,' he explained. 'Otherwise I wouldn't be asking.'

For all the interest he showed, the policeman behind the desk might simply not have heard him. He stood there quite still, staring back at Stan. And what he saw – the russet sports jacket, the orange shirt, the fawn trousers – he did not care for. The policeman was native-born: he had lived on the Island all his life and he disliked everything about summer visitors. It was merely that he disliked this one more than most; with that floppy linen hat, the dark glasses were, he reckoned, just about the last straw.

Seeing that he was making no impression on the man, Stan bent forward. Dropping his voice, he spoke sideways into the policeman's ear.

'It's Government business,' he confided. 'I want the Admiralty.'

That was when, because Stan had thrust his head up so close to him, the policeman detected the smell of whisky on Stan's breath; and having detected it, he realized that this was one of those moments when the customer has to be played along gently.

He pointed up at the Station clock.

'They're bound to be closed by now, sir,' he said. 'Better try again in the morning.'

A sense of helplessness came over Stan and he found himself trembling again. The policeman noticed it, too, and made a mental note; junkies were something else that one had to be on the look-out for nowadays.

'It doesn't matter what time it is,' Stan told him. 'There's always a Duty Officer on duty. That's the one I want. I want the Duty Officer.'

By now the policeman was quite clear in his own mind about what he was up against; and, for the moment, the part he played was more that of male nurse than police officer.

'Is he expecting the call, sir?'

Stan shook his head.

'And may I have his name, please?'

'I don't know it. He's just the Duty Officer.'

'And would he know your name, sir?'

Again Stan shook his head.

The policeman pursed up his lips and began tapping with his pencil. Then he spoke slowly and deliberately, keeping his eye on Stan throughout to make sure that he was being understood.

'So you don't know the gentleman's name you want to speak to, and he doesn't know yours, and everyone else has gone home and he's not expecting to hear from you. That's about the long and the short of it, isn't it, sir?' Stan nodded.

'Why not forget all about it, sir? Just go off home and get a good night's rest. I take it you're staying over here?'

This time the policeman was quite unprepared for what happened. Stan reached across the counter and caught hold of him by his sleeve.

'But I tell you it's urgent. Very urgent. It's life and death.'

The policeman disengaged his arm.

'Now, now, sir,' he said, 'don't get vahlent. We can't have vahlence here.' He had carefully taken a half-step backwards out of Stan's reach, and he felt that he could afford to humour him once more. 'If it's as urgent as all that,' he suggested, 'perhaps you'd like to tell me about it. If I don't know what's on your mind I can't help you, can I, sir?'

Stan had taken off his dark glasses. After the day's strong sunlight, however, the effect was rather strange; the rest of Stan's face was in the bright pink of early sunburn but, around his eyes, two large white circles were showing. It gave him the forlorn, startled expression of circus make-up.

'That's what I can't do,' he admitted, being careful to keep his voice down. 'It's confidential, you see. Highly confidential. I'm the only one who knows about it. I can't tell anybody else, only the Duty Officer.'

'Then I'm afraid I can't help you, sir.'

The policeman turned away as he said it. But Stan was leaning across the counter again.

'You've heard of "Top Secret", haven't you?' he demanded. 'Well, that's what this is. It's Government Priority. I demand to be put through. If I can't have the Duty Officer, I want the Prime Minister.'

Because the policeman did not even bother to turn round, but merely regarded him disapprovingly over his shoulder, Stan lost his temper.

'If you don't do what I tell you,' he shouted, 'I'll come round and do it myself. That's what I'll do. And don't you try to stop me.'

He was leaning even further across the counter as he said it and, for a moment, the policeman thought that Stan was about to climb over. The policeman was not naturally a quick mover. Nor did he like having to exert himself. But he knew his duty. It was no good going on being patient any longer.

He lifted the flap in the counter and came round to Stan's side.

'I'm afraid I shall have to charge you, sir,' he said.

The Station sergeant, too, knew all about holiday-makers. Year after year he'd seen it happen; too much fresh air and a touch of the sun, and they all started behaving like mental cases. But you still had to be careful, still had to keep your eye open for the genuine article, the real nutter. That was why, as soon as they had got Stan safely down below, he sent one of his young men round to Pineland Colony to make a few enquiries.

The young man was in plain clothes, and inconspicuous. With his denim trousers and his open-necked shirt, he might simply have been any summer visitor from one of the cheaper camps. He was, as a matter of fact, rather pleased to be visiting Pineland; resorts of that class were a bit off the regular police beat, and he was more than half prepared to find that he had been given a false address.

But here he had done Stan an injustice. The girl at the Trapper's Lodge reception desk knew all about the Pittses. Straight on down Sunset Trail, she told him, past the clock golf and Wolf Wood, and he'd find Hiawatha second on the left.

When he got there, however, only Marleen was at home. And she was sulking. Out on the front porch she was lying back in one of the folding chairs, not doing anything really, just sitting there with outstretched hands, waiting for her nail varnish to dry.

But the sight of the visitor put all thoughts of nail varnish out of her mind. For a start, he was even taller than the butterfly swimmer in the black trunks; Marleen liked all tall men, and this one had nice wavy hair, too. She was only sorry that she couldn't help him more, because she didn't want him to go away again so soon. It was no use, however. She hadn't seen her Daddy since lunch time, she told him, though she was certain that her Mummy would be about somewhere. Provided the young man promised to stay there until she got back, she even offered to go off and try to find her.

The young man lit a cigarette and waited, looking after Marleen's retreating figure: she hadn't hesitated, he noticed. On she went, her curls bobbing, past the clock golf, alongside the Beaver Pool and down Chyne Canyon towards Bachelors' Row. That was where he lost sight of her. But he had no need to worry. Marleen was on a bee-line. She bounded up the shallow front steps of Powhattan as though she had lived there all her life.

It was disappointing that the double doors, with their ornamental louvres, were closed on her, and she got no answer when she knocked. She waited, and knocked again. Then, when there was still no reply, she went round to the back where the bedroom was. The shutters were closed, too. But Marleen did not pause. Reaching up she gave two smart raps.

'Mum, there's someone to see you,' she said. 'I think he's a policeman.'

Chapter 28

It was the bit about the floppy linen hat and the russet sports jacket that worried Beryl most.

'It does sound like him,' she admitted, 'but it couldn't be. Not my husband, I mean. Not him. He'd never do anything like that. He's not that sort. He's more the quiet type like. He's . . .' She paused. After all, she didn't really know this tall, wavy-haired policeman who was driving her; certainly not well enough to begin exchanging confidences with him.

They had reached the Police Station by now. There were only two steps down to the cells but, as she descended them, she felt as though she were entering a deep cavern. It was partly a trick of the light. The lamp fittings in the corridor carried low-wattage, economy-class bulbs, and they were set high in the ceiling covered by a thick wire mesh. What brightness managed to escape from them was sucked up and absorbed by the dark green, waist-high dado that ran round the walls.

And inside the cell it was even worse. Beryl could not help feeling angry with Stan for ever having got himself into the place at all. The sight of him, perched on the hard upright chair in those ridiculous cruise-wear clothes of his, made her want to give him a good shaking. Not that there was any danger of that. The policeman who had brought her down had stood himself between them, so that she had not been able even to touch Stan's hand.

'Well?' she demanded.

Stan did not look up at once when she spoke to him; and when he did raise his head, his appearance shocked her. He looked as though he had been crying. His voice, however, was quite calm and steady.

'It's all a mistake,' he said. 'A great big mistake. I wasn't really going to fight the policeman. That's why I need a solicitor. He ought to have been here by now. There's nothing you can do. Not now there isn't.' He gave a long, weary sigh as he said it. 'So you go back to Marleen and don't worry. Just leave the rest to me. I'll be all right.'

Beryl drew herself up.

'You've got sunstroke,' she told him. 'That's all that's wrong with you. It isn't a solicitor you want. What you want is a doctor.'

She was still saying the same thing to the wavy-haired policeman as he drove her back to Pineland; and he agreed with her. There was always a lot of it about at this time of year, he said. Nasty at the time, but no after-effects; right as rain she'd find him when they let him out in the morning.

And that was what Cliff said, too. She could not imagine how she could ever have got through that long, awful evening without Cliff. He had been there on the front porch of Hiawatha, with his arm round Marleen's shoulders to comfort her, when the police car drew up on the return journey, and he had refused to leave them ever since. At least, not quite refused. Once he had slipped across to the side-counter marked 'Treks' inside Trapper's Lodge and come back with three portions of Uncle Remus's Kentucky chicken and fried potatoes; and the other time he had gone over to collect a bottle of Scotch that he had brought down with him. Until Beryl had recovered from the shock of Stan's arrest, he said, it was better for them to be on their own like that.

Remembering where poor Daddy was and how it had upset poor Mummy, little Marleen kept bursting into tears. But already the intervals between the outbursts were becoming extended; and, in between, she kept looking across at Cliff and wondering what it would have been like if she'd had him for a daddy instead.

As for Beryl, she had given up all pretence. She had tossed a cushion down onto the floor at Cliff's feet and was sitting there resting her chin upon his knees. He kept passing his hand across her hair, stroking it caressingly and saying 'darling', and she kept giving little stifled sobs that showed that she was still awake. Marleen, looking on, envied them both.

Beryl had intercepted Cliff's hand by now and kept giving it little kisses and holding it pressed up tight against her cheek. And why shouldn't she? she asked herself. She knew that Marleen knew; and Marleen knew she knew.

Next morning Cliff was round again before breakfast; and he took care to come in his Mustang so that it would be there all ready to take Beryl round to the Police Station afterwards. The sheer thoughtfulness of remembering to do such a thing brought a lump to Beryl's throat. And it was thoughtful in another way, too, because she could not help noticing how strangely small and insignificant their own little hire-car

Morris looked now that she saw it alongside a really full-sized one. Somehow she felt that they would be bound to be nicer to Stan down at the Station once they saw the class of friends he had.

The events of the previous evening had upset Marleen's nervous system. She couldn't eat any breakfast, and kept saying that she felt faint. When Beryl told her to go and lie down until they got back the symptoms became suddenly worse. She felt sick, too, she said, and she had a headache. Indeed, it wasn't until Cliff said that she could come along with them that she began to recover.

When they got to the Station, however, the sergeant refused to allow any of them to see Stan. He'd got his solicitor with him at the moment, the sergeant explained, and then he was about due to go off to the Magistrates' Court. They'd see him there, he said.

As he was speaking a small saloon car, like the one they had come down in, slid past the window behind the sergeant's desk. Marleen was the only one who happened to be looking, and what she saw was a glimpse of a russet-coloured sports jacket.

She gave Beryl's sleeve a tug.

'Mum,' she told her. 'He's started.'

Even the tears had dried themselves up by now. Her little face was still a trifle pale, but she was herself again. In her eyes was the excitement of the chase.

The Magistrates' Court was smaller than Beryl had expected; and shabbier. The brass facings of the stair-treads that led up to it had been worn paper-thin and, in places, the woodwork was already showing through.

The smallness was in itself a bit disconcerting. It was all right for the magistrates; they at least had a boarded-off private platform all to themselves. But down below in the body of the Court room it was turmoil: clerks, solicitors, ushers, witnesses, policemen all huddled up together and getting in each others' way in a space the size of a church vestry. The public gallery, to which Cliff and Beryl and Marleen were directed, consisted of a bench over at the far end.

Stan's solicitor might have been supplied in kit-form along with the Court room. He was small, frayed and worn-looking, too. Motoring offences, summonses for dog- and TV-licences, drunkenness, petty larceny and the swearing of oaths were his specialities. He came bustling up, tired, anxious and apologetic. He had been trying to contact them at the holiday camp, he explained, but they had left before he could get hold of them. In any case, everything was in order. Just a few formalities to be seen to, one or two small details to be ironed out; and then, after the imposition of a purely nominal fine, the whole family, he was sure, would be back at Pineland in plenty of time for lunch.

Hand in hand, Cliff and Beryl sat and waited. It was only Marleen who disturbed them. She had lost the watch glass of her Ingersoll, and kept searching for it. More than once Beryl had to grope about to find her hand so that she could slap it and tell her to sit still.

Then the solicitor came over again. There were, it appeared, complications: he couldn't yet tell them what they were because he had only just heard about them himself. Not that there would be anything to worry about; everything was in order like he'd told them. He went away still muttering it. Next time he came across, however, he seemed less confident. There might be further charges, he had just learned, and even the question of bail might arise.

That was where Beryl found it so marvellous having Cliff with them. He was inclined to treat the whole thing as a bit of a joke.

'Oh, the naughty boy,' he said. 'I wonder what he's been up to.'

Then, giving Beryl's hand an extra squeeze before he released it, he turned to the solicitor.

'About the bail,' he said. 'Put it down to my account.'

The solicitor appeared surprised.

'Up to what limit?' he asked.

Cliff gave a little smile before replying.

'The sky,' he told him.

Beryl drew in her breath sharply as she heard him say it. Cliff, she reminded herself, was born that way: doing the big thing came naturally to him.

She was just about to whisper her thanks, when she had to break off to speak to Marleen. One more question about why anybody should have to stand bail for her Daddy, Beryl told her, and she'd find herself outside in the corridor where she belonged.

Even that bit had to be said under her breath because the Court was really filling up by now and twice she'd had to move further down the bench so that somebody else could sit down. She now had a total stranger, a man, jammed up close against her; just the sort of stranger, too, that she would have expected to find in a Magistrates' Court: someone who was common and shifty-looking. Come to that, glancing down the row she noticed that, in their various ways, they all looked pretty common and shifty.

Her party – Cliff, Marleen and herself – were the odd ones out. The magistrate would be sure to notice that, she felt; and then he would see how ridiculous it was that they should be there at all. In the meantime, she found it difficult to forgive Stan for having dragged them down into the mire in this way; with a sensitive and impressionable child like Marleen it was the sort of nightmare memory that would go on haunting her forever.

Even when eventually the Court did get going, Stan's case did not come first; not that Beryl was in the least surprised. With a solicitor like the one they'd got she would have been quite prepared for it if his cases always came last. There was, however, nothing that they could do about it. They just had to sit back and listen. The cases were all so pathetically trivial, too; trivial and mostly sordid. They were about unpaid water rates; about uncleared garbage; about unattended vehicles; about child neglect. Then, quite suddenly – before they were ready for it, in fact – they heard the usher say: 'Call Stanley Pitts.'

It didn't seem a very nice way of calling him, Beryl thought. The use of the prefix, 'Mister', would have been more polite; as it was, it made him sound just like all the others. And she couldn't bear it when he did appear. He seemed somehow so small and so defenceless. She wanted to go right over and put his collar straight. If only she had known that he would have to stand there like that, she'd have arranged for Cliff to drop in at the Station with his proper clothes; the russet check sports jacket seemed somehow disrespectful in those surroundings.

What came as a shock to Beryl was the speed with which the law can work when it has to. There was a horrible precision to the whole thing as though it had been carefully rehearsed and timed beforehand. Disorderly behaviour was the charge, and Stan's solicitor did not even take the trouble to dispute it. Then, just as the magistrate seemed to be on the point of saying his standard piece about a three pounds' fine and the remembering to exercise more self-control in future, the policeman who had brought Stan along started to say something else. It was to tell the magistrate that he had to ask for a remand because further charges were pending. Even that, however, should have presented no difficulty. It was not until Stan's man, in a last desperate effort to remind everyone that he was still on the job at all, got up, that the nastiness occurred. He asked for bail and the policeman told the magistrate that he had to oppose it.

Beryl heard – felt, almost – a ripple of astonishment run round the Court as he said it, and she saw a young man who she didn't know was a reporter start scribbling in his notebook. There was a hurried conference between the magistrate and his clerk, and the magistrate agreed that Stan should be remanded in custody.

That was all there was to it. Less than three minutes after his appearance, Stan had been taken away again. It had been the last few seconds that were the worst. The magistrate had finished speaking, and the policeman who had conducted Stan up into the dock had tapped him on the shoulder to let him know that he wasn't wanted any longer. Then, quite suddenly, he looked up.

Until that moment, he had seemed to be unaware of what was going on around him; just standing there, head bent forward, unseeing and unhearing, in a sort of daze. But when he did look up it was to look straight at Beryl. She could tell at once that he had known perfectly well what was going on. His eyes were fixed full on her and the corners of his mouth were turned down in a way that she had never seen before. But, worst of all, he was shaking his head at her. Not a word was spoken but the message was clear enough.

He was trying, desperately trying, to break it to her that the whole situation was now quite hopeless.

Chapter 29

It was the mug of HM Prison tea that restored him. Hot, sweet and milky, it might have been prepared specially for reviving accident victims. And Stan was certainly one of those. It had all happened so suddenly, too, just the way accidents do occur: one day out taking colour shots of red sails against blue seascapes and, the next, sitting on the edge of a fixed wooden bedstead wondering if there really was a view out of the small barred window set six foot above floor level.

The strange thing was that he was already getting used to it – used to the metal mug, used to the door with no handle on the inside, used to being treated not as a normal human being but as an inmate. And not even an ordinary inmate at that; there was something special about Stan. You could tell that from the way they treated him, and from the type of visitor that he received. The Governor himself had just been down to see him, and now Commander Hackett was waiting for him in the interview room.

Stan was very glad to see the Commander. He provided the first real link with the outside world, and made Stan feel in touch again. Not that the meeting was an entirely easy one. There is something about all prison interview rooms that tends to inhibit smooth conversation. And Commander Hackett himself, Stan could not help noticing, seemed distinctly self-conscious. He shook hands almost as if apologizing, and reminded Stan not once but twice that he needn't say anything at all, unless he wanted to, without having his solicitor present all the time.

That part was all very formal and correct. The Commander would have liked to keep it that way, but he found it impossible. He could not forget that he and Stan were old friends: they had shared the same table in the Frobisher House canteen, gone turns with the same HP sauce bottle and the same sugar sifter, even played ping-pong together. And, after his second warning, the Commander could stand the strain no longer. He just gave up and blurted out what he was really thinking. 'Well, bless my soul,' he said. 'You of all people. I still can't quite believe it.' With that, he offered Stan a cigarette, took one himself and rocked back as far as he could go on his chair, trying not to look self-conscious again.

Stan was the first of them to speak; he didn't mind in the least about the solicitor, he said. They could perfectly well start up without him. Secretly, he was rather relieved that the solicitor wasn't present; there was an air of anxiety about the man that Stan found rather unnerving. Also, he had one particularly upsetting habit: it consisted of drawing in his breath in short, disapproving hisses as though he felt that whatever it was that he was hearing would ultimately prove to be to his client's disadvantage.

Now that he had abandoned the official manner, Commander Hackett made no attempt to rush things. He asked Stan what kind of a night he'd had and agreed that all police cells ought to be provided with proper bathrooms. Then he came round to the real purpose of his visit.

'How long's this been going on?' he asked.

Stan did not reply immediately. In his mind, he was working backwards.

'Since February,' he said. 'That's when it all started.'

'All what?' Commander Hackett asked.

It was ten past eleven when he put the question and, two hours and a whole packet of cigarettes later, he was still asking questions and Stan was still answering. By then, Stan had been given the regulation prison lunch on a tray and had munched his way through it, talking all the time so as not to keep the Commander waiting. The Commander, for his part, had merely had a cup of tea, one of the hot, sweet, milky kind. He was beginning now to wish that he'd accepted the warder's offer and had taken his own share of sausages, boiled cabbage and tinned baked beans, too.

But he couldn't possibly have broken off. Stan had far too much to tell him. And all so frank, too. It came out in a rush of Boy Scout honesty. There wasn't a thing that Stan kept back – the existence of his dual-purpose wrist-watch, the lonely lunchtime photographic sessions down there in the basement, the regular assignations in faded and obscure hotels.

What particularly delighted him was Stan's description of Mr Karlin. It was so exact: the smile, the large, smooth hands, the raincoat with its belt, and storm-flap at the back. If he hadn't skipped the country already, Commander Hackett reckoned that the other branch would have him inside within forty-eight hours. There was only one thing that Stan hadn't told the Commander about Mr Karlin, and that was about his association with Helga. Stan himself had seen very little of Helga. And what he had seen hadn't been very nice. She had deceived and betrayed him. He knew all about that. But, no matter what happened to Mr Karlin, Stan couldn't bear to think of getting Helga into any trouble with the authorities.

As Commander Hackett listened, he glowed. In the small hours of the morning, when he had been telephoned at home and told to leave immediately for the Isle of Wight, he had feared the worst. Apparently, under his very eye, in the one department for which he was personally responsible, a Top Secret leakage had occurred. It was like the worst days of World War II all over again, with the threat of immediate court martial hanging over him and any thoughts about pension rights and civilian retirement thrust somewhere away into the background.

It was only as Stan went on talking that he began to feel better. Much as he liked him, he saw quite clearly that Stan was done for. With a confession of the length of the one that Commander Hackett had got in his notebook, nothing on earth could save him. On the other hand, that self-same confession would prove to be the Commander's own salvation; it was really a matter of presentation. Phrases like '. . . had been under observation for some time' and '. . . significant change in life-style had not passed unnoticed' should still enable him to keep his job.

His thoughts were interrupted because Stan was addressing him again. Only this time it was not to tell him anything but simply to put a question.

'How long do you think I'll get?' he asked. 'Now that I've owned up about it, I mean.'

Loyal and steadfast, like the true friend whom Beryl had always known him to be, Cliff took charge of everything.

And how she needed him. The solicitor Stan had been given had proved useless, absolutely useless. When he heard that bail was not going to be allowed, he went to pieces; looking more anxious than ever, he just kept drawing in his breath, making it quite clear that this was not the sort of case in which, with his kind of practice, he wished to become involved.

And, at the Prison, he could not even manage to arrange another meeting for Stan and Beryl so that they could talk things over. Away for some considerable time, when he did at last come back, it was only to report that there was nothing doing because Stan was being moved; what was worse was that it turned out that he had been unable to discover where he was going. Of course, he would be keeping closely in touch, he assured them but, beyond that, he could for the moment tell them nothing more. No doubt, he added as an afterthought, Stan would be brought up before the magistrate again tomorrow, and then they would all know what really was going on.

It was the indefiniteness of everything – and the shame and humili-ation of it all – that made Beryl angry. Tense and tight-lipped, she sat there in the Prison car park, silently waiting. She had, indeed, become so remote and isolated that Cliff grew anxious about her. Even when he gave her hand a whole series of little squeezes there was hardly any response at all. She seemed oblivious of everything.

With Marleen it was all rather different. It was the first time she had ever been allowed to share fully in adult affairs. And she was enjoying herself. She recognized that the margin of acceptance was a narrow one: a single word out of place and she might find herself being excluded again. In consequence, she played her part very care-fully. Like her mother, she said nothing. But she remembered what was expected of her. Passive and demure, her hands folded disconsolately in her lap, she glanced up furtively from time to time; and, whenever there was anyone looking, she would give a little gulp and struggle bravely to stifle and choke back her tears.

They were just getting ready to leave when a young man came hurry-ing up to them. He was from *The Isle of Wight Guardian*, he said, and his editor wondered if he could be given any indication as to the nature of the new charges that were impending. He had a photographer with him.

This again was where Beryl was so relieved to have Cliff beside her: he knew exactly how to handle the Press. First, he raised his forefinger vertically to his lips to indicate that what he was about to say was highly confidential. Then, he jerked his head over to one side to make it clear that he wanted the young man to move in closer; and, when he did speak, it was in a hoarse stage-whisper.

'He was planning to steal the Needles,' he told him.

The young man smiled politely.

'No, seriously,' he said.

Cliff appeared to be surprised.

'That's serious enough, isn't it?' he asked. 'National Trust property, you know. All belongs to the Queen.'

The young man had pencil out in readiness, and he was still very painstaking and polite.

'Friend of the family?' he enquired. 'Might I have your name, please?'

Cliff did not hesitate.

'Douglas Fairbanks,' he replied. Then, after a short pause, he added: 'Senior.'

The reporter wrote it all down.

'And the young lady?' he asked, pointing the end of his pencil at Marleen. 'Is she the daughter?'

Again Cliff gave the secrecy signal with his forefinger.

'No, the aunt,' he said.

Cliff was still smiling to himself as he switched on the engine. Not that he'd found it difficult to put the reporter from the local paper in his place. There was really nothing in it; either you had the knack, or you hadn't.

It was so hot and sunny on the way back, and the car radio was on so loud, that they drove along, not talking. Beryl was trying to scratch a speck of dirt off her white jacket, using the tip of her fingernail as though it were a scalpel, and Cliff was thinking about the Naval catering contract. You could never be sure of anything until it was signed and witnessed – he was always reminding himself of that. Even so, he wasn't in much doubt about this one; and he had certainly put everything he'd got into it. But, once into Service supplies, you were really onto something. Uniforms and equipment were only just round the corner. And with them . . .

Marleen was preoccupied, too. But her thoughts were purely personal. She hadn't liked seeing the young man teased in that way, and still thought that it was horrid of Uncle Cliff to have behaved like that; after all, the reporter had only been doing what his editor had told him to do. And, even if he was a bit on the short side, Marleen had noticed that he had very nice eyes.

Because Beryl had an uneasy feeling that, back at Pineland, they would all be talking about her, Cliff suggested that they should lunch out somewhere; and, after a Pimms beforehand and a bottle of hock with the meal, other people's curiosity seemed less important. All the same, it was annoying. When they finally returned to Pineland, the young reporter from *The Isle of Wight Guardian* had got there before them. When they arrived he was already deep in conversation with the clerk in the reception office. And the clerk appeared to be keeping nothing back.

'. . . friend of the family you might call him, I suppose,' he was saying. 'Spends most of his time over there with her in Hiawatha, you know.'

It was Cliff's arrival that had interrupted him. The reception clerk turned away and pretended to be hanging up some keys. But the reporter remained unruffled and professional.

'Good afternoon, Mr Fairbanks,' he said as Cliff passed by him.

Almost as soon as they got indoors, the telephone rang. It was the solicitor, and it was to say that he was on the way over. He was speaking fast and rather loud.

As soon as Beryl had put back the receiver she turned towards Cliff.

'He says there's been a development or something,' she told him. 'He made it sound like it was something serious like.'

Cliff, however, did not appear to be unduly concerned. He said that it was probably only that they wanted the bail money after all, and would like a little on account. The best thing the two of them could do, he assured them, was to sit back and take things easy. While they were waiting, a little drink wouldn't do them any harm, he added; and he offered to go across to the store for some more Scotch.

He got up and stepped outside onto the front porch as he said it. But, to Beryl's surprise, he was promptly back indoors again.

'That bloody little reporter's hanging about outside,' he said. 'And he's got a photographer with him.'

Beryl started nervously.

'Where's Marleen?' she asked.

'She's out there, too,' he told her.

And through the open door, they could see her. Marleen was still wearing her Court-room dress – the simple, all-white one with the sailor collar. But there was a difference. She had undone the top button of the jacket and, with one leg up on the top step beside her, her skirt had become raised a little. In her right hand she was holding a strawberry ice cream cornet.

Beryl thrust forward, her hand ready to dash the ice cream from Marleen's lips.

The reporter looked across to the photographer.

'Make it a two-shot,' he shouted.

In the end, the strain had proved too much: not surprisingly, Beryl had collapsed under it. She was in the hands of the Colony's doctor by now, and it was tranquillizers that he had prescribed. In consequence, she was not really with them any longer – just drifting about on Cloud Seven with a medicated pad across her eyes and a glass of iced water within arm's reach in case she should need a sip.

At first, Marleen had sat there at the bedside with her in case she should need anything. Then, when it became apparent to Marleen that she would not be needed, she had got up and tip-toed from the room. She was now down beside the Pool, book in hand, quietly waiting for someone nice to come up and speak to her.

On the veranda outside the chalet, Cliff and the solicitor were both sitting. They were waiting for Beryl to wake up.

'Of course, with those extra charges, it becomes quite a different kind of case, you see,' the solicitor had just said. 'This'll have to go to the Old Bailey.'

'Old Bailey?'

Cliff brought himself bolt upright in his chair as he heard the words.

'Bound to be,' the solicitor told him. 'Official Secrets, you see.'

Cliff did not reply immediately; instead he started to draw his left hand slowly up and down his face as if he were massaging it. His right hand was still holding the glass of whisky-and-soda that he happened to have been drinking.

'But things aren't really likely to get that far, are they?' he asked. 'Not when you think of the sunstroke and all that? Not when they get character witnesses?'

This time it was the solicitor who paused. Not normally an unusually observant man, he was surprised to notice the sudden change in Cliff's appearance. The air of easy confidence had vanished completely, and even his polka-dot bow-tie seemed somehow mysteriously to have wilted.

'Too late for character witnesses now,' the solicitor said, with a note of trained professional regret in his voice. 'There's the confession, you know. Can't get around that one.'

'The confession?'

Cliff was disappointed in himself: it seemed that all that he could do was to repeat whatever had just been said to him.

The solicitor nodded.

'Ten pages of it,' he replied, drawing his breath in with a hiss as he uttered the words. 'Ten pages. All voluntarily given and without my knowledge.'

Cliff continued to run his hand aimlessly across his cheek. He had put the glass of whisky-and-soda down by now.

'What's it say?' he asked.

The question struck Stan's solicitor as significant. For a moment, he even wondered whether Cliff could be involved, too, he seemed so much concerned. Then he dismissed the idea. Small-time lawyer though he was, he could still recognize guilt when he saw it. And he could tell at once, this wasn't guilt at all: it was fear.

Nor did he see any reason why he should spare him. Cliff hadn't ever been to any pains to be particularly nice to him: on the contrary, he'd rather gone out of his way to make him feel smaller than he really was.

'Oh, the usual,' he said pointedly. 'Motive. Opportunity. Accomplices. Financial transactions. Family background. Marital circumstances. Domestic circle. It's all there. Nothing missing.'

'Marital circumstances . . . domestic circle': Cliff found that he was repeating the words. Only silently to himself, this time. And, as he did so, he saw that it would be no good now attempting to deny anything. There was too much against him for that. There was the news picture of the three of them when he had given the press photographer the fancy name of Fairbanks; and there was the Court offer of bail in his own name; and, looking back, it was distinctly compromising remembering where Beryl had been found when the young policeman had called round to see her.

'Does . . . does he mention me?' he asked.

The solicitor noticed the hesitation with which Cliff put the question; also, he could not help noticing that the customary incisive ring to Cliff's voice was no longer there.

'Oh, yes, you figure in it,' he said. 'But only in a general way, of course. Just as a friend, you know. Just someone who was close to him.' He paused. 'They'll be wanting a statement from you, naturally. They'll have to follow up all the ends they've got.'

But Cliff was no longer listening. All that he was thinking about was his Naval contract, the one for general supplies. And he was being quite realistic about it: he could see that any hope of Service catering had gone up in smoke as soon as Stan had so much as mentioned him. Nor need it necessarily end there, he realized: *they* would be on to him; and, at the thought of policemen coming round for a statement, he went clammy.

There was only one thing that he wanted, and that was his own solicitor: the little man on the Isle of Wight was of no use to him any longer.

He got up hurriedly.

'Have to excuse me,' he said. 'Got to make a phone call.'

The evening bell, the one that chimed out to announce that the Trapper's Bar was open and that fire-water was already being served there, had just sounded: and still Beryl was sleeping soundly.

Until now, the afternoon had proved to be a disappointing one for Marleen; the only people who had spoken to her had been mothers with children younger than herself. Then, just when she was getting miserable and had begun to sulk, a rather smart woman with a kind face had asked if she would like to go down into the little town to be with her while she went shopping.

That was how it was that Marleen came bursting into Beryl's room to wake her up.

'Mum,' she said. 'Mum, I've just seen Uncle Cliff. He's on the ferry. Last car on. Why's he going off like that? He said he'd booked till Monday; will he get a refund, Mum? Will he?'

BOOK THREE

Trial and Punishment

Chapter 30

If it was hot down there on the Isle of Wight – real heatstroke weather as Beryl still believed – it was fairly sweltering up in London. Tarry patches had begun to appear on road surfaces and, all round the Serpentine, the grass was littered with half-bare sun-bathers. Fleet Street, in particular, was being baked-out and desiccated. Not that there's anything very remarkable in that. It's the same every time there is a heat wave. There's something in the architecture of the place that does it. In the early afternoon, with the western sun pouring down on it, great pools of burnt-up air begin forming outside the Law Courts. Then, about three o'clock, the dam bursts and the whole accumulated load goes cascading down, past Chancery Lane and Bouverie Street, towards Ludgate Circus, to remain trapped there in the basin, sullen and suffocating until nightfall.

The *Sunday Sun* building was the last on the left going towards St Paul's, and the time was now four-fifteen.

In front of the Features Editor's desk stood Mr Cheevers, the author of the signed 'Crimeograph' series. He was in shirt sleeves; but, because he was a neat, tidy sort of man, they were neat, tidy sort of shirt sleeves, with an expanding metal bracelet fastened round the turn-ups. In his hand he held a teleprinter tear-off.

The Features Editor was in shirt sleeves, too. But he was quite the other kind of man – large, shapeless and crumpled-looking. The ends of his shirt sleeves were loose and flapping.

'It's O.K. if you want to go down there,' he said.

Mr Cheevers, however, only shook his head.

'She won't be staying on,' he replied. 'Not now. Not with those charges hanging over him. She'll be on her way back home with the kiddie. They all do it – go to ground for a bit.'

'Got the address?'

Mr Cheevers nodded.

'And the man's?'

' "Mr Fairbanks's", you mean.'

'Real name?'

'Clifford Hamson. I'll be seeing him afterwards.'

Mr Cheevers ran a smooth, freshly-laundered handkerchief across his forehead. It came away limp and sodden. The Features Editor was scratching himself.

'All right to put the two of them up somewhere – just till we've got the story?'

'Keep the price down,' the Features Editor told him.

'Go up to two?'

The Features Editor shook his head, and went on scratching.

'Fifteen hundred,' he said.

Mr Cheevers had re-folded his handkerchief. Dry side outwards, it was now back in the breast pocket of his shirt.

'Leave it to me,' he replied.

But the Features Editor was no longer listening. Not that it mattered. He usually let Mr Cheevers have his way. Besides, he was too tired to argue. He had gone over to the corner cupboard and taken out the whisky bottle and a single glass. He knew that Mr Cheevers did not drink.

'Don't buy it unless it looks big,' he said.

Mr Cheevers allowed himself a little smile. It was a knowledgeable, professional kind of smile.

'But what about the car, Mum? Who's going to collect it?'

Beryl did not answer. She was staring out of the train window, watching the trees, the cows, the cottages go past. She was, in any case, too preoccupied to think about the hire car; too preoccupied even to think about Stan. All her thoughts were concentrated upon Cliff.

Deep down in her heart she was sure that Cliff still loved her. It was just that circumstances had conspired against him. If only he'd not got mixed up with Service catering and had stuck to cheap watches and Japanese binoculars, she did not doubt that he would have been there beside her at this moment. But he'd always been one of the ambitious sort; reaching out for the stars, was how she liked to think of it.

For the first time in her life, she realized that she was alone in the world; really alone, with no one anywhere to turn to. It was Marleen who destroyed the thought.

'Did you pack my sun hat?' she asked.

Again Beryl did not answer. But Marleen was getting used to that by now. And, in consequence, she was bored. She leant back in her seat and kicked the upholstery opposite; under her breath she recited long passages from 'Hiawatha'; twice she warned Beryl that she might be going to faint.

It is always quicker by train. But to Beryl the journey seemed endless; same trees, same cows, same cottages. All that she wanted to do was to get back to Kendal Terrace. She knew, though she could not explain it, that once she had got inside No. 16 and had shut the door behind her, she would feel safer. Somehow, she and Marleen would be able to hold out there. They wouldn't be quite so defenceless.

Then she remembered about money. Would there even be any? she wondered. Did the Civil Service go on paying members of their staff who were remanded in custody? Or did National Insurance cover it? And suppose the worst happened, and they found Stan guilty? How would she be able to meet the bills for Marleen's dancing lessons then? As it was, it had been difficult enough to get Pineland Colony to cash a cheque just to pay for the railway tickets.

It was the end part of the journey that worried her most. From Pineland to the ferry and on to Waterloo had been all right. But Waterloo to Crocketts Green was something else again. Not that Beryl could have done anything else about it; with all Stan's luggage as well as hers and Marleen's, they'd never have allowed her onto public transport.

It had not been pleasant, however, watching the taxi meter tick up, and wondering if she'd have enough money to pay it. By the time they reached Kendal Terrace she reckoned that they would be just about all right, but only just, provided the driver was ready to give her a hand with the two heavy cases and then wasn't going to expect too much in the way of a tip.

It was then that, for the first time, Beryl met Mr Cheevers. He had been standing in the shadow of the rowan tree just beside the front gate.

'Mrs Pitts?' he asked.

Beryl, taken by surprise, admitted it.

'Then please allow me to look after this, madam,' he said. 'I'm from the *Sunday Sun*. You go inside. I'll see to the driver.'

Distressed as she was, Beryl did not forget her manners. As soon as the driver had been paid off, she invited Mr Cheevers inside to have a cup of coffee. And, because it was the first time they had met and because he had come a long way to see her, she brought out the best china. She even remembered to fill the little urn-shaped sugar basin with sugar of the multi-coloured kind.

Mr Cheevers was trained to take stock of his surroundings. He noted the glass-cased, all-electric clock; the triangular, marble-topped occasional table; the perpetual-motion drinking bird now temporarily stationary because its water beaker had not been re-filled.

In his mind he recorded, too, the brocaded rayon curtains, all on their patented tramline runners, and each with its individual draw-string; the pale Chinese rug spread in front of the cream-tiled fireplace; the standard lamp; the TV set; the telephone. All significantly above the general level for Kendal Terrace, he reckoned; and all so beautifully kept, so spotless.

He had plenty of time to look round because Beryl had been forced to leave him alone there. That was while she was upstairs making herself presentable. She changed hurriedly into her dark blue two-piece, switched over to plain gold earrings and did something to her hair.

It was the state of her hair that worried her most. Somewhere on the journey the white streak had become disarranged. Half of it was now on one side of the parting and half of it on the other. The effect horrified her; it looked as though she really were going white. That, and her eyes. They were terrible, too. But there was nothing that she could do about them. Red-rimmed as they were, it was obvious to anyone that she had been crying. Not that this mattered, she decided. For Stan's sake the last thing that she wanted was to appear callous and unminding.

Seated at her dressing-table she had been careful to leave the bed-room door open. That was to make sure that Marleen's door was kept shut. The last thing she wanted was to see a full-length interview with Marleen spread all over the front page of the *Sunday Sun*.

She was all prepared for her own interview, however; had been composing it, in fact, while she was still dressing. She was rather taken aback therefore when Mr Cheevers kept on stressing that it was to be exclusive.

She toyed with her coffee spoon, stirring it round meaninglessly in the half-empty cup.

'I don't know about being exclusive like,' she told him. 'I mean some of the other newspapers might want to interview me, too. It wouldn't seem fair if they couldn't, would it? Not if they asked me like.'

Mr Cheevers was trying hard to sum her up. And he was baffled.

Even distraught and tear-stained, she remained so ladylike. While pouring out the coffee she had even found time to talk about the weather. She had told him that she wouldn't be surprised if it thundered: indeed, the way things were, she rather thought it would. The fact that he was prepared to offer her money appeared altogether to have escaped her.

'It's got to be exclusive to be of interest to the *Sun*,' he told her. 'Exclusive or nothing. I'm sorry, but I'm afraid that's the way it is.'

Beryl did not reply immediately.

'I don't know. Really I don't,' she said. 'I ought to ask . . .'

And there she had to break off. Because that was what was so dreadful: there was no one she could ask. She was all by herself now. That was what she had to remember. Slowly her eyes wandered up and down the trim, pin-striped figure of Mr Cheevers. He looked honest and reliable, she thought.

'What would you advise?' she asked.

Mr Cheevers was an expert bargainer. Always first on the spot, he had more than once managed to secure a front-page feature at away-page rates. And this time he could tell that the Editor was going to be amazed by the deal that he was about to pull off.

'Exclusive,' he said. 'Five hundred pounds for the exclusive story.'

Beryl clinked her coffee spoon on the side of the cup before answering.

'How many newspapers are there?' she asked.

The question surprised Mr Cheevers. He had thought that things were proceeding faster than that.

'Just the Sundays,' he told her. 'You can forget the rest. Just three or four of the Sundays that pay big money.'

'Three or four.' Beryl slowly repeated the words after him. She seemed temporarily to have gone into a daze-state, a coma. Her lips were moving but she was not saying anything. Then, at last, she spoke.

'If they all paid five hundred that would be two thousand like, wouldn't it? It's not a lot when you think of it that way, not really it isn't, is it?'

Mr Cheevers found Beryl's habit of ending all her sentences with a question strangely confusing. He was never quite sure which it was of the questions that he was supposed to answer first. He decided to go on explaining to her about exclusives.

'But if all the papers carried the same story there wouldn't be any reason for our readers to go on buying our paper. They could buy just any old paper. That's why we pay top prices for exclusives. Our readers expect to get something the rest of them haven't got. Otherwise they'd be disappointed.'

For a moment, Mr Cheevers thought that Beryl had seen the force of the argument.

'Oh, I wouldn't want that to happen,' she said. 'Not if they'd actually bought the paper like. Not paid for it, I mean. It wouldn't seem right somehow, would it?'

Mr Cheevers smiled encouragingly.

'That's why I'm in a position to . . .'

It was a chime on the musical front-door bell that interrupted him. Beryl put her coffee cup back onto the table.

'Please don't disturb yourself,' she said. 'I'll answer it.'

Outside in the hallway, he could hear Beryl using her ladylike voice; it was the same one which she had used when welcoming him.

'There's another gentleman heah already,' she was saying. 'If it's an exclusive you want, Aim afraid Aye shell hev to ask you to wait out here in our little daining room. The lewnge is occupied, you see.'

When she returned, she gave Mr Cheevers a quick nod of understanding.

'You were right,' she said. 'He *was* after an exclusive, too. That's why I made him wait out there. I mean we can't all talk at once like. Not in front of each other, I mean, can we?'

Beryl's accent, Mr Cheevers noticed, had returned to normal. This pleased him. It showed that she was no longer treating him as a stranger. And it was encouraging that she should have come straight back to him in this way, shunting off his competitor as she did so.

But clearly there was no time to lose. He ran his hand down the knife-crease of his trousers to make sure that they were not riding up, and gave a little twitch to the handkerchief in his breast pocket.

'Mrs Pitts,' he said, 'to avoid placing any further strain upon you in having to be worried by people whom you need not see at all, I am prepared to increase my offer. And not merely increase it. I am prepared to double it. I will, here and now, on behalf of the *Sunday Sun*, offer you the sum of one thousand pounds for the exclusive rights.'

But Beryl did not appear to be listening. She was staring up at the motionless bird on the mantelshelf.

'Poor thing,' she said. 'It can't have had a drink for over a week like, can it? It's probably stuck like that forever.' She started to move towards it and then checked herself. 'You did say there were four Sunday papers, didn't you?' she asked. 'I mean four like who'd want my sort of story?'

Mr Cheevers blew his lips out.

'That's right,' he said.

And, because for a moment Beryl wasn't saying anything, he intervened.

'It's your husband's story, too,' he reminded her. 'His and yours. Our readers will expect to read both sides.'

Beryl nodded.

'I see that,' she said. 'It's only what's reasonable, isn't it? After all, it's his story like, really, when you come to think of it. I mean they wouldn't want to read about me, would they, if it hadn't been for him like.'

'Well, what about it?'

Mr Cheevers had discovered that the terse, almost rude approach was often the best when it came to rounding off awkward negotiations. Not, however, with Beryl.

'But that only makes two,' she said. 'You in here with me and that other gentleman out there in the kitchen. There's still the other two like, isn't there?'

Mr Cheevers's eye caught hers.

'Fifteen hundred.'

Beryl continued to hold the gaze. She appeared to be pondering. But before she could say anything there was another chime from the musical front-door bell.

'Perhaps that's one of them,' she said.

Mr Cheevers thought of his position in Fleet Street, his reputation for top exclusives, his invincibleness.

'Okay. Two thousand it is, then.'

Outside in the corridor there was the sound of voices. They were men's voices. Mr Cheevers listened intently, but he could make nothing of the conversation. Then he heard Beryl's social voice again.

'But of course, if you hev a search warrant, do please come rait in,' she was saying. 'You'll hev to excuse us, you know. We've only just got beck like. Aim afraid it's all a fraitful mess.'

275

Chapter 31

Next morning the papers were full of it.

There was a picture of Stan that had first appeared years ago in the staff magazine when he had just won some competition or other: it made him look young and very innocent, with the whole sweet promise of life still stretching out before him. Then there was the two-shot of Beryl and Marleen, with the top button of Marleen's jacket tantalizingly undone. And finally, there was the close-up of Cliff. In some, the name Mr Clifford Hamson was given. In others, it appeared as Mr D. Fairbanks, Mr Douglas Fairbanks, or even as Mr Douglas Fairbanks, senior. One or two of the papers resorted to quotation marks. Not that it mattered. Because, considering the circumstances in which it had been taken, it was an excellent piece of portrait-work and, no matter what it was entitled, the likeness was plain and unmistakable.

The one thing that Beryl did not like was the inset picture of No. 16 Kendal Terrace. The photograph showed a bit of both Nos. 14 and 18, with the Pitts's house in the middle, ringed round in white; done that way it made it look small and unimpressive, with no hint of all the imaginative modernization that had gone on inside.

It gave Beryl a funny feeling, too, waking up in a strange hotel bedroom and seeing a picture of her own home on the front page of the morning newspaper that had come up on her breakfast tray. But Mr Cheevers had been quite right when he had recommended, even practically insisted, that they should – to use his own words – go to ground until the heat was off. Clare Hall Private Hotel out at Chartley Wood was the place that he had selected for them, and the accommodation had been reserved in the name of 'Thompson'. Beryl did not feel too badly about it because, after all, the *Sunday Sun* was paying for everything.

And the move had certainly not come a moment too soon. By the time they had left Kendal Terrace there had been two police cars, a radio van, a mini cab, two newspaper pool cars and a television shooting-brake all parked outside. It was only because Mr Cheevers used his influence with the police and had a few whispered words with them that they were able to get away at all. As it was, Beryl and Marleen were half blinded by a photographer's flashlight as they left the house. But with one of the police cars deliberately parked across the rather narrow thoroughfare behind them, pursuit was mercifully impossible.

Mr Cheevers was helpful in other ways, too. He rang up the hire car company to tell them that their Morris 1100 would have to be collected. And he seemed to be in almost hourly contact with the paper's stringer on the Isle of Wight. This was the young man from the local *Guardian*. Mr Cheevers was very pleased with him; and the young man was very anxious to go on pleasing Mr Cheevers. It was from the young man, via Mr Cheevers, that Beryl learnt that Stan was being brought back to London. Tomorrow probably, he said.

This piece of news made Beryl feel a whole lot better. She hadn't really wanted to go away and leave him all alone like that. It was simply that, once Cliff had walked out on them, there had been nothing else that she could do. Besides, if they wouldn't let her see Stan, she kept telling herself, what was the point of being there at all? Once Stan was back in London, Mr Cheevers assured her, she would be able to see him every day if she wanted to.

And, in the meantime, the Clare Hall Private Hotel was really very comfortable. Admittedly, in conversation with one of the permanent residents, Beryl learnt that the menu never varied, just went on repeating itself week after week, month after month, over and over again, throughout the whole year. But for Beryl it was of no importance. A week at the outside was all that was needed, it seemed, for public interest to die down. It would, of course, be revived, Mr Cheevers told her, when the trial came on. But, for the time being, there were bound to be other sensations, other tragedies, other scandals that would hit the headlines instead.

Mr Cheevers spoke with authority on such matters.

When the warder came in, Stan was seated on the end of his bunk staring blankly down at his feet. Shoulders hunched and head bent forward, he could not have looked more abject. All during the night, he had certainly been pretty low. Around two o'clock, with everyone else asleep, he had been so miserable, so despairing, that he had fixed his teeth in the back of his hand and bitten down hard simply to prevent himself from crying out. But not at this particular moment. Indeed, as he heard the key turn in the lock he happened to have been thinking how surprising it was that there had never been a really good album of prison photographs. The long corridors, the pattern of light from the barred windows, the spectacle of the exercise yard on a wet morning – they would, he felt instinctively, make a complete art-collection in themselves.

He was a little surprised, too, when the warder told him that he was to go along to see the Governor, and wondered if something had gone wrong somewhere. Not that it could be because of anything that he had done; he felt quite sure of that. He hadn't given anyone the least little bit of trouble from the moment he had set foot inside the place. He had even finished the piled-up plates of prison food, with their great helpings of mashed potatoes, feeling that it might look rude, even rebellious, to thrust the whole unappetizing mass away from him.

It came as another surprise when the Governor told him that he was being sent up to London. There was nothing in the least dramatic in the way the Governor put it: just a plain statement. The interview was, in fact, entirely impersonal. If Stan had been a crated-up consignment and the Governor's office the Despatch Department, the whole routine could not have been more standardized.

It was only at the end that Stan held things up a bit. That was when he started to explain about the hire car and how Beryl didn't drive. But the Governor cut him short: Stan's solicitor, he told him, would attend to all that. Two minutes after entering the Governor's office, Stan was outside again.

And immediately the Despatch Department routine started up again. He was taken along to the Personal Effects room where the contents of his camera case – lenses, light-filters, flash bulbs and all – were spread out on the table in front of him. Another warder – a sitting-down one, this time – pushed a piece of paper towards him, and extended a large, fleshy finger.

'That's where you sign,' he said. 'They're all there. You can count 'em if you want to.'

Stan signed.

'And your hat,' the warder reminded him.

It was the floppy, white linen hat that came down rather low over his ears.

Stan signed for that, too.

278

The visit to the prison doctor was even briefer. The doctor took one look at him.

'Any symptoms?' he asked.

Stan shook his head.

The doctor, however, did not even seem to have noticed. He was already busy writing. When he had added his signature, he tore the page out of his Medical Pass book and looked up.

'That's all,' he said.

Streamlined as the procedure all was, the note of humanity had not been entirely suppressed. Before they left the Administration Block, the warder halted and turned to Stan.

'Want to use the toilet?' he asked.

And in the Reception Hall, with the barred door to the Prison on one side and the solid wooden door to the outside world on the other, it was still the same. A stout, friendly-looking man in a brown, chalk-stripe suit was standing there. He nodded reassuringly.

'I'm taking you up,' he announced.

Stan did not know quite how to reply.

'Thank you,' he said. 'It's very . . . very kind of you.'

For a moment, he even thought of adding that he hoped that it wouldn't be out of his way. But he decided that it would be wiser not to do so; the man in the chalk-stripe suit might think that he was trying to take the mickey out of him, beginning to get fresh.

The man in the brown suit came forward.

'Better have these on,' he said.

He pulled up the sleeve of Stan's yellow and magenta sports jacket as he was speaking and Stan felt something cold go round his wrist. It was the first time he had ever been in handcuffs.

'Well, let's get moving,' the man said. 'You keep up close to me and no one will notice.'

And, as though to remind Stan that he was there, he gave Stan's wrist a little tug.

The very thought of being outside in the open air with life going on all round him had come like the promise of a birthday treat. But somehow it wasn't working out right. For a start, it just didn't happen to be true that if he and the man in the brown suit kept close together, other people wouldn't notice about the handcuffs. If he and his companion had been Siamese twins they could not have kept closer: even so, all the way over in the saloon of the British Railways ferry a young couple had sat staring at them. Or, not so much at them as at their two wrists joined together. Every so often, the girl would bend over to her friend and whisper something. Head to head they would mutter together. Then, with a little giggle, they would separate again and go on staring.

Chapter 32

Mr Cheevers had been quite right. It was only one week later. But already an air crash, a local Government corruption case, and a particularly daring bank raid had thrust Stanley Pitts back into oblivion. There had been no mention of him in the papers for the last three days, and Beryl prepared for her return to Kendal Terrace.

What's more, she was determined to do the thing in style. She wore her new blue two-piece with a turquoise scarf and a pair of over-large gilt earrings with which she had been intending to surprise them all at Pinelands. It was only her hair that was the trouble. It certainly needed to have something done to it. But with hair like hers she could not afford to take chances; and out at a place like Chartley Wood she didn't know whose hands she was likely to get into. In consequence, she played safe and wore a turban. With the turquoise scarf and the two bright discs of the earrings, the whole effect was really quite striking. Even openly defiant.

Not that she was expecting to run into any kind of trouble with the neighbours. She was glad now that she knew so few of them. There was, of course, the exception like nice Mrs Ebbutt from next door. It was wonderful having her: she was always so calm and sensible. And so reliable. Practically a second mother to little Marleen, in fact; ready to put herself out at a moment's notice, even though she hadn't got a single labour-saving device in the whole house: just the original stone sink in the scullery and an upright, black gas stove and that appalling bath-tub upstairs standing there on four squat legs like a hippopotamus.

As the car turned into Kendal Terrace, Beryl felt a sudden pang. Everything was so familiar, so ordinary, so normal. It looked the kind of street in which nothing unusual could ever happen. And so it was, except for the fact that, nowadays, the householder from No. 16 wouldn't be leaving to catch the 8.10 in the morning, and that there would be no mustard-coloured Mustang parked outside on summer evenings. But after a bit even that, Beryl supposed, would stop being unusual and become just another part of the overall ordinariness.

She was glad now that she had made Marleen wear her white linen dress with the plain leather belt. It looked so restrained, so suitable. And she was now more glad than ever that she had bought that set of matching luggage for the Isle of Wight. Seeing them being lifted one after another out of the boot by the uniformed chauffeur would in itself have been sufficient to disappoint any spectator on the look-out for signs of panic, distress or even hesitation.

Once inside the front gate, however, all was not quite the same. Not only had one of the gnomes – the one sitting on the heavily-speckled toadstool – had half his head chipped off, but one of his companions – the fishing one – was entirely missing. There was nothing there except for the dent that Stan had made in the cement for the little chap to stand in; the dent to show where through wet and shine, summer and winter alike, he had once dangled his plastic rod with the nylon line and the bright red metal float.

The state of the doormat came as something of a shock, too. It looked as though everyone in England had been writing. As well as the electricity bill and the telephone account there were anonymous post-cards conveying veiled mysterious threats; letters from Civil Rights movements, circulars from money-lenders and second-mortgage firms; expressions of sympathy from the vicar and the bank manager; and a request for a sitting from a firm that called themselves Court photo-graphers.

Beryl was still sorting through the correspondence when there was a ring at the bell. It was the calm, sensible, reliable Mrs Ebbutt; but calm, sensible and reliable no longer. At the sight of Beryl, she threw herself upon her.

'Oh, you poor dear,' she said, all in a rush, with the words tumbling over each other as they came out. 'How terrible for you. I haven't slept a wink since it happened. I've just lain there thinking about you all the time. And I've prayed. How I've prayed. Prayed that it must all be some terrible, hideous mistake. It *is* all a mistake, isn't it? Tell me there's no truth in all the awful things they've been saying. Tell me.'

And, overcome by emotion, she clutched at Beryl for support.

Beryl could not feel other than flattered that Mrs Ebbutt should care so much. It showed what a dear she was. On the other hand, Beryl found herself somehow resenting it. After all, it was her ordeal, her own private tragedy, not Mrs Ebbutt's, and it seemed that Mrs Ebbutt was getting more out of it than she was. The bit about not having been able to sleep was what particularly annoyed her. Because out at the private hotel at Chartley Wood Beryl had, as it happened, been sleeping exceptionally well.

It was little Marleen who managed to restore the balance. Seeing Mrs Ebbutt in tears, she began to cry, too. And she could cry louder. She howled. She let herself go. She flung herself about. She buried her face in the sofa cushions. She hit things.

After a while, Beryl could stand it no longer. Putting Mrs Ebbutt down in the nearest comfortable chair, she went across and slapped Marleen. Then, remembering her mother-image, she drew back and smiled across at Mrs Ebbutt.

'Poor little mite,' she said. 'She's missing her Daddy, that's what it is. She's all torn apart like inside her. Only she can show her feelings, and I mustn't.'

In her heart Beryl knew that it was the shopkeepers who would be the worst. Before going along to the High Street, she had to brace herself. Not that she could have taken exception to anything that was actually said; it was the unspoken bit, the sideways glances, that she minded. And the most painful moment of all had come in the Wide World Supermarket when she had been least expecting it. The Wide World was one of those shops that she knew by heart. She and Marleen – and Stan, too, on Saturday mornings – had been going there for years. She had just paid the bill and stuffed the carton of ice cream into the carrier-bag along with the wholewheat biscuits and the Ty-Phoo tea, when she felt a hand come down upon her own. It was the female cashier's hand; and it was a brown hand. Beryl turned and found herself looking down into a pair of dark Indian eyes, already half brimming over with tears. There was nothing but human pity and affection shining out of them.

The hand was meant well: Beryl knew that. All the same, it was upsetting. It upset her so much, in fact, that she realized then and there that she would never be able to go into the Wide World again. And that would be a real loss, a proper set-back, because the Wide World was one of the few shops that she really knew by heart. She could have gone round the shelves with her eyes shut, picking up the chosen dainties one by one, not faltering at the invisible dividing lines where the tinned fruits turned suddenly into household cleaners, or the frozen foods became cocktail wafers and salted almonds.

It was different, of course, with Monsieur Louis (late of the Ritz).

Somehow she had never thought of him as keeping a shop. He was more of a professional man really; someone with gentle, understanding hands. She didn't in the least mind if he tried to be consoling to her. As he put the pale, lilac-coloured gown around her and tied the little draw-strings at the back, she could feel herself settling down in the chair as though she belonged there.

Watching him in the mirror, she could see how quick and deft he was. And appreciative, too. He ran his hand across her hair as though polishing it, breaking off to give it little pats, letting strands of it trickle through his fingers for the sheer pleasure of feeling it in such perfect condition. There was one habit he had that had always fascinated her. As he removed the pins he would hold them, two or three in his hand together, and then place them between his lips while he went on unpinning. With anyone else, it would have disgusted her. She would have refused to allow him to use the same pins when he came to put her hair up again. But Monsieur Louis was so nice that somehow it didn't seem to matter.

In the ordinary way, time spent in the hairdresser's had always seemed to Beryl to be among the most restful moments in the whole working week. She would close her eyes and dream; quite often she would really doze. Not today, however. Suddenly, in the midst of this warm, safe world of comfort and attention, it all came back to her. She could see the expression on Stan's face as he shook his head at her from the dock; she re-lived the awfulness of the journey back with just the two of them. She remembered Cliff. And, as she remembered, she wept. Not openly, not so that anyone could hear; just little muffled sobs, spasms that she could not suppress. Monsieur Louis pretended not to notice. With all his old skill he simply went on piling her hair up again, working on the white streak as though it were a piece of ornamental inlay work.

But it had only been pretence. As Beryl was leaving he thrust a little packet into her hand; and, considering what it was, hardly such a little one, either. It was a bottle of scent – real scent, not toilet water – and there was a small, sticky patch on the top where he had scraped off the price label with his fingernail before giving it to her.

For some reason, just thinking about it made her want to start weeping again.

Not, by any means, that Beryl kept thinking only of herself. On the

284

contrary, she knew only too well what an ordeal it must be for Marleen to have to go back to Crocketts Green High on that first day of term. That was why she insisted on walking down all the way to the school gates herself even though Marleen protested that she could perfectly well go alone. But Beryl was not deceived. She knew how much like her Marleen really was, how never for a moment would she admit how much she dreaded meeting all her school friends again. And outside the school, Beryl bent down impulsively and kissed her. It was something that she had not done since Marleen had gone up from the Junior School and had, quite abruptly one day – even rather rudely, she recalled – asked if she would stop doing it.

It was now the eleven o'clock interval. In the large, asphalt-surfaced playground the girls were all standing round, straws and milk-bottles in their hands; and it was around Marleen that they were standing. Her colour was high as though she had been running, and she was talking rather fast, even though she was careful to keep her voice low in case there were mistresses around.

'. . . and then the other lot of policemen, the plain-clothes ones, came back again,' she was saying, 'and they slashed everything open, the couch, the cushions, the mattresses, everything. There wasn't a carpet left in the place when they'd finished. Naturally, Mummy was hysterical. I didn't know what she was going to do with herself. It was only lucky for her that I was around. I went up to the medicine chest in the bathroom and threw away everything that had "Poison" written on it. I even hid the aspirins because it was a full bottle, you see.'

She broke off because she could see the day monitor coming out into the playground ready to ring the bell; it was only a matter of seconds before everyone would have gone inside again.

'Next day Mummy thanked me,' she concluded simply.

Chapter 33

Stan's new lawyer, a Mr Marbuck picked at random from the Legal Aid List, promised to be a real winner. Indeed, it was hard to believe that he could be a member of the same profession as that frightened little muddler down on the Isle of Wight. Mr Marbuck was small, shrill-voiced and Napoleonic. Whatever he did was done briskly and rudely, other people being brushed aside on the way. It was to the police in particular that he showed himself at his rudest, his most aggressive, making it plain from the outset that he wasn't going to believe a word that any of them might say. From the very moment he heard the charges, his nostrils curled. Even without going into the case he could detect the old, familiar smell of trumped-up evidence, fraudulent witnesses, confessions obtained under duress.

It was Stan's signed confession that brought the two of them into conflict; that, and Stan's natural obstinacy.

There, in the upright-chair discomfort of the private interview room, with the lid of a tin box on the plain deal table for an ashtray, Stan sat facing him.

'It's very good of you,' he was saying. 'Very good indeed to go to so much trouble. I'm very grateful. I am really. But there's no point in going on about it. Because it all happened just like I said. I did take those photographs, and I did get paid for them. So, while I can't thank you enough . . .'

Suddenly Mr Marbuck could bear it no longer. He stumped out his half-smoked cigarette in the tin lid, and got up.

'But the plea,' he said. 'The plea. We agreed all that yesterday. It's going to be Not Guilty. Those confessions were forced out of you, remember. You'd have said anything, you were so frightened . . .'

But, even if he were disappointed in his client, Mr Marbuck thought very highly of Beryl. She was a woman after his own heart. Her recent experiences had led her, too, to be distrustful of policemen; and every day her circle of dislikes was widening. Her additional hates already included court ushers, magistrates' clerks, magistrates themselves, warders and prison governors.

'Well, it must be some sort of vendetta or something, or they wouldn't all be against him, not all at once like, would they?' she had asked, her large dark eyes fixed firmly upon him. 'Not if everything was fair, I mean. Not really fair.'

Mr Marbuck had agreed with her; and, encouraged, Beryl had continued.

'Because he couldn't have done the sort of thing like they said he did, could he? Not him, he couldn't. Not Stan.'

'But the confessions,' Mr Marbuck had impressed upon her. 'We must clear up the matter of the confessions.'

It was because of those confessions that Beryl was now sitting in the prison waiting-room; and there is something strangely lifeless and dispiriting about all waiting-rooms. They are rooms not made to be lived in. A pair of slippers beside a chair or a plate of sandwiches upon the table would be unthinkable. And, of all waiting-rooms, prison waiting-rooms are the worst. They are designed to discourage visitors rather than pander to them. The décor alone is enough to achieve this purpose. Pale oatmeal-coloured walls descend to a spinach-coloured dado; and, where the oatmeal stops and the spinach takes over, there is a thick khaki stripe to separate the courses.

The chairs, too, are unaccommodating. They are not built to be sunk into; with an HM Prison chair, it's at attention or nothing. No carpet on the floor, either. Just polished brown linoleum, crinkled in places where the floor boards run across. And the whole place entirely pictureless. Merely notices. Notices everywhere about not smoking, not carrying fire-arms, not swearing, not causing a disturbance, not committing a nuisance, not attempting to pass over money, alcohol or cigarettes. And all made more dismal, too, by the harsh glare of the bare electric light bulbs dangling down from the plain white-washed ceiling.

Nor was this one improved by the visitors who were using it. Beryl thought that she had never seen anything like them since the Magistrates' Court on the Isle of Wight. One glance would have been enough to tell her that they were drawn from the criminal classes. And she was not in the least surprised to find that such a high proportion were not British. Not proper British-British, that is; more Pakistani-British and West Indian-British like.

With both windows of the waiting-room shut fast, the atmosphere wasn't too pleasant, either; a bit too spicy for Beryl's taste, too curry-ish. Try as she would, she could not help wrinkling up her nose. As she did so, she noticed that one of the Pakistani ladies was wrinkling up hers, too.

Only hers was a jewelled nose. There was a white stone mounted in the side and, every time she sniffed, the stone twinkled. What was more, the Pakistani lady kept turning her head from side to side clearly searching something out. And, when she came to Beryl, she stopped. It was evident that, if Beryl did not like the odour of chutney and chilli sauce, the Pakistani lady did not care for Monsieur Louis' presentation bottle of perfume.

Beryl remembered her manners and kept her dignity. She gave a final sniff and simply looked away.

Not that the Pakistani lady had been without some right on her side. It was an undeniably powerful perfume that Beryl had been given; at once both pungent and lingering. And penetrating in its own subtle fashion. It was the first thing that Stan noticed when Beryl entered the interview room. And to Beryl's intense annoyance, Stan himself began sniffing, too.

Looking back on it afterwards, Beryl recognized that this was what had made the whole visit so forlorn, so heart-breaking. But, at the time, she had been helpless; trapped, as it were, by her own loving kindness in being there at all.

'Well, what's the matter with you?' she asked. 'Don't you like the way I smell, or something?'

She was sorry to have to put the question to him point-blank like that in front of the prison officer who was sitting at the end of the little table, only a few feet away from them, pretending not to be listening.

But she could not restrain herself. It was the third time she'd been to see him inside that dreadful place and he simply didn't seem to realize what a strain it was for her; what an ordeal, what torment.

And Stan's next remark made her wish more than ever that she hadn't come this time.

'Did Cliff give it to you?' he asked.

She did not attempt to answer him; could not have done so, in fact, because already she was having to choke back her tears. Nowadays, as she kept telling herself, the very name 'Cliff' was a dagger directed straight towards her heart. Nor could she possibly explain; the shame of saying that he had walked out on her would have humiliated her more than she could bear.

There was a long pause, during which the prison officer looked up to see what was happening. Then she gave a loud, involuntary gulp.

'You haven't even asked how little Marleen is,' she said, her voice faltering. 'Not even enquired after your own daughter.'

'Well, how is she? She's all right, isn't she?'

A note of sudden anxiety had entered into his voice. It was just what Beryl had intended.

'With all the other girls knowing that her father's in prison?' she demanded. 'What do you think?'

Stan shrugged his shoulders.

'I'm sorry,' he said. 'There's nothing I can do about it. Not now there isn't.'

That was when Beryl lost her temper with him.

'Oh, yes, there is,' she said, not even attempting to keep her voice down so that the warder would not hear her. 'There's plenty. And don't you forget it.'

'Like what?'

'Like withdrawing those stupid confessions of yours. Like saying they were all lies.'

'But they weren't. They were true. Every word of them.'

Beryl could feel her hands tightening up in anger.

'Well, you don't have to go on saying so, do you?' she snapped back at him. 'Stop thinking of yourself for once. Try to remember about me and Marleen.'

This time it was Stan's voice that faltered.

'I do,' he told her quietly. 'I remember about you and Marleen all the time.'

'Then tell 'em it was sunstroke. Say you were all confused like and can't remember anything about it.'

Stan did not reply immediately. He just sat there, silent and tight-lipped.

He was about to speak when the prison officer interrupted him.

'I'm sorry,' he said, 'but that's all for this afternoon. I've given you an extra couple of minutes as it is.'

It was not only Beryl and Mr Marbuck who were worried about Stan's obstinacy; there was Mr Cheevers as well.

Mr Cheevers, indeed, was in the worst position of them all. He had already chanced his arm, and his whole professional reputation was now at stake. Fifteen hundred pounds the Features Editor had said, and Mr Cheevers had gone up to two thousand; been driven up to it, rather. And if, as Mr Cheevers had heard, Stan really had made a full confession, there wouldn't be anything for the front page at all; just a side-column piece headed something like 'ADMIRALTY CLERK ADMITS SELLING SECRETS'.

It was in order to get hold of as much of the drama as was still rescuable that Mr Cheevers paid another of his visits to Crocketts Green. Using one of the company's pool cars the journey took him only just over forty minutes. That was because he had come to know the route by heart. Turning right at Whitecross, thus skirting Mandley Green altogether, meant that you could cut out the notorious traffic black-spot of Crocketts Green High Street; and it was a tip worth knowing. Nowadays Mr Cheevers reached Kendal Terrace via Derwent Gardens and Fell Road, and *not* down Westmorland Avenue at all.

Once inside No. 16, it was the orderliness of everything that so impressed Mr Cheevers. And it was always the same – nothing out of place, everything freshly polished, no finger-marks, no dirty ashtrays, no squashed-down cushions on the three-piece suite; altogether, it might have been a show house, something in an Ideal Home Exhibition designed to set an example for the newly married. Mr Cheevers made a note of the fact and, as he did so, a disturbing thought came to him. It was only in a dominantly feminine ménage that everything could have been kept so perpetually neat as all that. Mr Cheevers found himself wondering how well Stanley Pitts had fitted into those surroundings; and, for an instant, the extraordinary thought flashed across his mind that it might have been in a mood of sheer rebellion that he had suddenly broken out.

Beryl herself was as immaculate, as poised, as ever. It was her Mexican housecoat, the one with the Sun God buttons, that she had decided to wear. And the decision had not been reached without something of a struggle. Beryl was naturally sensitive on all matters of etiquette, and on matters of dress etiquette in particular. There must, she felt, be something that was *right* for a woman whose husband was in prison to wear, something that wasn't too much like mourning, as if in her mind poor Stan was condemned already and, at the same time, wasn't too modish and might make it appear as though she simply didn't care.

Mr Cheevers had just reached the point of explaining to Beryl that she would have to cast her mind back to that single moment in time when she had first learnt of Stan's arrest, and then deliberately re-live the whole episode in her memory. Only by this means, he assured her, would she be able to recapture the authentic mood of anguish; and that, he went on, was what the readers were waiting for.

'Just tell me simply in your own words,' Mr Cheevers was advising her. 'It doesn't matter how they sound. I can always re-phrase it for you so that our readers will be able to understand what you were up against.'

'Why couldn't they understand like I told it to them?'

Mr Cheevers smiled.

'It's really a question of what they're used to,' he said.

'And they wouldn't like something different for once? Not something to take them out of themselves like?'

Mr Cheevers told her that he did not think so. Sunday newspaper readers, he stressed, were a strangely loyal band, practically a mystic society; a brotherhood that reassembled every sabbath. Beryl understood. She and Stan had been readers of the *Sunday Sun* for years.

'You ready?' she asked. She had closed her eyes by now, and she was breathing deeply.

Mr Cheevers nodded and then, realizing that she could not see him, added: 'Carry on.'

'What was it like when I learnt that my husband had been arrested on a charge of espionage?' she started, speaking very rapidly. 'That bit goes into italics because that's not like me speaking. This is me now. New paragraph. Black type.'

'But ...'

Mr Cheevers tried unsuccessfully to intervene. Beryl, however, was determined to continue.

Beryl kept her eyes closed and began again. Her voice had dropped to a low monotone, and it was almost as if she were reading. Mr Cheevers's shorthand notebook lay open on his knee.

'It was like an Atomic Bomb, capital "A" capital "B", exploding in my heart scratch out "heart" and make it "soul" ', she said. 'Everywhere was darkness. I was left numb, speechless, obliterated. Above me hung a great mushroom cloud of misery. For myself I was nothing. All I could think of was poor Stan and little Marleen . . .' She paused.

'Go back and say "My thoughts were only for my man and for our child." Then go straight on. "How can I save them? How can I avert disaster?" I kept asking. But no answer came. It was a moment when prayer itself was without avail. It was the abyss.'

This time when she paused it was only to take breath. Mr Cheevers, however, was trying hard to check her.

'Keep it personal,' he said. 'I want little things, like making yourself a cup of tea or having to take an aspirin.'

Beryl nodded.

'Horrified I drew back,' she resumed. 'The tempest of my fears raged round me. I . . .'

It was Marleen's return from school that cut Beryl short. The child looked flushed, and it was obvious that she had been crying. She ignored Mr Cheevers completely.

'Tracey kicked me,' she said.

Beryl got up, smoothed the housecoat down as she rose.

'Manners, darling, manners,' she said. 'Come and say how-do-you-do to Mr Cheevers.'

Marleen came forward. It was a hot, unwashed hand that she held out, and Mr Cheevers was surprised to find how damp it was; Mr Cheevers did not like children.

'How's little Marleen?' he asked.

The 'little' had slipped out quite unintended; Marleen was actually far bigger than he had first expected.

Marleen stared back at him.

'All right,' she said.

This was where Beryl had to come to Mr Cheevers's rescue; it was one of her rules of life that visitors had to be put at their ease at all times.

'Now be a good girlie and run along,' she said. 'Because Mr Cheevers is interviewing me like. I'm telling him what happened so he can write about it in the newspaper.'

'Why?' Marleen asked.

'Because Mr Cheevers writes about all the big trials where they have judges and that kind of thing, don't you, Mr Cheevers?'

Mr Cheevers gave a little smile.

'That is so,' he said modestly.

Marleen's gaze softened.

'Have you ever met a murderer?' she asked.

It was one question too many. Beryl wanted to go on with her own reminiscences, and not have to listen to other people's. She went over and gave Marleen a nudge with her elbow.

'Your tea's all ready for you,' she said. 'There's fresh pineapple juice in the fridge.'

It wasn't really fresh: it came out of a collapsible waxed cardboard container like everything else nowadays. But it said on the label that it was fresh, and so Beryl supposed that it must be; fresher at least than all the other makes that didn't even pretend to be fresh.

'Well, go along with you,' she said.

But Marleen didn't move. She had turned to Beryl again.

'You will write a note, won't you, Mum?' she asked. 'Because Tracey's got it in for me. She kicked me on purpose. And can I have a Band-aid to go over the place, Mum? It's all bleeding.'

Beryl had her arm round Marleen's shoulder by now, and had managed to work her over to the door.

'Band-aid in the get-well-soon box in the corner cupboard,' she said, using her specially-musical voice this time, the one that sounded as though she could never possibly get upset about anything.

Out of sight behind the shelter of the half-open door, Beryl was able to give her a little push. Then she turned back to Mr Cheevers.

'Was what I was telling you all right like?' she asked. 'Is it what the readers are waiting for?'

Before he could reply, the telephone had started to ring, and Beryl went across to answer it.

The room, even with its Summerland extension and the sliding aluminium doors leading onto the patio, was still only a small one. And the telephone itself was a comparatively new instrument, with a powerful diaphragm in the ear-piece. Mr Cheevers could overhear every word perfectly.

'That you Beryl?' the voice asked. 'Cliff here.'

It seemed to Mr Cheevers that, for a moment, Beryl hesitated. He noticed that the fingers of her free hand had suddenly closed up as if she were grasping something. Then, as suddenly, she released her grip again. And there was no hesitation whatever about her reply: this time it was not even her musical voice that she was using, merely her social one.

'Aim afrayed you heve the wrong number,' she said, speaking slowly and distinctly. 'Aih doan't knoew anyoen of thet naeme.'

Having said it, she put back the receiver. Everything that she had done had been neat and controlled and orderly. It was only that, in Mr Cheevers's opinion, she had put the receiver back rather more firmly, more decisively, than is usual with just an ordinary, everyday wrong number.

Chapter 34

Even though it had only been a matter of weeks – four-and-a-half to be exact – that Stan had been lodged in Cell 16, second landing, D Block in Her Majesty's Prison, he now felt as though he had lived there all his life.

Everything about it was now familiar – the size; the colour; the smell; the noise; the texture of the mattress; the red-bound Bible with the words 'Holy Bible' at the top and 'Property of HM Prison Commissioners' across the bottom; the antique-looking slop pail.

Already, he had discovered several very interesting things. About the bars at the window, for instance. They were what had worried him most when he had first gone in there; they were what had produced that zoo-like, caged-in feeling. But not so any longer. He had found out that if you faced up square to the window and gazed at it long enough, the iron bars slowly disappeared, eventually vanishing clean away to nothing, leaving you staring out at clear sky and clouds and the occasional bird that might with luck be passing over. Admittedly, it wasn't very comfortable because the window was set so deliberately high in the wall. Indeed, it was obvious that the prison architect had put it up there specially to discourage peepers. This meant that you had to tilt your head right back, with your throat drawn tight as though waiting to be shaved by a barber. You couldn't, in fact, go in for very much of that kind of window-gazing because quite soon you got a high-pitched ringing in the ears and then, if you persisted, you went dizzy. More than once Stan had been forced to sit on the edge of his bed with his head between his knees simply to recover.

That was where he was sitting at the moment. But there was nothing wrong with him this time. He was just meditating. One after another, a whole procession of disconnected thoughts had been passing through his mind. He had been thinking, for example, of how strange it was that the number of his cell should be sixteen which was the same number as his house in Kendal Terrace. That had put him on to wondering how Beryl's cottage-type dish-washer was working; labour-saving though it could be – with a complete three-cycle wash *and dry* all executed within sixty minutes – it did tend to go wrong rather too frequently. Stan knew just where the design-fault lay: that was why he was able to put things right so quickly. But, without his help, Stan reckoned that by now poor Beryl would probably have been driven back to the indignity of the washing-up bowl. And this made him feel very miserable because he knew that, of all household tasks, washing-up was the one that Beryl most detested. Then, before he knew what was happening to him, he was back into his old trick of talking to himself.

'Well, there you are, Stanley, my lad,' he began. 'It's nobody's fault but your own. You're the one who's got her into all this trouble. If it hadn't been for you, she'd be living a happy, contented life like other people. It's quite a nice little house really. But she'll never forgive you if she can't finish off that attic-conversion idea of hers. She's set her heart on getting the attic right. That's something she's bound to be angry about.' He broke off and, hands folded in his lap, stared blankly at the wall in front of him. For no particular reason he was recalling how Beryl had lost her temper when he had first told her that he wouldn't withdraw anything in any of the confessions that he had made. And as it came back to him, he started up the conversation again. 'Perhaps it's just as well for you that's the way she does feel,' he re-assured himself. 'It's better that she's mad at you. If she was just sorry that would really break your heart, that would.'

Because the edge of the bed was a hard one, and because he had been sitting there for some time, he felt the pain of pins-and-needles running all down his left side. He stretched himself, and re-crossed his legs. And that time it was about Marleen that he consoled himself. 'She'll be all right. I know she will. Nothing to worry about there. Beryl'd never let anything happen to her little Marleen.'

It was strange about Marleen. He was very fond of her; proud of her, too, when he came to compare her with other people's children. But she had never been really close to him; she had always been Beryl's little Marleen rather than Stan's little Marleen.

With his mind more or less at rest for the moment, he blew out his cheeks and allowed himself the luxury of a long, deep sigh. 'You did the right thing, Stan, when you signed that confession of yours,' he said. 'It was the only way. You wouldn't have wanted to have all that on your conscience for ever.'

Then from nowhere and with no warning, all the old anxieties came crowding back. What was worse was that one of them, the most pressing one, wouldn't go away again.

'If you go to prison,' a different voice kept asking, 'what's going to happen to your pension? And if your pension stops, what are they both going to live on? That's what you've got to think about – not about how much better you feel simply because you decided to come clean.'

That was when he got up and kicked the painted brickwork beside the door.

'I suppose I'll have to say it was sunstroke,' he said. 'Tell 'em one big lie and be done with it.'

There's a lot that can be said against the law – that it's unjust, antiquated, inhumane. But no one can say that it rushes things. Stan's four-and-a-half weeks had become three months by now, and still there was no sign of the trial coming any nearer. All that had happened so far was that they had moved him up to the third floor – cell 22 this time, the exact duplicate of his old one, merely one storey higher.

Also, for no reason except that he'd had nothing else to do, he had grown himself a moustache. It was not really much of a moustache, because Stan's hair was too thin and pale for it to show up properly, and it didn't bristle outwards as much as moustaches should do. It was simply a limp band of down. But Stan was pleased with it. He kept stroking away at his upper lip; even at times wondering what Beryl would say if he should decide to grow a beard as well.

Because of the delay, Mr Marbuck had practically given up seeing him. He had, indeed, only been to the prison on Stan's account once since Stan had been moved up a floor. Not that Stan held it against him in any way. Mr Marbuck had done everything that could have been expected of him; and, ever since Stan had agreed that the confessions must have been forced out of him, Mr Marbuck had become his friend again. What was so strange about it was that he was beginning to believe that they had been.

As it happened, Beryl's visits were becoming less frequent. Last week, for instance, she had skipped it altogether, merely telephoning through a message about not being well or something. It hadn't, however, upset Stan too badly; had hardly upset him at all, in fact. Beryl's other visits had all proved strangely upsetting – they had reminded him too much of the other world outside. And this was something that he had to avoid at all costs. Stan, indeed, was in process of learning the first great law of prison life – and that is to live it.

It's the same with soldiers serving overseas. Letters from home aren't always the little rays of sunshine they are supposed to be; quite often they simply unsettle distant sons and husbands who have grown used to being away. There's very little room for sentiment where armies or prisons are concerned.

And remember that Beryl had her own problems. Like the prison social worker, for instance. The woman had arrived at Kendal Terrace without prior notice and had straight away begun asking her questions.

What's more, the timing could hardly have been worse. It was three o'clock in the afternoon when she got there. Beryl had taken off her dress and was lying down on the large double bed with the pillows humped up in the nape of her neck so as not to disarrange her hair-do. The curtains were half drawn; last week's issue of *Woman's Own* was spread face downwards, open upon the bedclothes; and, on the oval bedside table, lay a half-eaten Mars Bar. Beryl was just beginning to feel sleepy, drifting gently away to nothingness, when she heard the chimes of the front-door bell.

Because it was a bay window, it was just possible to part the curtains and peer down onto the doorstep. The canopy was an obstruction: it cut off the upper part of anyone standing there. But it left the whole of the feet and legs showing. These were feminine and looked respectable enough, not like the feet and legs of anyone likely to be selling things. Beryl grew curious and put on her dressing-gown.

The visitor had the advantage of experience on her side. There was no doubt about that. She had called not merely on dozens but on hundreds of other women in Beryl's position, and she knew exactly how to put them at their ease.

'It is Mrs Pitts, isn't it?' she asked, speaking throughout at top speed, as soon as the front door was opened. 'I do hope this isn't inconvenient for you. I know what a nuisance people are when they drop in like this, but I wanted to have a word with you about your husband. I'm from the welfare department, you see. You don't mind, do you?'

In the end, it proved to be quite a long visit; nearly a full hour, in fact. That was because first Beryl had to excuse herself while she went upstairs to put a dress on – the one that she had been wearing, the blue check one with the open neck that was draped over the back of the bedroom chair didn't somehow seem quite suitable; then she had to go through to the kitchenette to make some tea for both of them; and finally, quite deliberately, she kept her visitor back showing her photographs of little Marleen as a baby, simply dragging things out long enough for her to be able to show off little Marleen herself on her return from school.

The way things had turned out, Beryl found herself enjoying every minute of it. She saw so few visitors in any case, and this one proved to be so sympathetic, so understanding. She knew exactly the right questions to ask, the probing ones that really made it possible for Beryl to open up. And, in the result, they talked about money, and sex, and nervous shock, and the unfairness of life, and the strain of bringing up even one child, and interior decoration and hairdressers, and the pangs of sudden bereavement, and cut-price supermarkets.

It was while she was talking that she realized what a relief it was to have found someone who really wanted to listen. Stan himself had never been a good listener. She had always suspected him of thinking about something else even while he pretended to be paying attention; and more than once she had caught him out afterwards.

But there was more to it than that. It wasn't just the sheer pleasure of being listened to that counted: it was the way it took your mind off things. And this was funny when you came to think of it. Because the whole, the sole reason of the visit had been Stan; and, looking back on it, they had hardly even mentioned him. More talked round him like.

There was only one thing throughout the whole fifty-five minutes that had kept on worrying her and that was the way her visitor was dressed. She could not understand how any woman in her official position – especially anyone who had to go around meeting people – could carry a black handbag when she was wearing a blue dress and brown walking shoes.

All the same, Beryl hoped that she would come round again some time. And Marleen hoped so, too. Marleen liked her. The lady had said what pretty hair Marleen had.

Nowadays, however, there is more to human welfare than just welfare workers. There are psychiatrists as well. Stan, in fact, was on his way to see one at the moment.

It was quite a walk, too, from D Block over to G where the medicos lived. That was because the prison had been built on the wrong-shaped site. Seen on the map, it resembled a capital 'L' with the base and upright both the same length. To reach G, Stan and the warder had to go along the length of the exercise yard, past the chapel and the bakery, through the courtyard leading to E, and then turn right by the clock tower and keep straight on to F, bearing off to the left a little to reach the laundry, the mortuary, and eventually the dispensary and the sick bays.

Stan was rather glad of the walk. Apart altogether from the pleasure of being in motion, it was nice to be actually going somewhere, not simply round and round the asphalt pathway that fringed the exercise yard. And the warder – or rather the 'screw' as Stan had now learnt to call him – was one of the friendly sort. He talked: Association Football was his subject and he brought Stan up to date on everything in the game – results, gates, transfer fees, penalties, sackings. Stan kept nodding his head, and thanking him for the information.

But Beryl had been quite right about him. He wasn't really listening. He was thinking of his desk down in the sub-basement at Frobisher House, and wondering who was sitting there now. Even though he had never liked it so much as his old desk upstairs with the view down the corridor, it hadn't proved too bad once you got used to it. It was quiet; and it was private. In fact, one way and another, you could have a perfectly good time down there amid the filing cabinets and the card index systems – that is, if you didn't mind working in artificial light and re-circulated air the whole time.

When Stan finally got to G Block, he could tell at once that it wasn't a regular prison doctor, not a staff man, that he was seeing. All prison staff had the same pale, waxy look as the other inmates, whereas this one seemed fairly brimming over with good health. He was surprisingly young, too; younger than his patient, Stan reckoned. And well dressed in a smart, trendy kind of way. No baggy trousers protruding from under a long white overall for him. No clip-on thermometer. No stethoscope.

'Come in,' he said to Stan. 'Sit down. Make yourself at home.' Then he turned to the accompanying warder. 'Shan't be needing you,' he added. 'Not just now, that is. Give me twenty minutes. Better make it half an hour. Thanks for coming over.'

It was certainly a change from ordinary prison life, hearing people being spoken to like that. Even the room itself was different; deliberately, defiantly different. The walls were peach-coloured, and they had pictures on them. Two of them were of country landscapes – one of winter and one of harvest time. But it was the other two that attracted Stan's attention. One of those was a French colour print of a small boy relieving himself into a pond of what would otherwise have been fresh drinking water. Stan remembered that he had seen it before in a print-shop window and had always considered it to be in pretty poor taste.

What surprised him more, however, was the one over the fireplace. That was a matt print of a good-looking studio nude. The photographer had posed her up against one of those old-fashioned cheval-glass mirrors so that, in a single shot, most of both sides of her were showing. The lighting was good, distinctly good. Tungsten probably, Stan thought. By any standards it was a thoroughly professional sort of job.

While Stan was looking at the photograph, the psychiatrist was observing Stan. And the psychiatrist was very pleased with himself. The nude photograph trick was something that he had devised himself. It was now an integral part of his clinical technique and, once again, it was working perfectly.

'Would you like to have taken that photograph?' he asked.

Stan did not reply immediately. He was too busy admiring the sheer mastery of the lighting. Now that he'd had time to study it, he was really envious.

'Not half,' he said, running his tongue across his lips as he said the words.

The psychiatrist allowed himself a little inward smile. By old-fashioned conventional methods it would have taken weeks, months probably, to elicit such an admission, and here the patient was blurting it out before he'd even had time to sit down. No wonder that the psychiatrist's latest paperback, 'Sex and Sanity', was prominently displayed on all the bookstalls, and that the BBC was repeating his series, 'Your Other Self', on the Third Programme.

He decided to probe a bit deeper.

'You could have done, you know. You've got a camera, haven't you?'

The mention of his camera suddenly made Stan feel very unhappy. He'd been missing it terribly. Also, he had been reminded of those awful girls that Helga had brought along to the little studio off the Edgware Road. Looking back on it, that had been where all his trouble had really started.

He shook his head decisively.

'Not my line,' he said.

The psychiatrist did not attempt to press him.

'Come over here and sit down,' he said. 'Just take it easy for a bit.'

Again it surprised Stan that the psychiatrist should take the hard swivel chair and give him the low, upholstered one.

'And put your feet up,' he went on. 'You'll be more comfortable that way.'

The cushions gave out a gentle wheezing sound as he sank into them, and he found himself wishing that he could have had an easy chair like this one over in cell 22 in D Block. He closed his eyes for a moment in sheer pleasure.

'And how is your wife keeping?'

It was another of the psychiatrist's catch-questions; something tossed out quite casually as though by an old family friend.

Stan did not know what to say. The last few visits hadn't gone off at all well, and he did not want to be reminded of them. But he remembered his manners. If the psychiatrist was polite enough to ask, he supposed that it was up to him to show a little politeness, too.

'Pretty well, considering,' he said. 'In all the circumstances, you know.'

'You must be missing her.'

Even though it wasn't a question at all, Stan reckoned that it called for some kind of an answer, and a pleasant one at that. But, try as he would to think of something nice to say, the words seemed to stick in his throat. The best that he could manage was a low, meaningless gulp.

Even so, it was enough: it told the psychiatrist all that he wanted to know. He recognized instantly that here, stretched out on the couch beside him, was a man who, in layman's language, was heart-broken.

Glancing down at the case-notes in his hand, he decided to probe deeper.

'And your little girl?' he asked.

'What about her?'

This time the psychiatrist decided to put the question the other way round. It was another of the little professional tricks that he had worked out.

'I expect she's missing you,' he said.

Stan thought for a moment before replying.

Again, to the psychiatrist, the pause was every bit as good as a reply. It disclosed the battle between truth and falsehood that was being waged within. There was indeed one simple law that governed all such pauses: even first-year men soon got to know that the longer the delay, the greater the untruth.

And in a moment, sure enough, out it came.

'Not really,' Stan told him. 'She's got her mother – and her dancing, you see.'

The psychiatrist gave a little inward-looking smile. If he had prepared the answer himself, it could not have been more revealing. In simple terms it meant that Stan was tortured by the thought of the suffering that he had inflicted on his daughter and, purely for his own self-protection, had invented the myth that she had not been hurt at all.

It was apparent that the moment had now come for other areas to be explored. But the psychiatrist was not rushing things. When, at last, he did address Stan he spoke as though the question had only just come to him.

'Suppose you could have anything you wanted – anything you cared to ask for – what would it be, I wonder?'

This time the psychiatrist was not expecting a prompt reply. After all, the option was a large one; overwhelmingly wide-open, in fact. Nevertheless, Stan's answer was immediate.

'I'd like a decent cup of tea,' he said. 'I don't want anything fancy. Not China or Earl Grey. Nothing like that. Just an ordinary cup of tea that really tastes like tea.' His voice tailed off, became almost inaudible, and the psychiatrist thought that Stan had finished. But here the psychiatrist was wrong again. Stan had not yet reached the important part. 'And no tea bags, either,' he added emphatically. 'Just proper tea.'

With a laugh, a deliberately casual, disinterested kind of laugh, the psychiatrist tried again.

'We'd all like that,' he said. 'I haven't had a decent cuppa for years. But I meant something bigger. More important. Something to hit the headlines. Like winning the Pools. Or marrying a Beauty Queen. Or scoring a century in a Test Match. Or being Knighted. Or being voted Man of the Year. Something like that.'

This time Stan did not hesitate. His answer came back loud and clear.

'I'd like to get it over with,' he said.

The psychiatrist leant forward. This was the point to which all his questions had been leading.

'You will,' he said. 'You will. You'll be back in civilian life again, back with your family, before you know where you are.'

'That wasn't what I meant,' Stan said.

The psychiatrist ran the back of his fingernail up the side margin of his typed-out case-notes.

'Then what did you mean?' he asked, using the same flat, casual-sounding voice that he used at all these interviews.

'I meant the trial,' Stan told him; and, without any further prompting from the psychiatrist, he continued. 'Well, it's not right, is it?' he asked. 'Not just keeping me waiting. I'd like it to happen.'

The psychiatrist gave another of his little inward smiles.

'Then you're looking forward to it, are you?' he asked.

Stan pondered the remark for a moment.

'I suppose I am rather,' he replied. 'After all, I did it, and I've got to pay the price. That's what punishment's about, isn't it? It wouldn't be fair otherwise. At least, that's the way I see it.'

Stan seemed to have nothing to add to his last remark, and the psychiatrist made no attempt to prompt him. In the meantime, it was essential to preserve Stan's confidence, to win him over as a friend. The psychiatrist did not underestimate his powers. He knew that these mind-searchings, no matter how compassionately conducted, could be very painful to the patient. Quite often it was a human wreck with raw nerve-ends rather than a man left lying there when it was all over.

Slowly, so as not to alarm Stan in any way, he opened his cigarette case and held it out to him.

'Care to smoke?' he asked.

But there was no reply. The chair had proved too comfortable, the cushions too soft and too pneumatic.

Head on shoulder, Stan was fast asleep.

Chapter 35

I

Not that Stan need ever have had any misgivings about the delay. The law was taking its course all right. Already Mr Jeremy Hayhoe, QC, had been briefed for the defence, and things at last were moving.

What's more, Stan could not have been better pleased with Mr Marbuck's choice of counsel. It meant that he had been moving upwards all the time. First, there had been that natural-born loser on the Isle of Wight; then the battling Mr Marbuck with his built-in distrust of all police evidence; and now the prosperous-looking and imposing Mr Hayhoe.

You could tell at a glance that Mr Hayhoe was somewhere at the very top of his profession even though, when he was not in court and without his wig on, it might have been difficult to pin-point the profession. The made-up buttonhole, with the spray of fern tucked in behind the flower, could have belonged to an actor or a stockbroker. On the other hand, the ring with an over-large diamond set in it could have been the property of a well-to-do bookie or a bingo magnate. It was his face that betrayed him. Even a casual glimpse of the profile revealed something sterner, more Nero-like.

Stan began to feel better from the first moment he met him. It was nothing less than a privilege to sit opposite to someone so expensively equipped. Stan could not help noticing the thickness of the gold cuff-links and the thinness of the gold wrist-watch. There was the chased, gold fountain pen as well, and even Mr Hayhoe's little loose-leaf memorandum pad had gold corners to keep the leaves in place.

Mr Hayhoe was so reassuring, too. He nodded his head in sympathy with every reply that Stan gave him, and went out of his way to reassure him. 'Leave it all to me,' he kept saying. 'Just answer the questions as I put them to you, and I'll see to the rest.' By the end of their first interview, Stan had quite forgotten his old feeling of helplessness. Indeed, he could not help reflecting on how lucky he had been because, if things had turned out differently and the Civil Service had

305

given him that promotion that he had applied for, he'd have been above the salary limit for Legal Aid. And then, heaven knows what quality of man he would have been able to pick up.

Everything considered, Stan reckoned that he had a lot to be thankful for.

When at last Mr Marbuck told him that the date for the hearing had finally been fixed, Stan was so excited that he felt like crying. They had been too long, those weeks on remand: it had been like re-living a broken-off piece of childhood and waiting for a birthday that, it seemed, would never come.

Not that there was very much of the birthday spirit about it all. To and from the courtroom can be a pretty uncomfortable affair; indeed the whole of the day-trip and excursion side of prison life leaves much to be desired; up too early; a lot of hanging around; uncomfortable transport; no morning paper to help speed the journey; and all the fuss about handcuffs.

The handcuffs were what Stan most disliked. They were hard and cold and humiliating. And heavy. To be even reasonably comfortable in handcuffs you have to sit with your hands folded in your lap as though knitting. And that is part of the trouble with all Black Marias. There is nowhere proper to sit. All that the accommodation provides is something more like a shelf than a seat; and not even a properly padded shelf at that. Anyone who has made the trip in one of these mobile prisons will tell you what it's like to be perched up, half-standing, half-sitting, in the little, narrow cubicle when the driver takes a side turning a bit too fast or has to brake suddenly.

But it still meant something simply to be in motion. And as Stan felt the Black Maria beginning to move he wondered what route the driver was going to choose, and whether it would take him near anywhere he knew. Not that he could have seen a thing: the narrowness of the windows in Black Marias and the opaqueness of the glass are among the commonest causes of complaint; and, in any case, drivers aren't allowed to choose. The route is all there, down on paper, and can't be varied. The duration of the journey is specified, too, though of course it varies a bit because these cross-town passenger trips have to be made at the height of the morning rush-hour. According to the regulations a full forty minutes had to be allowed from the front gates of Stan's prison to the reception bay at the Old Bailey.

Stan himself was one of the early ones. The clock in the reception hall showed nine-thirty, and he wondered if they were missing him over in Frobisher House; he supposed they must be because there was bound to be something about the trial in the papers. But, as he hadn't seen one, he couldn't tell.

And that was something else he had against Black Marias: no radio.

Another early arrival at the Old Bailey had been Mr Cheevers. He always liked to get there early, take a look at the public entrance to see if any queue was forming, walk round to the courtyard which the Judges used, pass the time of day with the constable on duty and be in his place in the press gallery while the ushers were still going round arranging things.

In Mr Cheevers's view the reporting of any trial was a work of art, and no pains should be spared to make it as perfect as possible. This, moreover, was not simply any trial. It was one of Mr Justice Streetley's trials. Mr Justice Streetley was still at the height of his powers and, like the conductors of famous orchestras, Mr Justice Streetley could be relied on to draw his own audience. And that was where Mr Justice Streetley was one up on the conductors; Mr Justice Streetley's remarks were regularly quoted in all the Sunday papers.

As it turned out, Beryl had been one of the comparatively late ones; only just before the Judge, in fact.

But that had been British Rail's fault, not Beryl's. The eight-thirty-two from Crocketts Green had drawn up and waited outside Perrott's Junction for a whole quarter of an hour – which meant that when the train did finally get to Cannon Street she had to make a dash past the barrier, and find herself a taxi.

And that was something else that Beryl disliked: the thought of having to say 'Old Bailey' to the taxi driver. The taxi, however, had not proved such a bad idea. It gave her somewhere to see what was wrong with the skirt that she was wearing: for some reason the silly thing kept twisting round, leaving the row of buttons that should have been in front, sticking out all along the side. This upset her because it was specially for Stan's trial that she had bought the suit. Navy blue, with contrasting collar and cuffs, was what she had chosen, and she had allowed herself a new navy blue handbag, too. If it hadn't been for her hair-do, she would have bought herself a new hat as well. But Monsieur

Louis had made that impossible: she would have to have had a hat with a full nine-inch crown, and they don't make that sort nowadays. There was nothing for it, therefore, but the everlasting headscarf again, worn peasant-woman fashion and tied ever so loosely under the chin.

Inside, the Old Bailey was more like the Crocketts Green Town Hall than Beryl had expected. And busier. There wasn't just one Court, either. There was a whole collection of them, all set out on a notice board like a railway station indicator.

But what particularly impressed her was the politeness of the policemen. They were all so gentle and smiling and considerate; not a bit like policemen really. It was very nice, too, to have Mr Marbuck's clerk come forward to meet her; he would take her to her seat, he said. All the same, Beryl had more than half expected that Mr Cheevers himself would be waiting for her. But even as the thought came to her she could see how unreasonable it was. Mr Cheevers was probably somewhere upstairs with the Judge; chatting over the more interesting legal aspects of the case, most likely.

II

The courtroom was larger than Stan had been prepared for. Coming up the steep flight of stairs leading from the cells, he could see it widening out all round him. And the dock itself was enormous: a whole football team could have been put on trial there. And he could not help admiring the rest of the general lay-out. The four large wall arches, the circular ceiling light, the raised sword over the Judge's chair, the green leather upholstery, even the glass sides to the dock itself, all seemed in excellent good taste; restrained, but still imposing. Dignified, too, in a negative, impersonal kind of way.

As he looked about him, it occurred to Stan that he had never seen any decent photographs of the inside of the Old Bailey; not when there had been a trial on, that is. Whereas, the whole place was absolutely built for it. *Judge's-eye view of Prisoner*; *Prisoner's-eye view of the Judge*; *Judge's-eye view of the Jury*; *Jury's-eye view* . . . ; and so forth. With a good camera, even with flashes not allowed, Stan reckoned that he could have made up a complete double-sided, twelve-page album.

And when, at last, it happened Stan could not resist a gasp of sheer admiration as the Judge came in. The effect of the scarlet robes against the panelled walls and the green leather was nothing short of blinding: it clashed and blended both at the same time. And the grey wig was another master-stroke. Nor was that all. There had been the *sound* of Mr Justice Streetley's arrival – the sudden scraping of feet and the rustling of gowns and papers as everyone stood up. It was something on which Mr Cheevers himself had remarked in his own little manual of Court procedure. 'Like the noise of a great flock of birds taking off, or a sudden landslide' was how he, with his instinctive gift for words, had described it.

Mr Stranger-Milne, QC for the Crown, was a lifelong acquaintance of Mr Justice Streetley's; same prep school, same public school, both at Trinity, and finally, a shared staircase in the Temple. Mutual dislike at first sight had, over the years, ripened and become something deeper. In consequence, they were always excessively polite to each other both in their Club and in open court. There were always compliments and politeness on both sides; and, behind it all, a keen personal resentment of each other. And envy: Mr Stranger-Milne for Mr Justice Streetley's elevation to the Bench, and Mr Justice Streetley for the reported size of Mr Stranger-Milne's income.

It was the 'how-do-you-plead?' part that presented the first problem, and Stan made a complete mess of it. He was so self-conscious that he could not even raise his head. Fortunately his voice, in consequence, was curiously muffled and indistinct.

'G . . . uilty,' was the best that he could manage.

Immediately, he was aware of a sudden disturbance down below in the body of the Court where Mr Marbuck and Mr Jeremy Hayhoe were sitting, and he remembered what he had promised them. He hurriedly corrected himself.

'Not guilty, I mean. That's it, not guilty.'

He still had his chin down on his chest and was not looking up at anybody. Mr Justice Streetley meanwhile had removed his spectacles. Others of the press who, like Mr Cheevers, were familiar with the performance held their pencils at the ready.

'The plea,' he observed, 'must be either "Guilty" or "Not Guilty", and it is plainly necessary that I should know which. As things are at the moment, first I seem to hear one thing and then I seem to hear the other. Would you kindly assist the Court, Mr Hayhoe.'

Mr Hayhoe rose and bowed respectfully.

'As your Lordship has so acutely observed,' he replied, 'the acoustics of this Court are notoriously difficult. I will endeavour to make amends.'

But it was not easy. Stan did not want to raise his head: what had upset him was the sight of Beryl sitting there. She looked somehow so out of place, too. The navy blue two-piece with the contrasting collar and cuffs was conspicuously smarter than anything that anyone else in Court was wearing, and the headscarf had an almost holiday-ish air about it. But that wasn't what Stan objected to. He didn't like the idea of Beryl being there at all.

For her part, Beryl would have been quite ready to give Stan a wave if he had looked in her direction. Her last two visits to the prison had not been very consoling to either of them; and, on reflection, she felt inclined to blame herself. Even now, a wave and a smile just to show that she was ready to forgive him for all the trouble he had caused might, she felt, help him to put up a more convincing performance.

Mr Stranger-Milne for the prosecution was certainly nothing if not thorough, like starting off by asking who Stan really was, for instance; and where he lived; and what his job was and how long he had been employed there. Stan was amazed: if they didn't know even that much about him he reckoned that something must have gone wrong somewhere. Then it dawned on him. Something *had* gone wrong. But not this time. It must have been in some earlier case that there had been carelessness, and they were taking every precaution to avoid a similar mix-up this time.

And it was the same with Stan's confession. Sentence by sentence, he took him through it again, and it all came out – about Mr Karlin and his picture agency, and the kind of hotels he stayed in, and the payments in notes at a hundred pounds a time, and the camera that looked like a wrist-watch.

Beryl listened with amazement, tapping with the heel of her navy blue calf shoe until she found that she was jogging the person seated next to her; and she was glad now that she hadn't been able to wave to him. Mr Karlin and the cheap hotels and the fake wrist-watch did not interest her so much; what she wanted to know was what had happened to all those pound notes. Gazing up at the ceiling she tried hard to remember the rate for fourteen days at Pineland Colony and what she had paid for the matching travel cases and how much a Morris 1100 car cost to hire. Try as she could to fill it in, there still seemed to be a pretty sizeable gap somewhere.

As it happened Stan was gazing up at the ceiling, too, and he was wondering how Beryl was taking it all. It must, he realized, come as something of a shock to any woman to think that she was married to just an ordinary kind of chap and then suddenly find out that he was top criminal class really. The odd thought occurred to him that it might even make her admire him just a little bit.

But already Mr Stranger-Milne was back to his examination. It was hardly the lethal, ding-dong stuff that Beryl had been led to believe went on all the time at the Old Bailey, and she began to wonder what Mr Cheevers could see in it.

Q. You say that this Mr Karlin made you a number of payments?

A. That's it, sir.

Q. And how many would that be?

A. Four or five, sir.

Mr Stranger-Milne put the fingers of his two hands briefly together, and then separated them again as though momentarily breaking off from prayer.

'I must ask you to recall,' he said, 'that you are under oath. It is the truth, the whole truth, that I require. And "Four or five" is not an answer.'

Mr Justice Streetley leant forward, thrusting his arms out of his long scarlet sleeves as he did so. Then he put his hands together precisely as Mr Stranger-Milne had done. Mr Justice Streetley's hands, however, were paler than Mr Stranger-Milne's, and his fingers conspicuously more tapering.

'Mr Stranger-Milne,' he said. 'I do not have to remind counsel of your standing that consideration of the mentality of the prisoner is of the utmost importance in these matters. Indeed, I have heard you rightly so argue in this Court. The prisoner whom I now see before me is a clerk, but not a legal clerk. It is unreasonable to assume that he has any knowledge or understanding of the law. He must therefore be protected against his own confusion. Accordingly, I must advise you that the reply, "Four or five" *is* quite definitely an answer. It might not be a satisfactory answer, but it is an answer nevertheless.'

And, having intervened, Mr Justice Streetley then withdrew. There was something of the air of an elderly tortoise retreating into the shelter of its own gorgeous coloured shell.

'As your Lordship pleases,' Mr Stranger-Milne replied in his most courteous tone. He had learnt from long experience that nothing annoyed Mr Justice Streetley more than to have his rebukes bowed-to and acknowledged almost before he had finished speaking.

Without a pause, he resumed his questioning.

'Do you mean four or do you mean five?' he asked.

'One or the other. I don't remember.'

'Why don't you remember?'

'Because I've forgotten.'

Mr Stranger-Milne grasped the lapels of his gown.

'I put it to you that you remember perfectly well. I further put it to you that you are refusing to answer me.'

There was no response. It was as though Stan had not even heard Mr Stranger-Milne's question. The silence was so long, indeed, that Beryl bent forward to see what was happening. And it was impossible to tell. Stan looked all right. Looked better than she had expected, in fact; but that may have been simply because he wasn't wearing that dreadful Isle of Wight sports jacket of his.

Mr Justice Streetley leant forward, too, this time without the rather self-conscious shuffling with his sleeves.

'You have to answer Counsel's question, you know,' he told Stan. 'That is what you are here for.'

His voice was noticeably warmer, more human, when talking to Stan than when addressing Mr Stranger-Milne.

'But I haven't been asked a question,' Stan explained. 'All the other gentleman said was . . .'

Mr Justice Streetley raised his hand to stop him. Then, with a little bow, he turned towards Mr Stranger-Milne.

'Perhaps you could find some other way of putting it,' he said. 'Clearly the prisoner does not comprehend.'

Mr Stranger-Milne was equally polite.

'I am most grateful for your Lordship's intervention.'

He twisted round to face Stan again.

'Could it have been only on three occasions that he gave you money?' he asked.

Stan shook his head.

'More like four or five,' he told him.

'Or six, possibly. Tell me, was it six?'

'Not so many,' Stan told him. 'More like . . .'

This time it was Mr Stranger-Milne who raised a hand to stop him. Beryl felt rather sorry for Mr Stranger-Milne. She knew what Stan could be like when he was in one of his obstinate moods. At this rate the trial could go on forever, with Stan not budging and Mr Stranger-Milne not getting anywhere, either.

But Mr Stranger-Milne was already trying a fresh approach.

'And what did you do with all this money? You didn't pay it into your own bank account, did you?'

'No, sir.'

'And why not, may I ask?'

Mr Stranger-Milne was still on about Stan's Number Two account, the one that he had opened under an assumed name, when the Judge decided that he, for one, had already had enough and would adjourn things until after lunch.

There was no difficulty about lunchtime for Stan; for the prisoners, the Old Bailey has a perfectly good meals-on-wheels kind of service with your luncheon tray carried right into your own cell for you. The Judges and Counsel – and the jury, too, for that matter – are all quite nicely looked after. It is the interested parties, the hangers-on, who are least catered for. And, even at the best of times, the City doesn't have very much to offer to the single woman in search of something light. Beryl might have done better if she had turned up Holborn Viaduct: there are one or two little places there, hidden away between Hatton Garden and the Gray's Inn Road. But she chose Newgate Street instead. And that was fatal. In the result, she finished up in Cheapside, practically by the Bank of England, still without having found what she wanted. And this surprised her because she remembered that, when she had been a girl, every street you went down was fairly bristling with a Lyons' and an ABC and an Express Dairy; and a Fuller's, and Slater's, too, if you wanted something a bit more substantial.

In the end, she sat herself on a high stool up against the counter of an establishment that specialized in selling sandwiches. She was lucky. The seat had only been vacant for a second before she pounced on it. But that was evidently the spirit of the place; pop in, bolt something down and dash out again.

Anyhow, she was past caring. She had, at last, realized how old she was; how old and how disastrously out-of-date. All round her were eighteen-year-olds, fresh and pretty and bouncy, happily carrying off paper-bags containing cheese-and-tomato or sausage-and-chutney that they were going to eat among themselves, with the bag balanced on top of a typewriter somewhere. And there she was, thirty-fourish and nine stone five in weight, dressed all wrong for the City and with only the Old Bailey to go back to.

Nor had Stan read her mind aright when he thought that those revelations in Court about his ingenuity might have made her admire him just a little. On the contrary, the disclosure of the second banking account had really upset her. It meant that, all the time she had been trusting him, he had simply been holding out on her.

By now, she had finished all that she wanted of her egg-and-cress on rye; the other half lay uneaten in its Cellophane envelope. And she was saying something to herself. If there had not been so much noise and bustle in the place, the customers perched up on either side of her would have heard the actual words.

'Sneaky little creep,' she repeated quite audibly. 'Sneaky little creep to have me on like that.'

There is always a pervading air of somnolence about any Court after the lunchtime adjournment; even, on occasion, a marked reluctance to resume.

As with Mr Stranger-Milne, for example. For years he had made it a matter of principle never to examine either a prisoner or a witness at a time of day when, in the ordinary way, he would have been taking a short nap. In consequence, so far as he was concerned, two o'clock to three o'clock every day was junior counsel's hour; their playtime, as he teasingly used to refer to it. Once the young man, whoever he was, had got up onto his feet, Mr Stranger-Milne would perceptibly sink back in his seat, eyes half-closed, neither sleeping nor awake.

Not so Mr Justice Streetley. Severe with himself as with others, he made a point of always lunching lightly when he was on the Bench. One glass of sherry beforehand, ordinary tap-water at table, and meat, but no bread and no potatoes, was by now his regular diet. In the result, he was as wide-awake after lunch as he had been at breakfast time.

There was evidence of it almost immediately. Junior counsel was a Mr Crowhurst. He was short-sighted, studious and inclined to nervousness. Carefully following the notes in his hand, he put his questions pointedly and with precision. Mr Justice Streetley was watching him closely. Then he pounced. He shook back the cuffs of his gown and brought his two hands together; only the tips of his fingers were actually touching.

Mr Crowhurst heard the rustle and glanced apprehensively in his direction. Mr Justice Streetley had expected him to do so and was ready for him.

'I have been observing you,' he said. 'Are you addressing the prisoner or are you addressing those notes which you are holding? Because the notes cannot answer, can they? Only the prisoner can answer and, even then, only if he is quite sure that he is the sole object of your attention.'

'I . . . I stand corrected, m'Lud,' Mr Crowhurst began. 'I was intending to . . .'

It would, however, have made no difference to Mr Justice Streetley whatever Mr Crowhurst had been intending. Mr Justice Streetley had reasserted his authority and, for the time being, he was content. Motionless he now sat there, his long grey face staring out impassively over the silence of the open Court.

More than once Beryl found herself wondering whether it had really been worth it to come back at all. Mr Stranger-Milne, however, was by now feeling pleasantly refreshed and had decided to relieve his junior. Immediately things brightened up and the proceedings came to life again.

Q. Your hobby is photography, is it not?

A. Yes, sir.

Q. And what kind of photographs do you take? Are they landscapes?

A. More nature studies, sir. Trees and, of course, flowers, sir. (Pause). And swans, too, sir. I've done a lot of swans.

Q. And portraits. Do you take portraits?

A. Sometimes, sir. Not just head, though. More figure work.

Q. Nude figure work?

Stan took so long before replying that Mr Stranger-Milne had to repeat his question. The second time he said it louder. It was really this that woke Beryl up.

A. Only once, sir.

Q. And did you select the models?

A. No, sir. They were already in the studio waiting for me.

Q. Did you not expect to find them there?

A. Yes, sir.

Q. And will you now tell us what it was that made you decide to switch from nature studies – trees and flowers and swans and that kind of thing – and embark upon pictures of the naked female form?

A. They sell better, sir. There's more demand for them.

A sound like a snigger from somewhere in the public gallery caused Mr Justice Streetley to intervene.

'This is neither a Fun Fair nor an Amusement Park,' he observed. 'If there is laughter or other unseemly behaviour I shall order that the Court be cleared immediately. Pray continue, Mr Stranger-Milne.'

Q. So you did it for money, did you? For financial gain?

A. Yes, sir.

Q. Of your own free will?

A. Yes, sir. At the time, sir.

Q. What do you mean by 'at the time'?

A. I was being blackmailed you see, sir, only I didn't know it.

Q. And what was the instrument of this blackmail?

A. The nude pictures, sir. The ones that I'd been taking.

Mr Stranger-Milne raised his eyebrows and drew down the corners of his mouth. The expression was intended to convey pity mingled with astonishment. But Mr Stranger-Milne would never have considered asking any question unless he was already pretty sure of the answer; that was why his examinations usually passed off so smoothly, so effectively. In this one, he was intent on revealing Stan not merely as a common traitor, but as a greedy traitor. Any hint of blackmail would, he knew, be bound to excite the jury's sympathy, and he could not allow that to happen. He resumed his questioning.

Q. But these are the nineteen-sixties. Nude photographs no longer provide the blackmailer with his material. We are not living in Victorian times, remember. I put it to you . . .

He could get no further, however. Mr Justice Streetley disapproved of counsel who packaged and wrapped-up their questions. Not that he could possibly be seen to be seeking to correct Mr Stranger-Milne on a matter of Court procedure. That would have been unthinkable. Clearly what was called for was a correction of a more general nature. Already the loose red sleeves had been thrust back and the long, pale hands were beginning to appear.

'It rests upon me,' he said, 'to ensure that in the course of his examination the prisoner shall not be misled. That is of paramount importance. The reference to the Victorian age, an age which some of us much regret, cannot be held to have helped the prisoner to clarify his mind. Quite the contrary, in fact. Studies of the female nude were commonplace during the reign of Queen Victoria. Our public art

316

galleries are full of examples of them. The artists themselves were often elected to the Royal Academy, and even on occasion Knighted. It is not for us to ask ourselves why. It is simply a matter of historic truth that it so happened.'

The only other theatrical trick that Mr Stranger-Milne knew was that of raising his hands, palms upwards, in the manner of an Arab street-trader. He used it now. Helpless incredulity was what the gesture was meant to signify.

'I can only thank your Lordship for so succinctly putting the matter,' he said.

Then, with a little bow, he turned towards Stan again.

Q. Were they very *unusual* photographs that you were taking?

A. Oh no, sir. Nothing like that.

Q. Then how could you be blackmailed?

A. Because I was in some of them myself you see, sir. Someone else must have taken the photographs when I wasn't looking. And there I was, sir, arranging one model, and the other one was just standing there. She'd got nothing on either.

At first Beryl had just sat there, leaning forward in the chair, her eyes fixed on Stan, not believing what she heard. Then, as one by one the facts for which she was unprepared came tumbling out, she slumped forward, and was left staring into the lap of her new navy blue two-piece.

When it was all over, she suddenly sat up. With one quick movement she opened her bag and took out her handkerchief. Then she spat into it. What she wanted to do was to wipe the taste of Stan out of her mouth for ever.

It was not Beryl's fault that she had been neglecting Marleen. In the circumstances, it had proved unavoidable. The constant travelling, the prison visits, the attendance at the Old Bailey, the telephone sessions with Mr Cheevers anxiously seeking what he called 'background material', had occupied her increasingly. In the result, she had been tired out; so tired, indeed, that her unmotherliness towards little Marleen hadn't even occurred to her.

Not that Marleen had been in the least forlorn and miserable. Left more to herself than she had ever been before, she improvised. For a start, she used the telephone. There was only one of her schoolgirl friends whose family was on the telephone, and Marleen made a point of talking to her every evening. Even though they had been together less than half an hour before, they carried on long conversations about their other friends; about the mistresses at the School; about their favourite television stars; about new ice cream flavours.

But it was not merely social telephoning that consumed Marleen's time. Drawer by drawer she went through the papers in Beryl's desk, not finding anything particularly interesting, but still reading every line of everything just in case. Equally systematically, she checked over the contents of Beryl's dressing-table; and of her wardrobe, too, trying everything on while standing in front of the long bedroom mirror as she did so, drawing the garments in with her hands because they were too large for her.

It was because of the mirror and because she was alone that she tried some experiments with her hair as well, putting it up on top with the aid of a handful of Beryl's pins and even snipping some of it off with Beryl's nail scissors to see what it would look like if she should decide to grow a fringe.

That did not mean, however, that she had forgotten about Stan. Quite the contrary, in fact. Ever since that first moment of drama down there on the Isle of Wight, she had been collecting everything that had appeared about him. Where Beryl had angrily crumpled up a newspaper and flung it away from her, Marleen had retrieved and smoothed it out again. Just lately when the journalists had not seemed to have much else to write about, she had taken to spending her own pocket money on papers that she did not ordinarily see. Cuttings from *The Times* and the *Daily Telegraph* were now neatly pasted into one of her old exercise books along with pieces from the *Isle of Wight Guardian* and the *Crocketts Green Gazette*. On the front was a new label, lettered in bright crayon. 'MY DADDY,' it ran. 'THE DAIRY OF HIS TRAIL'.

School-work had always with Marleen come second to ballroom dancing and horse riding: there had been adverse comment on her spelling in more than one of her end-of-term reports.

III

The trial was now due to begin its third day, and there seemed nothing likely to prolong it. All that remained were the closing speeches for the prosecution and for the defence; and, of course, Mr Justice Streetley's own summing-up and sentencing.

According to the timetable that Mr Justice Streetley had worked out in his mind, the prosecution would probably be over by twelve or twelve-fifteen at the latest; if necessary, he could prolong it to twelve-thirty by making one, or possibly two, more of his interventions. His remark about Victorian nudes had been one of his most successful: both evening papers had carried it, and he was in 'Peterborough' and *The Times* diary as well.

Twelve-thirty, moreover, was one of the critical moments of the day. Anything earlier would have been derisory, and anything later meaningless. If he could spin it out until twelve-thirty, he could take an early lunch adjournment. Mr Jeremy Hayhoe could come on at two o'clock and have as long as he liked – which was practically without limit as Mr Justice Streetley recalled. Tomorrow, probably, he would be able to sum up. Then the jury would retire and give their verdict and the next day, no doubt, he could pronounce sentence. Mr Justice Streetley always liked to have a night's rest between verdict and sentence.

The only person who was left disconsolate was Mr Cheevers. All in all, he judged it to be one of the least memorable trials that he had ever attended. And his Features Editor had been quite right. Even with headings like 'PHOTOGRAPHER SELLS NAVAL SECRETS' or 'SPY WHO WENT IN FOR THE NUDE', the exclusive story wasn't worth the two thousand that Beryl had made him pay for it; somewhere in the one thousand to twelve-fifty bracket was where he would have put it.

Stan, on the other hand, was reasonably content. He was relieved to think that the prosecution had not pressed him as to who had taken the other, the incriminating, photographs. Because, no matter how many questions had been fired at him, he would not have revealed the truth. Helga – and it could not have been anyone but Helga – was, by now, a part of his own private fantasy. The thought of Helga was what comforted him when he went to sleep at nights. And this was strange considering that he'd never even had so much as ten minutes alone with her.

It all turned out exactly as Mr Justice Streetley had intended. Mr Stranger-Milne, for the prosecution, would have been through a full five or ten minutes too early if his Lordship had not intervened. As it was, the proceedings were brought to an end at five-and-twenty to one precisely, and everything was back on schedule again.

What is more, it proved to be one of Mr Justice Streetley's happier

319

interventions, something that was to be much quoted by his admirers and detractors alike. Mr Stranger-Milne, at his most dramatic, had suddenly thrust out his finger and pointed it accusingly in Stan's direction. The gesture was so abrupt and unexpected that, even at that distance, Stan felt himself instinctively recoil from it. And what Mr Stranger-Milne was saying as he glared at him down the length of his finger made it even more alarming. '. . . treacherous to the hilt . . . moral code of a Judas . . . most contemptible of motives . . . Quisling-type mentality . . . odious combination of high professional skill and low criminal cunning . . .' the phrases kept hitting into Stan like bolts from a crossbow.

But it was there that Mr Justice Streetley, noticing the time, saw fit momentarily to suspend the barrage.

'I very strongly deprecate,' he said, speaking slowly and distinctly, 'anything that may, in any way, interrupt the sequence and flow of Counsel's remarks to the jury – more particularly when they are so thoughtfully composed and so polished as I hear them to be today. Nevertheless, when there has been mis-representation – entirely un-intended, of course, but mis-representation all the same – it is my duty to act promptly. It is, indeed, one of the reasons why I should be here at all.'

Mr Stranger-Milne did not miss his cue. Eyebrows arched and with his hands again raised palms upwards, he turned towards Mr Justice Streetley, pausing long enough on the way for the jury to observe the martyrdom that he was being made to suffer.

'With respect, m'Lud,' he asked, 'in what way have I, in your Lordship's opinion – with which, when explained to me, I do not doubt that I shall concur – been guilty of this mis-representation to which your Lordship refers?'

Mr Justice Streetley consulted his notes.

'The expression you used was "high professional skill", was it not?'

'It was, indeed, m'Lud,' Mr Stranger-Milne replied. 'I was referring. to the photographic operation of the bogus wrist-watch.'

Mr Justice Streetley gave a little inward chuckle. He had laid the trap and Mr Stranger-Milne had walked right into it. Mr Justice Streetley, quite unnecessarily, consulted his notes again.

'But did you not tell us,' he asked, 'that all that was necessary for the taking of a photograph was for the wearer of the wrist-watch to twist it round so that it faced the paper and then press the winder? Did you not go on to say that the camera – for that is what it really was – was an instrument of fixed focus? And does not that mean that there was no call for the usual fiddling with the knobs and things that characterizes so much professional photography? And did you not further conclude that portion of your remarks by observing that the exposure was automatically – "electronically" I believe was the word you used – adjusted within the machine itself entirely without human intervention?'

Mr Stranger-Milne's sigh was, as he intended, audible to the whole Court.

'That was, indeed, the gist of my remarks, m'Lud.'

'Then I fail to see where the degree of high professional skill to which you have directed the attention of the jury, comes into it. A child, or a trained chimpanzee for that matter, could have operated such a camera. There was nothing highly professional about it. Nothing professional about it at all, in fact. Simply "click", and the whole job was done.'

Mr Stranger-Milne grasped the lapels of his gown, and squared up to his tormentor.

'I submit, m'Lud, that this is a technical point, a technical *photographic* point. With respect, I submit that it is not a legal point at all. The mere method of procedure involved in the taking of a photograph cannot be a matter of law.'

It was Mr Justice Streetley's prerogative to take as long as he liked before replying. On this occasion, he deliberately took rather a long time.

'Oh, but I assure you that it can,' he said at last. 'It can – and, indeed, does – bear directly on a point of law. Your actual words were' – here Mr Justice Streetley consulted his notes again – '. . . "a combination of high professional skill and low criminal cunning". No one could dispute your right in prosecution to impute the element of cunning or its criminal nature. But the skill and the professionalism simply do not come into it. They belong to a different case altogether. If the attribution of highly skilled professionalism remains, the jury will not know what manner of man it is who stands before them.'

Mr Stranger-Milne had one last try.

'As your Lordship will recall,' he started, 'I have been able to produce evidence to show that the prisoner is a highly skilled photographer, a professional in the best sense of the word. He has won many prizes and competitions . . .'

'But not for taking snapshots with a wrist-watch, Mr Stranger-Milne. Not, as I have said, for simply going "click".'

Mr Justice Streetley looked at his own wrist-watch.

'The Court will rise and we will adjourn until two o'clock,' he said sweetly.

Chapter 36

It had been anything but pleasant for Stan to have to sit there while Mr Stranger-Milne jabbed his finger at him. He had felt himself squirming. He was afraid, moreover, that some of the things that Mr Stranger-Milne had been saying about him were bound to have put the jury against him.

That was why he was so relieved that, at last, it had come to Mr Hayhoe's turn. And Mr Hayhoe showed himself to be in top form right from the very start. His manner was entirely different from Mr Stranger-Milne's. For a start it was apparently effortless. Speaking rather slowly and so quietly that even Mr Justice Streetley had to lean forward to ensure that he was missing nothing, he immediately took the whole Court into his confidence. A hush descended, and everyone present – except, of course, for Mr Justice Streetley himself and Mr Stranger-Milne and his junior – felt instinctively that, for the first time since the trial had started, the truth was being unfolded and justice was in the process of being done.

Mr Hayhoe opened straight away with the matter of Stan's admission of his own guilt.

'Let's begin by considering the matter of this so-called confession,' he said softly in that low, confiding voice of his; and, to show what he was talking about, he picked up the document and held it up for the whole jury to see.

It could not escape notice, however, that he was holding it by one corner, nipped gingerly between thumb and forefinger, as though closer contact with it might prove contaminating. 'There is more than one kind of confession in this world,' he went on. 'At its loftiest, its most exalted, a confession is an irresistible outpouring of the human soul. Every word within it is sacred.'

Mr Hayhoe paused. He was holding the document up even higher by now. 'And at its lowest, its most contemptible,' he reminded the Court, 'a confession may be nothing more than a mere string of lies, a worthless collection of frauds and falsehoods. And with such confessions' – here Mr Hayhoe suddenly loosened his grip and let the sheets of paper flutter onto the floor – 'we have to ask ourselves one question and one question only: "Why were they ever written?".

Stan watched him fascinated as Mr Hayhoe made no attempt to pick up the fallen papers; indeed, he appeared entirely oblivious of them. And the bland, honey-dew sweetness of his voice had changed to something altogether more tart and astringent. Stan was amazed. He even doubted whether, if the words had been spoken in the dark, Mr Hayhoe's own mother would have recognized him.

'I will tell you why such confessions are written,' Mr Hayhoe said. 'They are written because their authors are too alarmed, too terrified, to do otherwise. They are expressions not of remorse but of fear, not of penitence but of panic. I put it to you that this travesty of a confession was secured by subterfuge and written down under duress. There is, I suggest, not one vestige of truth in the whole document, not one word that has not been manipulated by other hands into a contradiction of its true meaning. And I will go further: I will . . .'

It was a characteristic of Mr Hayhoe's that he usually did go further. Sometimes much further – especially when he was enjoying himself. And he had already recognized this as being one of his better days, the sort of day that admiring juniors would long remember.

In his own way Stan, too, was full of admiration; indeed, listening to Mr Hayhoe, he didn't think that he had ever admired anyone more. Bit by bit, he had felt himself being compelled to come round to Mr Hayhoe's own way of thinking. He was entirely happy to sit back and leave his whole future in Mr Hayhoe's hands.

That was why Stan didn't mind in the least when Mr Hayhoe turned and slowly extended a hand in his direction. It seemed a friendly and endearing gesture. His voice, moreover, was at its gentlest again, its most dulcet. It was only the actual words that he was using that Stan didn't like so much.

'You have heard much,' he said, 'about the ingenious nature, the sheer technical accomplishment, of this imputed crime. "An exhibition of shrewd and diabolical cunning" were, you will recall, the words which my learned friend saw fit to use. My learned friend even went on to describe the author of the plot as "a veritable master-spy, a mixture of Machiavelli and Houdini, someone at once subtle and deceitful, slippery and evasive".' Mr Hayhoe paused. 'Machiavelli and Houdini,' he repeated the words, and there was a perceptible chuckle in his voice as he did so. 'You have had ample opportunity of seeing the prisoner and studying him and hearing him give evidence, and you will have drawn your own conclusions. Has there ever, I ask you, been a Machiavelli so bemused and bewildered by the attacks upon his character that he cannot remember to plead "guilty" or "not guilty"? Has there ever been a Houdini who floundered into every pitfall that opened up before him? Has there ever been a master-spy so pathetically, so innocently, adept at doing the wrong thing, so anxious it might even seem to incriminate himself by his own ridiculous admissions? That man whom you see standing there before you is another type of human being entirely; a little man in every sense of the word. He is a mere Charlie Chaplin of crime, someone incapable of any offence more heinous than that of travelling one stage too far on a tuppenny bus ride, or not going along to the police station with it if he came upon a half-empty box of matches lying on the pavement. It is for you, ladies and gentlemen of the jury, to decide in which category you would place him.'

With that, Mr Hayhoe abruptly sat down. Right up to the last sentence he had still kept his hand extended in Stan's direction. Then, with no warning, he dropped his arm to his side again and apparently lost all interest in his subject. He simply sat back, his feet resting on the crumpled pages of Stan's confession, his eyes unfocused staring vacantly up at the ceiling. The only indication that he had recently been so hard at work was that he was still breathing rather heavily.

The schedule was working out exactly as Mr Justice Streetley had planned.

Mr Hayhoe had been long, but not too long, and Mr Justice Streetley himself was poised, fully prepared and ready to the moment to begin his summing-up. Round about fifty minutes was what he proposed to devote to it. That would bring them to three-thirty. At that point he would rise and inform the Court that he would resume his summing-up the next day. The pieces were fitting perfectly.

In the matter of summing-up, Mr Justice Streetley was generally acknowledged to be a master. He allowed himself no tricks, no sallies. There was never anything quotable for the newspapers. Just the salient points, carefully selected, touched-up a bit, rearranged and strung together. As an intellectual exercise it was all highly stimulating in a rather chill, frost-bitten sort of way.

And in the case of Regina v Stanley Pitts, boiled down, it all came quite simply to this: that selling Admiralty secrets to anyone was in itself so grave an offence that all that members of the jury had to do was to keep it tucked away at the back of their minds. What they had to consider was whether Stan knew, or had reason to know, that he was trading with a foreign power. Mere cupidity – a favourite word of Mr Justice Streetley's and one which he always uttered with his lips drawn back and his teeth bared – was one thing: treachery which endangered the very throne itself was quite another. The jury should direct their thoughts to such a difference.

And, to end up, Mr Justice Streetley impressed upon them that, if on any point they were in the slightest doubt, it was their solemn duty to give the benefit of that doubt to the prisoner. ιΛr Justice Streetley's own mind had been made up long ago.

During the whole of Mr Justice Streetley's summing-up, Mr Hayhoe continued to stare at the ceiling. Stan himself did not know where to look. Hearing what was being said about him had a strangely ghostly quality about it, a spookiness. It might have been someone else to whom the Judge kept referring – a total stranger who had briefly entered into his life, destroyed it and then quietly slipped away again. It hadn't been the real Stan at all, Stan felt. Come to that, it wasn't even the real Stan who was sitting there in the dock at this moment.

He was, indeed, so much preoccupied in thinking about the oddity of it all that he hardly noticed when Mr Justice Streetley had finished his remarks. He did not bother either to turn his head when the jury stood up and began to file out in their two rows. It was simply the sound of shuffling that he heard. And even that was already getting fainter. The policeman who was standing behind him had to tap him twice on the shoulder before he realized that it was time for him to go below again.

He got up and turned, avoiding looking in Beryl's direction as he did so.

There are those who have gone through the ordeal of a long trial who say that the time spent waiting for the jury to return is easily the worst of all. Stan did not find it so. Instead, he was conscious of a great wave of relief to think that at least the prosecution and defence part of the proceedings was all over and done with, and that he wouldn't have to face either Mr Stranger-Milne or Mr Hayhoe ever again. In their separate and individual ways they had both hurt his feelings more than he would have been prepared to admit to anybody, and he was only sorry that Beryl had been there to listen to them.

Nor did he expect to have to wait very long before the jury came back again. He wouldn't have blamed them if they had reached a verdict inside the first ten minutes. Had he been in their place, he reckoned that was what he would have done. And then he changed his mind because he knew perfectly well that he wouldn't really have liked finding anybody guilty. And apparently the jury didn't like it either. They took two days over it.

In the meantime, the police couldn't have been nicer to him. They did all that they could to make things as pleasant as possible for him. They brought Stan large chipped mugs of thick, very syrupy tea, and said that he was welcome to another one if he felt like it. The sergeant even dropped his voice a little and said that if it would help to calm Stan's nerves to have a cigarette while he was waiting he believed that he knew where he could find one.

Stan very politely refused the cigarette, explaining that he didn't really, and that he and Beryl only kept them in the house in case any of their smoker friends should happen to drop in. But he accepted the second cups of tea. On the second day, he was just about to ask if he could have a third one when the cell door opened and a constable said that they were ready for him upstairs.

He only just had time to say thank you for everything to the sergeant before he was being led into the dock again. Those stairs seemed by now every bit as familiar as his own staircase at No. 16 Kendal Terrace; he might have been going up and down them for years.

The verdict was exactly as Mr Justice Streetley had predicted. He thanked the jury, congratulated them on their good sense and promised that they would not be called upon to do service again for at least another five years. Then with one eye on the clock and speaking very slowly and deliberately, he added that, in a case of such unusual complexity with so many and so far-reaching ramifications, he would postpone sentencing until the morrow. It was, as he uttered the words, six-fifteen precisely; and, even using public transport, Mr Justice Streetley knew that he would be back in nice time for a drink and a hot bath before his dinner.

As at most widowers' dinner tables, it was a silent, rather melancholy meal. The portrait of the late Honoria Streetley stared down at him from the sideboard end of the room and the lamb cutlets were overdone and tasteless. Not that Mr Justice Streetley minded. He was not thinking of his food. He was thinking of Stan. And his thoughts pleased him. That was because Stan fitted so perfectly into a criminological theory of his own.

Over the years, Mr Justice Streetley had observed that forgers, con men, dishonest bank clerks and the like all tended to be below average height; two or three inches below, in fact, and he supposed that the group could reasonably be enlarged to include disloyal civil servants. Stan was certainly the right size. Then, there was the colour of the hair. Brown, mousy and nondescript made up the general range and, again, that was the category to which Stan belonged. Finally, there was the common behaviour pattern. On this point, Mr Justice Streetley was explicit and convinced. Violent murderers – not poisoners: they could be classed with the con men – criminal assailants and armed bank robbers frequently carried themselves with an air of open and rather engaging defiance. He had even found himself secretly admiring one or two of them. But with the sneaky sort, the cheats and the tricksters, it was different. There was nothing in the least engaging or defiant about them. They made excuses. They tried to ingratiate themselves. They cringed.

Mr Justice Streetley was still thinking about Stan, still labelling and classifying him, when he went up to bed. And his night followed the old, familiar pattern – a few short hours of tossing, uneasy slumber and then suddenly awake again with the minute-hand of his mind ticking on from the precise point on the dial that it had reached the evening before. Mr Justice Streetley made no attempt to fight his insomnia. Instead, wriggling over onto his back, he lay there, going over the shape and substance of tomorrow's sentencing, polishing up a phrase here, strengthening a weak epithet there. By five-thirty he was word perfect and had drifted quietly off to sleep again, only to be called at seven.

Stan, for his part, had enjoyed close on eight hours of practically un-broken sleep; easily the best since all this trouble had started. In consequence, he felt thoroughly rested; refreshed through and through, even relaxed in a strange, slightly dreamlike sort of fashion.

Standing beside his bunk and looking up at the criss-cross of the window bars, he began one of his secret, private conversations.

'No more of this hanging-about business, no more back-and-forthing,' he told himself. 'Whatever it is, you can take it. What's five years –

what's ten years for that matter – if you've kept your health? You'll be all right. You won't have lost your knack when you come out. You'll still be able to show them what a photograph ought to look like. You'll have your own studio one day. You'll be a celebrity.'

There was always this oddly consoling note in what was said when one of the two Stans began talking to the other one. It was as though the first one, the one who actively did things, was the one who made all the mistakes while the other, the withdrawn one, knew how to put them right again. Quite often, it seemed to Stan Number One a pity that their two roles could not have been reversed.

In a desultory way, the conversation continued all the way to the Old Bailey in the Black Maria and, once there, right up to the dock itself. Stanley Pitts Number Two had just said to Stan Pitts Number One: 'You don't have to worry about Beryl. She'll be all right. The Press'll look after her. And there's always Cliff, isn't there? You know how much he cares. If you're not there, he can take charge. He can afford to. He's loaded. He won't even notice what little Marleen's social extras cost.'

The unheard conversation was still under way, with Stan Number One listening attentively, when Mr Justice Streetley entered, and the whole Court had to rise. Stan got hurriedly onto his feet and stood respectfully to attention, hands to his side Boy Scout fashion. Even so, he was not ready, not really ready that is, when Mr Justice Streetley addressed him. He was still hearing what Stan Number Two was telling him.

'. . . and have you anything to say before I pass sentence upon you?' Mr Justice Streetley was asking in his quietest, most neutral-sounding voice. 'Because now is the moment when you can speak.'

The question took Stan so entirely by surprise that he didn't know what to say. He only wished that Mr Hayhoe would come forward to help him. But Mr Hayhoe did not move. He remained entirely unresponsive, seemingly oblivious. Stan realized that it was up to him.

'No, I don't think so, sir,' he said, 'my Lord, I mean. Not the way things are. Not after what's happened. But thank you all the same for asking, sir. Thank you very much indeed.'

Mr Justice Streetley made no comment. He merely acknowledged Stan's reply by a brief nod of the head. Then, after a suitable pause, he began his own speech.

'It would seem,' he observed, 'that nowadays loyalty is the forgotten virtue.' It was here that Mr Cheevers gave a little tremor of delight as he heard the words: close student of Mr Justice Streetley as he was, he had never heard him phrase things better. But already Mr Justice Streetley was in voice again. 'Apparently patriotism is no longer fashionable,' he went on. 'Today it is the sentry who is on guard who opens the door to the citadel when he finds that the enemy brings gold . . .' There was quite a lot more in the same vein because in the night Mr Justice Streetley had lain awake for quite a long time. Stan did his best to follow him. It was not, however, until Mr Justice Streetley got round to the bit about the actual sentence that Stan found that he could really concentrate.

'Of all the offences on the statute book none is more grave than that of treason,' he heard him say at last, 'and no convicted traitor can expect leniency when he is brought before the law. It is therefore my clear and inescapable duty to impose upon you a sentence which will ensure that you are put away for a considerable period of your life. I do so in order not only to protect the realm but to serve as a warning to others as treacherous and greedy as yourself. The sentence which after reflection I impose is one of eighteen years imprisonment.'

That was when Beryl, who had been sitting there all the time, fainted and fell off her chair. From his place in the dock Stan could not see properly what it was that was happening. The policeman's hand was already on his shoulder when Stan remembered his manners.

'Thank you again, my Lord,' he said. 'I'm . . . I'm deeply sorry to have put you to all this trouble and expense on my account.'

BOOK FOUR

Grounds for Divorce

Chapter 37

On that last day of the trial, when Beryl heard the terms of Stan's sentence, it seemed that suddenly her whole life was over – and Marleen's too, for that matter. It was as though the earth had stopped. There was certainly no future that she could see for either of them. But in all human relations there is a kind of Newton's Law, just as there is in text-book physics. Equal and opposite forces are working against each other the whole time, and there is an aftermath to everything.

For Beryl, it came in the form of a telephone call. And it was about time for it, too. Ever since her return to Kendal Terrace she had been suffering one humiliation after another. It was on a Thursday that Stan had been sent down and, by the following Monday, a letter had arrived from the Admiralty. In impressively large type the writer explained that Their Lordships were obliged to observe Service Regulations to the letter and that, where Official Secrets were involved, the rules were decidedly on the strict side. There was apparently no way of getting round them. In consequence Stan was to regard himself as no longer merely on the suspended list: he was sacked.

Nor was that all. Parliament, it seemed, really had it in for people like Stan, and it was specifically laid down that in such cases all pension rights were forfeited, too.

What's more, with nothing short of ruin confronting her, Beryl got no comfort from the first of the prison visits which the authorities allowed her. Quite the reverse, in fact. Even at their best, prison visits are pretty unsatisfactory affairs; and the first one went wrong from the very start. Stan remembered to ask about Marleen, but forgot to ask how Beryl herself was. The sheer thoughtlessness of his behaviour so much upset her that she could hardly speak. And when he asked if she had seen Cliff lately, she snapped back at him.

'You mind your business and I'll mind mine,' was what she said.

The sudden venom behind the words astonished him. It was only after the interview was over that he began to understand. But it was quite obvious really. It meant that she and Cliff must be seeing a great deal of each other; every day, possibly. And it was only natural that

333

she wouldn't want to be questioned about it. You could hardly expect any nice woman on a prison visit to say 'thanks-for-asking-yes-dear-I'm-going-on-being-regularly-unfaithful-to-you'. And he could see that having to say it through the wire mesh of the interview grille would somehow have made it all that much harder.

Stan was glad now that he had always made a point of being so nice to Cliff, pretending that he was pleased to see him whenever he dropped in, not showing that he minded when Cliff made fun of him, laughing at Cliff's jokes, gratefully accepting the gifts, so many of them trade samples, which he kept showering upon them. It was a positive relief to know that Cliff would still be around, because it meant that Beryl's future was so much safer, so much more secure. He wouldn't let go of her now, Cliff wouldn't; he'd be there ready to chip in if things got difficult; that had always been the best side of Cliff's nature, his generosity.

The telephone call came when Beryl was at her very lowest; right down in the depths, in fact. She could tell that she had one of her headaches coming on, and had already drawn the curtains right across the bedroom windows. Eyes closed, she lay there in the half-darkness. Only her lips were moving.

'Oh Cliff, Cliff,' she was saying, 'where are you? Why have you done this to me? Don't you mind about me any more? Have you just stopped caring?'

The words were still going through her mind when she started up as she heard the *b-rrr b-rrr* of the telephone bell. Immediately, almost by instinct as it were, she knew who it would be: knew that her plea had been answered.

The phone – it was an ivory-white one because Beryl had always felt that the black sort somehow looked too officey inside the home – was in the front lounge. All the way downstairs she was afraid that the bell would stop ringing.

'Cliff, Cliff,' she said breathlessly as she lifted the receiver.

But it was not Cliff at the other end.

'Mrs Pitts?' the voice asked. 'Mr Cheevers, *Sunday Sun,* here. I'm in the neighbourhood, and I wondered if I might pop round for a moment?'

It was a follow-up story that Mr Cheevers wanted: 'SPY FORFEITS

PENSION – WIFE FIGHTS FOR CHILD'S RIGHTS' – that kind of thing. Already his book, *Birth of a Crime*, was beginning to take shape; and Beryl was the only person who could help him with it. From her he would have to learn, bit by bit, all that could be known about Stan – not just about his singular lack of promotion in the Civil Service but about his secret ambitions, his impulses, his little worries, his photographic successes, his comforts, his doubts, his failings and his fears.

Mr Cheevers was a skilled interviewer of the sympathetic, understanding sort. He felt confident that, given time, she would tell him everything. From long experience he knew that, once lonely people start talking, there is usually no stopping them; and Beryl was certainly in need of someone who would listen.

In the result, Mr Cheevers became a regular visitor to Kendal Terrace, and Beryl made no attempt to deter him. Basically nervous where women were concerned, he was careful to keep it all very cool and matter-of-fact, always ringing up first and not letting things degenerate into the casual, dropping-in stage. Ostensibly it was always to see if there were any developments, anything new for the great army of his readers. But, little by little, the formality began to wear off. Nowadays, he would arrive carrying a small box of chocolates for Marleen, or a copy of an illustrated magazine that he thought Beryl might like to see. Never flowers, however. That, he felt, would be going too far. Besides, it might make Beryl think that he was pursuing her. The very idea shocked and alarmed him. It offended his whole sense of professional ethics. To him, doctor, priest and reporter were all bound by a set of laws positively Koranic in their rigidity.

This evening, notebook in hand, Mr Cheevers was leaning forward in his chair. Altogether it looked like being one of his more fruitful sessions. Now that Beryl was beginning to know him she was becoming less discreet; even quite confidential at times. And Mr Cheevers was employing his well-tried techniques. He rarely asked a direct question; preferred instead to make a harmless-sounding, generalized observation and then sit back quietly and wait for the response.

'One way or another in my kind of life you come up against a lot of unhappiness,' he had just said. 'And there's one thing you can't help noticing – that's the way old friends rally round. Things go smoothly, and you never see them. Then something happens, and there they are standing right on your doorstep. That's life, that is.'

Beryl did not reply immediately. That was because she had not been listening to a word that he had been saying. Instead, she was looking down at Mr Cheevers's feet and admiring them. Men's shoes had always held a peculiar fascination for her; and these were the style that she liked best – half-brogue, tan calf with narrow laces. And Mr Cheevers was wearing exactly the right kind of ribbed socks. Stan himself had always been hopeless about his shoes and socks.

Dimly she became aware that Mr Cheevers had stopped speaking.

'I've been thinking about what you asked me last time,' she said. 'About the book, I mean. Because you never really knew Stan, did you? Not like knowing him properly, I mean. So I'd have to tell you everything, otherwise you wouldn't have anything to write about, would you? But if it was me talking it'd be different. More unusual like. After all, I could say things nobody else could, couldn't I? They'd sound all right coming from me. With your help, of course. That way it ought to be good enough to go into a paperback and be serialized like. You'd have to do the writing part, of course, because I don't know about the chapters and the punctuation. Well, I wouldn't – would I? – because I've never done anything like that before. But it'd still be me speaking, like it was in those articles. Nobody could tell it wasn't me, could they? Not unless they knew, that is.'

She paused and looked up at Mr Cheevers.

'Then, of course, we could share the money,' she told him. 'That'd be only fair, wouldn't it? Do you think people would buy it? If I really told the truth, I mean. Not just hinted at it. We wouldn't just be wasting our time like, would we? I wouldn't want that. Because it's only for little Marleen's sake that I'd be doing it. It's different for you. You're a writer. I'm a mother. I have my child to consider.'

Mr Cheevers was slowly recovering his professionalism. It wouldn't be by any means what he had intended. But he could still see distinct possibilities. And, after all, his name would be there on the title page: '. . . as told to Cyril Cheevers' the inscription would run.

Chapter 38

In one respect Stan was noticeably better off than most of the other inmates. There he was in a prison that contained a lot of very important people – ex-MPs, ex-Local Government officials, ex-company directors, ex-bank managers, even an ex-clergyman or two – and he was one of the few to have a cell entirely to himself. That was what came of being a high Security risk. All spies occupy a privileged position in the prison hierarchy; they are special.

Not that there aren't some disadvantages, of course. There's less social life, less mixing, for example. But, in the long run, most prisoners would opt for a private bedsitter in preference to doss-house conditions and half an hour of extra table tennis.

The arrangement certainly suited Stan perfectly. He had considered it carefully, and he was content. It gave him more time for communing with himself.

'Eighteen years the Judge said,' he kept repeating. 'And that means twelve if you behave yourself, my lad. You're no fool. You'll keep in step all right. You won't give them any trouble. It's only your brain you've got to think about. You don't want that to go stale. Not get soggy, your brain mustn't. You want to keep up with things. This is your big chance, Stan, if you use it properly. They're bound to have a library in a prison of this size. You get onto the subscribers' list. Nothing trashy, mind you. Nothing cheap – no sex, no murder stories. Something to improve the mind. That's what pays dividends – knowledge. Like French and history and economics. And accountancy, of course, and science. You've got time. And there's art, and literature. Read about them, too. Just play your cards properly and you'll be the best-educated man in the place. What about the Open University? How would you like to come out of here as Mr Stanley Pitts, BA? Well, why shouldn't you? This is your one big chance to better yourself. And you make sure you take it.'

As yet Stan's mind certainly showed no signs of sogginess. Already it was the matter of prisoners' correspondence that he was working on. He was quite prepared to accept that you couldn't have the plotting-and-breaking-out kind receiving letters by every post; with that amount of information in their possession, they would be up and over the wall and away in no time. But, with the reliable and trustworthy sort, he reckoned that a letter a day might do some of them a power of good.

If only the Governor had asked him, he would have found that Stan had got the whole thing worked out. A single sheet of paper to be handed to the new arrival as soon as he got to the prison was how he saw it; a single sheet that is, with three columns and three little boxes in which to put the ticks. Column one would ask, quite bluntly, how often the prisoner would like to hear from his wife, with three times a week as a cast-iron maximum; Column two was for solicitor and near relatives; with Column three in reserve for mere friends and acquaintances.

Outgoing mail, Stan reckoned, could be similarly handled, provided two things were properly looked after. The first was that no extra expense should fall on the tax-payer, which meant that to cover postal charges there should be a simple system of deduction from prison wages; and the second was an extra little tick-box in all three Columns to indicate whether it was first- or second-class mail that the prisoner had in mind.

Stan had not spent all those years within the Civil Service for nothing.

From the start, Stan had been against any suggestion of an Appeal. It wasn't that he didn't think that it would succeed. It was simply that everything at the trial had seemed perfectly fair to him, and he couldn't for the life of him imagine what there could be to appeal about.

All the same, it was rather nice to have something to look forward to, something to break up the monotony of the everlasting six-thirty roll call and nine-o'clock lights out.

That's what counts in prison; even if the prisoner isn't able to help in preparing his Appeal, at least he's allowed to attend the Court just to see how it's getting on. And that at least means a journey in the open air, with different faces, different sounds and, above all, fresh breezes.

Stan enjoyed every moment of it. It was like a trip to the seaside; brief but bracing. Indeed, the tonic effect became apparent straight away, and he could feel himself taking in deeper and deeper breaths. When he reached the Court, he was actually whistling quietly to himself; and he would have gone on doing so if the officer in the reception bay had not told him that, if not exactly forbidden, whistling

graph to help keep the story alive; and for the book itself, no ending could have been more perfect. The more he thought about it, the more enthusiastic he became and, to make sure that there were no unforeseen hitches, no slip-ups, he offered Beryl the services of the *Sunday Sun* legal department.

'Place yourself in their hands, and you need be put to no further trouble in the matter.' He paused, searching round in his mind for one parting sentence of consolation. 'Of course,' he added, 'I fully realize what a deep shock all this must have been to you. If there is any way . . .'

But Beryl was not listening. She had gone over to the mantelpiece and was tapping something.

'That's funny like,' she told him. 'It isn't working. I must have forgotten to fill the glass up or something.'

Chapter 39

Mr Cheevers had been getting on with it, too. He had his first, neatly-typed hundred pages to show for it, and was now well into his second clip-back folder. Not that it had been easy. Beryl was too impulsive a collaborator for that; too mercurial. Only last month she had suddenly asked: 'Why not start all over again and do it like it was Stan talking? Then it would be more interesting like, wouldn't it? More exciting. Stan wouldn't mind. I mean, why should he? After all, it's for me and Marleen that he'd be doing it.'

At the outset it had been only once a week that Mr Cheevers had made the journey over to Crocketts Green. But, of late, in order to get on with things he had been stepping it up a bit – at week-ends mostly, but sometimes even twice on week-days as well. And Beryl always seemed pleased enough to see him. She had even taken to buying little delicacies, like tinned soft roes and steak-and-kidney pie in tin-foil, for the nights on which she knew he was coming. And, like the gentleman he was, Mr Cheevers never turned up without a little something himself. He had got over his earlier objection to flowers and the front lounge was now regularly ablaze with poinsettias, cyclamen, Russian violets; Russian violets especially because they lasted so well.

Having Mr Cheevers in the house so often, Beryl had naturally begun to make use of him. She put him on odd jobs like changing electric-light bulbs and re-fixing dislocated curtain runners. Also, more often than not, she allowed herself a drink from the bottle of sweet sherry or Dubonnet which Mr Cheevers would occasionally bring over in place of the flowers. Then, in the presence of the tirelessly bobbing-up-and-down bird, they would sit glass-in-hand, facing each other across the fireplace, going over, episode by episode, the various stages of Stan's career, private and professional, right up to the moment of his eventual downfall.

Now that Beryl was getting to know Mr Cheevers so much better she was ready to tell him so much more. Only last Tuesday she had revealed to him that, during the few remaining months of his freedom,

Stan had taken to drinking heavily. In vivid detail she described the night when he was so intoxicated on his return home that she had been forced to take Marleen into her own bedroom, being careful to lock the door behind her as she did so. Mr Cheevers was delighted. It was little touches like that, he told himself, that would make the book.

In the circumstances, with Mr Cheevers in the house so much, it was only natural that Beryl should find herself comparing him to Stan.

More than once, indeed, she had not been able to escape noticing how much alike physically Mr Cheevers and Stan really were. For a start, they were about the same height; and, come to that, about the same weight. There was, of course, one big difference. Mr Cheevers's hair was dark, like hers; almost raven. Whereas Stan's had been so much lighter; sandy as you might say, even verging on the ginger.

'*Had been* so much lighter': with a shock Beryl realized that already she was beginning to think of Stan in the past tense! Everything about him seemed to be something that had once happened. It amazed her to think that she should ever have been married to him at all.

For the first time since he had started, Mr Cheevers really believed that he would get his Stanley Pitts book finished.

He had been at work on it for nearly a year by now, and it seemed only like yesterday when he had started. The last six months had proved particularly fruitful. Buying Beryl a tape recorder had been one of his happier thoughts. Even at the manufacturer's recommended price, it was not an expensive one that he had chosen. Mr Cheevers had, however, bought it at a shop in Holborn which specialized in ignoring recommendations. Hong Kong was where the little recorder had come from; and, though its tone may have been a trifle nasal and Chinese-sounding, the play-back capacity was quite remarkable.

Beryl fell in love with it at first sight. She enjoyed speaking into the plastic mouth-piece. It made something to do when she was alone; also, it made her feel important. No other woman of her acquaintance possessed a Sabuki personalized recorder; and no other woman, she felt sure, had so much to say into it.

Of course, to begin with, she made her share of mistakes: beginners always do. For the most part, the tapes consisted of false starts, sudden re-winds and the intermittent sound of heavy breathing. But that did not matter. What was important was that Beryl was still trying; and

341

Mr Cheevers felt sure that, sooner or later, she would get round to the subject of her relationship with Cliff.

The year hadn't been passing quite so rapidly for Stan. But that is not to be wondered at. It's impossible to keep track of time in prison; and so easy to get confused, too. Indeed, he was a whole month out when, on one of his evening visits, the chaplain reminded him that, by the end of the week, he'd have done his first twelve months.

But looking back he had to admit that there was certainly plenty to show for it. He'd managed to make himself pretty useful all round; practically indispensable, in fact. That was because he was so good at checking things. In the carpentry and woodwork room, for instance, he had introduced a completely new system of receipts for timber handed out and counter-receipts for finished articles returned. Again, during the week while he had been lent to the Infirmary he had succeeded in tidying up the prison linen distribution so that no piece of clean linen went out until there had been a soiled one to replace it; and any day now they'd promised him that he should have a go at the Library. He'd already had a pretty thorough look round in there, and he had seen enough to tell him that the whole lay-out was wrong; amateurish to the last degree, in fact. But, once he had the new card-index system of his own design installed and the books themselves in proper order, he doubted if there would be any prison Library in the whole country that could compare with it.

And, in the meantime, Stan was making good use of the Reference Section. It was mostly legal works that he was consulting.

Naturally enough, the stress of prison visiting – coming on top of having to make a home for Marleen as well as helping Mr Cheevers with his book – had begun to get Beryl down. She could not sleep and, when she did, her dreams were both disordered and disturbing. On the third successive night when Cliff had come into them and had kept her awake because she could not stop thinking about him, she decided that there was nothing for it but to see her doctor. A short course of Valium was what he prescribed; and he advised, moreover, that for the time being she had better get someone else to take on the prison visiting.

That was how it was that Marleen came to see so much of her father. Up to that point, she had been Beryl's little girl much more than Stan's. But those fortnightly sessions served to bring them together. For the first time in her life she became really close to her father; and Stan, for his part, became just as close to her. He only wished that he could have had his camera with him. A shot taken across the interview counter, with just a hint of the grille and the figure of the wardress and the barred window in the background could easily have turned into a prize-winner. *Across the divide* was what he would have called it.

The fonder Marleen grew of her father, the more she resented Mr Cheevers. She saw him not as a friend but as an intruder. And this resentment came quite unexpectedly to a head one evening. What made the whole affair so regrettable was that it could quite easily have been avoided; indeed, it had only been at the last moment that Mr Cheevers had finally decided to go over to Kendal Terrace.

For a start, the weather had been dreadful. Ever since tea-time, the rain had been coming down monsoon-fashion, with spiteful little side sallies of the sort that drenched people who thought that they were safely sheltering in doorways. If it had not been that Mr Cheevers was still determined to pin Beryl down about Cliff he would never have set out at all.

As it was, he got soaked through simply getting from his parked car to the front door of Number Sixteen, and Beryl made him take his jacket off to dry before they got down to work together. The sight of Mr Cheevers in his bright red braces seemed to upset Marleen; and when she asked him how much more he was going to take off, Beryl sent her from the room.

Apart from that, the session looked like passing off very smoothly. Beryl told Mr Cheevers all about Stan's bogus promotion and how he had made use of it as a cover-up to conceal where the extra money was really coming from. Then, to his delight, she brought Cliff into the conversation unasked. This was something that she had never done before.

'The real trouble about Stan' – for some time now she had stopped referring to him as 'my husband' – 'was that he didn't impress people. He was ever so good at his work, he was really, but nobody ever seemed to notice him like. He was the exact opposite of Cliff. He was the one in the picture, remember. Nobody couldn't help noticing Cliff.'

'And were they close friends, the two of them?'

Beryl smiled. She was determined not to give herself away; if Mr Cheevers wanted to talk about Cliff she would discuss him as she might have done a stranger.

343

'Yes. Funny when you come to think of it, isn't it?' she replied. 'They weren't a bit like each other, you know. Not a bit they weren't.'

'But they got on well together?'

Beryl smiled again.

'Oh, yes. They always did. Cliff used to tease him a bit, but Stan never minded. Not really, he didn't. Not so that it mattered.'

It was Mr Cheevers who deliberately let the conversation flag. His long experience in interviews told him that, at any moment now, he would be approaching the danger point. When he did speak, he was deliberately casual; scarcely interested, it seemed.

'And if he was Stan's friend' – Mr Cheevers, too, had slipped into the habit of calling him 'Stan' – 'I expect you and Marleen must be missing him. He used to be around quite a lot, wasn't he?'

Beryl did not reply immediately. She was removing a piece of cotton from her dress.

'On and off like,' she told him.

With that, she got up and Mr Cheevers knew that the only thing left to him was to close his notebook. He thanked her, and went out into the narrow entrance hall to pick up his driving gloves.

As soon as he had opened the front door, however, he could see what sort of night it still was. The rain was sheeting down, and the pool with the old bearded gnome fishing in it was overflowing again just as it had been on the night when Stan had brought home all those presents. Mr Cheevers spread his handkerchief across his head and ran for it.

A minute or two later, the front-door bell rang. It was Mr Cheevers again. He looked wetter than ever.

'Sorry to have to bother you,' he said. 'But my car won't start. Mind if I use your telephone?'

Half an hour later, Mr Cheevers was still there. Apparently, there was no garage in Crocketts Green that was prepared to come out on such a night, and the hire-car service was not even answering.

'I'll phone Daimler Hire,' he told her. 'I'll get them to come down and pick me up.'

It was Beryl who stopped him.

'Why not stay here for the night?' she asked. 'We can put you up like. There's Stan's room. You can have that.'

Mr Cheevers drew in his breath. It would be the first time that he had ever been upstairs in Kendal Terrace. At the thought of the wealth of background material that it would provide, a thrill of sheer, professional pride ran through him.

'If you're sure it's not too much trouble . . .' he began.

But Beryl stopped him.

'You stay down here,' she said. 'I'll just go and get things ready.'

Left to himself, Mr Cheevers ran over the evening's notes. There were nearly six pages of them. Pruned down and properly sub-edited they would make up another very useful paragraph or two. He was by now, he reckoned, at least three-quarters through the whole manuscript, and he was even working out possible publication dates when Beryl called out to him to come up.

Once actually inside Stan's bedroom, it was all more true to life – true, that is, to the life that he had imagined for Stan – than seemed possible. The very smallness of the room had a pathos all of its own, and the size of the miniature washbasin only seemed to accentuate it. The bed, too, was a narrow one. All in all, it was hard to believe that Stan's bedroom belonged to the same house as the front lounge with the built-in china cabinet and the television set or the dining alcove and the free-standing kitchen cabinets. Mr Cheevers felt that at last he was beginning to understand how it was that anyone as ordinary as Stan might have felt driven to break out.

A pair of striped flannelette pyjamas had been laid out on the eiderdown.

'You'd better wear those,' said Beryl, who was standing behind him. 'Stan wouldn't mind. Not the way things are, he wouldn't.'

She paused.

'And you may be needing this,' she said. 'Better have it anyhow, just in case.'

It was the blue-and-white sports robe that Stan had bought at the Colony's Trading Post for use when he was sitting beside the swimming pool.

'Well, I think that's everything,' she said. 'Good night. Sleep well.'

Mr Cheevers undressed slowly, looking round the room as he did so and treasuring every moment. 'Like the wallpapered cell of a lay monk,' the words came to him. 'Spartan, plain, austere . . .'

He was still repeating the words as he put on the sports robe, and began to make his way along the passage to the bathroom. He did not get far, however. The door of Marleen's room was flung open and she

345

stood there facing him. For a moment neither spoke. Then he saw that under her flimsy pink nightie her little bosom had begun to heave.

'No you don't, Cheevie,' she said. 'Not your scene. No way. Not now. Not ever.'

With that she flew at him and tried to rip the soft blue-and-white towelling off his shoulders.

Chapter 40

After 'the little scene', as Beryl always in her own mind referred to Marleen's attack upon Mr Cheevers, she was careful to keep the two of them as much apart as possible. They had, of course, to sit down together with her in the warmth and comfort of the front lounge and share the same folding-table in the alcove of the dinerette. But she no longer left them alone in each other's company.

Not that, in all probability, anything would have happened if they had been. That was because Beryl had already had it out with Marleen. She had slowly and patiently explained how important it was that the book should be published, and how necessary therefore Mr Cheevers was to both of them.

'If you think I want the two of us to starve just because your Dad's done something silly then you'd better have another think coming,' she had finished up. 'There's a lot of money in books if you know how to write them like Mr Cheevers does.'

With Beryl herself so much preoccupied with Mr Cheevers, it was only natural that by now Marleen should have become the family's chief link with Stan; and it was to Marleen rather than Beryl that Stan mostly wrote nowadays. It was probably just as well, too. Previously, Beryl had kept on getting upset by the unpleasant reminders on cheap, brownish notepaper; even the sight of the equally cheap envelope had been enough to bring on one of her headaches.

In the result, it was Marleen who was best placed to observe the change in Stan's condition; all for the better, too, it seemed. And it was the Library that had done it. In any prison, the post of Librarian is, next to that of the Governor himself, about the most cherished position in the place. And Stan was certainly the man to fill it.

The transformation of having someone under forty, and still with a zest for good filing, was really quite startling. In the six months or so during which he had been there, a renaissance had taken place: loose pages were pasted in again, broken spines repaired and traces of chocolate and chewing-gum scraped off covers. The Library became, after the Chapel, the show-piece of the whole prison. Journalists,

Howard Leaguers, foreign visitors, well-intentioned Peers and documentary film producers were all taken there, and Stan was introduced to the whole lot of them. Never in his entire life had he felt so important or so deeply appreciated. And it was apparent in his appearance. Despite the awful, ill-fitting prison clothes, a change had come over him. He had acquired a new dignity, and an air of calm and self-possession; it was the air of a man who after long deliberation had finally arrived at a big decision.

Even so, Marleen was entirely unprepared for it. As Beryl herself was. And this time it was to Beryl that the inferior-looking prison envelope was addressed. The enclosed letter made no mention of Marleen.

The tone, moreover, was so quiet, so reasonable, that it might have been that of any husband and any wife conferring together about their domestic future. It began by reminding Beryl that, though he had already served nearly two years of his time, there was still a solid block of over ten years ahead of him, even allowing for a maximum reduction for good conduct: by then, he would be nearly fifty and Beryl herself would be forty-six. That being so, he felt it only fair to remind her that she should start thinking about getting a divorce just as soon as she could. He'd checked up how to go about it and apparently it was all quite simple and straightforward: more of a formality than anything else, really. He'd fully understand, he said, if she wanted one, and if she wanted to get married again he wouldn't mind about that, either. All that he was thinking about, he assured her, was her happiness and Marleen's.

It was the extreme neatness of Stan's handwriting that upset Beryl. If the whole thing had been scrawled, tear-stained and crumpled, she might have been able to understand, even to forgive. But this tidy, formal little document, never! The left-hand margin was as straight and upright as though he had used a T-square; and, at the bottom right-hand corner, Stan had drawn a short, diagonal line and had inserted the letters 'PTO' in the resultant triangle.

As it happened, the letter came on the same day as one of Mr Cheevers's evening calls, and naturally she turned to him for advice. Mr Cheevers, it turned out, was all in favour of the idea: he made that clear from the outset. The whole thing, indeed, seemed part of a pre-arranged pattern: if he had designed it himself, he could not have improved on it. News of the divorce would make a useful little para-

was nevertheless frowned upon. It was enough to put the Appeal Judges against him from the start, he added.

Nothing came of the Appeal, of course. All three of the Judges agreed with Stan that the whole trial could not have been more properly conducted; and that, with nothing less than the safety of the Realm at stake, eighteen years was a very reasonable sort of sentence.

The only thing that worried Stan was the matter of his cell. By now he had become used to No. 16 in D Block and, on the whole, rather liked it. The thought alarmed him that, in his absence, the room might have been let to a new arrival.

All that Stan wanted was to be left alone where he was and be allowed to settle down and get on with it.

POSTSCRIPT

Au revoir, Mr Cheevers

Chapter 41

It may even have been part of a prearranged plan – though Mr Cheevers was not to see it like that at the time – that Mr Cheevers's old mother should have passed away on the very day on which Beryl's speeded-up divorce came through. Whatever it was, the outcome was inevitable. 'Two lonely hearts' was how Mr Cheevers put it to her; and Beryl found herself agreeing with him.

In the result, Beryl's new address, as Mrs Cyril Cheevers, was No. 10 The Pallisades, Wimbledon Common. Admittedly, it was not quite so central as she might have wished, nor so fashionable. It wasn't by any means the sort of apartment block she would have been living in if she had married Cliff. But it was modern and, even though she had been there rather less than three years, she had largely forgotten about Kendal Terrace by now. It might have been another woman of the same name who had once happened to live there.

For a start, there was none of that everlasting money-worry that had nagged at her during all those endless, wearing years with Stan. This showed itself in all sorts of different ways. Nowadays, for instance, on those occasions when her sugar-hunger suddenly became unbearable, she no longer had to slip into the nearest confectioners' to buy a walnut-cream-milk-flake, pretending that she was buying it for Marleen: instead, there was always a box of Dinner Mints or assorted chocolates standing by all ready on the occasional table in the living-room.

And it was the same with her clothes. There was no need now to go to a back street suburban dressmaker, with a copy of last month's *Vogue* under her arm, and a length of material bought in the January sales. These days Beryl was exclusively a High Street shopper. Her dresses came from the smarter of the Wimbledon boutiques, Estelle's or Maryon's or Jeannette's; and very smart some of them were, too.

The greatest difference in Beryl's appearance, however, had come about because of her hair. With no Monsieur Louis, late of the Ritz, to guide her, she had allowed herself to be talked into utter recklessness. In the end chair in one of the new open-style salons she had, on impulse, agreed that she would have her hair cut short.

Not that the operation had passed entirely without incident. Twice at the thought of what was happening she had broken down completely and, with two of the junior assistants called in to help, had needed to be comforted. Then, after it was all over and she saw her hair, *her* hair, lying there discarded on the side-table with the white streak showing up pathetically amid the mass, she collapsed again. This time it required Osborne biscuits and Nescafé to restore her.

Indeed, it was not until her hairdresser suggested that, professionally mounted as an ornamental hair-piece, what had just been cut off could be worn again whenever she wanted to, or all the time if she felt like it, that she became calm once more.

Her one great consolation was an inner, private one. It was all part of today's preparation for tomorrow. Everyone told her that short hair made her look much younger; and this was now all that mattered. She was now thirty-six, getting on for thirty-seven; and, for the future to be perfect, she could not afford to look one day older than thirty-one, or thirty-two at the outside.

The only trouble was that there was one room too few in the new apartment. Beryl had done all she could, of course: she had made the best of things. The end bedroom, Marleen's room as they had called it when they moved there, had been completely redecorated. In place of the pale, satin-finish wallpaper and the Regency curtains, there were plain white walls with a stencil design of rabbits and windmills and baby elephants, and the dado of funny ducks all carrying shopping baskets; even the glazed chintz curtains carried scenes from Disneyland.

And in less than four months now, as Beryl kept reminding herself, the brand-new little room would have its brand-new little occupant.

The one person who did not in the least mind about the loss of Marleen's room was Marleen. She was down in Berkshire at a training establishment doing stable-lad duties and loving every moment of it, even the mucking-out part.

By now she had entirely given up all thought of exhibition dancing; and this was just as well perhaps because she was no longer the right shape for it. The transformation had occurred some time during her sixteenth year. From then on she had slowly and progressively thickened. By the time she reached Berkshire she was a well-set, even muscular, young woman with strong hands. The old elfin air had mysteriously evaporated.

Her hair, too, had darkened. The silver-gilt sheen was there no longer and, in its place, had come a rich, dark tint of demerara. Not that there was much of it to be seen anyway. She had got rid of the curls as soon as she had left home, and mostly wore a cloth cap nowadays.

The only time she came up to town was to see Stan. The second Sunday of every month was set aside for it. By now, the prison staff greeted her like a friend even if they happened to meet her in the roadway outside.

They meant a great deal to Stan, these visits of Marleen. Instead of playing ping-pong with the others in the prison recreation room, he now made a point of reading the racing pages in the daily papers simply to learn the names of the winners, the trainers, the jockeys. Before going to sleep at night, he used to say them over and over to himself until he was word perfect; and, as the Sunday for Marleen's visit approached, it gave him a nice, warm feeling inside to know that they would both have plenty to talk about.

As for Beryl, she never came into the conversation at all. At one time Stan had always begun by asking after her. But it had proved unrewarding. Marleen had been quite unable to tell him; it was over a year now since she had even seen her mother.

In any case, Stan didn't want to probe too deeply into Beryl's private affairs. Unresentful as he was, he could not help feeling that, in a way, he had been cheated. It was for Cliff, and for Cliff alone, that he had stood aside and made way. Mr Cheevers still seemed to him an interloper. That, however, wasn't why he hadn't sent Beryl a note of good wishes on her second wedding day. He hadn't sent it because he thought that it might upset her.

Beryl's bedroom in Flat No. 10 was the best room in the whole apartment. The window opened onto nothing but gardens and, in springtime, the whole place was full of bird-song. In the ordinary way she shared the room with Cyril. But not at the moment. She was far too restless and on edge for that. Any time now, the doctor had told her; and, propped up against rather a lot of cushions, she counted the hours and tried to remember what it had felt like while she had been waiting for little Marleen to come.

Not that she was in the least panicky or frightened. Just not able to settle down to anything. And this was strange because, underneath it all, she had a deep-down feeling of peace and contentment. Everything was working out exactly as she had wanted it. Or would do as soon as she had put just one thing right.

'Cyril,' she called out to him.

'Coming, love.'

The reply was instantaneous, and from very close at hand. Ever since the doctor had warned them to be on the alert, Mr Cheevers had slept on the long settee in the adjoining drawing-room.

Tonight, however, he had not even been asleep. He was lying, with his chin propped up on his hand, thinking; very pleasant thoughts they were, too. The three-hundred-page manuscript, entitled *Natural History of a Crime* and containing the life-story of Stanley Pitts, Civil Servant Grade B2, had eventually been delivered and the proofs were at last within his hands.

The publisher was certainly enthusiastic about it. In his opinion it would immediately become recognized as a classic of its kind, and could not fail to soar triumphantly into the best-seller lists.

Arrived at Beryl's bedside, Mr Cheevers was already more than half-dressed. Ever since a midnight scare nearly three weeks ago, he had made a point of being ready.

'You all right, pet?' he asked anxiously.

But he could tell at once that this was not an emergency call. Beryl was sitting, propped up against the pillows, polishing her nails, and seemed strangely calm and self-possessed.

'I've been thinking . . .' she began.

Mr Cheevers moved over to sit down on the end of her bed to listen to her, but Beryl waved him away again.

'Too hot,' she said briefly.

Then she gave a little cough. It was the kind of cough that he had heard a hundred times before when interviewing people. Experience warned him that it meant that she was about to say something that he wasn't going to like very much.

'I've been thinking,' she resumed. 'It's about the book. About Stan, I mean. I don't think it's very nice, not now it's over, bringing it all up again. Not now that it's by me. I think it's best just forgotten. Like it had never happened like.' She paused and, for a moment, rubbed away hard at her thumbnail. 'In any case,' she went on, 'it's different now I'm going to have a baby, isn't it? I wouldn't want baby to think that Mummy would ever have married a man who would do that kind of thing, would I? It wouldn't seem right like. Not thinking of the baby, I mean. Not when baby grows up and begins to meet people.'

Mr Cheevers tried hard to soothe her.

'But I tell you, darling, it's all printed by now,' he reminded her, speaking ever so gently. 'The publisher's all ready to send it to the bookshops.'

Beryl did not answer immediately. She was sobbing by now.

'Then tell him you've changed your mind like,' she said jerkily. 'Tell him he'll have to publish something different.'

'But . . .'

Beryl smiled the very sweetest of her smiles, the one which over the years had won first Clifford Hamson, then Stanley Pitts and now Cyril Cheevers himself.

'You know I mustn't let anything happen that may disturb me,' she said. 'So promise. Please promise. Just for baby's sake, promise. You will, won't you?'

There was a long pause. Then Mr Cheevers took a slow, deep breath.

'I promise,' he said faintly.

And what about Stan?

While Beryl and Mr Cheevers were still talking, Stan was fast asleep in his old cell in D Block. The light in the ceiling was full on, but he had long since grown accustomed to it; by facing the wall and rolling over on his side he could still get a perfectly good night's rest.

In any case, he was unaware of his surroundings. He was dreaming: dreaming about a night long, long ago when he had just won the Departmental Photographic Competition and, out of his winnings he had bought a silk scarf with views of Old London for Beryl, a chunky, leather shoulder-bag for little Marleen, and a bottle of Beaujolais just so that the family could celebrate. And, in anticipation of his home-coming, he was smiling.

At this moment, Stan was one of the happiest men in London.

Norman Collins was a Fleet Street journalist and then a publisher before turning to television. He has been the Controller of BBC Television and is currently a Director of Associated Television Ltd., and of Independent Television News Ltd. He is author of twelve previous novels of which DULCIMER STREET, published over thirty years ago and subsequently made into a highly successful motion picture, is soon to be reissued in this country.